THE CHAPMAN LEGACY

JOHN NEELY DAVIS

FIVE STAR
A part of Gale, a Cengage Company

Farmington Hills, Mich • San Francisco • New York • Waterville, Maine
Meriden, Conn • Mason, Ohio • Chicago

LIBRARY OF CONGRESS CATALOGING-IN-PUBLICATION DATA

Names: Davis, John Neely, author.
Title: The Chapman legacy / John Neely Davis.
Description: First edition. | Waterville, Maine : Five Star Publishing, 2018. | Identifiers: LCCN 2017055251 (print) | LCCN 2017061468 (ebook) | ISBN 9781432842789 (ebook) | ISBN 9781432842772 (ebook) | ISBN 9781432842765 (hardback)
Subjects: LCSH: Gunfighters—Fiction. | Ranchers—Fiction. | Fathers and sons—Fiction. | Pecos River Valley (N.M. and Tex.)—Fiction. | Mexican–American Border Region—Fiction. | West (U.S.)—Fiction. | BISAC: FICTION / Historical. | FICTION / Sagas. | GSAFD: Western stories.
Classification: LCC PS3604.A9643 (ebook) | LCC PS3604.A9643 C53 2018 (print) | DDC 813/.6—dc23
LC record available at https://lccn.loc.gov/2017055251

First Edition. First Printing: June 2018
Find us on Facebook–https://www.facebook.com/FiveStarCengage
Visit our website–http://www.gale.cengage.com/fivestar/
Contact Five Star™ Publishing at FiveStar@cengage.com

Printed in the United States of America
1 2 3 4 5 6 7 22 21 20 19 18

DEDICATION

This book is dedicated to my father, John Brown Davis (1900–1975). He instilled in me early the love of the American West. Although he did not follow mustangs across the plains but instead followed mules across deep furrows of west Tennessee farmland, he was a cowboy at heart.

Also, I want to remember all the little boys who, seventy years ago, rode those river-cane stick horses and fired at the bad men with pistols fashioned from dogwood branches. We were never thrown from a bucking horse, never lost a gunfight, and never kissed a girl. Like the heyday of the gunslinger, our time has passed.

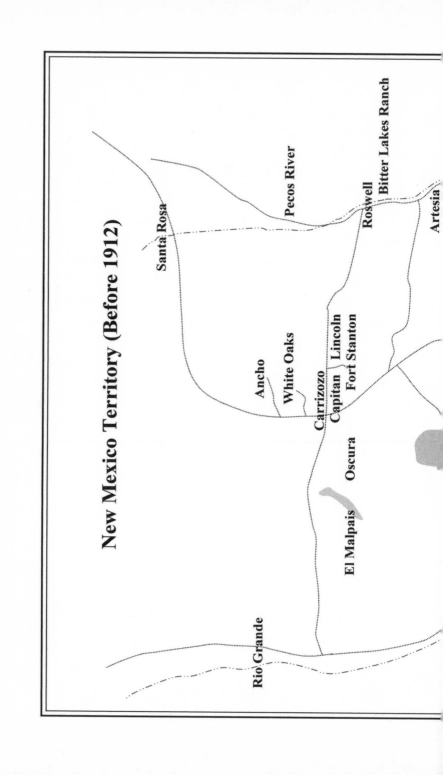

New Mexico Territory (Before 1912)

Santa Rosa

Rio Grande

Pecos River

El Malpais

Oscura

Ancho

White Oaks

Carrizozo
Capitan · Lincoln
Fort Stanton

Roswell

Bitter Lakes Ranch

Artesia

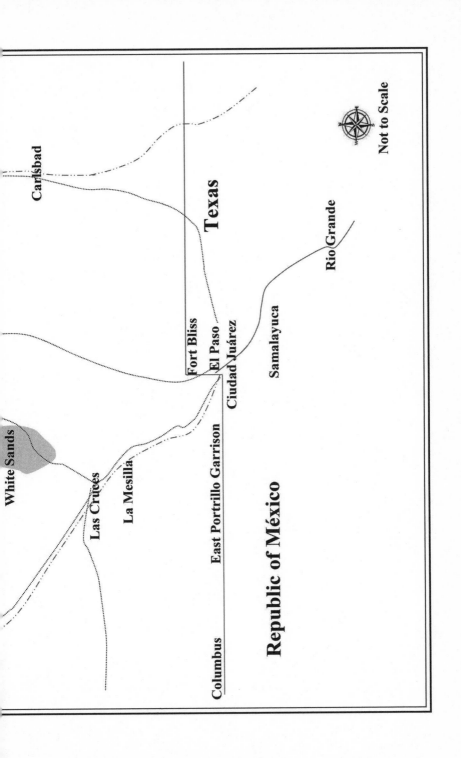

ACKNOWLEDGMENTS

These words would have never been published without the help of many people. The Harpeth River Writers of Franklin and the Scribblers of Brentwood labored with me over this book, pointing out inconsistencies and poor sentence structure. Leticia Salazar helped with the unfamiliar tongue.

I would never release any manuscripts without the oversight of Jerry and Gayle Henderson.

My girls, Cindy and Melissa, continuously encouraged me—"Come on, Daddy, finish it, for goodness' sake!"

My wife, Jayne, read every word, laughed, and cried in all the right places. Sixty years of marriage causes that kind of connection.

PROLOGUE

As long as there is anyone on earth who remembers you, it is not over. People leave behind strange little remembrances of themselves. Everyone has been gifted with at least one: an old hat, a thimble, a worn pocketknife, a war medal, an empty box containing a scant scent, a snatch of a tune hummed mindlessly. Maybe it is an old rifle. It could be a crudely sketched drawing of a dragonfly or perhaps a red, wooden chair leaning against a cantina on a wind-blown street corner in Samalayuca, Mexico.

The memories may sink beneath the plane for a hundred years, but eventually they surface and hold someone captive for a heartbeat.

Chapter One:
1950s

North Korea

The ground froze so deep they could no longer dig a foxhole or bury their own dead. The corpses of B Company were in the macabre positions of violent deaths or, ironically, children frolicking in the snow.

He crouched in his foxhole, watching the ridgeline. In late November, the rain stopped, and a cold front from Siberia descended over the Chosin Reservoir. The temperature plunged to minus forty degrees. Silver-dollar-sized snowflakes swirled in a huge vortex reaching from the Funchiln Pass to the north and Chosin Road as it snaked southward.

His platoon's weapons malfunctioned: artillery rounds fell short, firing pins froze, lubricants gelled, and batteries died. Medical supplies were useless: morphine syrettes required defrosting in a medic's mouth before injection; blood plasma turned to purple jelly. Rations and water froze solid. At this temperature, fire had no warmth.

The orders were to hold the enemy until the M-25 tanks could open the seventy-eight-mile road down to Toktong Pass. When the battalion's withdrawal was complete, then his company could retreat in an orderly manner. "A blocking position," the Battalion Commander called it; ground troops called it FUBAR.

Yesterday morning, his men were staggering with fatigue, malnourishment, and the brutal effects of debilitating, mind-numbing cold and strength-sapping wind. They operated on sheer determination and will power. And fear. He decided that fear was a hell of a motivator.

Last night, Marine Corsairs furiously napalmed the Chinese army as it crossed over the ridge toward his position. The jellied gasoline charred hundreds of the enemy. Others raced off into the darkness, human torches seeking a relief they would not find. Phosphorous and incendiaries fell so heavily that the barren slopes still smoked this morning.

He lost two of his remaining three men to indiscriminate napalm during the Corsairs' final run. The planes would not be back tonight. Neither would the EVAC helicopters, ever.

Before him, the ridgeline erupted with the glow of flares. He could see the silhouettes of the enemy, could hear whistles, bells, bugles, and the oncoming enemy beating metal canteens with bayonets. "A fuckin' Gook birthday party," Billy once described it.

Billy was the toughest man in the platoon—maybe the toughest he had ever known. It had taken most of the day for Billy to bleed to death; small seepages of blood surfaced through the dressing on his chest and then disappeared when he took a breath. Since noon, the tough guy pleaded: "Shoot me!" They made a pact about mortal injuries, and now he couldn't live up to his end of the agreement. Finally, Billy asked for a grenade, held it against the gaping hole in his chest, and turned over onto his stomach; his life ended in a muffled explosion and a sticky, red mist spewing up from the foxhole.

His frostbitten feet would no longer support him. Even with his broken leg tied to an ammo-case board, he could not crawl over to cover Billy's mangled body. He removed his unlined parka and emptied two syrettes of morphine into his arm. The demonic cold started to slide into a crinkly place in his mind.

He wasn't a religious man, but some Baptist Vacation Bible

School lingered. Until yesterday, he could recite The Lord's Prayer. A single mortar shell dropped into a foxhole shared by the lieutenant and the chaplain. Now he couldn't remember how the prayer started.

"Well, God," he said. "Looks like it's just You and me. And I'm in a helluva mess." He removed his dog tags and threw them onto the frozen snow. "I'm checking out now. I've had it. You get anything that's left. I reckon it's every man for himself, and the devil take the hindmost."

The Gooks came down the ridge. Every fifth man carried a sputtering flare. They were close enough he could make out the details of their ragged uniforms. They carried their weapons in the port arms position, confident the deadly cold had conquered their enemy.

Coatless and without a helmet, he sat on the edge of his foxhole and lit a cigarette. The morphine hummed a sweet melody to his brain. For the first time in weeks, he smiled.

The Pecos River Valley

"It's been more than two years, Papá," Matilda said. "He is dead. I know it . . . I can feel it in my bones."

Her father, Romero Luna, sat in the shade of a pecan tree. His father set the tree out in 1891, and now Romero was the second generation that watered it with the saline water of the Pecos River. He believed God saw him and the tree as the same age. Pecan nut casebearers attacked the tree by burrowing into the tips of the nuts. He applied insecticide, but the moths seemed to outsmart him.

He, himself, had been similarly attacked by his children after his third gas well started production. Not really attacked. However, they always seemed to have a need: a car, rent money, help with utility bills, always something. Sometimes he wished there was a spray available for grown children.

"Papá, are you listening?"

Romero stared out at his small patch of unpicked chilies and wondered about the pepper weevils. April, he decided, April. He would plant later this year, and the chilies would prosper in the July and August heat. Maybe he would just make *ristras*. Sell them at the Guadalupe Park market in Artesia. Decorate them with seedpods, dried flowers, and small clusters of garlic. Maybe he would carry cigars and a thermos of hot coffee and share with his best friend, Freddy.

He knew what his youngest daughter wanted: his blessing. Blessing to marry that little weasel-eyed Osweldo Gómez. Romero knew the Gómez family; knew they were worthless. They were no more than common goat thieves. Osweldo would not make a good husband for Matilda. Or father to her young son, Pete, his sweetest and favorite *nieto*. Romero closed his eyes. Maybe his daughter would tire and go away so he could concentrate on the *ristras*.

Matilda stood close and ran her fingers through the old man's hair. "Papá, I know you don't want me to be a widow. I'm only twenty. I am a young woman. I have most of my life in front of me. My husband is dead! The government says he is only missing in action. But I was his wife, and I know he is dead.

"I didn't want to tell you this . . . for fear that you would think I was crazy. But he comes to me in dreams and tells me. He wants a daddy for Pete. A living daddy."

Matilda was his youngest. She was like her mother, may her soul rest in peace; Romero had never been able to deny anything to either of them. He nodded and kissed her forehead.

He watched his daughter walk away, sinuous, skin copper in the winter's sun, hair dark enough to make a man's heart ache. His blessing caused her eyes to sparkle like new coins. No man ever refused her anything very long; she carried their hearts in her hand like a captured *trofeo*.

16

Kunu-ri, North Korea—Death Valley

At some point after his capture, he decided he could hide in his own mind.

The trip northward was more than hell. The Gooks had beaten him with rifle butts until they decided he wasn't faking and that he couldn't walk. Two soldiers out of the Oklahoma flat country made a litter from tree limbs and filthy blankets and carried and dragged him for two months. In the beginning, the agony from his frostbitten feet almost drove him insane. One night when the temperature dropped to ten below and a guard stole his thin blanket, he shivered until his joints gouged his swollen flesh like jagged steel. He decided *screw it* and separated his mind from his body.

Off and on for the next three months, he mentally lived in the warmth of the Capitan Mountains of western New Mexico. He, his son Pete, and his dad fished the New Mexico snowmelt-gorged streams. His wife, Matilda, always welcomed them back to the fishing camp with a smile and a sweet kiss for him. She had been his first girlfriend and cheered from the small grandstands as he roped steers. It pained him to think about her, and sometimes, when the pain was the worst, he would exclude her from his mental trip because he didn't want her around such an awful happening.

His dad, Chapman, came into this dry country sometime in the late 1800s and, as a young man, learned the cowboy business from Abijah Quezada and then worked as some kind of a U.S. marshal in southern New Mexico. Dad loved to reminisce, and his old tales of gunfights, range wars, and chasing horse thieves thrilled Pete. The three of them had wonderful conversations, sitting in the pine needle carpet watching buzzards ride the invisible sky currents and, once, they made a trip south for the horse races. They ate *pozole,* tacos, and beans washed down with strong, sweet coffee.

He remembered his father's hands: strong, usually a cut or a bruise, or a healing blister. The old man would weave blades of bear grass into the form of a dragonfly, add narrow twigs for wings, and give them to Pete. "One of my favorite things," he would tell the boy, "graceful and fragile. Kinda like the days of a man's life."

His mind continued to protect him when the guards hosed water over his freezing body, pierced his flesh with heated bamboo spears, and burned his testicles with lighted cigarettes. The brave Oklahoma kids' hands were bound behind them with wire, and they were told to run. They stumbled down the frozen road. The guards shot them and then for sport bayoneted their emaciated bodies.

Starvation was a constant companion. Prisoners boiled their boots to make a thin, evil tasting soup. What few rations allotted usually ended up in the guards' plates. He could barely eat the half-cooked, weevil-infested rice balls anyway.

The mind trick worked until the morning a Korean surgeon came into his miserable tent with a pair of garden shears and cut off three gangrenous toes. No anesthesia—just snip, snip, snip. He vomited from the pain and over the next four days removed two more infected toes with his fingernails.

For months, he looked after Henry, a young, blind marine. Fed him and tried to keep him comfortable. Three Chinese scientists implanted chicken livers under the blind man's armpit; perhaps a cure for frostbite they said. He was dead within a week. Henry's wasted body was dragged out into the snow and fed to the camp's dogs.

Later in the day when the guards returned, he attacked them, screaming every Korean curse word in his vocabulary. They beat him with their rifle butts, stripped him naked, and locked him in a four-by-four iron box. Daily, for the next two weeks, a handful of uncooked rice and a cup of water were thrown through a slit in the door into his private hellhole. In the darkness, he searched frantically for rice grains and licked the water droplets from the frost-covered floor and walls.

His misery reached an unfathomable level. And he gave in and asked Matilda to visit him.

He and his father had cut hay and stored it in the barn down by the river. He took Matilda there to see the harvest and a newborn colt. A light rain shower pelted the tin roof, and with a childlike contentment, they lay in the sweet-smelling hay dreaming dreams reserved for the world's most innocent—the dreams Adam and Eve had before the serpent encroached into the Garden. A heat rose up between them. He removed his shirt, then her blouse, and they lay facing each other in the hay. He had never seen a naked woman; she had never seen a naked man. Then the snake brought its knowledge to them.

He relived that in his mind for four days—and then told Matilda she had to go, and she could not come to him again. He could not stand for her to see him reduced to this, and he did not want the woman he loved so deeply to see him die. He pounded his face against the icy floor of the iron box until he was senseless.

Only when he was taken from the dark and cold box did he become aware that his right cheekbone was shattered and the eye was torn from its socket. Dr. Snip-Snip came and severed the ocular muscles.

The periods in which he could not remember his name became more frequent and longer.

June 1954, he and three other prisoners were trucked to the DMZ and dumped as if they were garbage. Naval corpsmen recorded his weight as sixty-nine pounds.

The Pecos River Valley

As Matilda slowly drove up the road to her papá's house, the yellow Hudson Hornet's shininess was dulled by the fine dust; Osweldo would not be happy. Soon after their marriage, Matilda learned her happiness depended on Osweldo's. He was quick with foul words and almost as quick with his fists.

Pete was the recipient of much of Osweldo's anger. He mostly called her son—"little Anglo *mierda.*" Once she pointed out that Pete was only half-Anglo, and that his dead father had been a good man and had given his life for their country. Osweldo laughed and spit on the floor. When he became angry at her, she could take him into the bedroom and drain his heat. Pete did not have that option.

Matilda recognized Osweldo's slyness: He was always respectful to her papá. And respectful to her in the old man's presence. Once Papá found bruises on Pete's ribs and questioned her. "He was playing in the irrigation ditch and fell against the sluice gate," she lied. It was only the second time she ever lied to her papá; the first time was when she told him her husband had come to her in her dreams saying he was dead. She was afraid. She was carrying Osweldo's sprouting seed in her stomach, and no child in her family had ever been born without a father.

On her wedding day, she became ill and emptied her stomach twice at the church. Her papá told his friend Freddy it must have been nervousness that caused her sickness. She tried to hold back the tears, but she knew it was God's way of punishing her. A young priest at Our Lady of Grace once said, "Certainly, an evil person will not go unpunished, but the descendants of righteous people will escape."

She vowed to become a good woman so Pete could escape her sins. And her unborn child would be pure and unstained.

Matilda found her papá sitting in the shade of a Russian olive tree in the back yard, sharpening a grubbing hoe. She pulled her dress away from her enlarged stomach, hoping he would not notice she was so soon with child.

Softly, she crept behind the old man's chair and kissed the back of his neck. "It's me, Papá. Your favorite daughter. The one who reveres and loves you the most."

8076th Mobile Army Surgical Hospital—South Korea
A Sikorsky air ambulance chopper came hammering in over the drab-colored hospital tents and, in a great flurry of pebbles, settled onto the concrete pad. Corpsmen unloaded two outboard litters and then scurried up the hill to the canvas tent of C Medical Company. A Marine gunnery sergeant sat in the rear seat of the chopper. Up at the DMZ, he carried the emaciated, one-eyed soldier on board the aircraft and then cradled him like a baby during the thirty-minute flight. In the rear-facing mirror, the copilot, his eyes hidden behind his aviator's sunglasses, watched the battle-hardened sergeant cry.

The critically ill soldier presented a major problem at the hospital: He was obviously part of the Allied forces and surely American, but he didn't have dog tags and was nonresponsive to questions. IVs sprouted from his body. Other tubes drained infections. For a month, nurses going off duty were sure he would be dead when their shift resumed. He lay still. When he regained consciousness, his eye opened and scanned the room without seemingly grasping the significance of his surroundings.

He became a mystery man, muttering pidgin-Korean and unable to sleep without powerful sedatives. The staff piled blankets atop him, but he remained cold. A South Korean interpreter sat by his bed for hours while scribbling indecipherable mutterings.

One afternoon, the interpreter announced, "He is saying

'wife and son.' And sometimes he says 'daddy.' I think he wants to see his family."

His physical recovery was so minute that once it was measured by his ability to open and close his finger twice more than the previous day. When he gained two pounds in a single week, the nursing staff declared a day of celebration and wore their caps backward and served cake and ice cream. But there was no way to measure mental progress because there was none.

Just before Christmas, he was moved to Walter Reed General Hospital in Washington. The medical staff in Korea, while they saved his life, believed they had failed, and several nurses wept bitterly when he was loaded onto the C-54 Medical Transport. They knew no more about him than when he had arrived months ago.

Some things only time can fix.

Capitan, New Mexico

Chapman was in his late thirties when he married and didn't figure there'd ever be kids in his life. His wife, Zella, was ten years younger. They had one child, a boy. She'd died about five years before the army took him. It would have killed her to see their son go off to war. Probably worse yet, she never got to see her grandson, Pete. Folks said Pete looked so much like his daddy that it was as if he'd spit in the dirt and Pete got up and walked out of it.

Chapman and his son bached after Zella died. He taught the boy to make cathead biscuits, barbecue a brisket, break a horse, repair a fence, rope, and just act like a man in general. But then, the boy married a cute little Mexican gal from over around Artesia. He'd rather the boy have married an Anglo, but he wasn't the one getting hitched. Hell, he'd probably have done the same thing when he was his son's age.

Now in his seventies, time had taken a toll on Chapman's body. His fingers were arthritic and long ago started pointing in unintended directions. When he was still young enough to rope and brand, a steer hooked through his thigh, and now it hurt like the devil when he swung a leg over the saddle. He'd spent too much time breaking horses, and most days his spine ached like hell. He took aspirin by the handfuls.

His mind told him that he was old. But it was worse when sometimes his mind didn't tell him anything. It used to piss him off something awful when he couldn't remember a feller's name or a familiar place. Sometime last year, he started getting used to it, and now those moments just slid on by like an evening shadow.

After his son went to the army, Chapman moved near Capitan, in Lincoln County, just south of the Sacramento Mountains. Capitan wasn't more than just a broad spot in the road. The old men who sat around the town's only store said it was getting smaller every day.

He bought this rough, eighty-acre spread and ran a few cows and a half-dozen horses. It took him and a couple of Mexicans more than a year to build his three-room house. It wasn't much to look at, but then he didn't need much and he didn't spend much time looking.

He put up his own hay—such as it was—tended a few stands of bees, and, optimistically, planted a fruit orchard. On summer mornings while it was still cool, he carried water up the hill from Magado Creek to water his tomatoes and young peach trees. Sometimes a month might go by and he'd not see anyone.

Matilda brought his grandson, Pete, over in the summers.

Pete didn't know Grandpa Chapman was old and worn out. The little boy loved his grandpa. They'd go camping and fishing. The grandfather told stories of Billy the Kid, Pat Garrett, gun fights up at La Mesa, the goings-on at Fort Sumner, and ghost stories about crying women wearing long, white veils haunting hotels.

Late afternoons, Chapman took his grandson out in the arroyo behind the barn. They'd rest his engraved Winchester on a bag of sand and shoot at tin cans; even with his deteriorating eyesight, the old man was deadly at a hundred yards. They would spend thirty minutes cleaning the gun; Chapman was always teaching.

Pete was awed by his father's father. He told Matilda, "When I grow up I want to live in the mountains with Grandpa Chapman. Gonna be a cowboy. But I want Papá Luna to come and spend summer vacations with us out at the ranch."

Chapman never learned to drive—"Don't trust the fool things," he said. But he caught a ride over to Roswell to hear U.S. Senator Joseph Chavez make a campaign speech. The yellow brick walls and the green terracotta-tiled domed roof of the courthouse made a great backdrop for the senator's public relations team to take photographs of the mostly partisan crowd. With his long, silver hair and sweat-stained, black hat, Chapman stood out in the mass of onlookers.

A group decked out in white, heavily-sequined mariachi suits and matching fiesta sombreros entertained the crowd, and the local high school band played three patriotic songs followed by the national anthem. Senator Chavez stood on the speaker's platform and raised his arms like a prophet blessing his followers before their pilgrimage into the desert.

The next day, the *Albuquerque Journal* reported that the senator's eight-minute speech was interrupted fourteen times with applause. However, they did not comment about the silver haired rancher who stood at the front of the crowd and shouted repeatedly at the senator: "You've killed my son, you son-of-a-bitch. He's dead over in that goddamned Korea." Nor did they report that the senator's security force cuffed the old man's hands behind his back and roughly dragged him to the backside of the courthouse.

Chapman sold all his horses except Deep Ruby. The mare's coat was the same color as Zella's hair when he first saw her.

He took two forks of hay out to feed Ruby and opened the gate into the pasture. He sat in the corner of the corral in the warm spring sunshine, and the fluttering behind his left shirt pocket went away—it always did. He thought about his boy and wondered what kind of hell he went through. He thought about Zella and how much he still missed her and was glad she was spared the awful death of their son. And he thought about Pete. It would be tough to be raised up without a daddy. He thought about his daddy and his grandpa buried back in the Tennessee hills, and all the changes they'd seen in their lives. He wondered how they felt when they got old.

Slumped against the fence, he sat through the night and the next day and the next night. Blow flies came and laid their eggs. Then the deer mice and the wood rats showed up. The raccoons, testing the air with little black noses, arrived and studied the still form. During the third night, the coyotes came. They were secretive eaters and carried parts of him through the peach orchard to a tamarisk thicket down by the creek. Ants took away what was left. After two weeks, it was as if he had never been.

Matilda took Pete to the ranch twice that summer. They didn't find Grandpa Chapman either time, nor did they see Ruby. The house had never been locked. They went inside on both visits: The first time things were intact; the second time the doors and windows had been smashed and the house vandalized.

Matilda had her hands full at home with Osweldo and their

girls. She told Pete his granddaddy must have moved without telling them. Pete argued with her, had a little-boy fit, and then cried as the car descended from the mountains and made its way over the bumpy roads back to Artesia.

Walter Reed General Hospital
Under the care of the Walter Reed staff, he gained weight but still showed little interest in the world of the hospital. The doctors noted one bit of progress: He no longer flinched when someone entered his room unexpectedly.

Pajamas buttoned to the top, he listlessly thumbed through *Collier's, Life,* and *Saturday Evening Post.* Photographs depicting the violent aftermath of the war, he tore from the magazines, crumpled, and threw on the floor.

The doctors wrote in his charts: enigma, inscrutable, closed book, challenging, puzzle. But the biggest mystery continued to be—Who was he? No dog tags. No entry into his mind. Nothing.

A nurse, Jill Bateman, joined the staff. The young doctors took notice. Her hair was thick, short, blond, and swept back as if she had just returned from a sunny afternoon ride in a convertible. She'd spent much of her teen years as a competitive gymnast. Her body still had the leanness ingrained from hours of practice and high-level competition. She had the look and the demeanor of someone unaccustomed to losing; she was bright and cheerful, but inexperienced.

She was not much younger than the wounded soldier. He became her special project. "I can bring him around," she said, in a Monday morning staff meeting. The nurses and doctors who had worked with him unsuccessfully for more than a year wished her luck.

One day in early April, she brought an overcoat, a fresh patch for his still-healing eye socket, and a wheelchair to his room. "A road trip," she told him. "I've got a van from the motor pool. We are going down to the Tidal Basin. Going to see the cherry blossoms."

Expressionless, he watched the government buildings slip past the van's window.

She rolled him out into the glorious clouds of the pink blossoms, and they sat in the warmth of spring sunshine. A National Park Service ranger helped him into one of the paddleboats, and she toured him about the lake. Having recognized the military nurse and suspecting the crippled man with her was a soldier, the ranger was waiting when they got back to the dock.

At a concession stand, they bought coffee. The wind blew a cherry blossom petal into his coffee, and he stared dully at it, uncertain what to do. A troupe of young female dancers bought ice cream, and they laughed as happy young girls do on a spring outing. Then, they pantomimed all sorts of happiness. He stared at them; the nurse thought he almost smiled.

One of the young women pretended to jump rope. "One, two, buckle my shoe, three, four, shut the door," she sang. The others joined in, then tired of the game and flitted away.

He stared up into the cloudless sky, and tears gathered in his eye. His lips moved slightly and mumbled: "1-2-3-8-8-3-1, *sir.*"

Stunned, the nurse whispered, "Oh, my God. My God."

She and her patient returned to the hospital at twilight. Senior staff was gone for the day. She filed her evening report. The next morning, the supervising nurse called her into the central conference room where two doctors were sharing her report.

"He said these exact words?" the oldest doctor asked.

"Yes, sir," the nurse replied. "I wrote the numbers almost immediately after he said them."

"He did not repeat them?" a younger doctor asked.

"No, sir, just said them once."

The doctors leaned away from the table and conferred.

The younger doctor scribbled something on a pad and hurriedly left the room.

The older doctor rested his elbows on the table and leaned forward, palms against his temples. "I've been in the service for almost twenty-nine years. I believe I know what those numbers represent. Believe it or not, I started as a medic in the infantry. We were assigned weapons in those days. That is the serial number of our mystery man's weapon—I'll bet a month's pay. If I'm right, we will know his name before the sun sets tomorrow."

At afternoon break the next day, an army courier delivered a worn manila envelope. The older doctor placed the envelope on his desk and called the younger doctor and the nurse into his office. He took the last swallow of tepid coffee and stubbed his cigarette out in a crowded ashtray. "Here goes nothing," he said as he unwound the red string securing the envelope's flap.

He placed three sheets of paper on the desk. To anyone not in the military, the information would have been almost indecipherable: dates in military format, capitalized acronyms, scrawled initials, various colored stampings, routing stations, and equipment issues. A black and white identification photograph was attached to the first page with a paperclip.

The doctor read aloud, as he scanned the data. "Born Roswell, New Mexico, in August 1930. Finished the eighth grade. No high school. Sworn in at Fort Sill, Oklahoma, in September of 1949. A-positive. Christian. Finished basic training at Fort Sill. Expert Marksmanship badge with rifle and pistol badge bars; Distinguished Shot badge. Deployed to Inchon in August 1950. Received a Purple Heart. Missing in action: December 1950 at the Battle of Chosin Reservoir. Weapon number 1-2-3-8-8-3-1.

"Listed relatives: wife Matilda and son Peter, Seven Rivers, New Mexico; father F. E. Chapman, Artesia, New Mexico."

The doctor flipped back to the first page and slid it across the table. He pointed to the caption under the photograph. "So now you know our mystery man's name. Martin Chapman. It is a solid name, don't you think?"

The Pecos River Valley

Osweldo had plenty of time to make plans. He was serving six months in the Chaves County Jail for cutting Rick Reyes during a crap game.

He knew Matilda's father, Romero, had to be in his seventies, maybe older. The old man had gone through a couple of strokes, and the doctor warned him about fatty foods and too much wine. Of course, he didn't do much: walk around and look at his pecan trees, plait *ristras,* worry about bugs laying eggs in his pecan blossoms and chili weevils eating his peppers. And rain: the old man worried about not enough rain.

Nueces River Operating Company took Romero's royalty check down to the bank the first of each month. Gas leases, drilling, production, and exploration were a mystery to the old man. If he had his way, he'd rather have pasture and cows than oil wells, service roads, and pipes meandering across his land. He never spent money, wore the same old raggedy shirt and patched jeans, drove an ancient, floppy-fendered Dodge pickup he purchased just before World War II.

Matilda did whatever little looking-after Romero's money required. Now, Osweldo was looking after Matilda.

He knew about the old man's money when he asked Matilda to marry him; wasn't like she had much choice unless she wanted to tell her daddy she was going to have a baby and didn't have a husband.

Marrying into a family that had producing wells was, he believed, a smart move on his part. Besides, Matilda still had an easy-to-look-at ass and the best set of tits this side of Ciudad Juárez. He figured to put up with Pete until he could whip the little *mierda* into shape.

As far as old man Romero, after he was buried, Osweldo would be moving onto Easy Street.

His friends called Osweldo *El Calculadora*. He always looked for the angle. Most of the time, his best plans ended in disaster, but it was not because he had not calculated the risk; it was because he was just not bright. He'd tried to sell a twice-stolen pistol to the original owner. Once he'd broken into a store on the north side of town only to encounter the owner's vicious cur waiting inside when he came through the window. But he was right this time, and he knew it.

Back when he courted Matilda, she had been lonely. She had a child, and her husband was surely dead. Osweldo slicked his freshly-cut hair, shaved, rubbed his face with Bay Rum, and even put a little in his armpits. He chose his shiniest red shirt and the western boots with the silver toe-covers. He studied himself in the mirror, loosened the top buttons of his shirt, and puffed his chest out until the fake gold chain glistened against his skin.

It took three times: once they went to mass together; the second time he bought her a soda; the third time they'd parked by the river, and she'd put her face on his chest and told him of her sadness. He consoled her. In every way he could imagine.

Later, he bragged that Matilda melted in his arms.

Osweldo stood by the jail window, clutching the bars. He would party Matilda many times when he got home. Maybe they would make a baby. He rubbed his hand across his crotch. Maybe even two. Now the only thing he had to worry about was the next twenty-nine days in this stinking cell. Or was it twenty-eight?

Walter Reed General Hospital

Having the addresses of his next of kin didn't help unravel the mystery of the wounded soldier. The DOA sent registered letters informing them he was recuperating in Walter Reed; they were returned stamped *Moved No Forwarding Address.* After the second letter came back, he would not leave his bed for a week, just lay facing the wall.

When he became responsive again, the young nurse started physical therapy at a more intensive level. His feet were malformed. The loss of toes and subsequent surgery left him with little more than stubs. Standard issue army shoes were uncomfortable. The nurse found canvas gym shoes were appropriate, and, until he regained strength, a wheeled walker added confidence.

He required more time than other patients. Although his mood swings appeared to diminish, they were still significant; a single day would encompass periods of optimism, sullenness, and despair. But, generally, the staff saw progress, and the young nurse was asked to present a paper at a two-day, New York seminar explaining the methods of rehabilitation she found most successful.

Staff detected the soldier was becoming attached to the nurse, and on her days off or when she was away he sulked. During her absence, he lay in bed with the sheet pulled over his head.

Each week, she carried him to a different restaurant. Occasionally, civilians stared at the slender man, hands folded in his lap and one eye covered with a black patch. He slumped in the wheelchair as the petite nurse pushed him through the crowds. But most of the people who frequented this part of town were accustomed to seeing damaged men. Walter Reed seemed to house more than its share of men mangled by the terrible machine of war.

Soon he sat on one of the hospital's open decks, a blanket around his thin shoulders, and watched the peacefulness of swans swimming in a small lake. He was proud of his new-found strength and the ability to shave and take a shower unassisted. His memory of imprisonment started to erode, but, strangely, he retained the ability to remove his mind from his body and exist in an entirely different place.

He had become reconciled he would forever walk painfully and with a lurching gait. Doctors confirmed that the tips of his fingers would remain partially numb from the severe frostbite, and drainage from the nasal cavity behind the shattered cheekbone would be intermittent.

He joked with the young nurse one morning that considering he had only one eye, was crippled, snot ran from his nose most of the time, and was only partially crazy—he was in damned good shape. He didn't have many light moments, and staff considered this black humor to be a progression of his mental health.

The lieutenant colonel and his aide stood beside the soldier's bed. The officer called the medical staff into the room and made a big ceremony presenting him with a couple of medals and a written commendation.

He was not impressed with either men or their medals. "Desk jockeys, the both of them," he told the nurse later.

"Considering what you've been through," the colonel said, "you have been awarded a leave of ninety days and, after proper authorization, will be discharged. Of course, you've accumulated pay for the period when you were held illegally by the North Korean army. And for your stay of recovery here at Reed."

The soldier looked at the aide's soft, perfectly shaped hands and hated him.

The colonel continued. "We will arrange military transportation to Walker Air Force Base in Roswell. I believe a medical escort down to Walker would be appropriate."

The aide nodded in agreement and made a note.

The Pecos River Valley

Osweldo and Matilda lived in the poorest section of Artesia—the part of town where failed cars rested on concrete blocks and small heat-generated dust devils skipped and played along unpaved streets as if they were lively children. To the east, pecan groves ended before the Pecos River, and, past that, red-grainy hills spotted with gas wells and spidery service roads continued for five miles before giving way to open rangeland.

Osweldo complained he was cursed with bad luck. Promised jobs at the refinery did not materialize. He was jailed occasionally for selling stolen property. He believed common field labor was beneath the dignity of a man like himself—particularly a man married to a woman whose father owned three gas wells. Osweldo missed the birth of their second child because he was in the Carlsbad jail. He claimed he had been misidentified as a participant in a grocery store burglary.

Matilda refused financial help from her papá; it was part of her deal with God. She watched her siblings take money from their father and then spend it wastefully—she considered it sinful and evil. She remembered the young priest's words: *"Certainly, an evil person will not go unpunished, but the descendants of righteous people will escape."* She was determined to be a righteous person. Her part-time jobs at the feed store, the pecan store, and The Range Inn motel supported the family.

★ ★ ★ ★ ★

Most of the time, Pete stayed at his grandfather's. It was Matilda's way of protecting her son from Osweldo's violence. It suited Romero to have his grandson live with him. They made a good pair, tending the chilies and watering the pecan tree.

Romero bought Pete little toy soldiers. In the afternoons after school, children sat on the bank of an *acequia* in the back yard and dug miniature foxholes to protect the soldiers. Flipped pebbles were artillery rounds, and they never hit the troops. "We're the good people," Pete told a buddy. "Good people don't die in the war."

"My folks said your daddy died in the war," his buddy said. "I thought he was a good man."

Pete cried himself to sleep that night.

Without the old man's nurturing, Chapman's fruit trees suffered death from dehydration.

Varmints searched his house for bits of food and sought shelter from the elements. Two coyotes denned under the tattered remains of the old man's bed. Soon it became a full-time job to feed the lactating mother and the three buff-gray pups. A male cougar watched the coyotes for days and learned their habits—the female hunted at night and the male during the day. Just before dawn on a cool morning when the male was mouth-feeding the young, the big cat quietly invaded the house and claimed the domain of the coyote. He toyed briefly with the pups before dragging the dead adult coyote out into the fresh morning air.

The C-54 Skymaster en route to San Diego from Washington diverted and landed at Walker Air Force Base in Roswell, New Mexico. A young nurse and a slender man deplaned. The man struggled to walk, his one-eyed face something from a bad dream. The warm desert wind swept the airport. No flags snapped in the wind. No trumpets sang. No drums rolled. No crowd cheered. No applause. Just the dry wind.

A jeep took the two back to the terminal. He stood in the center of the building and breathed the once-familiar desert air. She called an automobile rental agency in Roswell, and, within an hour, they were driving south along Highway 285 toward Artesia. He insisted all four windows be down.

As they drove, she wondered about this alien country. The dry rangeland slipped past, its desolation occasionally altered by a windmill, a cattle pen, or a dry creek bed. In ten miles, she saw three oversized mailboxes. And two cows—or at least that's what she thought they were—standing in the shade of a scrawny tree, their swishing tails fighting a losing battle against a swarm of hostile flies. A rabbit the size of a small deer hopped across the road in front of them and stopped to look at the automobile, seemingly curious at this strange machine. She wondered how in heaven's name people existed in this barren land.

He must have sensed her thoughts. "There's good land east of here, close to the river," he said almost defensively. "Grow good alfalfa and cotton. Maybe if you stay around a while, we can go see it."

She'd formed this strange attachment to him. It was not love, but instead, like. When he came to Reed, she'd washed his scaling legs and lotioned his misshapen hands and feet. When he'd been so detached from humanity, sometimes when her shift was over she'd go home and cry, wondering what she was doing wrong. Now, when they were approaching the end of their journey together, she wondered if there would have been anything between them if they'd met under different circumstances.

The nothingness of Artesia rose from the plains. She asked if he was hungry. He said he reckoned he could eat a bite. She ordered burgers and coffee at a roadside café. They sat on a slatted bench and ate. He watched the passersby, searching for a familiar face. Not one.

They drove, the mid-afternoon sun heating the right side of the car. "We're comin' up on Seven Rivers," he said. "Don't blink or you'll miss it. Up there. Past that grove. Just before the feedlot, turn left."

She'd never seen a feedlot nor even knew they existed. The steers stood in the fenced lots among unbelievably high mounds of manure. She innocently assumed beef just somehow appeared magically in the grocery coolers, and it was not easy for her to imagine a steak could come from something that smelled so awful.

He grinned at her. "I used to work there. Was a pen rider. Kept the cows fed, looked after the sick ones, stuff like that. Colder'n hell in the winter and hotter'n hell in the summer. You get used to the stink. Well, I did; Matilda didn't. Folks around here say it smells like money."

Dust elevated behind them, and, from a distance, it might have looked like a brown wedge pushing the automobile. He pointed to a road paralleling an irrigation ditch. "That one. We live down at the end. Moved down there soon after Matilda and me got married. Pete was just a baby. Crawled all over the place."

They stopped in the yard of a small adobe house. The windows were missing, and the front door had become unhinged and leaned against a porch post. At the back of the house, a few scattered tin cans and a child's tricycle with the front wheel missing. Tumbleweeds assaulted the back porch and were encroaching into the kitchen. Four dried okra stalks huddled together in the barren garden, leafless sentries guarding nothing.

He appeared emotionless, she thought, or maybe he was stunned. He put the broken tricycle in the back seat.

They drove back out to the highway, turned northward, and back toward Artesia.

Late afternoon, they turned eastward along the Lovington Highway. If she thought the trip down to Seven Rivers had been through a hostile country, she revised her opinion on the road to Maljamar. Once they crossed the Pecos, there was nothing but a sea of carefully spaced gas wells. The hundreds of walking-beam heads moved up and down unsynchronized. The sour smell of the wells caused her to roll up her window. She hoped he'd realize her distaste and do the same, but he seemed to enjoy the breeze and didn't notice her actions.

Abruptly, the gas wells and the Jacob's beams with their nodding horse heads were behind them. The land was devoid of growth taller than a man's belt buckle. Just miles and miles of nothing. Inwardly, she cringed.

"See those mailboxes up there? Turn left. Dad lives up that road. We moved there after Mama passed on."

They drove by two ranch-hands' houses. At the first house, a woman was unloading a horse from a gooseneck trailer. She turned, shaded her eyes from the sun, and touched the front brim of her hat; he waved back. The second yard was filled with stock dogs and children. They raced the car along the fence, the kids shouting and the dogs yipping.

"Over that little rise," he said.

Her female intuition warned her about impending . . . something—something they were not expecting. The house was being used by a service company as a field office, and the yard and horse lot were covered with drilling equipment and battered pickups. She gave him privacy as he stood outside the car and wept. This time, he didn't even walk into the yard.

★ ★ ★ ★ ★

The woman had tied her horse beside the trailer and was brushing him with a rusted currycomb. They stopped, got out of the car, stretched, and made introductions. She'd lived on this ranch less than a year, and the man who lived down the road—she thought his first name was Chapman or maybe that was his last name—was long gone when she got here. Somebody said he'd moved out around the Capitan Mountains—maybe somewhere close to El Malpais.

It was dark when they got back to Artesia. It'd been a quiet trip; he'd slumped down in the seat, crossed his arms defensively, and closed his eyes. She had no idea what to say.

She rented two rooms at The Range Inn, the best motel in town. He'd wanted to pay, said he had plenty of money. She paid. The government military per diem covered the cost of getting him acclimated.

He declined dinner. She ate and checked on him at 7:00. Got no answer. An hour later, he knocked on her door. "Would you like to go over and get a cup of coffee?" he asked.

He took his coffee with double cream and leaned back in the Naugahyde-covered seat. "We are oh-for-two today," he said. "I looked through the Artesia phone directory tonight. Found a Romero Luna. Called the number, and a man answered—sounded like an old man's voice."

"Did you talk with him?" the nurse asked.

"No. I hung up. I'm not ready. I don't have a good feeling about this. Matilda gone and all. All those registered letters the government sent returned. There is a big hole here, and I can't seem to reach the bottom." He took a drink of coffee. "Do you understand?"

She thought for a bit. "I think so. It's about facing things, isn't it? Unknown things?"

He nodded. "I reckon. I've got to know about Dad. Then

Matilda and Pete. Maybe saving the worst for last." He looked out through the café's tinted window and for a few seconds watched the yellow shafts of headlights gliding down the street. "If Dad did move to the mountains, I know where he is at. A little town named Capitan. We used to go over there deer hunting. He always said that a man could find peace there."

"Sounds like a plan," she said. "How will we find him?"

"We'll go to the Lincoln County courthouse in Carrizozo. Look for a deed. Work on it from there."

They crossed the street to the motel. She slowed her pace to match his hobbling, then searched her jacket for the room key.

He stood by her door and smoothed his eye patch. "Can I ask you a question?"

Without even hearing the question, she was worriedly forming answers. "Sure, go ahead."

Then, he took a few steps, unlocked his door and pocketed the key. "Would you—" his voice wavered. "I'm sorry . . . maybe later . . . not tonight."

Once inside, she studied her face in the bathroom mirror. "God," she whispered.

There was strangeness at breakfast. He seemed hesitant, and she desperately sought to regain the relationship they shared since leaving Washington.

They rode along through the desert, and, at mid-morning, low mountains interrupted the smoothness of the horizon. There was greenery and a scattering of ranches with weathered headquarters buildings. They stopped for gas at a wind-blasted service station. He went in and bought cigarettes. She had never seen him smoke. "It's not good for you," she said.

"I ain't found much lately that's good for me," he said.

In Carrizozo, Mrs. Zamora, the county clerk, found a record of the deed where Chapman purchased eighty acres. She marked the location of the property on a county map.

They drove the twenty miles back to Capitan. He chain-smoked, and she shook her head disapprovingly. Even with the sunshine and the freshness of the mountains, sweat stains darkened the underarm parts of his shirt.

This time, there was no mailbox, just a weathered plank with a crude image of a dragonfly cut into it. "That's Dad's mark," he said. He got out and opened the barbed-wire gap; she drove the car through, and he fastened the gap. They drove up the rutted road. He smiled—it had been a long time since she'd seen his smile.

She was a city girl, but she wondered why the road did not show sign of travel. Maybe Chapman just didn't come out much. Maybe he was happy with his own company. She wanted these maybes to be true.

He searched the road in front of them for tire tracks. Dad never fully trusted anything with a motor. Perhaps his father traveled only by horseback—maybe that was the reason for no tire tracks—or maybe he walked. He desperately wanted a reason for the untraveled appearance of the road.

The road turned sharply, and there before them was the house and barn sitting on a narrow bench of rock overlooking the creek. From a distance, everything appeared commonplace, and he was able to breathe normally without the tightening in his chest or the hammering of his heart.

Her vision was sharper than his—two eyes versus one—and before he could see, she saw the weed-filled garden and tattered rags and bits of paper scattered across the front yard and captured by the brush. A sheet of tin roofing had come loose, and one end moved beckoningly in the wind. There was no smoke from the chimney, and the glassless windows opened into darkness. She wanted to turn around and maybe come back another day—a day when Chapman would ride out of the shadows and greet his son, and she could witness a joyous reunion.

They came to the last barbed-wire gap, and she stopped the car. He got out and opened it but this time did not wait for her to drive through. He ran with his hobbling gait through the weeds and mesquite toward the house, fell, and ran again, but this time he howled like a dog struck by a car. An alarm inside her went off: this might be too much. She was in this terrible isolation with a man who may have been pushed over the edge, and she was afraid—afraid he might be taking her with him.

These were her options: Drive away and leave him here; go and try to comfort him—after all, she had been trained for situations like this; or stand here and wait for him to come back.

She took a deep breath and let it slip out as a soft mutter . . . *Please let him be all right, please.* She got out of the car and worked her way through the weeds and bushes toward the house. She could hear him inside, shouting and cursing, breaking glass jars and splintering wood.

She was almost to the house when he charged through the door and out onto the porch. He stood, weaving, and then pounded his head against the porch post. Then he turned toward her, hands at face level, clenching and unclenching his fist. The mesquite or broken glass had cut him, and his arms were bloody. She could smell him—smell the adrenaline-powered sweat and the anger. Mucus from his damaged sinuses lay across his upper lip. His eye patch had slipped off, and a dark, reddish-brown liquid drained from the vacant eye socket.

He glared at the nurse and clawed at his face. "Goddamn you, you bitch, this is your fault, all your fault."

Something inside her agreed with him. It *was* her fault.

It was Matilda's weekend to work the front desk at The Range Inn motel. Osweldo had not come home last night, and she needed a ride to work. Her father's truck was in the shop. "Call my friend Freddy," he suggested. "He will be glad to take you to work." She found his phone number.

"Be there soon as I finish my egg," Freddy said. Ten minutes later Freddy's dusty Chevrolet sedan, trailed by a thin cloud of blue smoke, stopped in front of her house.

Once before, she had ridden with Freddy. Some time back, he'd broken his glasses, and his foggy vision caused him to have several fender benders—nothing major: he'd hit a phone booth, demolished mailboxes, narrowly missed a neighbor's dog, and did hit the corner post of his yard fence. But, in his defense, he drove slowly, and neighbors soon learned to avoid the erratically moving Chevrolet.

The ride this morning was typical Freddy. Matilda was relieved to arrive at the motel in one piece. She thanked the old man and kissed his cheek. The gears clashed a couple of times, and soon the car swayed and swerved down the street.

Inside, she made fresh coffee and vowed to find Osweldo; he *would* pick her up at work tomorrow night.

She took last night's receipts from the cash drawer—management required payment in advance—and started matching them against the occupants. She usually studied the guest register, liked to see the names—the far-away cities where they lived. The motel had regular customers: oil field engineers, salesmen, and cattle buyers. She sugared her coffee and ran her finger down the guest register. She recognized most of the names.

Adjacent rooms 120 and 121 were rented last night and again for tonight. Home address of the occupants was Washington, D.C. The first signature was delicate, obviously feminine. The second was a childish scrawl, almost unreadable. Matilda leaned away from the counter, and her elbow brushed the coffee cup. Everything moved in slow motion, the cup tumbled dreamily downward, and then the black coffee spread sluggishly across the tile floor. She recognized her husband's signature.

Matilda fled to the manager's office. Her mind sought a peaceful hiding place in her brain—a place where she couldn't see the shaky signature. She dialed home and then her father's number; neither answered.

She called the clerk on the previous shift. His name was William. He never forgot anything and viewed everything suspiciously, made mental notes. He'd been robbed once at another motel and wasn't able to give a good description of the robbery or getaway car. "Makes you look closer," he'd told Matilda.

"He's gone to see his mother in Socorro," his wife said. "Be back next week. His mother doesn't have a phone. Sorry."

It had been almost eight years since she last saw her husband, and, last night, they slept in the same town. She had been almost sure he was dead—almost wanted him dead. She needed to go on with her life. Now he was back.

The office door opened and buzzed. Matilda looked through the peephole in the door and was relieved to see the housekeepers had arrived. They came behind the counter and looked at the list of rooms that needed service. She came out and made the assignments while Claudia, the youngest of the women, cleaned the spilled coffee from the floor. This woman was a recent employee and spoke almost no English. The older woman, Rita, busied herself collecting fresh linen and towels and loading them onto her work cart.

Matilda flipped through the registration cards until she found the license plate number the occupants of 120 and 121 had given. She wrote the number on a card and gave it to Rita saying, "See if this automobile is in the parking lot."

Rita circled the U-shaped parking lot and came back shaking her head. "Nothing matching these numbers."

Matilda felt some relief; at least he was not at the motel this morning. But with the rooms reserved for tonight, it was almost certain he and the woman companion would be back.

How was he here? The government had not notified her he was dead. Missing, but not dead. But it had been so long. And things changed here. A husband. Other children. And now he is here. In this town. This motel.

Why had he not contacted her or the family? Where had he been? How would he react if he came into the office and saw her? What would she do? And Pete . . . he probably did not even remember his father. Osweldo! He was insanely jealous. How would he react to the reappearance of her first husband?

Now her tension increased as her thoughts frantically ran through little avenues of her mind like mice seeking escape from a cat.

Matilda searched the phone log from last night. Room 121 made one call. To her father! The log showed zero minutes. That meant either her father had not answered, or the caller terminated the call almost immediately.

Rita pushed her work cart out of the office and onto the sidewalk. She turned and waited for Claudia to follow. "One moment," Matilda said. "I need help from Claudia."

Matilda took the master key from the desk drawer and motioned for Claudia to follow. Together they walked along the front of the motel until they came to room 120. She knocked on the door, called "housekeeping," waited seconds, then knocked again. She gave the key to the housekeeper and followed her into the room. The unmade room was tidy: blouses and slacks hung neatly, a closed makeup kit, a robe hung on the bathroom door and a pair of shoes aligned perfectly in the closet. The shower had been used but the motel soap and shampoo not opened; the woman, probably not trusting the quality of the motel's, used her own.

They went through the same knocking procedure before entering room 121. The bed covers were wrinkled but not turned down—whoever slept in this bed last night must have been restless because the pillows had been wadded and lay in the corner of the room. A canvas duffle bag had been thrown into the chair by the window. A paper cup of coffee rested atop the heating unit. A Dopp kit sat zipped on the bathroom vanity. A Texaco road map of New Mexico partially opened on the nightstand tented over something, maybe a book or other personal item. Curious, Matilda lifted the map with her thumb and index finger and saw a metal-framed photograph of a young woman. It had been turned to face the bed. The woman in the picture stared, unsmiling, straight at the photographer, maybe searching for the future, and not yet aware of life's uncertainty and things she should hope to never see.

The housekeeper studied the photograph, then asked, *"¿Quién es en la fotografía?"*

Matilda pressed both hands against her cheeks and for a moment could not breathe. *"Soy en la fotografía.* It's me in the photograph."

Freddy and Romero walked to the corner grocery for a soda and salted peanuts. Freddy offered to drive, but Romero declined; he had once ridden with his old friend and made the sign of the cross when he was safely out of the car. He decided not to challenge the charity of the saints on such a fine day.

As old men of leisure frequently do, they sat in the warmth of the winter sunshine and reminisced. They had been friends since childhood. They worked in the fields together gathering chilies and digging irrigation ditches. Romero married first; Freddy envied his friend's happiness, and soon he, too, married. Their children grew up together. Their wives died in the same year, and the old men consoled each other. Like old entwined grapevines that had grown beside each other through the seasons, what affected one affected the other.

The trip from Capitan to the motel in Artesia was just over two hours. She tried to make conversation, but he sat stoically, eyes locked on the road.

It had been the most intense situation she had ever encountered. The three months' training in the psych ward had not prepared her for anything like what she had experienced earlier in the day. For five minutes, he'd stood on the porch and cursed her. Then he went back into the house, and the crashing and banging started again. The next time he came back to the porch, he might have been calmer, but he continued to berate her. "Everything is your fault," he shouted. "I should have died in the hospital. Then I wouldn't have gone through this. Wouldn't have known that my wife had deserted me, and that my father was gone. I wanted to die, but you kept shooting drugs into me. Look at me now. Is this what you wanted?"

He hobbled up and down the porch, clawing at his face, pounding his head against the wall of the building. She did not move for fear of what might happen if she showed any emotion.

He wanted to kill this woman, this person who brought him out to this desolate place. She put him into a metal box and starved him. His feet ached after she cut the toes from his feet. She had made him cold and blew his friend to bits with a hand grenade. She must have known that his father was gone, known that Matilda and Pete were not at their home, and known that their house was abandoned. If she would only run, then it would be proof that she was guilty and had almost accomplished her evil plan. And he would run after her and tear the flesh from her bones. But she stood silently and watched.

In all but the most insane, man's madness has a limit.

He thought of the boat trip on the lake and the kindness of the park ranger. The little girls playing at jump rope and quoting the numbers. The nurse bandaged his hands and feet, rubbed lotion over the healing flesh. They had eaten at nice restaurants, and she was not ashamed of the way he looked. The cherry blossoms floated down from the leafing trees, and their pinkness covered him. It came to him about kindness and gentleness.

The madness softened.

Finally, he sat on the edge of the porch, and she sat beside him. She put one arm around his shoulder and with the other hand wiped away the dark, reddish-brown liquid draining from the vacant eye socket. The anger left his mind, and he cried.

At the edge of Artesia, he asked if he could have a beer— tallboys; he wanted Budweiser tallboys. And a sack of chips. He wanted to go into the liquor store by himself and buy the beer. Yes, he knew he was a mess, but that didn't bother him anymore. This was who he was and who he would always be. After today, he was past all that. He wanted her to drink a beer with him, needed to apologize—again and again.

Matilda watched through the curtains as the dusty sedan parked in the space reserved for room 120. The two people disappeared from her sight as they got out of the car and went into the rooms. She stood and watched; she hoped for a better look. Within minutes, the young woman and a crippled man with a blood-speckled shirt came out and walked to the gazebo that sat under the locust grove in the center of the parking lot. He carried a large paper bag as if it were a baby.

Matilda could see him better now. When they married, he had been muscular and wrestled steers at the local jackpot rodeos. His thick hair had been reddish brown and curly; now it was completely gray and cropped short. His body was slight and stooped. He hobbled to the trash can with two empty beer cans, and with the last light illuminating his features, she could see the eye patch and his terribly twisted face. Here was this man from her past—her husband—and he was unrecognizable.

Once when they were teenagers, she stood waiting for the school bus in the mid part of first morning light. He'd come loping along the dirt road on his horse and tipped his hat to her. She could still see the gray hat, sweat stained, high-crowned, a small hole where the pinch and the crease met. Matilda waved—timidly, in case her Papá was watching. Chapman passed, then wheeled the horse and, with a great pounding, swept down upon her. He kicked free from the left stirrup and reached out—"Put your foot in the stirrup," he'd shouted—then pulled her up behind him. She'd wrapped both arms around his waist, her young breasts pressed against his back. She never looked at another boy.

She wept. She had not intended to, but this powerful feeling of pity and loss had come over her like a chill; she lost control and screamed into her cupped hands.

She watched them as long as it was light, and with the darkness they became shapes almost without form. They sat and drank beer, and occasionally the tip of his cigarette glowed angrily in the darkness. Matilda locked the front and went through the back door and, keeping in the shadows, moved until she could understand a few words of their conversation: "Chapman . . . Seven Rivers . . . Maljamar . . . Pete . . . Walter Reed . . . scared."

The man said the word *Matilda,* and her soul ached.

There was no laughter, only weariness in their bodies and sadness in their voices.

Matilda went inside and closed the curtains. She got her purse from the manager's office and searched behind the slit lining until she found the creased black-and-white picture—a carnival photograph made the day after they married. She looked at the young woman in the picture, narrow waist, heavy bosom, happy smile. Her hair was shoulder length and tied back with his bandana; he said she favored the movie star Yvonne De Carlo. He wore a checkered, short-sleeved shirt. The sleeves were turned up a couple of times, and his biceps strained against the cloth. After all these years, she could still feel his strength. Just teenagers! They leaned in against one another, and their heads touched. They thought life would be like this forever.

She placed the photograph on the counter and took stationery from the drawer. She would write him and explain what happened. Explain that she thought he was dead, Pete needed a father, and she was lonely. She would tell him her papá encouraged her to marry, that he wanted her to be happy, this was the right thing to do, and he gave his blessing. She sat at the typewriter and wrote these things. She would not tell him that she was with Osweldo's baby.

It was almost a quarter past nine when she finished. The lies bothered her. She covered these words with Mistake Out until the page embarrassed her. It was almost like the glossy whiteness was shouting *lie, there's a lie under here.* She crumpled the typing paper with its untruths and tossed it into the trash can, bought a pack of Chesterfields from the vending machine, and made a pot of coffee.

She telephoned her father. He was asleep and probably did not hear the phone. The young priest at Our Lady of Grace did not answer his phone either.

The manager didn't like for her to smoke in the office. She walked into the office restroom, dropped the half-smoked Chesterfield in the toilet, and flushed. She watched the cigarette circle the bowl, fighting the pull of the swirling water, and then surrender to the inevitable conclusion.

Matilda removed the name tag from her blazer, lit another cigarette, and dialed room 120.

★ ★ ★ ★ ★

The phone buzzed three times before the nurse sleepily answered. Matilda told her there might be a problem with the bill, and it needed to be cleared before she could close the accounts for the day. There was a long silence. Shouldn't take more than a couple of minutes.

The nurse was a levelheaded person with a generous streak of kindness. However, this had been the most chaotic day of her life; after driving miles and miles across deserts and mountains, she had dealt with a man who teetered on the edge of lunacy. She had taken a double Cutty Sark and then luxuriated in a warm, ten-minute shower. Tomorrow had the potential to be just as stressful as today—now the desk clerk was trying to reconcile her account. She put on her blouse and slacks and walked to the motel office. *Jesus H. Christ!*

She is not much younger than I am Matilda thought when the nurse, her short blond hair still damp, entered the motel office. But the word *intimidating* ran through her mind. "I apologize for this inconvenience," Matilda said. She explained she simply needed verification of the automobile license plate and a couple of other items. The auto had a Utah tag, and they had given Washington, D.C. as an address. Her boss had a policy of matching license plates and addresses—once police chastised him after a robbery about a registration mismatch. She was terribly sorry to be so much trouble. She was just taking orders from management.

The nurse understood taking orders. She made it clear that it was a rental car from Roswell. As far as the addresses, both she and the man in room 121 were from Walter Reed Army Hospital in D.C. She assured Matilda that she was not a bank robber, and they shared a quick giggle as women do when they are a bit unsure in an unusual situation. She explained she was a nurse, and the man was a former soldier, a patient under her care.

Matilda made the notation on a supplemental registration sheet. Her writing was shaky, and she felt perspiration gathering in the small of her back. She gave the nurse a weak smile. "I hope he is doing well. Did he once live around here?"

The nurse returned the smile. She knew the desk clerk was fishing. Why not just get this over with so she could get sleep. "Yes, my patient is improving. He had been a POW in Korea." She had been assigned to get him reestablished so the government could release him. It was unusual for the government to provide such a service, but his circumstances were also unusual.

Matilda wiped her brow and licked a drop of sweat from her upper lip. The room was too warm—maybe it was the thermostat. She felt lightheaded. Then she knew it wasn't heat, it was the smothering stress.

Preparing to leave, the nurse collected her purse from the counter. "Tomorrow, we will search for his wife, Matilda, and their son, Pete."

Matilda took the faded black-and-white photo from the drawer, the one made soon after she and her husband married, and timidly pushed it across the counter. The nurse slid it to the side and away from the glare of the overhead light. The day had been long, and the night was stretching out. The nurse needed rest, and now the motel clerk was showing family photographs. "Do I know these people?" she asked and was chagrined at the irritation in her voice.

Matilda pointed to the woman in the photograph. "That's me," she said. "We had just gotten married." She shook her head. "Innocent. We were so innocent. We had no idea what lay in front of us. How the war would change our lives. And Pete's."

Maybe it was the stress of the day, maybe the double scotch, maybe the surreality of the search for his wife and child ending so simply, but it took the nurse a couple of heartbeats to connect reality with what she just heard. This time, the nurse said,

"Jesus H. Christ! You are Matilda, his wife? This is him before
. . . before he was . . . before the awful—?"

She hadn't smoked since nursing school because she had
seen the damaged lungs and gasping for breath. Matilda
watched the nurse glance at the pack of Chesterfields a third
time before she slid it and the lighter across the counter. Even
forgotten rituals remain ingrained; the nurse tapped the end of
the cigarette against the back of her thumbnail. She flipped the
Zippo, lit up, and pulled the smoke deep into her lungs.

What followed was a purgation of the two women's emotions.

Matilda told of watching him leave on the train to join all
those fresh-faced boys, some of them too immature to shave.
Off to a war no one understood! Then the fear after the government notified her he was MIA, and then the loneliness set in,
and she was frightened that she would raise Pete by herself. She
looked out the window into the darkness, confessed her mistake
of having sex with Osweldo, and how it would pain her father if
she had a second child with no father. She felt like a rat hemmed
between unknowns. She cried after admitting Osweldo's cruelty
to her and to Pete. Then she sat, stoically, staring at the floor.

The nurse told Matilda of the months of care she had given
the wounded soldier. She talked about his depression and how
his despondency weighed on the entire staff. She told of the day
of the cherry blossoms, and the little girls and how that led to a
partial solution of who he was, and where he was from.
Yesterday, they had driven to Seven Rivers where the soldier
once lived and then to Maljamar where his father had lived.
Today, they had driven to Capitan. Still no luck. Matilda sobbed
loudly when the nurse mentioned finding the broken tricycle.
She cried again when she learned about Chapman's abandoned
ranch.

During the next three hours, a pot of coffee, and a pack of

cigarettes, the two women formulated a plan. Together, they would meet with an attorney to resolve the marriage issues. Pete would want to see his father—Matilda would arrange that. Because of Osweldo's violent nature, they would allow him to remain in the dark, at least temporarily.

The nurse needed an opportune time to tell the soldier what she knew about Matilda, her second marriage, Osweldo, and Pete. Perhaps it would be best in a public place—maybe the restaurant at breakfast in the morning—a place with people around. She didn't want to go through an episode similar to the one at Chapman's ranch again by herself. If things went well, he and Matilda could meet in the gazebo. If they didn't, well . . .

Her alarm went off at eight. Five minutes later, he knocked on her door and said he was hungry. She negotiated ten more minutes. He walked to the motel office, got a paper cup of coffee, bought a paper from the news rack, and wondered why the motel clerk was not on duty. He sat in the gazebo, smoked, and drank coffee. He tried to read the paper, but his mind would not concentrate and jumped from the past day's experiences to what might happen today. Last night, he'd dreamed of Billy, but he was alive and there was no sign of the exploded grenade. And Henry—except Henry wasn't blind and had not been mutilated by the Chinese doctors. The three of them drank beer and ate pretzels. The young Oklahoma boys joined them. Bayonets protruded from their backs and then everyone was wrapped with wire and thrown into metal boxes. The cold settled on them, and their breath became icy clouds. He would tell her about the dreams—maybe she could help.

Matilda stood behind the drapes and watched him. She saw his uptight movements: quick drag on the cigarette, fidgety sips of coffee, nervous flipping of the newspaper pages. This was not the calm man she'd married.

It was one of those New Mexico mornings when the air had a nip to it, but the sky was clear, and the mid-morning sun would drive jackets back into the closet.

He and the nurse crossed the street to Chan's Café. She modified her usually quick pace to accommodate his crippled hobbling. The customers were what you would find in any small town café in America: a couple of laborers hurriedly finishing sausage and eggs, a deliveryman refilling the dairy case, a postman getting his second cup, two policemen eating donuts and drinking coffee, a female real estate agent going over her listings, and a pimply-faced teenager hiding behind a comic book in a corner booth while sucking down a forbidden milkshake. The only difference from a café in Anywhere, U.S.A., was the smell of frying chilies. The waiter, a slightly-built Asian, brought coffee and water. She ordered two poached eggs, fruit, and unbuttered toast. He ordered three donuts, toast and jelly, and a pecan waffle. She chided him about his unhealthy diet; he ignored her admonishments.

He double-sugared his coffee. The POW years without sweets created an almost insatiable craving for the taste. He sat with both hands wrapped around the heavy, ceramic coffee cup; his nubby fingers were abnormally sensitive to cold, and he never missed an opportunity to warm them. Since well before daylight, he had searched for a plan to find Matilda and Pete. They looked for his family the first day. There was a sinking feeling after finding his son's broken tricycle at Seven Rivers. When there was no one at the ranch at Maljamar, he felt himself sinking into the darkness. Then yesterday at Capitan, the abandoned house and the desolation of the ranch forced him to admit his father was gone. He was edgy this morning—holding on—fingers slipping—losing his grip—falling.

He looked at the police and their heavy revolvers. He needed a gun. There was a way out of this misery.

She moved the eggs around her plate and ate only the cherries from her fruit bowl. She was aware of his mood. "I have some news," she said. "It's not exactly what we wanted but . . ." she couldn't find the words to put a positive spin on the rest of the sentence.

He looked at her, eye wide, the pupil contracted into a small dark point. His face was drawn and grayish, his short hair disheveled.

"I know what we are going to do," she continued. "I just don't know how to go about it. Last night, I found Matilda, or, rather, she found me."

The word *Matilda* penetrated his confusion. "Why didn't you tell me earlier? Is she all right? And Pete? Is he OK?" His hands were shaky, and he half-stood from the booth. Questions, disturbed hornets, swarmed his mind. Her response was not quick enough.

Agitated, he stood and bumped against a waiter refilling water glasses. Ice water cascaded down his back, and the memories of his captors hosing freezing water onto him came howling. Shouting Korean curse words, he attacked the surprised waiter, pounding the man's head with his fist.

The two policemen were only three tables away. One policeman tried to pull the waiter free while the second flailed the attacker across the shoulders with a nightstick. Even being so thin and emaciated, the officer found him to be strong and determined. While they couldn't understand what he was screaming, there was little doubt as to the intensity of his words.

The nurse was at first horrified and then irate as the policeman continued to pummel the soldier, except now across the head. She tugged at the back of the officer's shirt, and then, when she saw how ineffective this was, started pulling his hair and attempting to drag him away from the soldier. "He is sick, don't hurt him!" she screamed.

With the waiter freed, the second policeman turned and tried to subdue the nurse. "Calm down, lady. Get away from the officer. Put your hands behind your head."

Now she attacked the second officer, screaming, "You can't hurt him! He is sick. Can't you understand? He's sick. What's wrong with you, you asshole?"

With his hands cuffed behind him, the soldier lay convulsing on the floor, his empty eye-socket turned toward the ceiling. She wrestled free from the officer and then protectively covered the soldier's body with hers. His blood intermingled with the ice water.

Matilda watched them cross the street to the café. He didn't weigh much more than the nurse, she decided. The day clerk arrived; Matilda was free until the next weekend. Although it was more than three miles to her home, she thought the walk would do her good. Pete spent last night with her father, and the girls were with her sister. Only Osweldo knew where Osweldo was. Maybe she could catch up on her sleep with no one home but her. Three blocks from the motel, she heard the sirens but didn't see the blue lights and didn't see the squad cars slide to a stop in front of Chan's Café. She also didn't see the Artesian Funeral Home attendants load the gurney and its struggling occupant into their vehicle, nor the Artesia police drive away toward the city jail with the nurse handcuffed and huddled in the back seat.

Pete got off the yellow school bus and waved to his grandfather and Freddy. The two men were planting chile seeds in wooden boxes along the sunny side of the house. He liked to spend time with his grandfather. It was quiet here alongside the river. Romero didn't own a TV, but he was a good cook; refried beans and beef tamales topped with tomato sauce, cheese, and cream were his specialty. Matilda said that Grandpa Luna was not a clean cook, but his cooking suited Pete. They had a deal: Grandpa Luna cooked, and Pete washed the dishes. After supper, they played checkers or Forty-Two. Pete thought Grandpa Luna let him win if he'd had a bad day or if Osweldo had been mean to him.

The teachers at Yucca Elementary School agreed Pete was a sweet little boy. He was an average student, but his attendance was spotty. He'd not miss any days for a month, then be absent three or four in a row. "My Grandpa Luna was sick," he'd say, "and I had to stay with him, help him around the house." But the teachers would notice narrow bruises across his legs like a man's belt would make, and once he came to school with a split lip. One of the teachers lived near Pete's family, and she heard family fights more than once—Osweldo cursing; Matilda screaming.

Pete's Grandpa Luna saw these marks, too, and it made his stomach burn. Although he'd not wanted Matilda to marry a *gringo,* this man had not been a good husband nor made his daughter happy.

He wished Matilda had listened to him about Osweldo being worthless, no more than a common goat thief. But he was not *estúpido* and could count months on his fingers. To save embarrassment to her family, she'd married.

He discussed these things with Freddy and no one else. His old friend was a man of gentle spirit and wise thoughts. "Perhaps together, we might go and talk with Osweldo," Freddy said. "*Concejo* with him, help him see the error of his ways." But Romero did not think this advisable. Freddy was disappointed, because he wanted his friend to be *feliz* in this dusk of their lives.

Pete finished his homework, went outside, and stood until

Grandpa Luna saw him. Pete was a respectful child and did not interrupt the conversation the two old men were having—they both approved of his good manners. Romero motioned for Pete to join him. "Maybe we will go down to the store and get a *mortadela* sandwich for supper," Grandpa said. "Then, if you are in the mood, perhaps we can have a game of checkers."

Pete was in the mood for both.

Late in the afternoon, Matilda went to Chic's Beauty Shop. Once a month, she afforded herself this luxury, and, while Osweldo complained about the waste of money, it was money she earned, and she was willing to listen to his complaints just to have this small bit of pleasure.

Chic's was a wonderful place to hear gossip: who was having a baby, what man had been caught in the wrong bed, what kid got kicked out of school, what girl was in trouble, and who was sick. Today, everyone was talking about the altercation during breakfast at Chan's Café. Each woman had a different version. But one thing seemed clear: it had been caused by an army nurse and a strange-looking man fighting with the police. The nurse had been taken to jail, and the funeral home ambulance carried the soldier away. The waiter was bruised some, and Chan had given him the rest of the day off.

Matilda canceled her appointment and called her sister—the one who was keeping her kids and who had an automobile. Together they drove to the motel. The car with the Utah plates remained in front of room 120; the day clerk had not seen the occupants of either 120 or 121.

An observant motel clerk has friends in many places. The duty deputy at the Artesia Jail owed Matilda a favor. Two weeks ago, she allowed him to use one of the rooms without registration—"need to spend a little time with a friend," he told her. She asked no questions, but she knew the friend. A little time turned into six hours. And there were two friends. Both women.

"I'm not authorized to allow visitors other than family and attorneys," the deputy told Matilda.

"And I'm not authorized to allow anyone to stay at the motel without registering," she responded. *What goes around comes around!*

The nurse stood rigidly staring through the rusty bars, her back against the concrete cell wall, disheveled as a wet cat, and with wrists raw from the handcuffs. She didn't know much: didn't know what would happen to her next, didn't know what she would be charged with, didn't know anything about bail. But she did know where he was: Artesia General Hospital on North 13th Street. No, she didn't know if he was hurt. But one other thing she did know: she wanted out of this damned cockroach-infested dump with its drunks, whores, and shoplifters.

She gave Matilda a scrap of paper with her name on it, a phone number, and the name Major General Magnuson and his extension. "Call him and tell him what happened."

Some things happen sooner than later. When a major general makes a call to the Department of Defense, who calls a U.S. senator, who calls a U.S. representative, who calls the Artesia municipal judge, who calls the chief of police, there is no paper shuffling, no dillydallying. Before ten that night, the nurse and the soldier were back in rooms 120 and 121. Other than still being irate, she was okay. He had bruises and sutured cuts. He smoked a pack of cigarettes before he went to sleep and dreamed of policemen with Korean faces.

After his arrest, it became coffeeshop gossip that the man the community thought to be rotting in a North Korean prison camp or, even worse, dead, was alive. Rumor had it he started a fight in Chan's Café and seriously injured a waiter. A nurse at the hospital reported he was restrained the entire time during his brief stay, and he was a menace to the community. The most intriguing story was that he'd been a spy, and everything known about him was a hoax. Hearsay became truth, and his notoriety spread like a prairie fire.

The next day, the nurse and Matilda met with an attorney. A priest accompanied Matilda. Overall, the findings were not as they hoped: the attorney advised her not to raise the issue of a divorce from Osweldo; it might bring about bigamy and child custody issues. The priest agreed since there were two children fathered by her current husband, and, if she pressed the matter, there would be no winners.

The nurse sat quietly and listened to the counsel of the attorney and the priest. Although she was concerned with the welfare of the children and the happiness of Matilda, the mental health and well-being of the soldier were foremost in her mind. It would be her responsibility to convince him the decisions reached were the best for everyone involved. For the second time, she had the thought that she was not trained for something like this. But then, who was?

Matilda was relieved. While she had started to despise Osweldo, she loved their two daughters. Pete was almost lost to her anyway. A boy not welcomed by a stepfather can never be a happy kid.

After the two women left, the priest and the attorney sat in the richly paneled conference room and shared a drink of the law firm's finest scotch. "God-damndest thing I ever saw," the attorney said and then begged the priest's pardon for his vulgarity.

The priest nodded and held his glass out for a refill.

"I'll do what I can about child visitation rights," the attorney said and then added, "Of course it will be *pro bono* and will have to get in line behind my other work."

The priest adjusted his clerical collar. "I look after so many needy people, but I'll try to fit Matilda and her family into my prayers. My life is very trying . . . I don't know . . . maybe I wasn't strong enough for things like this."

The nurse would have sneered had she heard these remarks.

When the nurse got to the motel that afternoon, he was stretched out on one of the gazebo tables with a cup of melting ice in one hand and an almost-empty fifth of Casa Noble tequila at his feet. He was fairly clear-eyed and apologetic. He tried to explain his actions at Chan's Café yesterday: "Don't know. Cold water down my back and this Asian guy standing there . . . Just brought back too much bad stuff. Really sorry. But, on a brighter side, I reckon you never had the opportunity to spend a day in jail before, did you?"

She remembered the stench of the jail and didn't share in his sense of humor.

They walked two blocks through the last of the day's sunlight to the Pecos Rose for the night meal. They sat in a dark, corner booth and did not order anything with alcohol. The waitress brought salsa and chips. The nurse asked for time before they placed their order. It took an hour and three bowls of salsa to explain what she'd learned from Matilda—things she'd been about to tell when he blew up at Chan's. She watched tears well in his eyes and his deformed fingers nervously lace and unlace. She took a deep breath. Got that behind us. She explained the meeting with the priest and attorney.

He looked down, his eye tracing the intricate designs of the tablecloth for a couple of minutes as if trying to process the mess his life had turned into. "I reckon I can understand about Matilda. We hadn't been man and wife for a long time, but I loved her . . . God knows how much I loved her." He searched for words, "Couldn't expect her to keep waiting. Wasn't fair to her. Anyhow, I durned shore ain't much of a man now, anyways. But Pete . . ." He looked up from the table, and his eye seemed to change shape and take on a different hue. "That's a horse of a different color."

"Matilda promised to call me at nine tonight," the nurse said. "She'll arrange everything. We will go to her father's tomorrow after school. You can see Pete. Talk with him as long as you wish. If you want her to be there, she will; you don't, she won't—your choice."

They ordered, and he spent a while chewing on the tough end of a steak before answering. "I guess it will be OK. Hadn't seen her in so long we might have to be introduced. Hell, I'm not sure I'll even know Pete."

She wanted to hide her feelings. There was something exceptionally sad about hearing this broken man talk about what had been his family. Might not know his wife. Might not know his son. *Crap!* It had not dawned on him that they might not recognize their husband and father. But it sat heavily in her mind. She wanted tomorrow behind them.

The four-room house was common, even for Artesia. Forty years ago, Romero Luna and Freddy made the adobe bricks by hand. It was hard work building the frames, mixing the dirt and water together, pouring the mixture into the frames and waiting until it sun dried. It took them more than a month to make enough bricks for the house and then much more time to lay them. Because both men had other jobs, the house was built in the afternoons after work and on weekends. They were proud of their masonry work but swore they would never build another house. Romero raised his family in this house, and now that he had gas wells, his neighbors thought he would move to a better place. But he was comfortable here; it was his own making; it was full of happy thoughts. Sometimes in the darkness when he lost control of his thoughts, he could almost smell his wife's Palmolive-clean body next to him and hear their children laugh. He could not imagine living anywhere else. Not away from these sunset memories.

They sat in the rented sedan beside the convenience store waiting for the school bus. The nurse glanced at the soldier, saw his twitching hand movements, and prayed he could keep his emotions under control. Pete was the only child to get off the bus. My gosh, the soldier thought, look at how big he is, look at that mop of curly hair. Romero Luna met his grandson at the mailbox and put his arm around him. Freddy finished watering the chili plants, stood, and waved at the boy. Together, the three went inside.

Matilda, face swollen and red from crying, met the nurse and the soldier on the front porch and asked them in. The nurse kept her shoulder against his, and she felt his body stiffen as he searched Matilda's face looking for something, maybe compassion, a hint of love, something other than the dullness. She glanced at him briefly, shadowing her thoughts.

Pete stood beside his grandfather, staring at a man he mostly remembered from photographs. The soldier shook Romero's hand. The old man would not have known him if he met him on the street, and it was difficult not to show shock at the soldier's appearance: gauntness, gray hair, eye patch, and mis-shaped cheekbone.

The room was like a photograph: everyone was motionless, frozen with apprehension and the sadness of the moment. The nurse introduced herself to Romero, then, bending over, to Pete and told him how much his father looked forward to seeing him. This was like the removal of a keystone anchoring a stone arch.

Matilda placed her hand against Pete's back and gently urged him forward. The boy pressed his head against the man's chest and hugged him with both arms—for the first time in years, they were father and son. The nurse watched the soldier closely. Easy, easy, she thought, hold it together, hold it together; you can get through this, you can do it.

These six were together for almost an hour: the women talking discreetly in a corner of the room, the grandfather brewing coffee, Freddy stacking *tejas de almendra* on a plate, and the father and his son trying to repair bridges that had never been built.

The soldier took a small, black presentation case from his jacket pocket and gave it to his son. The boy opened it and looked at the heart-shaped medallion attached to a purple ribbon. He told the boy the casting in the center of the medallion was General George Washington and Washington's coat of arms. The boy looked on the back of the metal and slowly read the words aloud: "For Military Merit." He asked the boy if he would like to have it. The boy nodded, and the soldier pinned it to the boy's shirt.

The two sat together on the sagging couch. The boy asked the soldier if he knew his grandfather, Grandpa Chapman. The man explained that Chapman was his own father. The boy said that he was gone, and the man nodded. "It made me sad," the boy said. The soldier said Chapman had probably gone to live with the other brave men who lived in the stars. The boy asked if he could go there someday to be with him and maybe take Grandpa Luna.

"Bet we will all go there," the man told the boy.

The boy inspected the soldier's crushed cheekbone, touching it softly with the tip of his index finger, and asked if it hurt.

"Only when I smile," the man replied.

"What happened to your eye?" the boy asked.

"It got hurt and had to be taken out," the man said.

"Can I wear your patch and pretend I'm a soldier? I'll bet it would be fun."

"Maybe you won't ever have to be a soldier," the man answered. Then, "No, no, it's not much fun."

The guttural exhaust of Osweldo's Hornet broke the poignancy of the moment. Matilda whispered something to the nurse and then hurried outside. Pete ran to the window and then back to his grandfather, who patted him on the shoulder, seemingly assuring the boy everything was all right.

In the past, Pete had seen Osweldo hit his mother and then turn his anger toward him and his half-sisters. He knew Osweldo had always been on his best behavior around his grandfather. There was something different today in his grandfather's actions, perhaps just a bit of anxiety. Pete thought that Osweldo would be glad to see his real father, but the way his grandfather was acting it might be different from that. He wished he was back at school and that, maybe, his real father was not at Grandpa Luna's house.

It had not been a good day for Osweldo. He had been caught in a five-dollar drag race in Carlsbad this morning. It cost him a ten-buck bribe to keep the policeman from writing a ticket. Ten dollars was not always a large sum, but today—fifty bucks down in a chicken-shit bingo game last night—ten bucks damned near emptied his wallet. Thought he'd swing by home and maybe get a twenty from Matilda. She wasn't there, girls across the street with her sister, who had no idea where Matilda was. *Puta!*

Maybe her shift had been extended at the motel. No, not there either. He parked his car in the motel lot, walked across the street to Chan's, and sat in a booth behind two cops. Never could tell when they might drop something juicy, something about a raid or who was doing who. Little tidbits might lead to something bigger; Osweldo was always looking for an edge. He searched his pockets for change, found a dime, and ordered a small bowl of vanilla ice cream.

Big cop was telling a little cop about the fight here in the restaurant. "Couple of folks staying at the motel across the street, one of them some kinda wacky fellow jumped a waiter. Had a woman with him, and she got into it with a cop."

"Awww," little cop said. He was working the hospital this morning when they brought the man in—had him strapped to a gurney. One of the nurses knew the crazy guy. "How about this?" the little cop whispered loudly. "She said he was married at one time to Romero Luna's youngest daughter. Believe her name is Matilda. Something like that. You know, she's now married to that little ratty guy, Osweldo. You know, the little shithead we're always picking up for trying to sell stolen stuff."

The cops dropped a fifty-cent tip on the table and left; Osweldo hid behind a newspaper until they were gone. He took the two-quarter tip from their table when he left.

Osweldo hustled over to the motel office and asked the clerk to see the guest register. The clerk knew it was none of his business, but it wasn't worth getting into a yow-yow. Osweldo scanned the register and found two people from Washington, D.C., driving a car with Utah plates—probably a rental. Matilda had just worked a forty-eight-hour shift. So, she had probably seen the two people. One of them her ex-husband. Maybe they'd even connected up. The one common thing between them was Pete, and Pete was at that old fool, Romero Luna's, house. That is where he'd find all of them. He cranked the Hornet. This wasn't turning out to be a bad day at all. Not at all.

Osweldo stopped in front of Romero's house, raced his engine, and let the roar of the gutted muffler announce his arrival. He checked himself out in the mirror, adjusted his sunglasses, put an extra roll-up in his shirtsleeves, and flipped a

curl, just so, over his forehead. A month ago, he had the likeness of a tiger needled into the outside of his right forearm. He
rolled his fist and the tiger writhed.

Matilda met him at the edge of the porch. She started to
explain how this meeting came about. Osweldo brushed past
her and the screen door clattered shut behind him. He said he
needed to see his son; to see if he was all right.

Now the life seemed sucked from the room, and there was
nothing left except tension. Osweldo stood just inside the
doorway, opened hands perched atop his hipbones like buzzards
atop fence posts, feet spread wide apart, and rocked from heel
to toe. The nurse controlled a giggle; she thought he looked
ridiculously like an eight-year-old boy mimicking a gunfighter
in an old black-and-white western movie. Matilda stood partially
between her first husband and second husband. "Osweldo," she
said, "I'd like for you to meet Pete's father—"

Osweldo cut her off. "I know who he is. What the hell is this
cripple doing here scaring my son?"

Pete leaned in against his father. He'd seen his stepfather like
this before, and it usually meant a beating was about to happen.

The nurse watched her patient, watched for the wildness to
reappear in his eyes, watched for the madness to surface and
explode through the room like shrapnel. Instead, he stared
coldly at Osweldo.

She had formed an opinion of Osweldo before she saw him.
She thought that after what she had been through in the past
two days she was ready for about anything. "We were invited to
Mr. Luna's house by Matilda. We needed to see Pete. We will
arrange further visitations through legal avenues. Now, sir, if
you will step out of the door, we'll be leaving."

Osweldo was not accustomed to anybody talking to him like
this—especially a female.

The nurse took a step toward him. "Courage is fire, and bullying is smoke. You are in the presence of one of the most coura-geous men I've ever known. But I can see through you. I know what you are. You are just smoke. Now, I won't tell you again: move your cowardly ass out of the doorway."

The nurse and the soldier drove away; Osweldo stood in the front yard watching them leave, wondering what in the hell just happened. His tattooed tiger was no longer writhing.

That night, a seething Osweldo gloated to Matilda. "Well, he's such a big shot, guess he can pay child support and back child support, too. It has been a burden on me raising some other man's child—especially with the other man alive. We can use the extra money, me with my bad back and barely able to get outta bed sometimes." He smiled and flashed the gold fillings that rimmed his front teeth, "I haven't had an easy life raising a kid like Pete."

Matilda sneered at him. "Very little you've done. He has been at Papá's more than he has been here."

"*Puta ignorante,*" Osweldo said and backhanded her—then for good measure caught her with a forehand. She spit on him, and he hit her again. Wiping the blood from her split lip, she gathered their two little girls and ran across the dusty street to the safety of her sister's house.

The C-54 approached Walker Air Force Base in Roswell from the southwest and touched down. Refueling would last an hour. The nurse stood in the center of the terminal, breathed the dry-ness of the desert air, and marveled at the softness of the shadows the winter sun shoved across the polished floor.

She lit a cigarette—the tenth of the day, dammit—and reflected over today's happenings.

Breakfast this morning consisted of hot coffee, two slices of toasted whole wheat just touched with butter for her, three chocolate donuts and a honey bun for him. Rather than eat at Chan's, they chose Sandy's Sweet Shop; they had no history at the donut place.

He knew she was scheduled to return to Washington today. Without her support, he would be directionless, a kite without a tail. What if he went nuts again? He wasn't ready to be cut loose; he needed support—a crutch, something or somebody to hold onto. He had this roping buddy, Rudy Vega.

They drove back down to Seven Rivers, stopped at a forlorn, one-pump service station, and found that Rudy Vega was working at the feedlot. Accompanied by a steady bawling of cattle, dust and the smell of cow shit rose like a thin mist over the lot. It took them fifteen minutes of driving up and down the concrete feed rows to find Rudy. He had roped a steer and was pouring a vile, green gut-wash down its throat. Rudy was big. The nurse thought the steer wouldn't have a fighting chance even if Rudy didn't have the horse on his side.

Rudy greeted him with: "Damn man, what happened to you?" He told Rudy he'd been sick for a while, laid up in a hospital in Washington. Rudy looked him over and asked if he was job hunting. He said no, just for a place to stay while he was getting his stuff together. Rudy wanted to know what stuff, and he told him he was going to try to put Chapman's place back together. House needed a heck of a lot of work, and the fences were down. Rudy figured that was a job offer, and it sounded a hell of a lot better than doping sick steers. Right then and there, he decided he was about to become a carpenter. Besides, this feedlot work was just too damned regular.

Rudy untied the steer, coiled his rope, tied it to the wang-strap, and looped it over his saddle horn. "Would you open your trunk?" he asked the nurse. She would have done almost anything he asked. Standing in the middle of a ten-thousand-head feedlot was not her idea of a good beginning for her last day in New Mexico.

Rudy tied the roan to the fence, uncinched the saddle, gripped it by the horn, slung it up on the metal gate, climbed over while balancing the saddle, and dropped to the ground. "I'm Rudy," he said to the nurse. He had square, white teeth and a cleft in his chin. Clean him up, get some of the cow smell off him, have him spit the snuff out, he'd be good looking, thought the nurse. He wouldn't fit in D.C., but he would turn some female heads.

"Why don't you bunk in with me tonight," Rudy said. "I've got this old pickup; it's pretty rough lookin', but it'll haul lumber and fence posts. I got a wagon sheet we can stretch 'tween two trees. Make us a tent. You'll like my biscuits . . . well you'll like 'em after a while if you can't find nothing else to eat. I bet we will have that house livable 'fore the peach trees bloom."

"Can we put grape jelly on our eggs?" the soldier asked and grinned.

The nurse considered this bit of frivolity to be a good sign—finally a victory and a friend.

They took Rudy's saddle by his place: a three-room house, a barn with a definite lean, a horse lot with a couple of cow ponies, and a chicken yard with a half dozen Domineckers scratching for bugs beside their watering tin. "There she is," Rudy said, "be it ever so humble there ain't no place like it."

The three of them drove to Artesia to get the rest of the soldier's belongings. Rudy thought it would be a big comedown from the tidy motel room to his place. But there was no way he could ever know how much the soldier looked forward to the move.

The nurse wondered if she had successfully discharged her responsibilities. She would never see a patient as just a name and a number again. In the back of her mind, she speculated about ever seeing him again and decided the chances were slim.

At Seven Rivers, the two men stood by the corral and waved good-bye; they did not see the nurse's tears.

She packed and checked out of the motel. In the quietness of the trip back from Seven Rivers, she had mentally listed contacts to be made: an army attorney friend, who was a member of the New Mexico bar, who might be able to put pressure on the local attorney to move along with visitation rights and the child support issue; contact the board of discharges; look into disability payments; telephone Matilda's priest; look for any charges resulting from the Chan's Café fiasco, and gosh knows what else.

Matilda watched from the gazebo, and, after the nurse had loaded the car, they spent an hour talking much as new friends do after a short separation. Matilda promised to write. She would try to keep things smooth on the New Mexico end. It would be best if Pete lived with her father—at least more peaceful. The two women hugged good-bye.

The nurse drove northward to Roswell. She rolled down all the windows; she wanted to smell the mesquite, the desert, and the sour smell of the gas wells. Her nose didn't even wrinkle at the odor coming from a feedlot; she thought it smelled like money.

Like a tremendously awkward bird, the military transport rose with great effort from the sea of gray concrete, banked eastward, and leveled, and the flight engineer set a course for Washington.

Jill Bateman leaned back into the seat, closed her eyes, and massaged her temples. She didn't sleep; her mind would not allow it.

Below, somewhere in that brush-covered, gray landscape, Martin Chapman was searching for himself and trying to start a new life.

CHAPTER TWO:
1890s

The Pecos River Valley

On this July day, the temperature was just over a hundred, and a mischievous wind aggravated the dead tumbleweeds.

This place was only a broad spot in the road straddling the reddish-brown water of the Pecos River until, in 1866, Charles Goodnight and Oliver Loving drove vast herds of cattle along the Pecos, trampling the countryside into pewter-colored curds. They set up cow camps at Seven Rivers and southward along the Pecos. Later, John Chisum worked a hundred thousand head of his own Jingle Bob Ranch cattle through the valley, their cloven hooves stirring up bitter tasting clouds of dust that lingered for days.

Natives had grazed the area for centuries with small herds, so the valley was far from pristine when the big ranchers arrived, but their enormous herds did irreparable damage to the fragile desert ecology. It would be another century before recovery was even noticeable.

Now, the big draw was the mineral springs, and that brought Ab Quezada to this "Pearl on the Pecos." The springs were said to have the power to draw whiskey from a man's body; Quezada needed to have a considerable amount withdrawn. The development around the springs was simple: four small sheds, three horse troughs, two tamarisks, and one cottonwood tree.

Quezada sat naked under the smallest shed waiting for the mineral water to evaporate from his skin. His horse, Russ, stood in the shade of the cottonwood, its tail no competition for the eye gnats and bottle flies. Sweetie, his one-eyed cow dog, lay ten feet away in the shade of a horse-watering trough, observing.

Quezada wasn't the fastest draw in the Pecos Valley, but he could still kill a man in a gunfight. His secret: he could take a bullet and still put two in his adversary. The first one would be in the center of the chest about nine inches below the Adam's apple. There was always a second. If his opponent was standing, it would be between the eyes; if the opponent was on his back, dying, it would still be between the eyes. He had been the winner in nine gunfights. Now it would be ten, counting the one Francis Chapman was about to see.

Francis and his mother and father were traveling in a dusty double buggy a quarter mile behind Euther Battles, a collector of buffalo bones. They had trailed Euther for the past hour, betting he knew the best low-water crossing along the Pecos.

Occasionally, Euther turned and looked over his shoulder and speculated about his followers. There was a woman in the buggy, so probably he didn't worry about them being robbers or the such. He'd gathered buffalo bones for the past ten years, but the work was getting harder and harder and the bones scarcer and scarcer. He figured he had about fifteen hundred pounds of bones in his wagon, and that came to about nine dollars. Nine damned dollars for a week's work. And he'd camped out for six nights, sleeping under the wagon, rolling around on sandburs, scratching sand fleas, and smelling mule turds. If a man could have generated lightning and thunder, Euther Battles would have been a hell of a storm blowing into the springs.

Quezada dressed and watched the approaching wagon piled high with bleached bones and, past that, the buggy. Irritated, he thought the country was getting so damned crowded a man could not even take a bath without folks coming in on him. Sweetie pricked her ears toward the rattle of the bone wagon, and her nose twitched at the stink of the mules. The dog just dug deeper into the cool sand beside the trough, did that circling thing canines have done since they were wolves checking for enemies, and settled down in the first cool place she'd had all day.

Ten feet from the trough, the teamster's mules stopped and pricked their ears toward Sweetie. Euther stood in the wagon and shouted, "Get away from there, you sumbitch. My mules need to drink, and they ain't drinkin' over the top of a damned dog."

Quezada shoved his long, wet hair back over his head and trapped it with his hat. His voice was gravelly and deep. "Who you calling a sumbitch?"

"Well, it's that damned dog . . . or you. Whichever one it fits."

Quezada buckled his gun belt, then shoved it down to the comfortable place on his hips. He flexed his gun hand and wished it wasn't sticky with mineral residue. "Mayhap the dog don't speak nothing but Spanish, and you're talking English."

Francis pulled his horse to a stop a hundred feet from the bone picker's wagon, and the buggy wheels stopped their irritating screech. His father was whispering to his mother, partly comforting and partly trying to mask her ears from the profanity.

Euther reached under the wagon seat, dragged out his double barrel, and climbed down from the offside of his wagon. He walked to the front of the mules, the shotgun hidden against his hip. "Well, he better learn English 'cause if he don't move purty quick, I'm gonna lace his damned ears with buckshot."

Cheat a man in a card game: expect trouble. Steal a horse: get out of the country. Make a pass at another man's wife: run for the border. But, make a dog get out of a shady spot, that should not draw gunfire but—

Quezada stepped away from the shed and stood in the shadow of the cottonwood. "Well, he's my dog, and I don't 'llow him talking to strangers. So, perchance you'll have to take your quarreling up with me."

The teamster didn't move the shotgun away from his hip, just tilted the barrel upward and fired. The shot struck Quezada on the left side of his body; he spun, staggered to his right, and put a .44 slug in the middle of Euther's chest. Euther looked down, surprised at the blood gushing from the half-dollar-size entry wound. The shotgun slipped from his grasp, did a half roll, and fell onto the desert floor. He dropped to his hands and knees and studied the sand as if he'd lost a coin or something of great value. He surrendered his search and raised his head. From a distance of five feet, Quezada put the second bullet between Euther's eyes.

The mules bolted at the sounds of the gunfire and raced out through the cholla and horse crippler cactus, the wagon lurching and bouncing wildly. The rawhide lashings gave way, and the buffalo bones freed themselves and strung out across the prairie, the bleached skeleton of some elongated, hydra-headed, prehistoric beast.

Displaying more enthusiasm for life than he had the entire trip, the horse pulling the buggy snorted, reared, and lunged against the traces. Had Francis not leaped to the ground and grasped the cheekpieces of the animal's bridle, his mother and father might have been flung out amidst the buffalo bones.

Once he quieted the horse, Francis led it to the springs and tied it in the shade of a tamarisk bush. He helped his shaken parents down from the buggy and tried to comfort his sobbing mother—who seemed to be beyond soothing.

Quezada squatted in the shade, picking buckshot out of his left arm with his pocketknife. Apparently unfazed by the stampeding horse and mules and the gunfire, Sweetie simply moved to the other end of the watering trough and dug a new hole.

"Well, hell, son, don't just stand there," Quezada said to Francis. "Take my horse and go catch those fool mules. Perchance the wagon isn't in too bad shape. You can load the bones back up. Make a day's wages. When you get back, mayhap I'll have most of this shot picked out. We'll have a little man-planting to do."

The Santa Cruz River Valley

The Santa Cruz River flows northward from the San Rafael Valley and had for thousands of years when Jesuit priest Eusebia Francisco Kino picked his way through the Sonoran desert. "I have found a group of people that are docile, affable, and industrious," he wrote to the king of Spain. "They call themselves Tohono O'odham." The priests call them Pimas.

The O'odhams raised corn, beans, peppers, and squash in irrigated fields. Under the broiling sun, they built dome-shaped houses of bent saplings covered with brush and mud. They wove baskets of bear grass fibers, decorated them with black-bean pods, and bound them with yucca leaves. For centuries, they had been a peaceful people.

Father Kino was not the first priest to visit the valley; previous missionaries laid the foundation for his Catholic teachings. His followers built the Misión San Xavier del Bac, the Great White Dove of the Desert, and later a mission at Tumacácori. The priest taught the Indians animal husbandry and the cultivation of wheat and fruit trees.

Coveting the wealth that arose from the practices of the O'odhams, Apaches continually raided the country along the Santa Cruz River. Presidios at Tubac and San Augustin del Tucson sheltered the priest and the Indian women when attacks became unbearable.

Then in 1767, King Carlos III of Spain tired of the arrogance of the Jesuits and expelled them from New Spain. The Black Robes—as the Pimas called the highly-opinionated Jesuits—were taken in chains and put on ships bound for Spain. They were succeeded by the less aggressive and more compliant Franciscans, who were now in favor with the king.

However, one Black Robe, Father Avalia Quezada, left a permanent remembrance of his presence in the New World. Seven months after his departure, an O'odham woman bore his son.

Later, Mexico ordered all Spanish-born residents to leave the Santa Cruz Valley. The harshest winter ever known to the Indians fell on the valley; Tubac and Tumacácori were abandoned.

But the surname Quezada remained, and the descendants were many. They spread over the Santa Cruz basin and moved northward to what would become Phoenix and Tucson. These mixed-breed people were cattlemen, outlaws, guides, scalp-hunters, gunfighters, and adventurers. They became known for their intelligence and fierceness. And the coldness of their blue eyes.

These were the ancestors of Quezada.

Nashville, Tennessee

Lathel and Melba Chapman had been married three weeks less than a year when Francis was born. Melba was mortified; no respectful woman would deliver a child without being married at least two years; Lathel prouded around town handing out cigars, strutting like a Bantam rooster that laid a second square egg.

He was a civil engineer who specialized in the layouts of railroads and cities. With much of the railroad construction completed around Nashville, he found it necessary to look for work in an ever-expanding circle. He'd spent much of the past ten years living in Kansas and Nebraska.

Melba refused to leave Nashville and her English teaching position at Peabody Normal College. She believed she was cut out for the genteel life: starched white blouses, afternoon tea, the symphony, fine china, and candlelight suppers; a place where men stood when women entered the room. She hung on to this lifestyle tenaciously.

Francis grew up in his mother's world but voraciously read blood-and-thunder, yellow-backed novels. Melba was appalled. She advocated Shakespeare; she might as well have preached to a post. She was encouraged when Francis started reading dime novels—until she read one herself. She was relieved when he started reading Kipling and Scott. But always, he went back to Western novels. He had never seen a cowboy, but he believed it was unnecessary to have the ability to fly to want to be a bird.

"Let him alone, Melba; he'll get it out of his system," Lathel said.

"I don't know how. You keep going off to the west and then coming back here with your wild stories . . . feeding his imagination."

When Lathel received an invitation to come to the Pecos Valley and bid on the engineering for a proposed irrigation system, he thought it would be an opportunity to get Melba out of Nashville and let Francis see the west. Lathel packed maps; Melba packed elbow-length, white gloves; Francis packed two bandanas, one red and one blue.

The Pecos River Valley

It took Melba two days in a Roswell, New Mexico, hotel to recuperate from the train trip. Lathel and Francis rented horses and rode out to Silver Springs to see Chisum's Ranch. Francis had never sat on a Western saddle or anything other than a gaited mare. He told his father he had been born for the West and had simply been temporarily detained by fate of birth in Nashville.

After his parents retired for the night, Francis crossed the street to the saloon. Batwing-chapped cowboys stood at the bar, one foot resting on the brass rail; three gamblers sat at a table waiting for someone with enough grit to take them on in a five-card-stud game. Kerosene lamps lit the room, and a man wearing sleeve garters and a gray bowler pounded away at a corner out-of-tune piano. Francis smelled the cigar smoke, the beer, the scent of horses, and believed he was home.

Early the next morning, Lathel went to the livery stable and rented their finest hack. Within an hour, they were high stepping southward along the Pecos.

Every two miles, Lathel checked the flow of the Pecos and noted the growth of salt cedars, river switchbacks, and bank erosion. Melba, fearing death by dehydration or scalping by some primitive beings, sat in the rear seat under the buggy's canopy, a pained look on her face, eyes squinted, mouth a narrow straight line. Francis breathed the fresh air of the desert and considered replacing his black string tie with a bandana.

Lathel wanted to cross the river and survey the east bank. They tried three times and found either quicksand or the water too deep for the hack. Ahead, a wagon hauling bones left a wavering feather of dust rising shakily above the ocotillo and honey mesquite. "Ah, salvation," Lathel said. *"And the Lord went before them by day in a pillar of a cloud, to lead them the way; and by night in a pillar of fire, to give them light; to go by day and night."* He turned to Melba and smiled. "And we all know that the good book does not lie. So, we must be on the way to the Promised Land."

Melba shifted in the seat, squinted, adjusted her skirt, and did not acknowledge Lathel's half-hearted attempt at levity. She would do much more tightening, shifting, and adjusting before this day was over.

Unknown to Francis, this was the day that would change his life. Forever.

Lathel deposited Melba in the shade and, after a bit of fumbling, loosened the top button of her blouse. She was sure she was dying of heat exhaustion, shock—or maybe both. Her head lolled to the side, and her eyes fluttered; she wanted Lathel to witness and suffer from the hideous thing he had foisted on her. It would serve him well if she died right here in this godforsaken place. She longed for Peabody Normal and lemonade.

Francis was barely astride Quezada's horse when it tore out after the runaway wagon, jumping cactus and whipping through the stunted brush. He clung to the saddle, fearing he might meet the ground and death at the same time; it was the most exciting thing he'd ever done. It took almost a mile to catch the wagon and subdue the mules. With Quezada's horse tied to the rear of the wagon, Francis sat on the hard wooden seat, feet braced against the front gate, and came bouncing across the prairie back to the springs. The wagon was in worse condition than before the stampede but still serviceable. Francis was exceedingly proud of himself.

Lathel's anxiety level dropped when he saw his son approaching. Melba would have held him directly responsible if Francis had been injured or—God forbid—killed. Already he was having foreshadowing of future years: Melba's whining, her nightmares, her accusations, hot flashes and chills, and increased nervousness. Now he was convinced. His future happiness would directly relate to his ability to secure out-of-state jobs.

Melba believed her weakness was going away, and she might be recovering from witnessing the killing and hearing the profanity. She peered out through less-tightly-drawn eyelids at the dim image in front of her. Quezada came into focus: shirtless, pockmarked with bloody pimples, and leering. He was a most disgusting looking individual. She frantically clutched the opening at the top of her blouse and rose to a heretofore unseen state of primness. "Lathel, I believe I'm prepared to return to Roswell. We have need to vacate this heathen land and make travel arrangements back to Nashville."

Lathel shrugged. He was embarrassed for Quezada to hear Melba's tirade.

Quezada looked at Lathel, astonished that any man would allow a woman to act in such a way.

Francis adjusted the mule's harness. "I'm going to gather the buffalo bones, Mama. I'll be along later."

Melba gave him her sternest look. "Francis, we will make travel preparations for three."

Lathel looked at his son. *Do it, Francis. This may be your last chance. Do it.*

"Mama, I'm gonna stay here. I'm not going back to Nashville. I'm almost nineteen. I need to do this. Need to try something on my own. Buy me a ticket, and leave it with me. If I can't make it, I'll come home. But at least, I'd have tried."

"Francis! You listen to your mother, and I mean it. Stop this nonsense right now. You *will* be going back to Nashville with us. It's all your daddy's fault—sowing those wild ideas in your head about the west. You *will* listen to me. Do you understand?"

"No, Mama, I'm staying. I don't want to disobey you, but I've got to do this on my own."

That night, Melba shrieked, pulled her hair, and flounced wildly across the hotel bed. Lathel pleaded his son's case, but Melba was unceasing and adamant in her demands: Francis would not desert her and would not live in this uncivilized land.

To avoid his mother's histrionics, Francis slept in the hay at the livery stable. If he inherited only one trait from his mother, it was stubbornness.

Late the next afternoon, Melba and Lathel Chapman boarded the 4:05 northbound out of Roswell. Francis stood on the loading platform and waved good-bye, the afternoon sun hanging aglow like a gigantic, August-ripened tomato at his back.

Francis and Quezada unloaded the bones to a buyer. "Tell you what, son. There is fourteen dollars here. You keep the bone money. I'll keep the mule team and the wagon. Fair enough?"

Francis had no idea what to do with the bone picker's rig and quickly agreed. "Do you know where I can get a job?"

The man looked at the skinny young man: flat-sole shoes, dark suit now tinted with grayish sand, and thin, black necktie. "Yeah. Mayhap I'll hire you. Drive the wagon up to the Fort Stanton ranch. Give you fifteen dollars for that, and I'll give you ten dollars to get a pair of boots and some fittin' clothes. You look pretty shitty in that Eastern haberdashery. Wouldn't want nobody to drive my mules lookin' like that."

Francis shook Quezada's hand. "Deal," he said.

"One other thing: Is Francis your only name? I wouldn't want nobody named Francis bossing my newly acquired mules."

"My middle name is Elmore," Francis said, and he knew Quezada's response before he heard it.

"Hell, that ain't no better. What's your last name?"

"Chapman."

"Mayhap we just throw away your first two names and just call you Chapman?"

"I believe I'd like that."

Ab Quezada's Fort Stanton Ranch was west of Roswell in the Sierra Blanca range. Chapman traveled northward to Roswell. The off-mule had thrown a shoe, and, even as green as

Chapman was, he knew he needed the services of a blacksmith.

The smith's shop was little more than a tin-topped shed surrounded by the hulls of wagon wheels and other farming equipment in the final stages of death. Reeves, the smith, was a man of mixed heritage—Melba Chapman would have described him as *mongrelized*. He was squat, muscular, and talkative.

"Chapman . . . I believe you said your name was Chapman," Reeves said, as he leaned into the mule and raised the animal's front foot from the ground. He pulled three nails, rasped the hoof, and started fitting the new shoe. "I do believe that you ain't owned these mules very long. I shod them a few days ago. Man named Battles owned them. Believe he said he was picking up bones south of here. Hell of a sorry job, picking up buffalo bones. Yes, sir, hell of a sorry job."

Chapman squatted at the side of the mule and watched the shoeing process. In less than a minute, he decided this was a job he would never attempt. "Yes, sir, I believe that was the man's name, and he was gathering bones. Till day before yesterday."

The blacksmith talked from one corner of his mouth, horseshoe nails clutched in the other. "You said day 'fore yesterday. He quit the bone business?"

"Yes, sir, he did. Quezada owns them now. And the wagon, too."

Reeves straightened and stretched his back. "Don't reckon, you got any idea what he paid for them? It really ain't none of my business. I just like to keep up with things like that."

Chapman wasn't sure how to answer this question or if he should. "Well. Mr. Quezada didn't really buy them. More like he took them. You see, Mr. Battles shot at Mr. Quezada—"

". . . and Ab done him in," Reeves finished the sentence.

"Yes, sir. That's the truth. We, my family and me, we saw it. I'd say it was fair."

Reeves finished clinching the nails and lowered the mule's foot. "Yeah, that's the way gun fights wind up with Quezada. He don't ever come in second. Son, you need to remember that: Quezada don't ever come in second." The blacksmith hitched the mule to the wagon. "Give my regards to the man. Tell him I done you a favor. Stop back by when you're in town again."

It took Chapman four more days driving through the desert and over the mountains to reach Fort Stanton. He got accustomed to sleeping under the wagon at night, rolling around on sandburs, scratching sand fleas, and smelling horse turds.

Fort Stanton wasn't much more than a small army garrison plus three stores and a few dilapidated residences; the town had seen better days. Built in 1855 on the east bank of the Rio Bonito, it was one of a series of garrisons accommodating the cavalry tasked with controlling the Mescalero Apaches and aiding in the western migration of the white man. Controlling the Apaches was like herding antelopes. Although fearful of the Indians, the white settlers continued to move westward and saw themselves as the rightful owners of everything stretching out past the endless horizon.

The symmetrical parade ground impressed Chapman, but the buildings were deteriorating and the force reduced to a couple of dozen troopers. Three of these soldiers were haggling with a gnarled Indian woman over four pieces of turquoise jewelry. She spoke little English; the bargaining was mostly a series of grunts, hand motions, and head shakes.

Chapman had never seen an Indian. He stood and watched until the troopers ended the negotiations by walking away, leaving the woman in mid-word. "How much you want?" he asked the woman. She responded with a series of words totally unlike anything he'd ever heard. He opened his sweat stained wallet and offered her four bits. She shook her head and reached for more coins. Chapman backed away, and the old woman followed, tugging at his jacket and raising two fingers. He offered another two bits. She snatched the coins and handed him a pendant of turquoise encased with hammered silver.

He was pleased he'd talked and bargained with a real Indian; the woman was pleased she got three times what the shoddy piece of jewelry was worth.

A brittle old white woman in the post station pointed southward to Quezada's ranch. "Go along the river 'bout a mile; first big spread you come to. Got two of them big Aeromotor windmills out in the pasture—can't miss them. Headquarters is across the river."

Quezada sat on the front porch of a white, two-story, frame house, smoking a cigar, Sweetie asleep at his feet. "Son, where in the hell you been? I figured you took my mules and run off back to Tennessee."

Chapman didn't know if he should take Quezada's comments as a compliment or criticism. "Go feed them damn mules 'fore they collapse, and I'll have Felipe cook you a steak and some 'taters. We got a bunch of branding to do this afternoon. I don't want you to think that the life of a cowboy is just sashaying around all over the country in a wagon, vacationing, drinking whiskey, chasing whores, and the such."

Years ago, Quezada had built a three-room bunkhouse halfway between the ranch house and the barn. Chapman threw his gear on an empty cot; he liked to think of it as gear, but it was just an extra shirt and pants and the clothes he wore the day he met Quezada.

In the kitchen, Quezada and three cowboys sat at the table, wolfing down potatoes and beef. Melba would have been appalled at their table manners. They leaned against the table with their forearms, slurped their coffee loudly, and chewed with their mouths open. No one removed his hat.

Quezada made the introductions. "Boys, this is Chapman. He's got other names, but you wouldn't want to know any of them. He's pretty green. Been working as a teamster, ain't that right, Chapman?"

Chapman nodded, relieved Quezada's introduction was so generous.

The rancher continued. "This fellow here with the sideburns is Tollafson. He is a good bronc-buster if he ain't busted up his-self, which he is most of the time. Next feller is Evans. He's a good tracker; follow a cow before she even knows where she is going. Then that's Chance sitting there at the end. He's a helluva good rifleman. They cashiered him outta Stanton— something about disobeying orders—and he just come right on up the river and went to work for us."

The men paused briefly from their eating, nodded, and went back to chewing.

"Mayhap you'll meet some more of the boys this evening. They've been rounding up strays. Been out about three days; 'spect they'll be pretty rank when they get in."

Chapman wondered what *rank* meant, but he'd figure that out later.

Chapman followed Tollafson down to the corral, and the cowboy roped and saddled a horse. "This'll be your horse till you want something with more piss and vinegar. Ain't much to learn about being a cowboy. 'Member which end of the horse to face when you're riding and that payday is the last day of the month. You just kinda follow me around till you get the hang of things. I'm bunged-up with a bad back. We'll gather up some stock this afternoon, keep the fire going, and try to stay out of the way.

You'll learn. Might even learn that you ain't cut out for this shit. Decide to go back to wherever you're from."

The climax edges of the mountains were sharp, and a purple twilight settled along the river. The ranch hands were sitting on the porch smoking when they heard the cattle making their way along ◗ ҙ river trail. "Sounds like a hundred or more," Quezada said.

Then the bawling mass of cattle came swarming across the front pasture, and the outriders turned them toward the pasture behind the barn. To Chapman it seemed like a million animals escaping a Mogollon's bad dream, their shaggy coats and pointed horns ghostly illuminated by the fading light as they rebelled against the whistling and humming lariats of the cowboys.

The riders tended their horses and then came clomping across the back porch into the kitchen, the rowels of their spurs singing a jingling chorus. Chapman sat in a dark corner watching them: wind-burned faces, faded jackets, drooping moustaches, and wooden-handled pistols encased in stiff, leather holsters. The kitchen now smelled heavy with the scent of sweaty horseflesh and whiskey. The word surfaced, and he decided that's what they were: *rank*.

"Mayhap come daylight," Quezada said, "me and you and Tollafson will run a tally. Sort out anything that looks sick. Perchance have to do a little vet work. Sort out the mama cows and be sure they are with the right calf. Don't want no misbranding. Can't have a misbranded calf nursing a cow that don't have the same brand."

Chapman fell into step with Tollafson on the way to the bunkhouse. "I don't understand about the misbranded calves."

Tollafson walked on. "These boys swung a pretty big loop when they were gathering up livestock up river. We'll brand the calves tomorrow. Put Quezada's Slash Q on everything that's not wearing a brand. But we'll not overmark anybody's brand. Wouldn't be right. Quezada wouldn't stand for it. Fellow can get hanged in this part of the country having his brand on a calf sucking a cow with another man's brand."

Tollafson looked over his shoulder toward the other cowboys. "Cattle rustling has caused the death of many a man. Fellow get caught with a running iron, he's in bad trouble, 'cause ain't but one use for it, and that's to change a brand. A hanging offense in cattle country."

They branded twenty-five calves the next morning. The smell of burned hair and seared cowhide spoiled the freshness of the morning air.

Midmorning, last night's herd and the newly branded were mingling with the rest of Quezada's cattle in the river pasture, grazing on grama grass that came half up to the largest steer's hocks.

Chapman had been thinking about the running iron. "Tollafson, you ever see a man hanged cause he changed a brand?"

"Yeah," Tollafson said. "Twice. My brother. And a first cousin."

Sunday, after the chores, was a day Quezada's ranch hands could do pretty much as they pleased.

Couple of the younger hands rode up the river to Fort Stanton. "Gonna buy some cartridges and a shirt," they said, neglecting to say that they would also make a stop at a two-woman whorehouse. With most of the garrison's troopers reassigned, the whoring business was not good, and the choice of woman flesh was worse. But, being nineteen, inexperienced, and eager to learn, the two young men were not overly fastidious.

Most of the men wound up in a cottonwood grove by the

river. Some bathed; others washed clothes; others, having bathed just last week and not needing another one, played cards or napped in the shade. Avila, one of the oldest hands and the only Indian, did a brisk business trimming beards and cutting hair; he used the same shears he used to shear sheep and goats in the spring.

Quezada worried about the men. Experience taught him they became restless about this time of day on Sunday. Wrestling matches and fistfights were bound to break out. Most of these scuffles occurred from boredom, but dislocated shoulders and broken collarbones were a hindrance when working livestock, and Quezada didn't want hands hanging around the bunkhouse trying to heal—not with work to do.

He rode across the pasture carrying a bantam rooster under his arm. A hundred feet from the men, he leaned out of his saddle and tied the rooster to the top rail of the pasture fence. There was adequate string for the rooster to move along the rail a couple of feet in each direction but not enough so he could become a fugitive.

Quezada took a pint of whiskey from his saddlebag and set it on the tailgate of a wagon. "Mayhap we gonna have a little contest," he said. "It'll cost you two bits to enter. Evans, put your hat over there on the tailgate. Now, here is the way the contest works. First of all, I put up the rooster and the whiskey. So I make the rules. You ante up, and you get a chance to shoot at the rooster. You miss, and you're out. You hit the rooster, you get what's in the hat and the whiskey. But you gotta shoot him in the head."

"What happens if somebody hits him somers else?" a one-eyed cowboy asked.

Quezada glared at him. "Hit him in the body, you're disqualified, and you've got to pay me for the rooster. You all can shoot one round. Everybody misses, I get all the money, but I'll leave the whiskey. You boys ante up again, we'll keep doing this until somebody hits the rooster or everybody runs outta money. We'll draw straws to see who shoots first. Just to keep it fair, I'll not shoot. I'll loan Chapman my pistol, and he'll shoot last."

"We got to draw and shoot?" a man asked, as he loosened his pistol in its holster.

Quezada answered, "I don't give a damn how you shoot. You can shut your eyes for all I care."

Twelve cowboys anted up. The rail was centered twice and nicked a number of times. The rooster was excited and danced along the rail away from the previous shot. At each shot, he'd jerk his head and blink his yellow eyes, but he seemed to gain confidence after the rounds started kicking up dust behind him. Finally, he just squatted on the rail, excreted a vile black and white substance, and stared at the shooters.

Tollafson fired and missed. "Bastard put the evil eye on me," he said. "Trying to hoodoo me."

After each miss, there was a considerable amount of cursing and coarse kidding. Chapman's turn came. "I've never fired a pistol," he said. The cowboys took two steps backward in unison, almost a square dance routine.

"Hell, just aim it like a rifle," Quezada said. " 'Cept just use one hand."

Chapman held the pistol with his right hand, arm extended and locked, gripping his wrist with his left hand. He didn't aim, just slowly raised the .45 and fired. The rooster did not move on his perch.

"Hell," Evans shouted, "you never even made him doddle his head or nothing. What're you shooting at—the moon?"

Two seconds later, the rooster twitched once, toppled forward, and hung upside down, his body a slow, jerking pendulum. Its severed head fell atop the rail, yellow eyes unblinking and staring at the heavens.

A couple of cowboys threw their hats up in the wagon, and others shouted, "Sumbitch . . . lucky turd . . . beginner's luck . . . rooster died of a heart attack." And things much worse.

Avila made three trips back to the barn and came back each time cradling a rooster in his arms. Three more times, Chapman beheaded an unlucky rooster. Now, each a dollar in the hole, none of the cowboys wanted to compete anymore.

That afternoon, Chapman made twelve dollars and won four pints of whiskey. The cowboys grumbled they'd been set up since they'd never seen anyone shoot like that—especially a greenhorn. Their mood improved considerably after the whiskey passed through the crowd a couple of times.

Quezada stood beside Chapman. "Son, don't ever count your winnings in front of losers; that'll get you knocked in the head or something worse. The boys all believe you were sandbagging them. You can tell me. Where'd you learn to shoot like that?"

Chapman stuffed the coins, uncounted, into his pockets. "Really, Mr. Quezada, this is the first time I ever shot a pistol. I promise."

Quezada's eyes searched Chapman's face. "I believe you. But the boys don't. Mayhap you ever get back into one of these matches again, miss some. One other thing and I'll hush. How did you do that? You never missed. What's your trick?"

Chapman closed his eyes and studied before answering the question. "I pretended the pistol was my finger. I just pointed at the rooster and fired."

Quezada nodded. "Son, you decided to, you'd make a damn tough gunfighter. Mayhap a range detective, a regulator, or a lawman or something like that. If you've got the guts and the mean streak."

Chapman never went back to Tennessee, nor did he ever see his parents again.

They exchanged letters and gifts the first Christmas. Two years later, his father died in a railroad tunnel explosion in South Dakota. He had been buried almost a month when Chapman learned of his death. His mother remarried an English professor within a year. *God protect the man.*

Buenos Aires, Argentina

Late August, the Muñoz family left their posh polo estate in Mercedes and spent the night with friends in Buenos Aires. At noon the next day on board the steamship *Majestic,* they sailed out into the blue waters of the Atlantic. It would be days before they reached the port in Galveston. Still, days after that lay their final destination, Albuquerque.

Diego Muñoz was the premier polo pony trainer in Argentina. His horses brought a premium, and the training fee at his stables bordered on being unreasonably high. But the product of the Muñoz training was world class. "We are the *Mecca* of polo," he boasted. Few disputed his claim.

As warranted by a man of Diego's prominence, his wife, Soledad, was a breathtakingly beautiful woman: statuesque, glossy black hair, olive skin, and eyes the color of fields of amber grain. It had long been rumored that men contracted to stable their horses at Mercedes just on the chance they might have a glass of wine with her, or perhaps just a passing glimpse of her.

Lucho, by one year the older of the two Muñoz siblings, was an artist. He was delicately built and as handsome as his mother was beautiful. Women described him as gorgeous and, without the approval of their husbands, commissioned him to paint nude portraits—of them. Much to his chagrin, *hombres homosexuales* found him equally attractive.

His sister, Carla, had more than her share of Diego's genes. She was sturdy, more than average height for a female, and fearless. She played polo against men and never asked or gave quarter. They learned to give way to her charge or be trampled. "Only because you are a woman," one said; she called him a *porco chauvinista*.

Occasionally, she would goad an exceptionally obnoxious man to a steer-tailing contest, a *gaucho* game in which a horseman riding beside a running steer reaches down and grasps the tail, loops it around the rider's leg and then veers off. The animal is jerked off balance and usually lands on its back. Her father enjoyed seeing the men wrenched from their saddles and roll across the arena floor. "Where is a man that can duel my daughter?" Diego challenged. Soon there were none.

Diego Muñoz was a farsighted man. His family spoke Castellano, French, and English. And because they had business associations with Brazil, they spoke passable Portuguese. They traveled abroad and were comfortable in most settings. He insisted his family always have local currency in a money belt strapped to their midsection. "You might find a horse or some fiery bauble that you desperately need to add to your collection," he joked.

In addition to their formal educations, Diego insisted Lucho and Carla be proficient in other activities. Both were better than average trap shots; Lucho was superior to his sister with a handgun.

If Diego Muñoz had a failing, which Soledad stoutly denied, it was that he controlled the family too tightly and made all the important decisions without counsel from within. He was a retired *Teniente Coronel* in the Argentine army and much more accustomed to issuing commands than seeking input from anyone inferior in rank. This one familial failing would be disastrous in the future.

"You got a problem you can't handle and I'm not around," Diego was fond of saying, "call in the army."

★ ★ ★ ★ ★

Carla was self-assigned to care for the five Mercedes horses below deck. Once in Galveston, they would travel northward by rail with the family.

The final destination would be the Neva Tandy Ranch, one of the original Spanish land-grants that, even after division, contained more than 400,000 acres. Profits from their sale to the wealthy Albuquerque rancher would more than pay for the family's trip.

The Muñoz family rode the purple-colored swells of the Atlantic northward toward the port of Galveston. They dressed in tailored white linen; no one underestimated their social position. The meals were exquisite; the orchestra knew all the modern tunes; the formally attired staff was attentive but, as with everything in life, this too would end.

Galveston, Texas

In the late 1800s, Galveston was a vibrant city with a population of just over thirty-five thousand. It was the biggest city in Texas, mostly attributable to the natural harbor of Galveston Bay.

Two powerful hurricanes destroyed Indianola, a nearby town on Matagorda Bay, and Galveston residents assessed their similar location—a city constructed on a sandbar along the Gulf Coast. But the city of Galveston had weathered numerous storms with ease. Residents believed it impossible for any sizable hurricane to strike the town. They failed to consider that dunes along the shore had been pirated for years to fill low areas in the city, removing the protection they provided from the waters of the Gulf.

The storm's origin was not definable. Ship reports were the only reliable tool for observing hurricanes at sea, and these reports were not available until the ships put in at a harbor. The storm may have begun as a tropical wave moving off the western coast of Africa. The first formal sighting of the hurricane's precursor was a thousand miles off the Windward Islands when a ship recorded a large area of unsettled weather. Three days later, Antigua reported a severe thunderstorm followed by the hot, humid calmness that often occurs after the passage of a tropical cyclone. Continuing westward, the storm made landfall on Cuba, dropping heavy rains. It emerged into the Florida Straits as a tropical storm. Erroneously, Cuban meteorologists expected the storm to curve northeast along the coast of North America.

The storm passed north of Key West. Soon, large swells from the southeast raced across the Gulf, and clouds at all altitudes began flowing in from the northeast. These observations were consistent with a hurricane approaching from the east. The Galveston weather bureau office raised its two square red flags with a black square at the center.

Diego Muñoz was a meticulous planner. Months before his family's arrival into Galveston, he secured a suite of rooms at the city's finest hotel, the Paradise of the Gulf. The Paradise sat less than a hundred yards from the Gulf. "An unobstructed view and the sparkling Gulf waters are at your feet," proclaimed the handbills that accompanied Muñoz's confirmation.

A carriage waited for the family at the dock. "Lucky you got here this morning," the driver said, " 'cause we're gonna have a heavy rain this evening."

That night, winds of one hundred fifty miles an hour screamed ashore and devastated the city. Almost eight thousand people died. Every building fronting the Gulf splintered into a jumble of wood and glass; the Paradise of the Gulf was no exception.

Sierra del Tigre, Mexico

Sonora, Mexico, shares a border with what would someday become Arizona and New Mexico. Much of this border country is deserts, mountains, and scattered grasslands. It is a cruel and severe land. It produces harshness; everything here either bites, scratches, or is poisonous.

The region is dotted with sky islands—mountaintop islands in a desert sea. The peaks of these mountains extend upward above low hanging clouds and create an ethereal sense of peace and solitude. Migratory birds seek the mountains so they may rest and recoup their strength for the journey ahead.

Shadrach Cajón was born and raised in this godforsaken wilderness near the sky-island town of Sierra del Tigre. His mother was Chiricahua Apache, his father, Mexican. He inherited his mother's nickel-gray eyes. In anything less than the bright sunlight of noontime, his eyes appeared to be nothing more than vacant, colorless windows.

A priest attempted to start a mission in the area, and his lessons included the story of Nebuchadnezzar and the fiery furnace that sat on the plains near Babylon. Shadrach, Meshach, and Abednego did not translate well into Spanish. But the word Shadrach reminded the Indian mother of a similar word that meant warrior in her native tongue.

So her firstborn son, Shadrach, was saddled with a Hebrew name. Perhaps his life might have been better had he been named Daniel. Unfortunately, he would never share the royalty or nobility of his namesake. He grew up poor. As a young man, he hauled wood and loaded ore carts in the silver mines. He did not find either of these occupations to his liking.

From birth, Shadrach's father did not care for his firstborn son. As the boy aged, the father believed he saw the vicious disposition of the Chiricahua surfacing in Shadrach. He punished the boy mercilessly for minor infractions. At the age of fifteen, Shadrach threatened to kill his father. "I am not as strong as you," he said, "but I will bash your brains when you are sleeping." The father didn't attempt to discipline the boy again; he did not sleep at night until the boy slept, and he woke when the boy awoke.

The young man despised the poorness of his life. He had never known anything other than wretchedness, and he knew that somewhere there was something better. There had to be. And he intended to find it.

When he was nineteen, Shadrach traveled northward. He stole a cousin's mule and an uncle's rusted revolver. It wasn't until he was five days north of Sierra del Tigre that he felt safe and could sleep without fear as his nightly companion. Villages were scarce and so was food. He loaded the mule with a sack containing corn, peppers, beans, and dried squash. But he underestimated the amount of corn the mule required. Two weeks later, he was reduced to eating uncooked beans and sharing the corn intended for the mule. Both he and the mule plodded across the seemingly endless desert. He found dried streambeds with scattered pools of tepid water teeming with tadpoles and mosquitoes. Water was water; he and the mule had no choice.

Later, on a morning when the red and gold orb rose up from the east to scatter waves of heat across the glittering sand, the mule refused to stand. Shadrach talked to the mule about the consequences of his uncooperative ways. The animal remained prone, sides heaving, ribs making narrow, parallel indentations in the sand.

The rusted pistol would not fire. Shadrach's knife was dull, and it took a great effort and many attempts to saw through to the mule's jugular.

Shadrach cut a steak from the mule's hindquarter and roasted it over mesquite coals. An ancient Indian herder riding a donkey and trailed by his five sheep and dog crossed an arroyo to investigate the thin plume of smoke that lifted up in the desert breeze. Using hand gestures and grunts, the shepherd explained his village was less than a half day to the north.

The sheepherder, and perhaps even his dog, did not feel comfortable looking into Shadrach's eyes. The Indian was once a shaman back in the time when such knowledge was respected. He learned that the thoughts of men fall from the brain and lodge in the eyes. But avoiding Shadrach's gaze and not being aware of his thoughts was fatal.

It was not as difficult to cut the sheepherder's throat as it had been the mule's. The dog was skittish and stayed beyond Shadrach's grasp.

Galveston, Texas

The Great Storm destroyed Galveston's bridges to the mainland and all telegraph lines. It would be almost two days before accounts of the devastation reached the governor of Texas.

Rescuers from Houston found Galveston destroyed and the stench of dead bodies gut-wrenching. Most had drowned or been crushed as the waves pounded the remains of what had been their homes minutes earlier. Others survived the storm itself but died days later, trapped under the wreckage of the city and its relentless heat and humidity. Rescuers, guided by the weakening screams of the survivors, combed the debris.

Dead littered the city; burying all of them was impossible. First, the dead were ferried out into the bay and dumped overboard. But the gulf currents washed most bodies back upon the beach, where conscripted crews burned these remains. This job was so gruesome the city supplied unlimited amounts of whiskey to the men so they could complete the job, and they staggered from one mountain of debris to the next. Weeks after the storm, a cloud of bluish-gray smoke continued to hover over the city.

Days after the storm, an occasional dazed survivor crawled from the debris only to perish later from dehydration and injuries. But of those that did live, many had little recollection of what happened. Some of these survivors never regained their memories or sanity, and the book to their past remained closed forever.

Plains of Mexico

Riding the Indian's burro and trailed by the sheep, Shadrach skirted the dead sheepherder's village. The dog smelled home but remained loyal to the sheep.

In mid-summer, he crossed the continental divide and continued east through the barren desert before turning northward. He came to the Rio Casas Grandes. The water wasn't deep; he and the burro could cross it easily. But he knew the sheep couldn't swim, and he had been unable to find a bridge or low-water crossing. He lifted the sheep to his shoulder and, one by one, ferried them across the river. He had no idea of their worth, but he had traveled with them this far and had no thoughts of leaving them.

The dog was now dependent on Shadrach and ate from his hand. With the sheep safely across and grazing, Shadrach forded the river again. The dog sat, face and ears lifted expectantly. Shadrach tied a rope around the dog's neck and looped the other end to a cactus. Perhaps the gray-eyed wolf that had been following him for days would see this as a reward for not raiding the flock. The man felt a kinship with the stealthy killer.

Shadrach had never seen a town the size of Puerto Palomas de Villa. A blacksmith, a cemetery, and the pens of a cattle trader occupied the three sides of the *plaza*. One store and two cantinas sat on the river side of the square. The store was dark, but lamp light caused distorted shadowy figures to creep along the adobe walls of the cantinas and then become shredded by the grave markers. From the largest cantina, the haunted sounds of a guitar slipped out into the dirt road. Three goats, a workhorse, and a boney milk cow stood in the trader's pen and eyed him as if he were the purveyor of feed.

The dirt streets were so wide two carts could meet and each continue on its way. Bats patrolled the darkness, the *chee-chee* sounds of their cries barely audible.

Shadrach turned his livestock into the trader's pen and then lay in the softness of the grass on the outside of the fence.

The livestock trader was surprised when, through the foggy dawn, he could tell the number of livestock in his pen had increased since last evening. A gaunt figure rose from the fence-row and stood as expectantly as the hungry milk cow. The dealer was accustomed to having a waiting customer, but this man was different. His clothes were little more than rags, and his sandals were mended with strips of rawhide until little of the original leather remained. His eyes were deeply recessed and his skin burnt to the color of dried tobacco. Greasy hair fell below his shoulders, and his scruffy beard was matted. Too much desert and not enough food, the trader thought.

"I would like to sell my livestock," Shadrach said, his words heavily accented with the peculiar sharpness of the mountain people that lived to the south and west.

The trader looked into the mouth of the burro and estimated an age of seven. The sheep were thin and matted with burs. Along their flanks, the wool loosened and showed signs of mites or screwworms.

He was accustomed to gauging the needs of the seller as much as he was the value of the stock. He never expected to receive what he asked nor give what was asked. He held up five fingers.

Shadrach studied the trader's face.

The trader looked past Shadrach. He was not comfortable looking directly into those empty, nickel-colored eyes—it made him feel queasy in his stomach. For an instant, he wished he'd offered more money.

"*Sí, se puede,*" Shadrach said, and the coins changed hands.

The trader could not believe his luck. He purchased the gaunt man's sheep and burro for a tenth of their worth. When the ragged man pocketed the coins and walked away, the trader looked heavenward, made the sign of the cross, and smiled.

It was not until Shadrach found that the cost of a pair of sandals was three coins did he realize what happened. He wore the sandals out of the store and with the remaining two coins bought a chunk of stale bread and a live chicken. He returned to the river, roasted the chicken, and sat in the afternoon sun, dangling his feet in the river while considering the honesty of the livestock trader.

Darkness came, all heavenly light muted by low-lying clouds. The gaunt man returned to the trader's lot and waited under a stunted mesquite tree. He was patient and deadly as a desert scorpion.

After the evening meal, the dealer visited the *cantina*, where he told three friends of his cunning purchase of the sheep and burro from the gaunt man. In celebration, he bought a round of *cerveza* for his friends, and they, in turn, repaid the favor. He left the *cantina* to make a final check of the stock pen's gate. His trip across the *zócalo* was uncertain, his feet unsteady in the darkness, his mind clouded with alcohol. With fumbling fingers, he tied the gate with a piece of rope, looping a second knot for safety. An unusual sound, perhaps a chuckle, whispered from the mesquite bush at the back of the pen. He stumbled across the lot to investigate.

The merchant's wife became disturbed when ten o'clock came and he had not returned home. Her lantern lit the passage to the cantina and then to the lot. She found her husband slumped behind the mesquite bush, an evil opening in his neck and the trampled dirt around him blood crusted.

Her screams brought the townspeople. It was she who discovered his purse missing. His friends noted the missing livestock.

Three miles to the north on the American side of the border, the village of Columbus briefly broke the monotony of the flat desert. In the distance, bluish-gray mountains promised cooling comfort as the burning sun broke the eastern horizon. The proprietor of the single business establishment in Columbus swatted flies that unwisely squatted on a quarter of yellow, stale cheese. Midmorning, a gaunt and ragged man traded a milk cow, a burro, a workhorse, three goats, and five sheep for a clay-bank dun gelding and saddle.

From the dead livestock dealer's cash-filled purse, Shadrach also purchased an almost-new Winchester rifle and a serviceable Colt .45 Peacemaker revolver. The merchant inwardly shuddered at the malevolent stare of the gaunt man and threw in a box of shells for each weapon. After all, he wanted to be able to enjoy a peaceful night's sleep; a clean conscience would counter bad dreams of the gaunt man's eyes.

Although Shadrach was illiterate, he could read a couple of dozen Spanish words. Until he left Sierra del Tigre, he had not seen more than fifty English-speaking people, and their language seemed incomprehensible. It was too slow and without rhythm. Now after he crossed the border, he knew his lack of English handicapped him.

In Sierra del Tigre, he had little need to understand currency. He was paid only a few coins each day for his work in the mines or hauling wood. His father took those. Shadrach was never sure of the worth of a day's labor.

The five-finger sale in Puerto Palomas de Villa taught him a valuable lesson: all coins were not equal.

Galveston, Texas

Citizens left Galveston as if it contained a plague, and, in a way, it did. Buildings not destroyed perched at crazy angles amid debris and flotsam. Trees were uprooted or snapped off at ground level. The relentless pounding surf lashed the roadways until they were nothing more than paths interrupted by an occasional culvert. Those who lost immediate family were the most reluctant to leave. Short-term residents or those merely visiting the city gathered their scant belongings and fled as soon as they were able.

Survivors roamed aimlessly through the city calling out the names of their missing family. Seemingly in an incurable shock, one survivor had to be restrained at the beach where he tried to sort through the burning bodies. Tired of the constant struggle of dealing with the chaos, Galveston city officials callously loaded many destroyed souls on the single functioning train and hauled them to Houston.

Houston was ill prepared for this cascade of humanity. The Catholic churches sheltered masses of bewildered people, and soon other churches answered the challenge. Then, Houston took a page from Galveston's book and simply forwarded the next group of fifty survivors by rail to San Antonio.

Three Galveston refugees hid in an equipment compartment of the caboose while the train completed a coal and water stop in San Antonio. The train chugged westward through the night and part of the next day crossing the almost barren west Texas landscape. At dusk in El Paso, the three made their escape from the train as it entered the switchyard. Two hurriedly crossed the street and disappeared into the *barrio.* The third entered an alley, removed the contents of the cloth money belt, and studied the sodden American currency and the rotting envelope with the return address: "Tandy Ranch, Albuquerque."

Mexico Border

Shadrach stayed in Columbus for two weeks, living in a rancher's barn outside of town. He mucked out the stables and herded half-wild mustangs twenty-five miles northward to Deming. At night he sat in the cantina, listening; by day he practiced his English, talking to a manure fork. He learned it was almost one hundred-fifty miles from Columbus to Ciudad Juárez and El Paso. He had no idea of the size of the border towns and wasn't sure if El Paso was an American city or part of Ciudad Juárez, or even if either existed. He heard the city was light in the night as day and there were heavy-breasted women who wore yellow and gold and smelled of sweet perfume. He wondered if he could trade stolen cattle for one of these women.

Finally, he bought two pack mules, bacon, beans, and coffee and, dropping southward, traveled eastward along the border, crossing the invisible boundary as it suited his needs. It was simple to steal livestock north of the border and sell the stock in Mexico, but to steal cattle in Mexico and take them northward presented a problem. The language barrier was only slightly lowered.

It was a lonely trip across the nothingness of the desert. He came upon an occasional ranch: dilapidated cattle pens, a few cows, goats, broken-down horses. The people lived little better than those in Sierra del Tigre. Sometimes, Shadrach wished he had the shepherd's dog. He was almost sorry he had left it tied for the wolf.

Three months into his trip, in the edge of the low, barren mountains, he found a small village, Ag Gurita. *Gringos* visited this village in the fall to hunt doves and again in the winter to hunt wild pigs. The townspeople slipped from Spanish to English and back again as easily as Shadrach rolled a cigarette. He stayed there for a month, living in an abandoned pig shelter. A woman lived in this village with her three daughters. The mother was lonely; her husband had left years ago. The third night Shadrach was in the village, she made herself available to him. She was almost twice his age. "I do not find you attractive; your skin is dry and wrinkled," he told her, afterward, "but your oldest daughter . . ."

A week later, he approached the widow woman. "I will be leaving," he said. "I want your middle daughter to go with me—her English is the best. I will give you four coins and a new blanket. If you do not agree, I will beat you to death and take all your daughters."

The widow looked into Shadrach's eyes, felt the coldness of his heart, and knew he was speaking the truth.

The first night Shadrach was disappointed. The girl had small breasts and only a narrow strip of downy pubic hair. He was sorry he had not examined her before the trade. He believed he'd been cheated and considered taking the girl back and exchanging her for the older sister; maybe even taking the blanket back, but it would interfere with the trip, and he decided to make the best of the trade.

One night after he finished with her and had gone to sleep, she tried to escape. He found her hiding in a coyote den and beat her legs bloody with his lariat. Every night after that, he tied her ankle to his leg with rawhide. Her crying irritated him. She soon learned it was against her happiness to deprive him of sleep. He had only to touch his rope to remind her of what could happen.

Fort Stanton Ranch

Quezada found Chapman easy to like. The young man could read, write, and understood the mysteries of division and multiplication. And he was honest. Quezada sent Chapman into Fort Stanton on Saturdays to purchase supplies. Frequently, other cowboys sent money for their own needs, and the merchandise and the change always jibed with the money sent.

He even tutored two young cowboys on how to negotiate a two-for-one deal at the whorehouse. "And don't let them give you any of those whorehouse tokens for change, either," he cautioned. He said all this, but he had never seen the inside of a whorehouse.

Chapman became a good ranch hand. "Too damn bad he wasted so many years living in Tennessee," Quezada said.

Chapman's roping skills were fair, but he had a good eye for livestock and was a better than average range veterinarian. Summertime, Sunday afternoon's shooting contest down by the river continued. But Chapman no longer entered the competition. His skill developed far beyond the other hands, and something in the back of Chapman's mind prohibited him from deliberately missing—he did not want to plant that seed, did not want to develop the habit of pulling away from the target.

Only Quezada stood a chance against him. The pupil didn't want to compete against the mentor; it's a law of nature: there could be no clear winner, just a loser.

Chapman returned to the Fort Stanton ranch after having three horses shod at the fort. Quezada was in the tack room repairing a bridle.

"Mr. Quezada, talked with a government agent while I was at

the fort. He says Fort Bliss down at El Paso will buy forty steers from us if we can get them there in two weeks. Seventy dollars a head. Eight per cent bonus if none of them have pinkeye."

Quezada hung the bridle on a peg. "How much money is that, son?"

The younger man lowered his head and closed his eyes. "That would be . . . twenty-eight hundred . . . plus bonus of two twenty-four . . . total out at three thousand twenty four dollars."

Quezada did a low whistle. "Damn. They pay cash?"

"Same as. Government check with an eagle stamped right in the middle of it."

The Rio Grande Valley

Ab Quezada owned three ranches but favored the Fort Stanton spread because of the isolation and the coolness of the mountains. His second ranch was near Bitter Lakes, east of Roswell, and his third ranch saddled the Rio Grande near La Mesilla, south of Las Cruces.

"I've got enough steers at La Mesilla to fill their needs," Quezada said. "It'll take us about three days to get over there, and another three days to get the steers down to Fort Bliss. Six days in the saddle. See if you got any iron in your ass or not."

It was near the end of the first day on the way down to La Mesilla before Chapman understood the iron-ass business. They were still in the mountains outside of Ruidoso when Quezada dismounted and led his horse to a stream to drink. Chapman buried his foot in the left stirrup and slung his right foot over his horse's rump. Except his leg didn't move. He was numb from his knees to his belt, except his ass felt as if it were seared with fire. He took the horn in both hands, slipped clear of the stirrups, and eased himself to the ground. Couple of minutes later, he took a step and then another. He tied a rope to the horse's bit-ring and let the animal wade out into the water.

When the horse had his fill, Chapman led the animal to a fallen tree, gingerly climbed up on the log, and then eased himself into the saddle.

Quezada stepped back up into the saddle. "Ready to go, tender ass? Mayhaps we get to the ranch, we can find some cornstarch to rub on them raw spots."

Chapman wasn't ready to go, but he did.

Excluding the La Mesilla ranch, this was desert country, and other than scattered hills to the west and the jagged Organ Mountains to the east, the land's flatness was interrupted only by arroyos and the south flowing Rio Grande.

Level and verdant, the La Mesilla ranch is very different from the one at Fort Stanton with its mountains and woodland.

The ranch headquarters sat on a low hill overlooking the river. The adobe ranch house squatted in the heat like a sentry watching the sun relentlessly bake the countryside.

Quezada's ranch hands painstakingly built dams of intertwined sticks and rocks that guided river water into a main ditch and fed smaller ditches extending half a mile to irrigate pasture and hay land. Indians developed this *acequia* system long before the white man came to this part of the Rio Grande Valley, and, while primitive, it still worked.

On the day they arrived at the ranch, Quezada sat on the veranda, smoked a cigar, and drank tequila. Chapman changed horses and rode over the spread. He was getting the hang of ranching, and he marveled at the greenness of the pasture and the pones of fat on either side of the steers' tails. The animals were not as rangy as the Fort Stanton cattle, but they were in far better condition, and Chapman wondered if they underpriced the steers when dealing with the army agent. He counted more than a hundred head grazing in just one irrigated section.

Eastward toward the foothills, he came to Quezada's horse

pastures. Two windmills pumped water from a shallow aquifer into three tanks. Horses stood in the shade near these tanks and occasionally ambled over for a drink, pulling the cool water into their round bellies much as a man drinking a cold beer on a hot day. All the stock was either a dark bay or a related color, and most had some form of blaze. They raised their heads as Chapman approached and just as quickly lost interest in the solitary rider.

A wrangler, a slender man wearing scarred leather chaps, rode up out of a draw. Chapman identified himself, and, almost as quickly as the horses had lost interest, the wrangler touched the brim of his hat and continued along the fence line inspecting the barbed wire.

Intensified by a dust storm blowing down from Cookes Range, only half of the setting sun loomed atop the horizon to cast fire down on the headquarters' buildings. Quezada looked at the bottom of the tequila bottle and worked on his second cigar. His boots lay on the floor of the veranda, and his gun belt looped over the post of his rocking chair.

Chapman came across the open porch, the rowels of his spurs jingling. Quezada's face was slack and flushed. "Son, I've been thinking," he said. "We could put them steers on one cattle car and have 'em at Fort Bliss in less than a day. But I'm still leaning toward just herding them down there. The way I look at it, ain't gonna be too many more trail drives. We used to drive thousands, and this one will be way less. Pretty damn puny in a way. Old timers would laugh us right out of the saddle. But, hell, this may be your first and last opportunity to trail a herd."

"I kinda like the idea of trailing them down to El Paso," Chapman agreed. "After all, the feeling is coming back into my rear end. I've got some miles left in me."

Quezada took another pull at the tequila and laughed. "Beings as how I'm the oldest and own the steers, I'll ride point. I'll get a couple of the boys to ride flank. You get to ride drag; you are the man that'll keep the slow steers up with the rest of them. You are also the man that'll eat the dust. If I can't ruin the bottom part of you, I'll try the top part."

Chapman grinned. He'd been around Quezada long enough to know sometimes his bark was lots worse than his bite. "We gonna take a chuck wagon? Maybe a hooligan wagon, too?"

"Well, hell, son, ain't like we're going from South Texas to Montana. No more than fifty miles. Three days. We'll catch a couple of my old *compadres* going down. Worst thing that can happen is we sleep in a hay shed."

Chapman was disappointed. He'd looked forward to beans, biscuits, and beef. Now Quezada was making the trip down to Fort Bliss sound like a Sunday school picnic.

"Felipe." Quezada turned in his chair and called into the house again. "Felipe. I believe I'll have another bottle. And a little music, if you don't mind."

A couple of minutes passed. A man limped out of the house carrying a bottle in one hand and an oversized guitar in the other. He pulled the cork with his teeth, handed the bottle to Quezada, then walked to the end of the porch and sat on the floor, leaning back against a porch post. He strummed the guitar once, tightened a string, and strummed again, then nodded slightly as if in approval of his work and set out in a melancholy tune Chapman had never heard.

"Can't tell shit looking at him," Quezada said, motioning toward Felipe. "We herded more cows in three years than you'll see the rest of your life. Took four herds from down on the Nueces to the yard in Dodge. I never saw nobody that could clear a stray outta a thicket easier than him. I saw him run down a gray wolf, rope him, and drag him back to our cook tent. Shook his lasso off, turned that wolf loose right in the middle of supper one night—cowboys run like a pack of school girls—couldn't shoot at the danged thing—men going every which way, slinging snot and cussing."

Quezada took a drink and set the bottle back on the veranda floor. He lit another cigar, pulled the smoke down deep, and released it out through his nose.

"He's got a bad limp. Was he always cripple?" Chapman asked.

"Naw. He got jerked down, and the bull came back and got him. Hooked him something awful. Bull got his horn 'tween Felipe's leg muscle and the bone. Carried him about a hundred yards before I could get a rope on the damned thing. Tore Felipe's leg loose at the hip. Damn near bled to death. He got the first artificial leg I ever saw.

"Don't mean to make it sound like an everyday happening, but I saw a lot of good men get ruined. Lost two men in a stampede one night when St. Elmo's fire dripped off them longhorn's tips like purple water. Had an old kid from Dogtown get his foot hung in a stirrup and got dragged to death. Took about a dozen men into Abilene one night, damned if three of them didn't get shot in a saloon. Two of them died right there, and the other one died the next morning. Crying and calling for his mama.

"In a way, I never figured I'd make it this far. Didn't deserve to. Don't know. Reckon it was just never my time."

Chapman sat in the dark and waited for Quezada to continue to reminisce.

"Son, it's changing. Won't be long until men like me won't be around. Won't be no need for us. Man won't be able to carry a gun in public. Gonna be more fences and farmers. Open range will be a thing of the past. I hear tell that back east they are building wagons with motors in them. Don't even need a horse or mule to pull it. I don't believe I could live in that kind of world. Or that kind of world could live with me."

He stood on wobbly legs and said, "Felipe, let's help each other get back in the house. I'm out of tequila and cigars. And you're outta tune."

That night, Chapman threw away the last of his dime western novels.

Mexico

Shadrach named the girl *Poco Coño,* and she continued to cause him problems. She cried at night and called for her mother. But she didn't try to run away again. She wasn't the smartest girl in the world, but she was not stupid, either. She taught him English—not much, because she didn't know much. Each month she got sick and complained of a bellyache. He ignored her protestations as much as he did when his pack mules staggered under their load.

Although he couldn't count, it seemed to Shadrach it had taken almost half a year to reach Ciudad Juárez. Now with the sun starting to drop into the barren desert behind him, he could see the clouds of dust and smoke rising ghostlike to the east.

He pitched camp, started a fire, boiled coffee, and heated tortillas. He spread them on a flat rock and filled them with cold beans and strips of beef. He ate three and gave *Poco Coño* one. She complained she was not receiving her *parte,* but when he threatened to take her small meal, she sank to the ground and stuffed the single tortilla into her mouth.

Small fires twinkled in the distance like stars that had fallen to the earth, and they fanned out and disappeared to the south. To the north, Shadrach could make out a ribbon of darkness he reckoned was the river between the two border towns. North of the river, the lights were brighter but not as many. *Gringos,* he decided, were afraid of the dark.

He would not enter Ciudad Juárez tonight; he would wait for

tomorrow's light. He wanted to be able to see everything, to know what was around him.

He lay on the ground and pulled his serape over him. He made the girl turn her back and then pulled her against his chest.

She did not know it, but this would be her last night with him.

The sun hung halfway between the eastern horizon and its zenith, a pulsating ball that promised a searing mid-day. *Poco Coño* was tired and thirsty; Shadrach was eager to explore the dusty town that lay sprawled before them. He had never seen as many houses. He wondered if this was the biggest town in the world.

He planned to spend a couple of days in Ciudad Juárez, enjoy those women who wore yellow and gold and smelled of sweet perfume, and do some trading. He didn't figure to need the pack mules, because he would not be traveling across any more deserts. He could not imagine needing anything more than the Winchester and the Colt—except, maybe a shotgun, a double-barrel one. He'd become accustomed to the claybank gelding, so he wouldn't need another horse.

That afternoon, Shadrach and the girl walked the potholed streets of the dirty town. They made a most peculiar pair: the rangy, nasty man with the cold eyes and the filthy, disheveled girl. Even in a city where the dregs of humanity were common, the pair stood out.

As darkness invaded and shadows of the afternoon melted into blackness, Shadrach left the mules and his horse in a wreck of a barn on a dead-end street. He cautioned the girl against running away. "If you are not here when I get back," he threatened, "I will find you and I will cut off your tongue and then feed you to the dogs."

It never entered her mind that this was an idle threat, and she huddled silently in a dark corner.

At the intersection of Acacias and Oro, Shadrach found a cantina where women stood on the edge of the street and motioned for him to come inside. They were not as beautiful as he hoped, and they smelled sour, but they smiled at him and allowed him to buy them tequila. And two sat on his lap and, with their fingers at his crotch, challenged his manhood.

One grasped his hand and moved toward a back room. A fat man with a gun shoved in the waistband of his pants stepped between them and held up two fingers. Shadrach was surprised but understood when the woman told him it was for the bed. He dug two coins from his pocket and offered them to the man. The fat man looked at him and then went into howls of laughter. His enormous belly thrashed like the sides of a bucking horse, and the gold in his teeth flashed in the dullness of the lantern light. Then, the woman put her hand into Shadrach's pocket and found two more coins and four pieces of paper money. She gave the money to the fat man and then took Shadrach and shoved him into a small room that smelled of urine and sickness. She did not follow but, instead, closed and locked the door.

A candle, a straw mattress, a mangy dog in the corner, a toothless woman, and a crying baby in a wooden crib.

Five minutes later, Shadrach stood in a dark alley behind the whorehouse, the fire no longer burning in his loins. He had no more money than the day he was born. Nothing had gone right tonight. The woman with the big *tetas* had put him with the hag . . . these were not honorable people.

Near midnight, Shadrach returned to the barn. He whispered, *"Poco Coño."* She had burrowed into the straw and came out rubbing her eyes, shoulders rounded forward, fear in her thin movements. He put her on one of the mules, tied the second mule's halter rope to the tail of the first, and walked back the way he'd been. The women were still standing in front of the cantina and giggled when they saw him approaching.

"I would like to see *el jefe*, the fat man with the gold teeth," he said.

The man came out with two broad-shouldered young men and stood in the darkness away from the light of the lanterns. "You wished to see me?" the fat man asked.

"I want to sell you these mules," Shadrach said. "I want the same amount of money you charged me to go into the back room."

The man and the men with him snickered, a sound Shadrach found disrespectful. "Your relations might have been bad," the fat man said, "but it was much better than with a burro. You're asking too much. My *compañero*s would believe me a simple man if I made such a trade."

"I will include the girl," Shadrach said. "For no additional money. Just what I paid to go into the back room is all I want."

The fat man was surprised. "You are offering to sell me this little girl? To work? Here in my house? With the whores?"

"No," Shadrach said. "Only the mules will I sell to you. The girl will be a gift. You will find her suitable except she cries at night, but she does not try to run away."

The fat man turned and nodded to his *compañero*s.

A street sweeper, a man with weepy eyes and poor understanding, found Shadrach huddled under a watering trough, his eyes swollen closed and his ears smoothly severed from his head.

For two weeks, Shadrach hid in the rubble of the barn, waiting for his wounds to heal, his hearing to come back, and his eyes to return to normal. On a Wednesday night of the third week, when the moon was no thicker than the end of a fingernail, he found one of the fat man's broad-shouldered *compañeros* walking down the center of the street, over-served with *cerveza*. He left the man slumped forward in a church doorway, his neck broken, his mouth frozen forever in a silent scream. The next night, he clubbed the second *compañero*—who was stupid and not yet aware of the death of his fellow enforcer— with the wooden spoke of a wagon wheel and then hung him up on the doorpost of the cantina.

He pickled the bodyguard's ears in brine and enjoyed watching them shrivel. *Tal para cual.* Tit for tat, he thought and the corners of his mouth lifted to something resembling a grimace more than a smile.

The fat man, much to the irritation of the watchful Shadrach, chose to stay away from his job as operator of the house of loose women. Wisely, he decided to make an extended visit with his sister in San Elizario. When Shadrach learned this, he was not happy.

But he would wait as long as it took for the fat man to return. He got a job at a tannery, scraping hair and fat from hides. The odor was overpowering—so bad that his eyes and lungs burned, even in his sleep. He lost weight, and his gaunt frame resembled a scarecrow. He thought he might leave Ciudad Juárez and come back later to attend to the fat man on another day, perhaps in another year. But, even in his dreams, he could hear the fat man laugh and see his gold teeth. So he stayed.

Much later, on a warm night when the wind drove grit and sand down the dimly lighted street, the fat man returned. Although he had a guard with him carrying a shotgun, he still moved like a rat scurrying from one corner to the next but staying away from shadows. For a week, the pattern did not change. Shadrach watched and waited patiently.

A single-seated wooden *latrina* straddled a ditch behind the whorehouse. After a few nights, Shadrach decided to wait near there for a spell; after all, who takes a bodyguard with him to *mear*? On the eighth night, he was rewarded. The fat man cautiously looked out the back door, then hurriedly made his way toward the building, unbuttoning his pants as he waddled along like a human duck.

Shadrach stepped from the side of the building. Before the fat man could call for help, Shadrach put his knee in his back, grasped his head with both hands, and snapped his neck. He searched the dead man's pockets and was disappointed—a comb, nine thin coins, and a wooden-handled pocketknife. He felt cheated. The man was more worthless than he thought.

Shadrach studied the man on the ground, arms splayed, mouth opened in a distorted smile, gold-filled teeth mocking him. Using the whore-master's knife, Shadrach cut the gold teeth loose, pocketed them, and deposited the fat man headfirst into the *latrina*.

The next night, Shadrach swam his horse across the Rio Grande and set off for the mountains north of El Paso. He wore a most unusual necklace—a four-plait length of rawhide run through the ears of the fat man's *compañeros*.

El Paso
Frightened, uncertain, and still in shock from the storm, Muñoz spent the night in an alley, huddled behind a shipping crate. A thin fog rose off the river and ghosted down the street, little eddies of gray breaking off before fading into nothingness. The Argentine had never been as miserable.

Daylight came. Cattlemen stood in the stockyard café drinking coffee. They gave no notice to the longhaired youngster in the dingy, white, linen suit, who stood at the end of the bar and ordered, *"Huevos con panceta, por favor."*

The waiter lived in Ciudad Juárez but worked in El Paso at

the café during the day. He did note the accent and wondered if his customer was from Spain. After delivering the second cup of coffee, he told Muñoz, "That'll be two bits."

The Argentine reached inside the dirty shirt, extracted tattered bills and smoothed one out on the bar top.

The waiter was accustomed to being paid in American or Mexican, but he had never seen bills in such bad condition. "You don't try to keep your money dry when you swim the river?"

Muñoz did not understand the joke and was afraid there was something illegal about the money. If there was something wrong and a *crimen* committed . . .

The waiter was not a mind reader, but he recognized panic. "No, no, there is nothing wrong. It's just that I never saw money in such bad shape. You'll be lucky if you can pass those bills. Here it doesn't make any difference; nobody is getting in trouble over two bits. But out on the street. Well, I don't know.

"I don't recognize your accent. But I can tell by your clothes, you don't belong with a bunch of cowhands."

The waiter had to break off the conversation frequently to mop spills, refill coffee cups, and deliver orders. It took Muñoz almost a half hour to tell the story: the ship ride northward, the hurricane, the devastation, and the loss of the rest of the family.

"Damn. Can't believe you went through all that and lived to tell it. We knew it was bad, but that's the damnedest thing I've ever heard tell of. So, I reckon soon as you collect your wits, you gonna go back to Galveston and catch the first boat back to Argentina."

Muñoz was silent and studied the bottom of the coffee cup. "You've seen my money. It's disgusting, and you are right—I can't spend most of it. Even if I could, it's not enough to buy a ticket back to Buenos Aires. I'm . . . I'm in a . . ."

"A mess. A damned mess. You got any people around here?"

the waiter asked.

Muñoz looked down. "Father had a business client and friends north of here. We were taking horses to him. But the horses are gone, and the only thing I have is this envelope. I've got no idea of the location of the ranch."

The waiter studied the faded envelope. "Neva Tandy Ranch. Albuquerque. I'm gonna be able to help you. See that man over there in the checked shirt? He's a cattle buyer for a big English outfit. He'll know them if they are any size at all."

The waiter had a brief conversation with the cattle buyer. He was a big man with a booming voice, and he followed the waiter to the bar. "Hear your dad was taking horses up to the Tandy Ranch. I was up there less than a month ago, and they told me about you folks. They was pretty excited. 'Course, they didn't know about the hurricane. They're good folks. If you can get up there, they'll give you a hand. You can bet on it!"

Muñoz sat in front of the café and inventoried the contents of the money belt. Maybe twenty-five dollars was salvageable. The rest was getting mushier by the hour.

Diego Muñoz once said, if you needed help, call in the army. The Argentine army was not available, but the U.S. army might be.

Back inside, the waiter answered, "Yeah, you'll find Fort Bliss due north of town right at the foot of the Franklins. Can't miss it."

The Rio Grande Valley
Moving during the day and grazing in the coolness of the night, the cattle trailed from the La Mesilla Ranch southward toward Fort Bliss. Quezada led the herd along the river so water would be plentiful, and there would be a minimum of arroyos to cross.

Chapman ate the dust of the moving herd as greenhorns had done since the first Longhorn calved on the Great Plains. It was a relief anytime a steer made a break for freedom because Chapman got away from the dust, even if it was only temporary. In Nashville, he'd dreamed about this, and now he was right in the middle of it.

They spent two nights with rancher friends; Quezada slept in the house and Chapman and the two flank riders under the stars. It was refreshing to bathe in the waters of the Rio Grande. Even if it ran sluggish and compared no more to Tennessee streams than a snake to a bird, it was still wet. Chapman would wash the salt stains from his shirt and then put it back on still wet. Cowboys changed pants at least once a month, needed or not.

On the fourth afternoon, they swung east around the foot of the Franklins and turned north toward the red aura that seemed to cover Fort Bliss. El Paso and Ciudad Juárez lay to the south, the buildings faint and dancing eerily in the last of the day's sun.

Fort Bliss, Texas

The government purchasing agent met them at the gate to the stock pens and counted the cattle. "I'll have money for you in the morning," he said. "Our cashier took off early to 'tend to some business.' That's nice words for he got drunk last night and didn't make it in today. We got some barracks that ain't being used. Feel welcome to bed down tonight, and you can go to mess with me. Our grub ain't too good, but it's probably better that what you've been having."

Quezada paid the two men who had ridden flank. They set off at a canter toward El Paso. "Hey," the purchasing agent shouted toward the disappearing riders, "you fellows see that worthless sumbitch cashier, tell him to get his sorry ass back up here. I need money to pay for these damned steers."

Chapman saw to the horses while the agent and Quezada exited the fort gate to a saloon, the kind that invariably pops up like mushrooms around every army post across the world.

The bar teemed with troopers, their blue uniforms slightly pinkish hued from the red dust. Women, best viewed in the dim light, worked the troopers for watered-down drinks with promises of later favors. An unskilled piano player hammered out a bad version of *Dixie* while soldiers and their temporary girlfriends jostled around the crowded dance floor. Skill ran a distant second to body contact.

In the corner farthest from the door, a slight figure dressed in tattered linen clothes sat uneasily watching the crowd—a glass of beer purchased with money that came from within the dirty shirt.

A tall Mexican stood at the bar and, with depthless eyes, watched the crowd wolf-like. Even without the strange eyes, this figure would have drawn stares if for no other reason than the sides of his head were palm smooth and earless. Had his hair not been pulled back and held in place with a strangely decorated rawhide thong, the lack of ears might have gone unnoticed.

"Perchance you know that ugly fellow standing at the bar?" Quezada asked.

The purchasing agent shook his head. "Naw, he's been hanging around here a few days. Wouldn't hit a lick at a snake. Don't know what he does. But I can tell you, he's in every night, cocking his head like an addled rooster, lookin' at people, like he's measuring them or something."

"Uglier than my first two wives put together," Quezada said, and both men laughed.

The purchasing agent said, "You think he is ugly? Heard him tell somebody the other night that his name is Shadrach. Now that's ugly."

Chapman finished feeding and watering the horses and stood peering over the batwing doors. Quezada waved his hat, and Chapman worked his way through the crowd.

"Busier than the bar in Roswell," he said. "And louder, too."

Quezada looked over the crowd and turned to Chapman. "You gotta understand these men. They're trained to hunt Injuns. Sorta. But there aren't many of them around that need hunting, and if you can find them, they are peaceful, sitting around in the shade telling yarns. Now the troopers don't have much to do except ride across this godforsaken country in a formation that somebody in the Civil War dreamed up, shoot at tin cans, worthless shit like that.

"They're mostly Germans and Irish. Couldn't get a job back east, so they came out here. Now they are bored as hell and would run off if they had anywhere to go."

Quezada crooked an index finger and scooped sweat from his forehead. "They come down here at night, whoop and holler and chase women. They cuss a lot and try to act rowdy. Bet there's not half dozen of them that's ever even shot at a man. Get down to the nut cutting, fellow might be better off without them."

Before watches were common, the bugler drove the rhythm of army forts: Reveille, Mess Call, Call to Quarters, Tattoo, and, finally, Taps. This was the last call of the day and notified that unauthorized lights were to be doused.

In the boisterousness of the bar, few troopers heard Call to Quarters, but with finely attuned ears, all of them heard Tattoo. They downed their remaining alcohol and hurried away from the bar, leaving only a few male civilians and the bar girls. The women looked over the remaining men and, not seeing any prospects, called it a night.

"Well," Quezada said, "at least we can now hear ourselves

think. It sounded like cattle branding at La Mesilla." He signaled the barkeep for another round.

The purchasing agent continued to rail against the absence of the army cashier. "He is a sorry bastard, and we'll be fortunate to see him tomorrow. I tell you what, Chapman, that man—he's a bigger drunk than I am."

Chapman listened to his tablemates but watched the tall Mexican at the bar. Something about the way he stood, the way he looked at the stragglers in the bar, and the expressionless eyes troubled him. A hawk, that's what it was. A hawk perched on a post watching the grass for a rabbit or rat.

Ten o'clock came, and the bartender finished herding cigarette butts into a flat metal scoop, emptying spittoons, and then extinguishing all but one kerosene lamp. "OK, boys," he said. "I can't make you go home, but I can put you in the dark. However you look at it, you can't stay here tonight."

The linen-clad figure got up from the chair and almost paused at Quezada's table before crossing to the door and stepping out into the darkness. Chapman noticed the departure and then the quick exit of the earless Mexican.

The purchasing agent rested his head on the tabletop and began snoring while Quezada rolled a cigarette and then searched his vest for a match.

Something, a sound or a change in the night, moved Chapman, and he stood and looked over the swinging doors out into the darkness. The quickly disappearing solitary, white figure was enveloped by a shadowy mass that rose out of the darkness.

"Auxilio! ¿Puede alguien ayudarme?"

The bar was quiet and the words came again: *Auxilio! ¿Puede alguien ayudarme?*

Quezada came across the floor in long strides and shoved

Chapman aside. "Who is that hollering for help? What's happening out there?"

"Up yonder," Chapman said, and pointed in the darkness away from the light of the fort. "I was watching that fellow in the white suit, and all at once, he just disappeared like somebody had thrown a blanket over him. Just there one second and gone the next."

"Auxilio! Auxilio!"

Quezada clawed his pistol from the holster and ran toward the screams. Chapman followed, fumbling at his gun, his heart pounding.

"Auxilio! Auxilio!"

Quezada reached the struggling pair first. With his pistol, he lashed the attacker across the head and sent him sprawling into the dirt.

Now Chapman was near enough to the struggle to see the attacker was the earless Mexican.

The Mexican pulled the Peacemaker from beneath his serape and fired at Quezada. The rancher staggered from the impact of the .45 slug and then fired twice at the Mexican. Shadrach grunted two times as Quezada's shots found their target; he dropped to all fours, blood running from his mouth.

Then, Quezada violated his life-long principle by not finishing Shadrach with a shot to the head but instead turning his attention to the Argentine.

Chapman knelt beside the victim and was trying to quell the flow of blood from a face wound. Quezada dropped to his knees, pulled the neckerchief from his neck, and packed it into the gaping wound.

Shadrach staggered to his feet and, gripping the pistol in both hands, fired a single shot. Quezada made a huffing sound, leaned forward, and fell to his side.

Chapman stood, turned to where he'd last seen Shadrach,

and drew his pistol. There was no one there, but he emptied his revolver into the darkness toward the sound of the fleeing Mexican.

Quezada made an effort to stand and then collapsed. "Son," he whispered, "I'm hit. Bad. I can't feel my legs." Blood was streaming from a hole in his stomach. "Damn . . . I ain't never hurt like this. You got to help me up . . . shit! . . . I . . . I can't . . . breathe."

After sundown, the Fort Bliss post commander, Colonel Micker, issued a perpetual order that two sentries stand guard at the front gate. "In case of Indian attack," he said. But there were only drunk soldiers returning to the fort and no marauding Indians. Night sentry duty at Fort Bliss was cold in the desert during the summer and miserably bone-chilling in the winter. The wind whipped dust from the parade ground, and the major lifted a uniform protocol and allowed the sentries to wear kerchiefs over their faces.

Almost a dozen unevenly spaced shots cracked from the darkness out past the saloon. The sentries hurriedly closed and barred the gate. Major Warbel ordered a night squad comprised of eight troopers to assemble, and they rode out to investigate the gunshots.

Ten minutes after the squad departed, two troopers returned and requested an ambulance. "Two civilians involved," they reported, "one severely cut and the second dying."

The four-wheeled ambulance broke the silence of the moonless night as it raced through the fort gate, the pounding hoofbeats of the two mules beating a rhythm to the tempo of the jangling trace chains.

The night of the attack, Dr. Woods, the post doctor, cleaned Muñoz's wound and completed the stitches. "I've just got one thing to say, Muñoz—you did say your name was Muñoz, didn't you? You are one lucky son of a bitch. An inch further, and he'd have cut your jugular. That would have been it for you in about two heartbeats."

Two days later, Chapman waited outside the door of the army infirmary. Dr. Wood's white, starched coat was seeing third-day service and had grown a web of unintended creases and smears of undetermined origins.

"Dammit, son, I've told you a dozen times. It ain't *when* he walks, it's *if* he lives. And, yeah, you can go in and see him. But don't expect any miracles. Used my last one ten years ago. Don't be in there too long, or one of the women nurses will embarrass you by kicking your scrawny ass out the back door."

Quezada lay on his back, sweat pooled on his forehead, his lips fever chapped. A blood-encrusted bandage encircled his middle, and a green fly inspected a small freshly bloodied spot below the dressing. Chapman had not seen a dead man since Quezada killed the bone picker at the springs outside Carlsbad. He thought he might be seeing the next one.

"If it is all right, I'd like to wash his lips?" Chapman asked a nurse, who looked as bedraggled as the doctor.

"Pretty much a waste of time, but have at it. There's water over yonder in that bucket. Some clean rags in the cabinet. I believe he's about past caring anyway."

The night shift commenced at six in the afternoon, and they paid less attention to Chapman than the day shift. He spent the night in a wooden chair beside Quezada's bed listening to him mumbling about Tucson, Captain Fesmire, Apaches, and bars of gold.

The fever came and went. For two weeks, either Muñoz or Chapman sat in the infirmary caring for Quezada around the clock. Dr. Woods stopped by twice each day, examined and cleaned the wound, shook his head, and walked away.

The sun rose red and angry, and it cast a bright yellow shaft of light through the window and across Quezada's face. The sick man stirred and laid the back of his hand across his still-closed eyes. His upper body turned slightly, his lips moved: "I do believe I need a drink of whiskey."

"Well, hell no, I'm not staying here. I got livestock and three ranches to see after. I'm not dead; my legs just don't work. 'Sides, if I have to eat one more of them buzzard drum sticks that your cook favors, there might be some real shooting around here."

Dr. Woods looked up at Muñoz, over to Chapman, then back down at Quezada. "Well, you dang sure ain't riding a horse, and I don't see any angel wings sprouting outta your back. Reckon that means you won't be flying. And you are not walking. That bullet is laying right there against your backbone. I'm not taking the damn thing out, and if you dislodge it, you could wind up a whole lot worse than just paralyzed legs."

"No. Not only no, but, hell no. I'm going back to the La Mesilla Ranch. And I'm not riding in the back of a damn wagon like I was a sack of dried buffalo turds. And not one of those army ambulances either. Last trip I took in one of those things danged near killed me."

Dr. Woods was a short man with a shorter temper. He'd spent more than thirty years in the army, and he was accustomed to getting his way. "Who said anything about a wagon or an ambulance? I'll approve you taking a train. I'll send an orderly. That's it, and I don't tolerate no backtalk from a gut-shot civilian."

" 'You will approve' . . . 'your final words'! Hell fire, man. I don't need your approval for a damn thing." Quezada raised himself up on his elbows. "Chapman, I want you to take Muñoz here and go down to El Paso. I want a buggy with good springs and a top. And a big trunk box. I want a pacing horse that's broke to a buggy . . . no, I want two. And don't let them put some stringhalted nags off on you either. I want a black buggy, black horses, and black harness with silver trim."

Quezada flicked the ashes and studied the new redness at the cigar tip. "Mayhap you get going now, we can get the hell outta here 'fore supper."

It was not yet dark when Muñoz and Chapman came through the Fort Bliss gates in a shiny, new buggy pulled by an impressive black gelding, with a matching gelding tied to the luggage rack. They pulled up in front of the hospital, where Quezada sat on the porch in a military wheelchair, his gun belt and blood splattered jacket across his lap.

Chapman stepped down from the buggy, and Muñoz brushed the dust and sand from the shiny, black, leather upholstery.

Quezada looked over the rig and nodded in approval. "We'll put this blasted wheelchair in the trunk box. Doc said I could have it for a while, and it wouldn't break the army if I didn't bring it back. 'Course I don't figure I'll need it for more than a week or two." He leaned out and looked at the buggy again. "Perchance you two ain't too busy, you might kinda give me a hand off this porch and up into that rig."

Quezada was dead weight until he could reach the buggy top's steel bow and help pull himself into the seat. He didn't even grunt, but the back of his shirt was wet, and sweat covered his face. "I don't believe I'm quite up to driving today," he said. "I believe that perchance Muñoz is agreeable, he can drive me back up to the ranch. Chapman, you'll ride your horse and bring mine."

"Where you figure to spend the night?" Chapman asked.

"If both these pacing horses don't give out," Quezada said, "we'll not be spending the night anywhere. Next time I get down out of this buggy, we'll be at the La Mesilla Ranch—or, by God, I'll be dead."

Dr. Woods came out of the dispensary with two worn, drab blankets. "Tuck these around your hips" he said to Quezada. "If you bounce around too much, you'll start bleeding again—might even dislodge that bullet and shore enough cripple you up to your stubborn head."

Now the doctor addressed Chapman in an even sterner tone. "Don't bring his sorry ass back here. I don't care what happens to him. I'm done with the stubborn cuss." He leaned into the buggy and put a knapsack on the floor between Quezada and Muñoz. The contents emitted a faint clinking sound.

Muñoz grasped the reins, and the buggy smoothly moved out of the fort. Chapman followed, leading Quezada's horse. He'd ridden drag part time coming down here and he was riding drag full time going home; he just wasn't eating the dust of a herd of cattle this time.

Through the coolness of the desert night, Muñoz sat erectly in the seat, carefully steering around potholes and boulders. Somewhere to the north, the Neva Tandy Ranch was little more than a dream. Tonight Muñoz was with friends.

Darkness came, and now Chapman rode ahead serving as guide. For almost a year, Quezada had been his mentor. He remembered the older man's gruff guidance, and now it was his turn.

Quezada slumped over in the seat and leaned against Muñoz. From his hips upward, there were stabbing pains. From his hips downward, there was no feeling—no pain, no tingling, nothing. "Muñoz, reach down there in that haversack," he said. "If that sawbones is half the man I think he is, mayhaps there you will find a couple bottles of whiskey in there. I believe I'm about ready for the first one."

The sky in the east started to turn to the light pink color that is on the underside of Gulf of Mexico seashells. The Organ Mountains were still a blurred gray and undefined when the buggy and its weary occupants stopped in front of the La Mesilla Ranch house.

Franklin Mountains, Texas

For a week, just off a rocky trail leading through the Franklins but still in sight of Fort Bliss, Shadrach lay in the mouth of a shallow cave. He had fled through the darkness, cringing at the fusillade of bullets that swept past his head like angry bees. He was unaware of the grinding pain in his leg until he stumbled across a dead cholla and fell face first into a rocky arroyo. But raw fear drove him onward. He clambered across the gulch and then, making ungodly moaning sounds, scrambled like a wounded animal across the dead bear grass and sotol toward the mountains.

Quezada's first shot cracked the Mexican's fibula, the smallest bone between the knee and the ankle; the second tore through the sidewall of his mouth, slicing the cheek as cleanly as the cut from a straight razor.

Pain radiated up the leg and swept through his body until it assaulted his brain. He bordered on delirium. He had taken Muñoz's money belt on the night of the attack and, after finding it full of disintegrating bills and useless papers, used it as a bandage for his wounded leg. But red ants were attracted by the rotting cloth and invaded the wound. He built a small fire at the back of the cave, heated his iron belt buckle, and cauterized the wound. He stuffed the edge of the serape in his mouth to muffle his screams.

Earlier he found, much to his horror, that he could stick his tongue through the slit in his cheek. He concocted a paste from dirt and his own urine and sealed the cut.

Just up the hill from the cave entrance, he discovered a spring that dripped a single drop every ten minutes. An earlier traveler left a tin can at the seep, and Shadrach visited twice daily to drink, just after twilight and just before dawn. There was not enough water to either quell his thirst or calm his fever.

His movements were stealthy, and only a trained eye could have detected his presence in the dim light. Regardless of his thirst, he was patient as the scorpion that waited for the desert frog to venture from its secret place out into the coolness of the night.

He lay in the dimness of the cave watching the fort for activity. On the first night, he had feared the troopers would take up his trail and overpower or, perhaps, kill him in the barren desert. But it turned out they were not anxious to follow an armed man into the darkness—certainly not a shooter that gunned down an adversary as formidable as Quezada.

As the days passed, he ate little except a few mushy and bitter grubs and the pads of prickly pear cactus. Surviving off the cactus was slow and tedious work: first to find the cactus in the dimness of night and secondly to peel away the bristles and spines to access the fruit. Incessantly, his stomach growled and cramped from hunger.

He thought of *Poco Coño*. If she was here with him, he could. No. He didn't even have the strength for that.

Yesterday just before sundown, a buggy left the fort. Although the distance was too great to identify the three men, Shadrach recognized two of the four horses as belonging to Quezada and Chapman. The group edged the southern toe of the mountain and then turned northward up the Rio Grande.

Shadrach's mind swam through unfamiliar colors and lights. He dreamed of cool water and meat roasted over an open fire. Maybe *pollo*. Or *cabra* with the juices sliding down onto the embers and then vapor drifting upward to pleasure his nose. He was a boy back in the sky islands. His mother fried corn mush mixed with peppers, and he washed it down with goat's milk cooled in the village springhouse. In the coolness of the summer, his father sent him to fetch the goats, and he stopped at an apple tree to gather the red fruit. He continued up the mountain, his stomach filled with the sweet pulp, until the goat bells were pleasant in his ears.

Even in his stupor, he withdrew deeper into the Cimmerian cave as he heard the sharp, directionless sound of steel against stone and the rocks above him being dislodged. A young boy, face yet to be touched by a razor, came riding along the trail on a pony. Four goats were lazily grazing before him. He paused, dismounted, and curiously peered into the dullness of the cave.

The goats ceased their grazing, turned their heads toward the cave, pricked their ears forward.

The sounds of the struggle were brief, and when it abated the goats returned to their peaceful grazing, completely oblivious to the young herder's death.

Under the faint light of a new moon, the boy's pony carefully picked his way up the side of the mountain. Shadrach, his legs almost dragging the ground, rode until he felt the animal staggering under his weight. He stepped off the pony and continued up the mountain, grasping the saddle horn and hobbling along on his good leg.

The moon hid its faint illumination from the earth as it slipped slowly below the western horizon, disappearing into the desert, silently as it had risen.

He descended the western edge of the mountain and could no longer see the lights of the fort, so he felt comfortable building a small fire. When the coals were an ash-covered dull glow, Shadrach roasted the hindquarters of the youngest goat. He ate wolfishly until his stomach ached. Then he pulled the saddle blanket over his gaunt body and slept until the dawn's dew gathered in his beard and moistened his face.

Three miles. He covered no more than three miles the first day, sometimes riding and sometimes leaning against the pony. He traveled cautiously, constantly looking over his shoulder or scanning the desert below. His concern was not of discovery by the troopers but by the *bandoleros* that plied the rugged mountains and preyed on the unwary traveler.

He was unaccustomed to being defenseless. On the night he had been shot, he'd stabled his horse in a livery and hidden his rifle in a hay manger. He felt comfortable with just his knife and pistol. After watching the unusually dressed person that sat in the corner of the saloon for two nights, he didn't see the need for his rifle.

The stranger caught his eye because of the timorous movements. And the money belt. Shadrach had never seen one. But he watched the stranger fish under the dingy shirt, pull money out, and pay for whiskey.

He outweighed him by at least a hundred pounds, and the slightly-built person wasn't armed. This would be pretty simple. Just slit his throat and take the belt. Wouldn't even be a fight. Then he'd go to the stable, get his rifle and horse, and maybe drift back down to El Paso. It would be easy to cross back and forth over the border. While he felt comfortable in Ciudad Juárez, it was difficult to make a living there, and he didn't want to go back to the tannery. And the people in Ciudad Juárez were too violent. *Norte Americanos* seemed to be more interested in having the nicer things in life: bigger houses, finer horses, better clothes. They were softer; they would be easier to rob.

This should have been an easy robbery. He'd followed the Argentine until they were away from the light of the saloon. There had been almost no struggle: a slap across the head with his pistol, a quick slash of the throat, and a ripping away of the money belt.

Quezada—that was the bigger man's name. Quezada. He overheard the bartender call him that. The younger man's name was Chapman . . . that's what the drunken army man called him. He had not calculated he would have to fight them. But the screaming caused the two *Americanos* to come from the saloon and attack him.

He'd shot Quezada, and the big man started to fall. But then he'd straightened and fired twice: the first bullet slicing through Shadrach's cheek and the second breaking his leg, causing him to drop to his knees. He found it difficult to stand and fire his pistol, but he did, and Quezada's legs buckled and he'd fallen. This time he'd not gotten up. Quezada's companion, Chapman, fired wildly into the darkness. Had he not been in such pain, he would have returned and killed all three.

He limped along. The pain in his leg was fierce as the summer thunderstorm that ripped at the mountaintops above him. It was Quezada and Chapman's fault. They had no right interfering in his business. He had not seen them talking with the Argentine; they were not friends; they didn't even know each other. Now here he was, through no fault of his own, limping along through the mountains, his horse and rifle gone.

They had shown him great contempt, much as the cattle dealer and the whore-master had done. It was not of his nature to suffer disrespect without retaliation.

He knew the name of the two meddlesome men but little else. He'd heard Quezada speak of La Mesilla and Fort Stanton. And when he'd last seen them, they were going north up the Rio Grande. He would travel northward and find these towns. Then he would teach these two men something about respect.

Charon-like, Shadrach sat overlooking a dry streambed, planning their deaths.

La Mesilla Ranch

Constant pain, like water wearing at sandstone, changed the countenance of Quezada. His once erect carriage degenerated into a stoop, and he lost appetite. He operated the ranch from the veranda during the summer, scowling, moving from one end of the porch to the other on crutches and staying in the shade. German carpenters attached an office to the living room, and he spent the cooler months there, sitting in a chair made from gracefully curved long horns and the hides of range bulls.

Most mornings and afternoons, he and Chapman had a *sit down*. Quezada taught Chapman range management, animal husbandry, irrigation, and the cattle industry in general. In the main, he was patient, but on days when pain crept up his back like an evil, scaly snake and gnawed at the base of his neck, he would shout at his protégé. Later, he would apologize. "Don't pay no attention to me, son. I reckon it's just my way of getting back at the world . . . and, well . . . you just happened to get in the way."

He would pause and look out the window down toward the river. "I'm gonna get better. I'll throw these danged crutches away, walk again on my own. I'll ride a horse. I ain't near done. Mayhaps you didn't know it, but there ain't never been a Quezada that died in bed."

But still, he must have felt uneasy. He moved Chapman from the bunkhouse to the bedroom adjacent to his. Muñoz occupied a small bedroom behind the kitchen, and Felipe slept on a cot in Quezada's bedroom. "Case I need to get up during the night or something," he explained.

As time went along, Quezada had two constant companions, regardless of the weather or the time of day: Felipe and a bottle of whiskey.

If a trip was in order, Quezada sent Felipe long before daylight to fetch the Argentine with instructions to "Bring the buggy around, we're wasting daylight." They sat close together on the buggy seat, Muñoz handling the reins, but if they met a friend of Quezada's, the rancher would hurriedly take the reins. "Ain't no need to advertise that I'm a semi-invalid," he'd say. He said this lightly, but it was obvious to Muñoz that Quezada felt his manhood slipping away.

Chapman understood the older man. Sometimes the remarks were cutting, and another man might have taken offense, but he knew this was just the price of learning. He pondered this as he became an *iron ass* on the frequent trips to Fort Stanton and the infrequent trips over to the Bitter Lakes Ranch. He heard the men in the bunkhouse and on his regular ranch inspections call him *jefe* or "Quezada's man."

"Two horses and three cans of beans," Chapman bragged. "La Mesilla to Fort Stanton. The ride from Fort Stanton to Bitter Lakes Ranch is a four beaner."

He enjoyed the trips across the San Andres and the Sierra Blancas, sleeping on pine needles at night and drinking snow-melt. And while it was not pleasant, there was something about the beauty of the white sands and loneliness of the plains to the east that strongly appealed to him.

"Let me see your tally book," Quezada asked as soon as Chapman stepped down from the saddle after an inspection of the cattle at Fort Stanton and Bitter Lakes. The older man would compare the current count against the previous trip and nod appreciatively at any increase. But any decrease in count brought on a furrowed brow and stormy questioning. "You sure about this?" he asked. "You looked down along the river and back up in all the *barrancos*?"

Chapman learned how to handle the old rancher. "Naw. I didn't look in any of them places, and I only used one eye when counting. Probably missed half of what was there."

Quezada would glare at Chapman, and Chapman would

mimic his look and stare back. Little crow's-feet would grow at the corner of the old rancher's eyes; then they'd turn into laugh lines. And everything would be all right again between the two men.

Chapman learned there were times it was easier to break bad news than others. One of the best was when Quezada finished his second bottle of daily whiskey, and Felipe was preparing the bed. "You hadn't asked me about the horses up at Fort Stanton," Chapman said.

Quezada lit his last cigar of the day, tilted his head back, and inhaled. "Well, hell, son. Can't you tell nothing on your own?"

"We've lost six horses up at Fort Stanton. Four of them was in the mountain pasture, but two of them was taken outta the pasture behind the barn."

Felipe came from the bedroom and announced, "It's ready for you."

Quezada stood, and Chapman helped him toward the bedroom. The older man sat awkwardly on the side of the bed. "Well, I'll damn sure not put up with somebody stealing our horses. If I was a betting man, which I am, I'd bet it was part of the Bunker gang. Sorry bastards."

"Do I know any of them?" Chapman asked.

"No, they were pretty much wiped out before you came here. Part of that Billy the Kid, Lincoln County War, Pat Garrett bunch. When I was younger, and that was a long time ago, we hunted most of that gang down. Killed the last of them up around Fort Sumner. Or pretty much the last of them. Few still scattered around, I reckon."

"What do you think about me going up and looking for them?"

Felipe removed Quezada's socks and stood.

Quezada looked down and wiggled his toes "No, I reckon that would be overloading your wagon somewhat. Mayhap this is something I need to take care of."

"But you're—" Chapman stopped in midsentence when Felipe elbowed him in the side.

"Yeah. I know what you're thinking. 'Cept your thinking ain't always that good. But I'll tell you what you can do. Write to Tollafson. Tell him to gather up Chance, Evans, and some of the best shots there at Fort Stanton. Meet us at the hotel in Alamogordo on the twentieth. But before they leave, invite everybody in that part of the country on down to the ranch on the twenty-fifth. Tell everybody we are going to barbecue a couple of beeves and have a party."

"Is that it?"

"Hell, no. Let me finish. I want you to order a case of .45 and a case of .44 cartridges. Maybe a couple of cases of 44.40s for the Winchesters. We'll take the shells up to Alamogordo with us. Don't want you men looking rusty."

"Is that all?" Chapman asked.

"If I think of anything else I'll let you know. Now get outta my bedroom and quit bothering me. I need some sleep."

Chapman walked through the living room, cupped his hands behind the lamp chimneys, and blew out the lights.

The ranch hands polished Quezada's rig until it looked new. His two pacing horses had a separate corral close to the house and received extra portions of oats. On most days Felipe helped his boss down to the trap, where he curried their coats until they glistened. Quezada loved fine horseflesh.

With the ammunitions lashed in the back of Quezada's buggy, he, Chapman, Felipe, Muñoz, and four cowboys left La Mesilla on a fresh morning while the pink of sunrise was pushing its way over the craggy Organ Mountains. The night birds were retreating from the daylight; the day birds were emerging from their roost. Quezada looked behind him at the string of riders and told Muñoz, "Damn, looks like we are a raiding party going out to hunt for Mescalero."

The trip lasted two hot days and a night. Quezada insisted they cross south of the white sands of the Tularosa Basin at night. Around midnight, it was fifty degrees, and the winds sliced through the eerie darkness at forty miles an hour, shifting the dune fields and blasting the saltbrush to an even lighter gray.

The horses' tails blew tight up against their bellies, and their manes whipped back and forth as if trying to escape the torment. The men leaned forward over their saddles and braced against the pommel. Their coat collars blew against the back of their heads. If their stampede string was not tight, their hats became unseated and waltzed with the desert wind until captured by a patch of wind-whipped brush.

Daylight came, the wind lay, and, in the distance, they could see the ragged, barren hills and, past that, the canyons and low mountains east of Alamogordo.

Finally, the buggy stopped, and the riders gathered around. Quezada eased himself to the ground, braced against a wheel, and pulled the oilskin duster from his shoulders. "Well, by God, I hope you're happy," he said, as if crossing the desert at night had been the riders' idea and not his own. "We'll have a little bit of coffee. Big thing on my mind is to get the hell out of this sand—we'll eat at noon and still make town before dark."

The men stepped out of their saddles and commenced to shake the dust from their hair and clean out the horses' eyes. Chapman pointed his finger at Muñoz and whispered, "Don't you ever do anything that dumb again." They turned their backs to Quezada and had a good laugh.

Alamogordo

The hotel was less than a year old, the newness of the sawn

139

timbers pleasant to the sand-rawed nostrils of the La Mesilla riders. Tied to the hitching rail in front of the hotel, six of Quezada's Slash Q branded horses enjoyed the building's afternoon shadow. The riders from Fort Stanton sat on the long veranda nursing mugs of beer.

Chance and Evans stepped out into the edge of the roadway, leaned forward, and shook Quezada's hand. "Where you been, Boss?" Chance asked.

"Farting around in the desert last night. Looking for kangaroo rats and coyotes. Felipe here claims he even saw *Pavura Blanca* a couple of times. Women haints scare him pretty bad. Reminds him of his first wife."

Quezada stayed in the buggy until his riders took their horses to the livery. Muñoz and Felipe helped the rancher across the veranda and up to his room.

With the exception of Quezada, the men gathered around the hotel's dining table and ate as if they had never tasted grub this good. Finally, the last fork lay idle on the table, and the coffee-pot made the final circle. The riders leaned back and either tucked snuff behind their lower lip or built a cigarette.

Quezada stayed in his room, and Felipe took a plate of food up to him.

Chapman stood. "Boys," he said, "I don't know how much you fellers from Fort Stanton know 'bout how the boss is do-ing. He got shot down at Fort Bliss. Hurt pretty bad. But he is mending and gonna be all right. But it's going to take a while. You may not even see him walk; if you do, don't make nothing over it. He's pretty raw about it. About the whole thing. Whole time we're down here, he'll be in the buggy. On the day of the eating and shooting, he'll be a-horseback, and you'll act like it's plumb normal—you'll not act surprised or nothing.

"We are going to do a little shooting tomorrow. Gonna go up in one of the canyons out of hearing from the city folks and do a little practicing. Got plenty of cartridges. Want you to be serious about this. We gonna shoot until Quezada is satisfied that we are the best around. Day after tomorrow, we're going back up to Fort Stanton. You fellers a-horseback may get to the ranch 'fore we do, but we'll be along. Day after we get home is the barbecue. Tollafson is gonna set everything up and be waiting for us. We gonna eat some beef, drink a little whiskey, and then we're gonna have a shooting contest."

"What's the prize?" one of the Fort Stanton cowboys asked.

Chance laughed. "Well, if you don't do good, you're gonna be working for somebody other than the Slash Q before sundown. The way the boss figures it, if you're the best around, ain't nobody gonna be stealing any more Fort Stanton horses."

"Is that the prize?" another cowboy asked. "Ain't no second prize?"

Chapman laughed. "Second prize is you get to keep sleeping in the same bunkhouse with all these sweet smelling Slash Q cowboys."

Chance walked to a corner of the dining room, and brought a rectangular wooden crate back to the table. "Here in this box is a brand new Winchester '73. It's the most accurate rifle man ever made. Hasn't been fired since it left the factory. It's a One of One Hundred, which means there ain't more than ninety-nine rifles that is its equal. Anywhere. I know for a fact that Quezada paid a hundred and twenty dollars for it. I'll bet that there is not another one in a thousand miles. Any more questions about prizes?

"Oh, one other thing. See this engraving?" He raised the rifle over his head, and the deep etching shadowed in the dim light. "Says: 'Winner. Slash Q Shooting.' So, I guess I was wrong. There ain't another one like this in the world."

"Now, so you top-hand pistol shooters won't feel left out," Chapman said, "Quezada is gonna give a prize for that, too. It's that black stud horse he bought over at Ruidoso couple of years ago. Might not rank with the Winchester, but it is a hell of a horse."

Lamp light shown through a dozen hotel windows until well after midnight as cowboys cleaned their rifles and pistols to mint condition.

When the first rooster crowed, Felipe walked along the hall of the hotel pounding on doors and shouting, "*Levantarse! Levantarse!* Chapman wants you to get up." Breakfast was on the table when the cowboys returned from feeding their horses, and Quezada sat at the head of the table drinking coffee and smoking a cigar.

"Morning, fellers. Chapman and Muñoz are going out with you this morning. I'll bet that both of them can outshoot the best of you. So don't get a case of the red ass if they give you some help. Felipe and me will be out later." He took a pull from the cigar and dismissed them with, "Don't shoot off no toes, and don't shoot nobody."

The sound of gunfire bounced off the canyon walls; bullets went whining off into the distance. Most of the cowboys had carried a handgun since they were big enough to believe they needed one. But they were not good shots. Contrary to what they might have boasted in a saloon, none had ever shot at another human. They'd shot at wolves, an occasional wildcat, and maybe killed a sick cow—but never shot at another man. Since the night of the gunfight at Fort Bliss, Chapman knew the difference between target shooting and shooting at another man. It was the same difference as seeing lightning and being hit by lightning.

Muñoz took a can of red paint out to the canyon wall and painted a large X on scattered trees and a few boulders. Most of the first shots missed, but by mid-day, the riders commenced to get the hang of it and started to punish the trees or chip away at the boulders. Soon it became evident: Muñoz was the most accurate shot with a handgun. "Rascal has been sneaking off, practicing," one of the riders complained, and then he took ribbing from the others: "Ain't near as good as you thought you were, are you?"

Felipe came out at noon, brought mutton and bread, and made coffee. Quezada stayed at the hotel.

The riders took their saddle guns, a mixture of .44 Henrys and 44.40 Winchesters, from their scabbards. They were more accurate with these long guns. Muñoz tried to teach the cowboys to hold their breath and shoot between heartbeats, but the riders just laughed and said they didn't need to do that.

Their shoulders sore and bruised, and hands blue with powder burns, the men almost cheered when Chapman called it a day.

It was a hard trip through the mountains and up to Fort Stanton, but the weather was pleasant, and the men enjoyed sleeping in the pine needles. Filipe pitched a small tent for Quezada, and, once inside, the rancher came out only to take a leak. "He is not feeling good," Filipe said. "His back is hurting, and he moans in his sleep. Talks out loud. He shouldn't have made this trip. He should've stayed at La Mesilla."

The white, two-story house at Fort Stanton shimmered in the light of the setting sun as the group arrived. Chapman climbed up into the buggy beside Quezada and said, "Let's have somebody bring us a bottle. We'll sit out here on the porch. Enjoy ourselves."

Quezada shook his head. He leaned forward, and Chapman saw the rancher's blood-crusted shirt and pants.

Fort Stanton Ranch

Before eleven the next morning, cowboys started gathering in the pasture next to the creek: a couple of soldiers, half dozen Indians, a handful of Mexicans, and men with hair hanging down to the top of their shoulders. Chapman got to forty before he stopped counting.

The last four men rode in together. They had quick eyes, the kind that are almost never still but seemed to be looking for something before it is even there. Their Henry rifles were in leather scabbards scarred by brush and hard wear. Leather batwing chaps fanned over their Spanish-heeled boots, and the ornate spurs jingled when their feet moved. Silver conchos, worn smooth by time, ornamented their gun belts.

"Look at their horses," Chance murmured to Tollafson. "Can't even tell what their brand is. Or was. Somebody took a running iron to them and didn't do a very good job."

"*Vaqueros* from some ranch to the south, along the border," a couple of the older and widely traveled riders guessed.

Tollafson took charge of the event. Quezada's stud horse had been brushed until he glistened as only a black horse can, blacker than the wing of a bat and darker than sin. The horse danced sideways through the crowd, nostrils flared, muscles rippling with a life of their own. Tollafson displayed the Winchester and explained the significance of the One-in-a-Hundred designation. After he gave the rules of the shooting match, he laid the encased rifle on the chuck wagon's tailgate and tied the black stud horse to a nearby hitching post. While the horse was magnificent, the cowboys admired the gun as if it were a good-looking woman rising naked from a bath in the creek.

A Fort Stanton army cook came down for the day. Two beeves lay on iron grills over a charcoal pit. A lamb and a half dozen chickens laid on a second grill, and the drippings fell down onto mesquite charcoal, spawning smoke that flavored the meat. Using the army's kitchen, the cook baked pans of corn light bread, pots of beans, and two dozen apricot pies. The food was spread on tables in the shade alongside the river. When the men finished eating, there was barely enough left to feed Quezada's dog, Sweetie.

Sheriff Stotts was on hand to run the contest. He was a small man and had a receding hairline and dark eyes permanently narrowed against the wind. There was talk that in his prime he was the most deadly gunman in what would become Western New Mexico. As he aged, young men trying to make a name for themselves came and unsuccessfully tested him. He was a man without swagger, but, then, timber rattlers and desert scorpions don't swagger either.

Six silver dollars used as targets were embedded in the top run of a rail fence, the same rail where the yellow-eyed rooster met his demise. Twenty men lined up to shoot at the coins. These were confident, braggadocious men with hand-tooled gun belts riding low on their hips and holsters tied down to their thighs. For the most part, they were more interested in impressing their counterparts with their speed of draw and style. They were not very good shots. Only three coins had to be replaced, until the final shooter, Muñoz, stepped to the line. The Argentine raised the pistol and fired six evenly spaced rounds. Four coins moaned away from the rail and disappeared in the pasture grass. Straws were drawn, and one other gunman won an opportunity to best Muñoz. He fired four rounds, hit one coin, missed, then laughed and fired the two remaining bullets up into the crisp afternoon air.

Logs sawn into six-inch blocks were targets for the riflemen. Two deputies lined them against a low bluff at the end of the pasture and staked lines at distances of twenty-five, fifty, and one-hundred yards.

The shooters brought an assortment of saddle guns, braced

themselves—five at a time—and began firing. There were few misses. Those disqualified grumbled about puffs of wind, poor cartridges, hiccups, or full stomachs. At fifty yards, only four shooters—Chapman, two *vaqueros,* and one cavalryman—were accurate. After a second round from this distance, only the trooper, Chapman, and the oldest *vaquero* remained. The third round eliminated the trooper.

Chapman felt hollow making it into the round. He sensed if the two faced off against either of the two *vaqueros* and a life depended on accuracy and a steady hand, he might not fare as well. He could not erase his sense of inadequacy in the gunfight at Fort Bliss. A wooden target was one thing; a man returning fire was another.

Tollafson brought out two wooden kegs that had cooled in the river since last night. The first contained peach brandy. The second, a first run made a year ago by a Kentuckian who lived in the mountains on an adjacent ranch. Sheriff Stotts tasted both and judged them to be fit for human consumption.

The cowboys drank the whiskey keg dry. They gathered in small groups, wagering and discussing the merits of each shooter.

The Rio Grande Valley

Shadrach drifted northward toward Las Cruces, the City of the Crosses. He enjoyed the temperature and the safety the mountains afforded. His leg was healing, but he limped. And it hurt. When it pained him, he remembered the men at Fort Bliss, and the memory caused his temples to throb. The cheek healed quicker, but the scar looked angry. He ran his fingers along it frequently, and it itched as if a fuzzy worm were inching across his face.

The afternoon winds blew clouds of fine sand across the plains, just right to hide the actions of a horse thief. However,

Shadrach didn't consider it stealing; after all, most ranchers had more horses than they needed. He needed the money more than some *gringo* rancher did.

It was not easy for him to find a suitable job. First, he worked for a farmer digging and cleaning out irrigation ditches. This was hard work. The farmer expected him to labor sunup to sundown. From late morning to early afternoon, the sun was almost unbearable. His leg hurt, and the farmer urged him to work faster. At another time in his life, he would have drowned the farmer in the mud of the irrigation ditch, but the unsteadiness in his leg prevented that. He found employment with a Basque sheepherder. The sheep grazed on the open range in and around the Organ Mountains. While Shadrach didn't like people, he did become lonely when his only companions were a band of sheep. But the work was easy, and it gave his leg time to heal. Usually he sat in the shade and watched the ignorant animals to see they did not wander off the side of a cliff.

His life settled into dull routine: up before dawn and make a breakfast of cold bread and coffee; lead the sheep to a stream and fresh grazing; a noon meal of last night's leftovers; lead the sheep back to camp after stopping by the stream; cook the night time meal. He was not a good cook, and his skills did not improve.

One night a week, he rode his broken-down horse into Cruces, had a light supper, a beer, and a whore. His weekly pay was little more than the cost of this recreational night.

He had been a shepherd for six weeks; it felt like six years.

The stars were dimming against the early morning sky when Shadrach saw uneasiness and movement at the edge of the bedded sheep. Two weeks ago, a coyote had taken a lamb from the band. "The value of the lamb will be taken from your month's pay," the Basque said. Shadrach was sullen in his stare.

Shadrach limped in a great circle and worked his way up a

narrow draw until he could see the flock. A small shaggy-haired boy, maybe ten or twelve, clutched a half-grown lamb to his chest, one hand gripping the struggling sheep around the mouth and nose—the pitiful bleats silenced. The boy backed away from the sheep and directly into Shadrach's splayed hands.

"You are trying to make me a poor man," Shadrach said, as he wrapped his arm around the throat of the struggling boy and lifted him off the ground.

The Fort Stanton Ranch

The *vaquero* and Chapman resumed the contest. Four more rounds and then the *vaquero* missed. It was Chapman's turn. He took a deep breath, exhaled gently, and fired between heartbeats. The wooden target splintered from the impact of his bullet. He had powder burns on his right cheek, bruises on his shoulder, and a ringing in his ears. Later, Tollafson calculated the three finalists each fired thirty rounds.

Body partially hidden by a black duster, Quezada rode into the gathering just as the last shots were fired. He sat stiffly erect in the saddle, Felipe close to his side. Men gathered around the rancher, reaching to shake his hand. He never reached down but touched the brim of his hat in acknowledgement.

"I want to thank all of you for showing up today. I hope you enjoyed the whiskey and the vittles." Applause and shouting interrupted his remarks.

"I'm mighty proud of Muñoz and Chapman. I never thought about two of my hands winning the contest. Reckon next time I have a shooting match, I'll make the two of them stay at the barn and give you other fellows a chance."

There was more whistling and applause, and the cowboys elbowed each other in the ribs.

The keg of whiskey was dry and the shooting match over. Some of the cowboys were tightening their saddle girths and preparing to leave. Quezada raised his hand. "One other thing. I want you to note who the best shots were today. I also want you to notice that all my horses have the Slash Q burned pretty clear into their hides.

"Somebody has been making off with some of my horses. I aim for that to stop. I've told my men that if they see somebody riding a horse with my brand on it, they are to shoot the rider. Don't ask no questions, just shoot."

Some of the cowboys started to laugh; none of them were Quezada's hands, and the laughter abruptly ended.

He continued. "I want to tell you again how happy I am that you came by today. Come back anytime. We'll be glad to see you. But we catch you stealing one of our horses we'll use you for target practice. Boys, I want for you to know how serious I am. We'll shoot any horse thief, sure as I'm sittin' here on this horse."

Quezada's words had a sobering effect on the few cowboys that remained.

"Tollafson showed you the Winchester before dinner today. It goes to the winner of the rifle shooting. I'm almost ashamed to give it to one of my men. But Chapman won it fair and square. Evans, would you bring it over here?"

The foreman walked to the wagon and picked up the rifle crate. It was empty.

The Rio Grande Valley

The boy dropped the lamb and struggled violently, drumming his heels against Shadrach's shins and knees. The Mexican tightened his grasp and raised the boy still higher. One of the boy's kicks centered Shadrach's healing leg. He dropped the boy and leaned forward in pain.

The boy rolled away from Shadrach and scrambled to his feet. "Don't you touch me again. My uncles will kill you."

Shadrach hopped forward, backhanded the boy to the ground, and put a foot on his stomach. "Your uncles?" he gasped, nausea rising up in his throat from the pain in his leg. "Did you say your uncles? Are they women? They send a boy to steal my sheep, and you think I should fear them? My sheepdog will carry your head to them like pig *carroña.*"

The boy continued to squirm under Shadrach's foot. "They've gone to a shooting match at Fort Stanton. You don't let me go, when they return . . . they will tie you to a wild horse and let him drag you to death."

"You little *mierda.* I hold you to the ground like a snake, and you threaten me!" Shadrach said, but he removed his foot. "What is your name?"

The boy sat upright, rubbed the blood and snot from his face, and then inspected his soiled hand. "My name is Alberto. But that is of no meaning to you. What you need to know is the surname of my uncles."

Shadrach laughed. "I do not care their name. No man frightens me."

Alberto stood and beat the dust from his shirt and pants. "*¡No seas estúpido!* How have you lived this long being so stupid? Their last name is Soto. They will roast you over a pit and feed you to their barn rats."

Shadrach took a quick, shallow breath. He knew of the Soto brothers. They ran a small ranch further north in the foothills. One day their pasture would be empty of livestock; the next day it was full. Horses and cattle seemed to arrive one night and leave the next. Brands were always a mixture.

"Maybe," he said, "I'll pinch your head off and feed you to the coyotes."

"*Stúpido.* My uncles know where I am. They sent me here. They will be home tonight, and they will expect me back with a lamb. I should have given it to my grandmother by now but for your ignorance in detaining me."

Shadrach considered his options. He could kill the boy and hide the body. Maybe burn it to ashes in the campfire. But the Soto brothers sent him, sent him here to steal a lamb. So, they knew where he was. They would come searching for their nephew. Or, he could turn the boy loose. The boy would go home and tell his uncles of the abuse. And they would search him out to revenge the ill treatment.

It would be difficult for him to run. His horse was not much better than walking, and his leg was not yet strong enough for him to hurry. He was not yet ready to take on a foe as formidable as the Soto brothers.

Alberto was full of belligerence and smirked. If the Soto kitten acted in this manner, how would the Soto tomcats act?

There seemed no way for Shadrach to win.

The Fort Stanton Ranch

Quezada rode over to the chuck wagon and looked into the crate. He leaned back in the saddle, took a deep breath, and said, "Crap. Who would have done such a thing? Right under our very own noses. Shit."

Tollafson climbed up on his horse, shaded his eyes, and scoured the pasture and the land along the river as if he might see the thief.

"Don't reckon the thief is gonna be setting on his horse right out there in the road, waving the rifle over his head, do you?" Evans said.

Tollafson was not amused.

Chance moved over to Quezada. "You want us to go have a look for him? He can't have got too far. Bet three or four of us could run him down. What do you think?"

Quezada and Chapman had been talking. Chapman shook his head, "Naw, no need of that. We wouldn't know which way to look. Too many cowboys left going in too many directions."

Quezada agreed. "But it'll turn up. I guarantee it. Man can't own something like that rifle and not brag about it. Show it to his friends. Get too much to drink and run his mouth to the wrong people. It'll turn up. Pisses me off, but I've had worse things happen." He shifted uncomfortably in the saddle and grimaced. "A whole lot worse."

Filipe walked around where the shooters stood and came back shaking his head. "Looks like where that feller Custer made his last stand—never saw so many hulls in my life. And you men pretty much ruined all the rocks down at the end of the pasture. Just shot 'em plumb to hell."

Quezada turned toward Muñoz and nodded. The two rode up the dusty road toward the ranch headquarters.

Chapman was on his third cup of coffee and second breakfast before he saw Quezada again.

The rancher emerged from his room, walking gingerly as a man with a rock in his boot, and took his accustomed place at the breakfast table. "I'll have two, fried, if you don't mind," he told Felipe. "Tell you what, Chapman, last couple of days I've been doing a bunch of thinking. This back thing is damn serious. It's putting me in a pretty bad place. First thing in a long time where I don't have control, and I don't like that, either."

Chapman watched Quezada spoon three sugars into his coffee. "I'm sure it still hurts something awful, but you're getting better. It'll just take some time."

Quezada looked toward the kitchen impatiently. "Well, that just shows what you know. You ain't the one that's putting up with numb legs and have an aching back that feels like somebody's driving a nail in it."

Chapman wanted to encourage his mentor. "Oh, I don't know, it won't be long until you . . ." His words tailed off; he didn't know—and his inability to help was frustrating. The two men finished breakfast with the silence broken only by the sound of eating utensils scraping against the scarred surfaces of their plates.

Chapman tied his horse to the rail in front of the Fort Stanton headquarters. The private on duty directed him to a small building behind the stables. "You'll find him in there if he ain't gone fishing, but most likely he's on the back porch taking a nap in the sun. He ain't too much in demand, beings as how there ain't a handful of us still stationed here."

The doctor sat in a wooden chair balanced on the back two legs, their tops leaning against the side of the building. His misshapen gray hat was shoved forward and resting against the bridge of his nose. Chapman cleared his throat a couple of times before the doctor rocked forward, and the front chair legs bumped against the wooden floor. "Scare hell outta a man. What do you mean sneaking up on me like that?" The doctor fumbled in his vest and pulled a small derringer. "I could've shot you."

"Sorry to wake you up, Dr. Calendar. My name's Chapman. I work with Quezada, up the river."

The doctor broke the derringer open, checked to see if it was loaded, and returned it to its hiding place. "Hell, I know who you are. I was up there at the shooting contest. You're that keen shot with a rifle. Still don't give you the right to sneak up on me."

Chapman sat on the weathered porch, removed his hat, and looked up at the doctor. "Well. I can't do much more than apologize again."

"Well. All right, then. What can I do for you? You ain't having a baby or nothing like that, are you?"

Chapman laughed. "Hope not," he said. "If I am, I don't know it."

"OK. What's your damn problem? Can't you see I'm pretty busy?"

For the next thirty minutes, Chapman retold the gunfight at Fort Bliss, detailed Quezada's injuries, and his present condition. He finished with, "He hurts all the time. I'm afraid he is getting worse. Do you think you could help him?"

"Well, hell fire. You think I'm a sawbones that runs a general practice, just goes around curing sick civilians, stuff like that?"

"No, sir, but I just wondered . . ."

"Wondered if I would go and doctor Quezada? Me being under contract to the U.S. army, you think I can just light out and doctor any old cowboy that didn't have no more sense than to get in a gunfight?"

Chapman stood and stared at the doctor the same way he would have looked at a mangy dog. "Why, you old devil. I don't give a damn what you do. Don't reckon that oath meant nothing to you."

"Oath! I took that oath in Chicago. I was good at cutting umbilical cords and curing thrush mouth. Then I get this wild hair to join the army—see the beautiful west before its majesty is ruined by farmers and the such. So I sit here day after day occasionally digging an arrowhead outta some unlucky trooper's ass. But what I do mostly is distribute crab powder and try to clear up the clap in some sorry-ass cavalryman. Don't lecture me about an oath."

"I don't care about any of that," Chapman said. "I've got this sick friend. If you can't get it in your heart to go and see him, I'm gonna rope you like a calf and drag you up the river to the ranch. I'll make you wish you'd never heard of an oath or an umbilical cord."

"Well, there you go," the doctor said. "Now you're acting like a man that cares for his friend. I've known Quezada since the second day after I was assigned here. Let's go and saddle my horse. See what I can do."

Dr. Calendar spent an hour with Quezada. Twice, he called out, asked Muñoz for towels and another pan of warm water.

Chapman took the doctor's horse to the barn, brushed him down, and poured a scoop of oats into a trough. Felipe combined rice, refried beans, beef, and cheese and wrapped the mixture in a flour *tortilla*. He made *churros* and added extra cinnamon, since that suited Quezada's taste.

Calendar, rolling his sleeves down, followed Muñoz and Quezada from the bedroom. "Well, I believe that'll 'bout do it for today," he said and eyed the kitchen table. "Reckon part of that's for me?"

While Felipe scurried around filling coffee cups and water glasses, Muñoz, the doctor, Quezada, and Chapman ate. Between bites, Dr. Calendar talked about Quezada's care. "Since Muñoz is the only person around here with clean fingernails, that's who I'm assigning nursing duties. Clean the wound twice a day. I'm leaving some salve that'll help with the healing and a bottle of stuff that will help with the pain.

"Now there ain't gonna be any more of that horseback riding silliness for a while. Probably be the worst thing he can do. Gotta go somewhere, take the buggy. And I'm not talking about riding up to Albuquerque either. Short trips, that's all. Remember, we're trying to heal this fellow. He's gonna need a lot of rest and looking after. Y'all understand?"

Quezada frowned and pulled the plate of *churros* away from the doctor.

Muñoz was a great nurse and followed the doctor's instructions; Quezada didn't.

The following week, Quezada and Chapman sat in the kitchen having a second cup of coffee and discussing the sale of horses to the army. "We'll take two dozen up this afternoon," Chapman said. "You want to see them before we leave?"

"No. I trust you. While you are up at the fort, go by and see Dr. Calendar. Tell him I'm about out of that pain medicine. Gonna need at least two more bottles." Quezada lit his first cigar of the day, leaned back in his chair, and said, "Yes, sir, real good stuff, that pain medicine."

Chapman looked at Muñoz, who turned away and shrugged.

"Go get the book and give it to him," Quezada told Muñoz. "The one I showed you last night, the one at the end of the bookcase.

"Gonna give you something to read. We are gonna take a little trip tomorrow. Gonna ride over to Carrizozo. You and me and Muñoz. I need to see somebody over there. A lawyer. 'Nother person I want to see. Need you to see them, too."

Chapman stood from the table. "But the doctor said—"

Quezada raised his hand. "I know what the doctor said. You don't have to tell me. I was here. Remember?"

Muñoz returned and placed the book on the table in front of Chapman. The leather binding was cracked, and the edges of the cover were deteriorating. Embossed in the center were the entwined letters *CSA;* across the bottom and in much smaller letters: *Bob Stevens.*

The Rio Grande Valley
Shadrach drove the Basque's sheep into a narrow box canyon and pulled a windrow of cat claw acacia across the entrance. There was enough grazing for the day. They would get thirsty, but he would be back by dark.

He hurried down the mountain trail with Alberto and two lambs walking in front. "We will be at your uncle's house before they return. I will help your grandmother prepare the lambs. You will be a *héroe* because you returned with two lambs instead of one. I will leave, but you and I will be friends. You will not feel the need to tell—"

Alberto turned, looked over his shoulder, and made an obscene gesture. "This is for you," he said.

Shadrach's stomach knotted.

Alberto stopped. "You can do this for me," he said. "Tomorrow, I want you to drive five of the fattest sheep to *el mercado* in Cruces. Leave them with Juan. Tell him they are mine, and I will stop by later to collect the money. Do you understand?"

Shadrach's brow furrowed, and he stared at the boy. "This is what I understand. You are trying to take advantage of me. I feel that I will beat you to death and feed whatever is left to the mountain wolves. Do you understand me!"

Alberto nodded wisely. "You threaten me? My uncles will build a fire in your *entrañas* if there is not roasted lamb waiting when they return."

Shadrach crowded past the boy and waved his hands at the sheep. "*¡Date prisa!* Move. Move," he said. "We don't have time to waste."

Alberto's grandmother had fox-like features. Because she'd pulled her gray hair away from her face and fastened it with a ribbon, her face sharpened even more. She looked up from the iron pot where clothes were simmering in soapy water, stared at Shadrach, and frowned.

Alberto hugged the old woman and said, "He is very ugly, but he has been kind to me. He even gave me five sheep. Isn't that true, earless man, you have given me five sheep?"

Shadrach was troubled he would now have to admit before the grandmother that he was gifting sheep to the boy. His involvement with the boy was getting deeper and stickier. He was not accustomed to being bullied—much less falling victim to a scheming child.

"Yes, we have discussed such a . . ." Shadrach let his words trail away as the boy looked at him and frowned. "Yes. Yes, we decided it would be nice if that could be arranged."

"Grandmother, this earless man wants to meet my uncles. Will you approve of him staying until our night meal?"

Alberto was her only grandson. She had never been able to deny any request from his lips. "I believe that is acceptable," she said. "My sons will return before sundown, and then you can be on your way."

Shadrach thought of the sheep penned in the boxed canyon. If the Basque came to check on his flock and found them penned without water, he would hold him responsible. The man's temper tended to boil over when his money was endangered. But, if he left now, no one knew what type lie Alberto might tell his uncles and how they might respond. He'd been told of their violent nature. He wished he'd let the boy steal the lamb.

Shadrach looked at the old woman. She was small, bent with age, and her steps slow and unsteady. Although the boy had the mouth of a snake, he too was small with biceps no larger than Shadrach's wrist. What if he picked the boy up by his heels and bashed his head against the ground? The old woman could not run, and, even if she could, it would be of her nature to stand and fight. He could slit her scrawny throat, then put both of their irritating bodies in the house and fire it. The pinyon-pine-sided dwelling would almost explode, and the grease from the bodies of the old woman and the boy would feed the flames. In no more than a quarter of an hour, only ashes and hot coals would remain. He would be free.

Then the grandmother sent Alberto to find the cow; she wanted her sons to have fresh *leche* for their *café*. Now he could pounce on the old woman and rid her of her life, except Alberto was out in the brush searching for the cow. The child was canny. He would suspicion something when he returned and his grandmother was not stirring the clothes in the wash pot.

¡Hijo de puta! How did he allow himself to get into this miserable mess?

At sundown, the uncles returned. They were dusty and tired, their horses lathered with cream-colored sweat. Alberto and the grandmother greeted them as if they had been on a long and perilous journey.

Shadrach stood to the side, uncomfortable and unsure.

Alberto made the introduction. "This earless man here—Oh, how thoughtless of me. Other than Ugly, what are you known as?"

Shadrach wanted the boy's throat between his hands. He should have immediately killed him this morning. He lowered his eyes and muttered, "Shadrach."

Alberto bowed in the direction of the earless man. "My new friend, Shadrach, Shadrach the Beautiful, is caring for a band of sheep. He is considering selling them. Perhaps, after you've had supper and rested, you might consider helping him in this task. Maybe he would reward you for your effort."

Shadrach drew in his breath and prepared to deny this untruth. Alberto stood behind his uncles and made another obscene gesture toward him. He took measure of the uncles— heavily armed, tired from many hours in the saddle, hungry, ruthless men—and decided this was not the time to bring up the inconsistencies in Alberto's story.

The boy pointed to Shadrach. "He will be glad to feed and water your horses while you rest."

The Fort Stanton Ranch

Chapman and Tollafson drove the horses downriver to Fort Stanton that afternoon. The purchasing agent paid them and inquired about Quezada's health.

Chapman found Dr. Calendar sitting in his small office, adsorbed in William James's *The Principles of Psychology*.

He looked up and ran his fingers through his thinning hair. "Can't you see I'm busy? What do you want? Don't tell me you've come to invite me back down to the ranch for supper again."

Chapman frowned. "With your table manners? Probably not."

"OK," the doctor said, "now that we've got the insults out of the way, what can I do for you?"

"I'm not sure, Doc. Quezada says he needs some more of that pain killer. A couple of bottles should do it."

"What?" the doctor sputtered. "I left him a month's supply. What does he mean, 'a couple more bottles'?"

"That's what he said. Couple more bottles."

The doctor stood, belched, scratched his privates, and walked to his medicine cabinet. "You tell that boss man of yours that this is it. No more until I see him again. Tell him I'm not running a drugstore up here."

Darkness spread across the valley, and a light veil of clouds settled over the mountains.

Chapman and Tollafson unsaddled their horses and turned them out to pasture. "Don't like riding around in the dark anymore," Tollafson said. "I reckon we've pretty much scared the horse thieves away from ranch, but you can't ever tell."

The kerosene lamp was dimmed, and everyone in the ranch house was asleep. In his room, Chapman jammed a heel in his bootjack, slipped his boots off, and set them beside the nightstand. Sometime during the day, Muñoz brought the leather-bound journal from the kitchen and laid it on his pillow.

Chapman sat, leaned back against the headboard, and opened the book. The pages were stained and brittle from age. Two pages into the book, Chapman knew he was reading some kind of diary.

February 28, 1862   We arrived in Tucson today. There is about 200 of us. We are called the Confederate Arizona Rangers and we came from Dona Ana. Our job is to make friends with the O'odhams. We intend to help the Tucson militia do whatever is necessary to protect the town. They need help. There is not but about 25 of them.

March 1, 1862   We raised the flag today. Colonel Gideon and an escort have left at noon to Sonora. We will get support from the Mexicans.

May 4 & 5, 1862   Had two battles with the Apaches this month up in the Dragoons. First skirmish was pretty much even. We took them on the second try.

May 14, 1862   Got word today that Union army is coming from the north. Major Fooster ordered most of our troopers to withdraw. My squad is to remain and observe the Union approach. There is 10 of us. We might even be enough to whip the Yankees ass.

May 15, 1862   We were almost trapped. About 2,000 Unions came in from the west while we was watching the north. We run east toward the mountains. There was a bank on the edge of town. We busted in there and made off with a bunch of gold. Some coins but mostly bars.

May 18, 1862   Had a hell of a bad time. Got lost trying to cross the mountains. Run into this young man. He was hunting Indians. Selling their scalps for a two dollar bounty. He took us through the mountains but we come out way far north.

May 19, 1862   Isn't any better. We got a Union platoon after us. Last night some kind of Indians raided us and took 2 horses. We just counted the gold. Some more than ten thousand dollars. May not do any good.

May 21, 1862   Guide says we will make the malpais tonight. The Unions has give up. The Indians haven't. Scalp hunter says we will hold them off.

May 22, 1862   I had enough peace to look around today. This is God-awful where we're holding up. This malpais place. Lots of creosote bushes, mesquite, tarbush and cactus. We've found grama and sideoats to feed our horses. Scalp hunter killed a antelope yesterday. So we are eating pretty well.

May 24, 1862   Goddamn Indians won't let us alone. They come in pretty close last night. Stole 2 of our horses. We killed 3 of the bastards and scalped them. The hunter was happy. Said he made six dollars and that is good wages for fifteen minutes work. He's a tough SOB. Indians would have been curing our balls over a fire long time ago if it hadn't been for him.

May 25, 1862   Lost 4 men last night. It was hand to hand.

May 27, 1862   Joe Lee died this morning. Don't know what happened. He just died. Wished I'd stayed home. No business in a place like this.

May 30, 1862   Herman made a run last night. He never got a 100 yards. Indians brought him back and hung him up on a bush. We are running out of water and cartridges.

May 31,1862   It is getting dark. Ate the last of the antelope today. I am way too far from home. Tomorrow we will

Chapman turned to the next page. It was empty of writing as was the rest of the book.

The Rio Grande Valley

Shadrach returned from the corral to find only the necks of the roasted lambs and three malformed potatoes waiting on the table. "Eat all you want," Alberto said. "My uncles want to know how many sheep you wish to sell. They are thinking about riding down there tonight—after they've rested a bit."

I am not a prisoner here, Shadrach thought. I am free to go anytime I wish. Nevertheless, somehow, Alberto hooked him like a scavenger fish bumping along the bottom of a putrid pond. He walked to the stable and sat cross-legged on the packed dirt with his hat pulled over his face, feigning sleep.

Can leave anytime. Maybe hide from the uncles in the mountains. Perhaps they would never find me. But then, there is the Basque. He has many sheepherders working for him, and they pasture all through the mountains. Just by accident, they are apt to stumble across me.

Maybe it would be best if he worked with the uncles—sell the sheep. Then in the future when they respected him, he could just slip away, and they would not follow. Pass through the mountains and work his way toward the Carlsbad desert.

It was dark, and Shadrach dropped into a fitful sleep. Alberto's shout woke him. "Go saddle four horses, *pendejo*. They are ready to go and see the sheep. My uncles are sorry there is not a fresh horse available for you. But it is not a great distance, and if you trot you will be able to stay in front of them, and they will not be inconvenienced."

Shadrach saddled the horses and considered fleeing—now. He would have all the fresh horses; the uncle's horses were tired. Perhaps he might just strike out for Las Cruces. He would go into the busy part of town where there would be people. Surely, the uncles would not attack him when others were present. He decided this was best: take the horses and flee into the darkness.

He opened the corral gate, stepped into the saddle of the largest horse, and bent low over the pommel. He heard the unmistakable sound of a round being jacked into a rifle chamber. The oldest of the uncles stood in the edge of the darkness, a shiny rifle pressed to his shoulder. "I hope you are not planning to leave us without saying good-bye," he said. The horse moved nervously beneath him, and Shadrach knew if the horse bolted, he would be a dead man before the second breath arrived.

The Fort Stanton Ranch

Chapman lay in bed, sleep hovering just above his still body awaiting permission to descend. The name on the diary cover was Bob Stevens, and, according to the CSA insignia, he must have been a Confederate soldier. He never heard of the man. Yet Quezada had given him the diary that morning. Not said anything, no explanation. Nothing. Just gave it to him.

He opened the book and studied the last entry, May 31.

Earlier entries were dated 1862. I was not even born then, Chapman thought. Why no more entries? What happened to the man?

The second time the rooster crowed, Chapman rolled out of bed, dressed, and went into the kitchen.

Felipe had a fire going in the cookstove and a pot of coffee gurgling. Muñoz came into the kitchen, retrieved two cups from the cupboard, and filled them with coffee. Chapman poured three spoons of sugar into one and grinned. "What you think, reckon that's sweet enough?"

Muñoz smiled, took both cups, and disappeared down the hall toward the bedrooms. The cooked steaks were in the warming closet and eggs were frying when Quezada limped into the kitchen, a half-empty cup in his hand. He was stooped—giving way to the pain—and leaning against Muñoz.

"Did you get paid for the horses?" he asked, as a way of greeting. "And did you get a good night's sleep?"

Chapman nodded. "Yep, on both accounts. I'd have slept better if Muñoz hadn't left that diary or whatever it is on my bed. You gonna tell me about that or is it just something you are going to pretend you found on the side of the road?"

Quezada took a sip of coffee, made a bad face, and added another spoon of sugar. "Gonna do better than that. Tell you about it tomorrow, on our way to Carrizozo. Felipe knows the story. I'll tell you and Muñoz at the same time."

"But the doctor said that—"

"Don't tell me that again. I know what he said, and I know what I'm gonna do. The two ain't much kin.

"I'm guessing that old rascal grumbled about the medicine. But in the end sent some."

"You're twice right." Chapman said. "But he said he wouldn't do it anymore."

Quezada sluggishly moved his eggs around on his plate and suspiciously studied the steak as if he expected it to move. "Tell you what, Muñoz. Believe I'll take a shot of that pain medicine and mayhap a nap. All of you got a busy day in front of you. Gonna need the buggy cleaned up and the pacers' manes and tails trimmed. Felipe'll need to cook up some extra grub and pack it. We ain't gonna be passing no good cafés on the way over to Carrizozo tomorrow."

Carrizozo

Carrizozo, sitting on the high-plains valley floor between the Jicarilla Mountains, the Sierra Oscuro Mountains, and the El Malpais lava flow, wasn't much town. To the south, the great Tularosa Basin fanned out; to the north, the town of White Oaks snuggled in against the mountains. One rancher, one of the instigators and winners in the Lincoln County War, owned most of the grazing land. Nevertheless, the town was growing, mostly because it was one of the stops on the El Paso and Northeastern Railway.

There was a single hotel in Carrizozo, but two boarding houses pretty much met the needs of the railroad surveyors, the hunters, and the occasional fishermen who waded the waters of the South Fork of Bonito Creek.

Chapman chose the best looking boarding house and rented four rooms. The rooms were sparsely furnished and showed considerable abuse from the years of cowboy occupants. Big rowel spur gashes marred the wooden floor into nasty splinters, and would-be scribes left crudely worded messages on the walls. He and Filipe took two upstairs rooms, Quezada and Muñoz downstairs.

Quezada and his men, along with a semi-permanent guest, sat at a long dining room table. The main dish was antelope stew that was heavy with potatoes and light on antelope. Quezada lifted his spoon, let the thin stew cascade over the edge and settle into the bowl with scarcely a splash. "Invisible antelope," he said. "Named after a seldom-seen Indian I once knew." Everyone except the woman running the place laughed.

The boarding house's front porch ran the width of the structure and faced southwestward toward the summer's setting sun. Quezada and his men moved from the dining room and sat there watching the sun drop. "Out yonder," Quezada said, taking a pull of tequila, " 'bout five miles, is the damnedest place you ever saw. Looks like a place hell gave up on."

"I was there twice," Felipe said. "We were trailing a small herd of cattle, taking them north to a ranch up in the edge of the mountains. Had a bad storm, lightning and thunder like you never saw. First time I ever saw St. Elmo's fire. Balls of fire the size of your fist would roll down them steers' horns and drip off in long streams of greenish fire—scariest damn thing I ever saw."

The Mexican walked to the edge of the porch and spit into the sand. "It just buggered the hell outta the herd. Half dozen rank steers run off and got into the *malpais*. We hunted them steers half a day, like to have ruined our horses—cut up their legs, tore two or three shoes off. Trail boss said, 'To hell with 'em.' Smartest thing I ever heard him say.

"We come back down couple of weeks later, two of the steers were standing alongside the trail, bawling their heads off. Legs were cut something awful. They hobbled after us down the valley for ten miles or so, but they was so thin and give out that we just left them. Bet the wolves got them. Served them steers right."

"Pretty good description," Quezada said. "Only way a man can get across the *malpais* is if he is really pushed. Something pretty bad after him. Can't do it horseback. Gotta be afoot."

"You ever crossed them?" Chapman asked.

Quezada nodded and spent almost a minute getting his cigar lit to his satisfaction. "Once," he said and blew smoke out into the dry, afternoon air. "Part of them."

Muñoz hadn't said much but now leaned forward and asked, "You gonna tell us about it?"

Quezada looked down at his hands like a man does when he is buying time. "I don't believe it would help nobody none."

A little cloud came down the valley, and a light shower dimpled the dust. Filipe stepped off the porch and removed his hat. Just enough rain fell to make a thin stream from his nose. *"La lluvia bendita del cielo,"* he said. "Blessed rain from the heavens."

The Rio Grande Valley

"Espera, Espera." Shadrach patted the horse's neck and slid carefully from the saddle. "Just bringing them up to you," he said.

The uncle smiled and dropped the hammer on the fancy Winchester. There was a satisfying click. Shadrach softly exhaled. Something told him the uncle would have enjoyed shooting him. Just for the hell of it—bang—like shooting at a gopher or a tin can.

Alberto leaned out from behind his uncle and grinned. "We were hoping you'd try to run."

Shadrach pulled himself up straight. "It is not in my blood to be a coward," he said.

"So I've been told," the uncle said. Both he and Alberto laughed, and Shadrach wondered just how much the boy told. But a grinning Alberto pulled his ears flat against his head, and Shadrach knew the boy told everything—and probably made up things that hadn't happened. He felt like an animal caught in a snare. The more he pulled trying to free himself, the tighter the snare became.

The three other uncles arrived and stepped into the saddles. Shadrach trotted out of the camp along the winding, steep path, the wind lisping in his ears. The riders followed single file.

A small pebble bounced into Shadrach's boot. He slowed, then hopped on one foot while trying to remove the boot. The lead horseman bumped against him, sending Shadrach sprawling on the rocky path. "We must hurry to find the sheep before sunrise," the horseman said. "We do not have time to play children's games, hopping along like we are in a schoolyard."

Shadrach pressed his teeth together tightly and stumbled along the path, mindful of the precipitous drop just feet away. The first horseman rode still closer to him, the horse's breath pulsating warmth against his neck. Shadrach increased his pace.

They approached the canyon, and the sheep bleated at the clatter of the horses' hooves and the men's voices, sounds they associated with human caretakers. They had gone almost a day and much of a night without water, and they voiced displeasure.

Two of the uncles waited to block the trail while the other two and Shadrach circled the sheep and drove them out of their canyon prison. "They will follow us," one of the horsemen said, and he and the other wheeled and trotted down the trail in the direction of their ranch. Followed by the other two riders, Shadrach trailed the flock. The uncle who tormented him earlier followed even closer than before.

Shadrach's legs were weak, and his heart hammered in his chest. His stomach was rebelling against the partially cooked mutton. He was afraid to stop or even slow his pace. He vomited, and the vileness splattered across his sweat-damp shirt. He had to do something—now. I can handle one brother at a time, he thought.

Ahead of them, the trail narrowed. Shadrach slowed, and the horseman came alongside.

Shadrach whirled and threw his hat into the nearest horse's

face. The animal reared, its hooves slipped on the rocky trail, and, before the rider could regain control, Shadrach leaned in against the horse and shoved. Both horse and rider toppled off the cliff and crashed into the canyon below. The second horse shied and bucked as Shadrach dragged its rider from the saddle. The man sprawled on the ground pulling at his pistol. The earless man lifted a melon-size stone. The struggle lasted less than two breaths.

A hundred head of sheep crowding and bleating make considerable noise, and it was not until the trail flattened into a meadow and the flock spread out along a narrow stream that the front riders missed their two brothers and Shadrach.

Carrizozo

Not counting the hotel, boarding houses, a combination apothecary and doctor's office, two stores, and a blacksmith shop, Carrizozo—the locals called it Zozo—had a single office building. *Dr. M. A. Wright and Atty X. L. Diuguid,* a weathered sign proclaimed the occupants. As if tired of fighting the ceaseless wind and the rawness of the elements, the sign leaned against the front of the building and was disfigured by two bullet holes that splintered the last *d* in the attorney's name.

"Perchance an unhappy client," Quezada observed.

He and Chapman sat on a rickety bench in front of the attorney's office. Muñoz and Felipe were at the blacksmith's having a felloe repaired on the buggy.

Quezada had taken to carrying a silver flask in his jacket pocket so tequila was always available. He took his first nip of the day. "Man can never tell when he might get bit by a rattler and need medicine immediately—I try to get a head start," the rancher said when Muñoz quizzed him about it earlier.

For the third time, Chapman tapped on the office door, then peered in the dirty window. He checked his watch. "Half past ten," he said. "Wonder where the shyster is?"

"We know where he isn't," Quezada said and sprawled down on the bench and crossed his ankles. "Tell you why we are here today. I'm having my will drawn up. I want you in there with me while this is being done. I'm not figuring on dying any time soon, but you can never tell. I'm gonna leave the ranch at La Mesilla to a feller you've never heard of. Gonna leave the Fort Stanton ranch to another feller. You get the Bitter Lakes Ranch. It ain't much, and I don't want you gettin' a case of the big head just 'cause you'll be owning it. Fact is, I won it in a game of stud poker, and if it was the only ranch I ever owned, I'd have starved to death a long time ago. It's a little-old-bitty thing, and I'm kinda ashamed to be givin' it to you. I haven't known you very long. Maybe not long enough to know your bad side. But I know, if it is needed, you will see after Filipe and Muñoz. I'm right in that, ain't I?"

"Well, yeah. But why are you telling me this? And why are you talking about leaving me anything?"

" 'Cause it's mine, and I'll leave it to who I damn well please. Besides, I want to control it even after I'm in the grave. Whatta you think of that?"

Chapman was trying to sort this information out in his head. "I reckon it sounds just like you. And it's none of my business. What do I do with the ranch if I decide to do something else? Like being a gunfighter or a preacher or something like that?"

The rancher laughed. "I saw you acting like a gunfighter down at Fort Bliss. It would be my advice that if you had to be only one of them, you need to become a preacher. I don't give a damn what you do with your life, but, if I was a betting man, I'd bet that you will still be ranching the day after you die."

A portly man, dirty white shirt spotted with tobacco stains, came out of the general store and walked slowly, head down, across the dusty street. One gallous was tighter than the other;

one pant cuff dragged through the dust, the other cuff two inches above his shoe top. He neglected to shave this morning or any morning for the past two weeks.

"That'll be him," Quezada said. " 'Bout the most successful looking lawyer in Carrizozo, what do you think? 'Course, there's not 'nother barrister in town."

The lawyer stepped up on the porch and adjusted his loose gallous. He removed wire-rimmed spectacles from a shirt pocket and perched them on his bulbous nose. "My name is Diuguid. Spelt the same coming as going. May I be of service to you?"

An hour passed. The document was completed, signed, witnessed, and stored in the lawyer's safe.

Quezada and Chapman sat at the boarding house table drinking coffee. Muñoz and Felipe came into the cool darkness, the underarms and backs of their shirts damp with sweat. "It'll be tomorrow before the buggy is fixed," Felipe announced and shook his head in disgust. "Something about a freighter's mules needing shoes 'fore anything can be done for us."

"That's all right," Quezada said. "Mayhaps, I'll need a refill on my flask, and one more day's rest will do my back good. 'Sides, me and Chapman need to look at some horses up to the north on an old woman's ranch. And I figured to ride out and have a look at the *malpais*. See if they've changed any—got more civilized."

A hardware drummer sitting at the opposite end of the table laughed. "Hell, man, they've been there fifteen hundred years and ain't changed a smither in all that time."

Quezada turned slowly and looked at the man as if he had intruded on a sacred gathering. "Mister, you ain't got no idea how long it's been since I've seen them. Have you?"

The drummer sensed something. Something not quite right in Quezada's eyes. He'd seen it a couple of times before—once in a St. Louis doctor's office and once in the back room of a Chinese saloon in San Francisco. Nothing good came out of either one.

"No, sir, you're quite right. Now, if you will excuse me, I've got a call to make this afternoon."

Quezada stood and rubbed his hand across his hip. "Believe I'll take a short nap. Muñoz, you might see if you can find me a bit of that pain medicine." He took a step stiffly away from the table, then turned toward Chapman. "Maychance, you'll get the smoothest gaited horse in the livery stable and have it out front for me in an hour. We'll take that little ride. See about buying them horses."

The two rode westward until they encountered the great lava flow the Spanish conquistadors named *el malpais* or *tierras baldías,* the badlands. The lava flowed southward creating a barrier that is almost impenetrable to man. The tubes of lava collapsed on themselves, causing great tunnels and jagged slabs. A horse could not cross it; an antelope found it difficult; a desperate man pursued by death could.

Traveling along the eastern edge of the flow, Quezada stared at the almost barren landscape as if looking for a lost friend. At a narrow fissure, he stopped. "Perchance I'm right, Chapman, I want you to walk into that gap and tell me if you find a small cave. Its mouth will not be more than two feet high. And it will be facing south."

Chapman dismounted and entered the fissure. The pathway was barren and little more than drought-cracked dirt. The cave was to his right. "It's here," he shouted to Quezada.

"OK. Now you've got to trust me on this," Quezada said. "I want you to take a stick and rake around in there. If there's a snake, he'll rattle. If you don't hear one, I want you to reach inside 'bout as far back as your arm will go. Rake around in the dirt. See if you can feel anything. Ought to be five of them—two feet long, 'bout slick as glass. Holler and tell me."

Chapman dropped to his knees and looked through the narrow entrance into the dark. He threw a handful of gravel into the cave. Nothing. He found a dead mesquite branch and thrashed it around. Satisfied there was nothing alive in the cave, he dropped to his belly and extended his arm inside. He found a shallow mound of dirt and dug his fingers into it. Five smooth oblong objects, their edges touching, lay coldly in the darkness.

He retreated from the cave. "I reckon I found what you were talking about," he said.

Quezada dismounted and stood, both hands gripping the saddle horn, stretching his aching back. "Did you cover it back up?"

"I didn't."

"You didn't look at it?"

"No. Did you want me to?"

Quezada studied for a few seconds. "No. I think not. No need in it. Just cover them back up and let's go."

Chapman went back into the fissure, partially crawled into the cave, and raked the dirt back into place. When he came out, Quezada, face flushed and wet with sweat, was in the saddle.

"We best get going," he said. "Need to get over to White Oaks and see about those horses."

White Oaks

They bought a dozen horses at an exorbitant price. Quezada paid with cash. "I'll send some of the boys up to get them next week—mayhaps a little later," he said.

Two young men somewhere in their late teens and a woman, their mother, ran the ranch. The men were burly, black-haired, and had cold, blue eyes. Chapman remembered his mother speaking of an aging woman who lost her early good looks;

called her a faded rose. He thought this woman would soon be a faded rose.

The ranch behind them, Quezada and Chapman rode south toward Carrizozo.

"You gave too much for the horses," Chapman said and added quickly, "in my opinion."

Quezada pulled at the flask, fired a match with his thumbnail, and relit his cigar. "You think so. Well, I'll tell you something else. Ain't nobody going back to pick up the horses. What do you think of that?"

They rode along in silence. Chapman finally said, "This isn't the first time you've seen that woman, is it?"

Rio Grande Valley

Shadrach stripped the dead uncle of his knife, belt, and pistol. The horse had broken the cannon bone in the left leg, and, even if this had not happened, the mountainside was too steep for the animal. He pulled the fancy Winchester from the scabbard, leaned against the horse, and shouldered him off the trail. The horse squealed once and after the second crash was quiet. The uncle with the bashed skull followed, his lifeless body careening off the boulders and stunted trees.

Now armed, Shadrach scrambled up the incline, pausing every five minutes, and listened, sounds flowing directionless and confusingly into his mutilated ears. After eight hours, the earless man felt he was not followed, and he slept.

Ushered in by a light mist, morning came to the mountains quiet as a dove's heartbeat. Shadrach squatted by a miserly fire, ragged serape pulled around his shoulders. He'd raided a rancher's vegetable cellar, and now a turnip danced in the hot water of a can resting over the fire. A potato baked in the ashes, and a handful of coffee grounds swam in the boiling waters of a second can. He'd not eaten because he always believed he made his best decisions when hungry.

Somewhere in these mountains, two of the uncles were searching; perhaps they recruited men to help them. He had been lucky. Once. He was not a man to be foolish enough to believe good fortune would continue to trail him like a starving dog. The Basque would be furious at the loss of his band of sheep. This man had countrymen who also grazed sheep. Their livelihoods depended upon their reputation of retribution— otherwise thieves would steal their last sheep down to the smallest patch of wool. They could be as coldblooded as the uncles.

He was one against many. Even someone as ignorant as he knew these odds did not favor him. He learned at Fort Bliss and again with the fat man and his *guardaespaldas* in Ciudad Juárez. Surprise and time were the friends of a lone attacker. Separate his enemies, make it one against one. Time was on his side; surprise would be at his choosing.

He would retreat south toward the border, reside in Ciudad Juárez, regain his health, make plans, and return to take care of this unfinished business. The Mexican rubbed his index finger across the engraving on the uncle's rifle: *Winner. Slash Q Shooting.* He could not read the words, but he knew the gun represented power, and now it was his.

With the blade of his knife, he raked the potato from the ashes, halved it, sliced the swollen skin from the boiled turnip, and ate.

Carrizozo

Quezada turned enough in the saddle so he could look directly at Chapman. "Why do you say that 'bout the woman? You just developed hindsight? Perchance become a fortune teller or something. A backward looking soothsayer, you might say?"

"No. Nothing like that. But I felt something between you two that was not kin to any horse trading I ever saw."

They rode on, Quezada slumping in the saddle, hand pressing against his back. "Yeah. I've had dealings with her before, you could say."

"Same time you were dealing with Captain Fesmire? And the Apaches? And the gold?"

Quezada didn't turn, just continued on, watching the trail ahead. "No. You ain't quite ready to start telling fortunes just yet."

"But everything was tied together?"

"Yeah. Sorta. But Stevens's diary didn't tell you all that. You are putting two and two together and getting five."

"Well, I'm not plumb dumb. Somebody had to bring Stevens's diary out of that mess. And I didn't get it from him. So, I figure he's dead, and you were probably the only man to survive. Then you talked some about it when you was outta your head with fever down at Fort Bliss.

"I'm figuring somebody had to look after you after you escaped the *malpais*. If I can believe what I saw and what Stevens wrote in his diary, it was a pretty bad time and an awful place. Then another thing. Those bars of gold . . . that I was feeling in that cave. That was what the Rebs stole coming outta Tucson. Am I right?"

"Yeah. You're pretty close on the gold part. There was some more. We'll talk about that later.

"I wadn't hardly twenty when all that took place. If I hadn't been young and strong, I'd have died out there with them soldiers and horses. If I'd have been a better guide, we wouldn't have got caught out there in the first place. But the Indians was closing in, and we were running."

"You were twenty? Guiding soldiers and hunting Indians for scalps. At twenty?"

Quezada stopped his horse and waited for Chapman to come along side. "Yeah, twenty," he said. "Some folks grow up quicker than others."

"Like me," Chapman said.

Quezada laughed, the little low grunting sound he made when he didn't really need to laugh aloud. "I ain't calling no names."

"So, where does the woman come in?"

"Sounds like you getting smarter. Asking questions 'stead of telling. It was her mama that looked after me. I was in a hell'va bad shape. Damned near starved for water. Cut all to pieces."

"So, that's where you met the woman, the woman we bought the horses from?"

Quezada nodded. "But she wadn't no woman then. She was this little skinny, big-eyed girl. I called her Lee-Lee."

Chapman wove this new information into what he already knew. "So, you stayed there awhile. Then you moved on. You go back to Arizona?"

"Well, there was this thing of stealing the gold from the bank. And Johnny Rebs or anybody that helped them wasn't very popular in Tucson." Quezada laughed and continued, " 'Sides, wasn't too big a market for scalp hunters anymore."

He unscrewed his flask and took a drink. "Looking back, I've come to think that mayhaps I wasn't plumb civilized. If the Quezada tribe had a rough end, I musta come out of it. My way of life was ending—killing Indians and stuff like that. White Oaks was just getting started—the mining business was picking up every day. Overnight millionaires. So, that meant that the gambling, whoring, and banking was growing, too."

Quezada took a long pull on his cigar, coughed, then continued. "Lot of this country was just starting to get bad. Folks fighting over grazing land and just raising hell in general. People that was running White Oaks figured the best way to head trouble off was not let it even get in. And that's what they hired me to do. It was kinda dangerous. Nobody else wanted the job. I figured *what the hell*. I hired a couple of good for nothings in White Oaks for backup. Old boys had run off from the army, didn't have much to lose one way or the other.

"Word would get out that troublemakers were coming, the three of us would meet the bad boys couple of miles down the road on the other side of the graveyard. Try to convince them that they weren't wanted in White Oaks. If they wouldn't convince . . . well, the graveyard was right there handy."

Chapman laughed. "OK. I'm getting things straight. You know White Oaks pretty good. Even knew the woman since she was a little girl. Lee-Lee or whatever you called her."

Little laugh lines formed at the outer edges of Quezada's eyes. "Son, I'd say you are about ready for the range detective business. But not hardly."

And now his face was dark and brow deeply furrowed. "Her and her mama found me not more than a hundred yards from where I hid the gold. They said I'd a been dead in another day. Wasn't even enough of me to cause the buzzards to circle. I was starved, and my lips was busted open and bleeding, they was so dry. My knees and hands were cut to the bone."

"So, you *were* the only one that lived."

The sun was down, and the desert air was starting to chill. Carrizozo lay in the distance, its buildings a pale blue silhouette against the twilight that was grudgingly giving away to darkness. Scattered pinholes of light dotted the village.

"The only one. It was three weeks before I could close my hands. Cuts was awful. That lava is sharper than a knife, and there was a hell of a lot of it. It was another week before I could walk. My knees were in terrible shape. Cuts that were slow to heal. Some of the scabs were half the size of the palm of your hand."

Now it was dark. The night birds swooped in their patrol

across the sky. Two ghost-gray coyotes crossed the trail in front of the riders, then stopped and stood partially hidden by brush and watched silently.

"But you brought the gold? Bad a shape as you were in, you brought the gold?"

"Yeah. I did. I'd seen a handful of men die trying to protect it. They didn't need it. I was a poor man. A body that will hunt scalps for two dollars apiece is a poor man. But now I wasn't poor any more. Only thing I had to worry about was living."

"And the woman?"

"She was just a kid. Her and her mama was trying to make a living off of scrubby pasture. Running a few sheep, some goats. Had a dozen cows. She'd had a tough life—things you ain't got no business knowing about."

The horses slowed and picked their way through the darkness.

"Was she married? Lee-Lee's mama?" Chapman asked.

"Never saw sign of a man. Folks didn't ask questions like that back then."

"But you took to Lee-Lee?"

"No. I told you she wadn't much more than a kid—maybe eight or nine. But, in kinda an off-handed way, we kinda clicked. I . . . uh . . . got tired of shooting at men. And being shot at. Folks that run the town kinda got tired of me, said I was ruining White Oaks's reputation. Well, that was a damn laugh. Anyways, I crossed the mountains and took up a little ranch in the Pecos Valley.

"Every two or three years I'd go back up to see if the gold was still there. Then I'd swing by like I was goin to see some old buddies in White Oaks. Stop by Lee-Lee's mama's little spread. I watched the girl grow up, you could say."

Chapman laughed. "You call that clicking?"

Quezada's voice was coarse. "Well. What in hell would you call it?

"Went by one day and her mama was dead. Lee-Lee had buried her out behind the barn. Done it by herself."

"And she had these two boys?"

Quezada snorted like a man will do when he is trying to blow a mosquito outta his nose, and his horse turned his head at this unusual sound. "She . . . she didn't when I got there. One of them bed sheet miracles; she said she couldn't have no kids."

"How long were you there?"

"Long enough. Two . . . two and a half years."

Now they were at the edge of town. The sound of a piano. A woman laughed. A half-grown boy came down the street carrying a lantern and driving a pig before him.

"And you left?"

"Yeah. Don't take a genius to figure that out."

They'd stopped in front of the boarding house, and Chapman helped the older man from the saddle.

"What happened? You had the boys and—"

"She had her ways; I had mine. We didn't really fit. Hell, I guess I could've tried harder. But I didn't."

"So now you buy horses from her and never pick them up."

"Right."

"And that makes you feel like you're doing right by her?" Chapman asked.

"Pretty much. She's never wanted for anything. I've done good by her that way."

"Well, if you ask me, I'd tell you—"

Quezada held up his hand. "Don't. I ain't asking you."

At breakfast the next morning, Filipe announced the buggy was road ready. Quezada was late, his face flushed and pupils no more than just dark specks in his eyes when he entered the dining room. He drank coffee with a generous splash of tequila and shoved his food away.

Chapman and Felipe brought the buggy and road horses to the front of the boarding house. Even with the help of the three ranch hands, Quezada had trouble climbing up into the buggy. He braced himself against the back of the seat and looked around at the town.

Diuguid, the lawyer, stood on his office porch and tipped his hat. Quezada acknowledged by returning the gesture. "Place hasn't changed much in thirty-something years," he said. He turned to Muñoz. "I've got a little something to finish with Chapman this morning. Why don't you ride his bay for a while?"

Muñoz nodded, and Chapman climbed up into the buggy.

Miles away across the flatness, the *malpais*'s dark surface shown dully in the morning sun. They turned away from it and headed eastward. Quezada sat and looked straight ahead. Even when a herd of antelope bounded across the road, he showed no interest. Finally, he said, "Reckon I was a bit short with you last night. Man don't like to have his shortcomings pointed out to him—'specially all at one time. Anyway, a guilty conscience don't need nobody a-gouging it."

"Didn't mean to do that. Didn't need to pry in your business."

Quezada shifted in his seat, trying to find a comfortable position. "No, you were right in what you did. Just want you to know, I've looked after her and the boys—left a little sack of gold coins, twice. She could've left the ranch, moved into town, moved wherever she wanted to, but she chose to stay out there. Said it was a good place to raise the boys. Away from the world she knew. Told me wasn't no need of them facing it until they had to. And that was the end of that."

Chapman didn't ask any questions. He figured he'd let Quezada go on at his own pace.

"They are good boys. Gonna make good men. I've kept up with them. Know pretty much about them. They are honest, hardworking . . . maybe a little strange. Guess they got a right to be that way, raised out there in the loneliness and by a woman and all. Not too social. Crazy about their mother . . . I reckon I can understand that."

"You say you left gold with her."

"Yeah; don't know exactly how much it was worth. But a right smart. We was out riding one evening, and I showed her where I'd hidden the gold bars." Quezada removed his hat and mopped his brow with his shirtsleeve. "Said if she ever needed anything, make use of them."

"Showed her where it was?! Aren't you afraid she will take it and sell it? Or tell somebody where it is and—"

Quezada interrupted. "No. None of that. I know her too well. She's not that kinda woman. Don't 'speck she's even told the boys. Even if she had, they wouldn't have bothered it. They are as honest and as independent as their mama.

"Now there's at least three of us that know where it is at. I ain't gonna need it. She's not either. That leaves you. Don't think you ever will. But I look at it this way: it's like having it in the bank—no, probably better. If any of us ever need it, we know how to make a withdrawal. Believe that's called a joint account."

Chapman laughed. "Looking back . . . You got any regrets?"

The wind came up and started blowing sand across the desert. Quezada turned his coat collar up around his ears. "Don't look back much. But I've asked myself that same question a lot of times. The woman was too much like me for us to ever live together. I've agreed with myself on that. I'd have loved to have a shot at raising the boys. I probably couldn't have done as good as she did. But it would have been nice." He lit a cigar, and the blue smoke slid by the side of his face. "Yeah, it would have been nice."

Chapman worked all this through his mind like a man separating pebbles from sand by allowing the sand to flow between his fingers. "So, they get the two ranches?"

Quezada dragged the flask from his jacket pocket and took a couple of drinks. "Yes. The oldest boy gets the Fort Stanton ranch. I hope his mama will come with him, but I doubt it. It's a better place for a woman than La Mesilla. Not as many people around. Believe she might take to that, make things easier for her." He took another drink. "Anyway, I've tried."

The rancher squirmed in the buggy and pressed a hand against his hip. They rode along, Felipe in front, Muñoz following.

"Yeah, it would have been nice, to have a family, I mean. Guess I missed the train. You get a chance, Chapman, catch the damn train, and don't look over your shoulder. 'Cause there ain't much back there that you haven't already seen and culled."

An hour away from the Fort Stanton ranch, Quezada opened his second flask. "Chapman," he said, "I've always won. Mayhaps it took a long spell. But in the end, I won. Sometimes, a man had to die—couple of times it was more than one—but I always won. You get what I'm saying? Any time I cash in, I'm a winner. You following me?"

He twisted in the seat, seeking a hiding place from the pain. "This hurting in my back . . . feels like there's a big devil back there with a pitchfork gouging me every time I take a breath." He grimaced again. "But I'm gonna win this time, too. Just always remember, that I won."

The Fort Stanton Ranch

That night, Quezada sat on the front porch in a willow-woven rocker and didn't talk much. Felipe came out and played old Spanish songs. Chapman told Tollafson and Chance about the trip; told them they didn't find any horses worth buying. In the darkness, Quezada, listening to Chapman talk, smiled.

Muñoz came from the house to the porch. "I've heated bricks and wrapped them in a blanket. I think it will help your back. I can't give you a shot tonight. Our morphine supply . . . I'll get down to Fort Stanton in the morning. First thing. See Dr. Calendar. Get a new syringe. I'll be back about noon."

Around midnight, Chapman awoke from a bad dream of crippled horses and jagged lava beds. He heard the faint sound of whispers and what he thought to be men struggling. He pulled on his pants and, barefooted, slid silently along the hallway, gun in hand, thumb crooked atop the hammer. Muñoz sat on the edge of Quezada's bed, a damp cloth against the rancher's face. The bindings had come loose, and blood seeped from Quezada's back and lay a deep crimson on the bed covers.

A tearful Muñoz looked at Chapman. "He's in such pain. Sometimes he knows where he is . . . sometimes he doesn't. I've had a difficult time keeping him in bed."

"You go back to bed. Get some rest. I'll sit up with him until he settles down."

Three o'clock in the morning, Quezada's head cleared.

Chapman and Quezada talked. They reminisced about horse and cattle deals. The rancher talked about his past and his father, Terrol. He spent time talking about the woman he'd not married, the boys he'd not had a chance to raise. "Life is like a river, son," he said. "You can touch the water as it passes you by. Then it is gone, and you never have a chance to touch it again."

Daybreak approached. It is the time when night birds fear the light and quit singing, and the day birds are afraid of what is unseen in the darkness and won't sing. Quezada sat on the edge of the bed, feverish and swaying in pain. "I believe mayhaps a drink of fresh water would do me good," he said.

Outside, Chapman removed the cover from the well, lowered the bucket, and listened to the gurgle as it filled with water.

The roar of Quezada's .44 disturbed the gray of the dawn, and a single Aztec dove fluttered skyward, seeking peace.

Before noon on the day of Quezada's death, Muñoz laid a white cloth over the rancher's face and washed the blood from the body. Felipe burned the soiled bed coverings, then scrubbed the walls and floor of the bedroom. Chance rode down to Fort Stanton and got Dr. Calendar. He can't do any good, Chapman thought, but it just seemed to be the right thing to do.

Chapman saddled his horse and slowly rode along the river breaks. Now, away from the ranch hands, he cried. It came to him he wasn't sure why he was crying. Quezada was better off. He didn't hurt anymore. And then Chapman knew he was crying for himself. He wasn't finished learning. His own father was a good man, in his way, but Quezada knew life and how it worked: he was a teacher, and now there would be no more lessons. The tears trickled down his cheeks and splotched the front of his shirt.

Evans and the ranch hands gathered in the shade of the trees that grew near the edge of the horse lot. They smoked and talked in low voices. Most everybody had a story about the rancher, usually it was about his gruffness, and then it slowly came to the cowboys that the story always ended with Quezada doing something good for somebody, standing up for what was right, or just giving good advice. After a while, they became quiet and sat looking out across the pasture, seeing a man that was, but now was not.

Before he left for his solitary ride, Chapman sent Tollafson and two wranglers to dig a grave on a low ridge overlooking the ranch. He gave thought to the cemetery at Fort Stanton and then a family cemetery of early settlers. Then he thought of the solitude Quezada sought—the hours spent riding through the range, checking on the livestock—usually by himself. He wished he'd known more about the man, what he'd done, what he'd seen, and other thoughts he had about his life. Maybe all this was best kept a secret; seems as if Quezada thought so, anyway.

They buried the rancher just before sundown, that time when the mountain winds cease their restless movement. The cowboys made a ragged circle around the open grave and stood with their hats in their hands. These were hard men: men accustomed to spending long days in the saddle; accustomed to battling the harshness of this dry country; accustomed to making do and doing without, and holding their own against a cattle stampede or a bucking horse. They had hunted Indians, fought in range wars; more than one had participated in a gunfight or a stagecoach holdup or bank robbery.

Chapman knew this was something they would not experience again. He was aware theirs was the last generation of real cowboys, and that somewhere in the east men were making machines that would replace them. Their breed was dying, and they would never again see a man quite like Quezada.

At the graveside, Chapman read from Psalm twenty-three. Many of the passages were foreign to the riders and hard to grasp. But some stuck with them, and they discussed it later at the saloon in Fort Stanton.

The oldest of the ranch hands, a man partially blind who spent his days mending bridles and saddles, talked about *maketh me to lie down in green pastures: he leadeth me beside the still waters.* "Man gets my age, that lying down in green pastures and still waters part sounds pretty damned good. I reckon I'd settle for that any day."

Of all the Slash Q hands, Evans knew the most about Quezada. They had ridden together more than thirty years ago, at a time when the west was *really* wild. He bought a round of drinks that night—'cause Quezada would've—and reminisced. "Where Chapman was reading today about walking through the valley of death and not fearing, well, that was him all over. I never saw the man scared in all the time I was ever around him. Never saw him fear another man, and I'm not sure we walked through the valley of death, but we walked in some bad damn places. Come up against some bad men. He never knew what the word scared meant."

Tollafson nodded. "Reckon I remember some of the same things, but there was more. I'm from Shiloh. Raised there till I got too big for my britches. Guess you could say, Pa run me off 'fore I was twenty. We was pore as snakes. Most likely, he was glad to see me go. Anyhow, Pa cut a tree, and it fell on him, crippled him up so much that he wadn't worth nothing at working. Got a letter from Mama, said things was pretty bad back home. Bills come due. It wasn't much money, but they didn't have it. Hell, I didn't have two cents to rub together. Whole thing made me feel pretty worthless—folks needing me, and I couldn't help.

"Quezada found out about it. Said he'd take care of it. But— there was always a but with him—but said he never took me to raise. Said he had a corral of horses that needed breaking. I didn't know flitter 'bout breaking horses. But I learned. Damn near killed me, but I learned. Got done, and he said the debt was paid. Then damn if he didn't pay me a dollar for every horse I broke. Never had so much money in my life. Wrote Mama, she told me to tie myself to that man's belt and never get out of his shadow. I done it. He couldn't have run me off with a bullwhip after that."

Chance walked to the bar, bought a bottle, and brought it back to the table. He had the erect carriage of a man who had grown up in the military. "I put up fifteen years in the cavalry.

Got into it with a major that had a wife who had ants in her bloomers. We got caught out in the hay barn."

Chance poured a round. "Woman lied like a lizard, and, gosh, she was ugly. Said I'd kinda enticed her. Who do you think the major believed? They was going to court-martial my skinny ass. And the major wadn't going to let it go at that. He was working on getting me some time at Fort Leavenworth. That was a bad place. They was still building it, and if a man got time there, he wadn't worth much more than a mule. Quezada was hunting with the colonel and found out 'bout me. He'd had horse dealin's with the major and knew what a shithead he was. Truth be known, he ransomed me for a pint of whiskey and a hindquarter of deer."

Felipe and Muñoz sat together at a domino table at the back of the bar, neither drinking. The older man brought his guitar, a battered instrument with worn frets and an irregular hole growing in the face just below the strings. Felipe's features were craggy. His face had the cracks and wrinkles of an old man, the same as his guitar. His pinkie and ring finger dug at the base of the hole, and his thumb and middle finger traveled lightly across the strings. He closed his eyes and bowed his head. His voice little more than a whisper, he sang in Spanish. The song was soft and tender and gentle as a spring vine that climbs upward toward the warm sunlight.

As if not to interrupt the old man, the Slash Q cowboys lowered their voices and, one by one, moved and stood by the domino table to listen.

"What are the words?" Evans asked softly.

Muñoz shook his head and whispered a reply. "I'm not sure. I can't get all of them. But it is mostly 'bout a man being on earth too short a time but being sad isn't going to keep him here any longer. And that God wanted him, so he set him free."

★ ★ ★ ★ ★

At sunrise the next day, Chapman put a cotton hackamore on the rancher's black horse and led him down to the river. He opened the gate and led the horse through. "You were Quezada's," he said. "Wouldn't be fair for no one else to ride you. I'm setting you free." Chapman stepped back into the pasture and closed the gate.

The horse stood with his head raised, nostrils flared, testing the morning air. A band of mustangs roamed the mountains to the east, and they saw the strange horse and nickered. Quezada's horse answered their challenge. And soon he was no more than a broken image as he disappeared through the timber.

A butter-colored moon traversed the heavens and spread a dull glow across the desert, causing cactus to cast deformed shadows. Mesquite nodded slightly at the soft breeze, and tumbleweed skipped blindly through the night, pausing occasionally to do-si-do with an ocotillo. Coyotes moved silently around a herd of untended sheep; their cousin, a gray wolf, sat on his haunches and howled into the endless sky, exactly as his ancestors had for centuries.

Bathed by the moonlight, Chapman sat on a promontory looking out across the valley and worried about tomorrow and the day after that. Three days' ride to the south Shadrach, washed by the same light, worked his way afoot through the mountains toward Ciudad Juárez. At Las Cruces, seething, the Soto brothers walked up the corral path toward their house cursing the loss of their two brothers. Alberto followed, taking long steps, trying to step on the head of his moon-shadow. North of Carrizozo at the edge of the Jicarillas, a woman grown late in her beauty saddled a horse and felt the coolness of a dead soul flow around her.

Because of Chapman's raising—his father, Lathel, a civil engineer; his mother, Melba, an English teacher at Peabody Normal College in Nashville—he had always taken any responsibility as if confirmed with an oath before God. The day after Quezada's death, he wrote to the ranch foremen at the La Mesilla and the Bitter Lakes ranches and instructed them to make an inventory of livestock as quickly as possible and return it to him. He also wrote to Diuguid, the attorney in Carrizozo, and informed him of the passing of Quezada.

He had not seen the document, but Quezada told some of the details of the will. He knew two of the spreads would go to the rancher's sons, and he was to receive the ranch at Bitter Lakes. He had been shocked at Quezada's generosity. Although Chapman secretly considered the rancher to be a father figure and mentor, he was still surprised at the older man's generosity toward him. Of course, Quezada wanted him to see that Muñoz and Filipe were looked after. He would have done this without any prompting, but, as Quezada said, he wanted to control things even after he was in the grave.

Quezada had been mostly open with Chapman. They discussed ranch business, and Chapman believed he knew as much about the rancher's life and finances as anyone—probably more. After the will was written, and they made the sham purchase of the horses at White Oaks—from the woman who had Quezada's children—the rancher never used the real name of the woman or of their two sons. That was one of the mysteries that would be solved with the reading of the will.

Business at the ranch went on as if the rancher were still calling the shots. Chapman sold more horses to the army, and he made delivery to Fort Bliss and to Fort Stanton. Dr. Woods was surprised to learn of Quezada's death and said he figured the old bastard was too tough to die. Chapman saw no reason to give details of the death.

Two weeks after he wrote to Diuguid, the attorney, he received a letter saying the parties at White Oaks had been notified, and the will would be read on the tenth of next month at his office in Carrizozo.

Carrizozo

The mountains came into view slowly. One minute the purple mist hid them, and five minutes later the purple turned a burnt orange, and the sunlight lit the peaks with a fiery glaze—angel fire to the local Indians. The wind had not awakened yet, and the air was calm and sharp with the pungence of sage.

Chapman and Muñoz, breakfasting on coffee and sourdough bread, left the ranch bound for Carrizozo. Chapman encouraged Felipe to make the trip, but the gimpy-legged Mexican declined, saying he'd had enough traveling across that part of the country. Fort Stanton was still asleep when the two riders passed through. Midmorning, they rested the horses in Capitan and had a cup of coffee and a slice of day-old apricot pie. The Vera Cruz Mountains loomed to the west. "Get across those mountains," Chapman told Muñoz, "and it will be downhill the rest of the way."

"Yeah," Muñoz agreed, "then when we reach the desert it'll be like riding across a dirty tabletop."

Chapman grinned. "And just about as exciting. First thing we get into Carrizozo you get us a couple of rooms for the night, and I'll see if I can find Diuguid. He's not looking for us until tomorrow morning, but I'll sleep better just knowing that he'll be up and about before noon."

They arrived in Carrizozo before dusk. Muñoz took the horses to the livery, and Chapman walked down the street toward Diuguid's darkened office. Chapman knocked on the door; it squeaked open on balky hinges. Law books, some gaping as if awed by the wisdom of their content and some tented, littered the floor. The lawyer's battered desk was upended, the drawers' contents coughed out in small, irregular shaped mounds. The cast-iron safe lay on its back undaunted, the dial and handle battered but the door intact, the contents apparently secure.

Chapman backed out of the office and carefully pulled the door closed.

Leaning against a post, the Lincoln County deputy stood on the edge of the porch, a sawed-off, double-barreled shotgun lying across his arm. "Find what you're looking for?" he asked.

Chapman was taken aback. "Uh . . . I . . . I was looking for Mr. Diuguid. The lawyer. I . . . I . . . I've got an appointment with him in the morning. And some other folks. Opening a will. Uh . . . Ab Quezada's will."

"You're a little late, old son. Or maybe a little early." The deputy leveled the shotgun. "Somebody else came by to see him night before last. Don't know what they were lookin' for. Don't know if they found it or not. If it was in the safe, I'd say they never got it. But they got the lawyer or at least nobody has seen him. Hope your business wasn't pressing or nothing."

"But . . . it is important that we see him. I've got this letter and it—"

"Well, it must have been more important that somebody else see him. Or least they beat you here. Who you supposed to meet?"

"Ah . . . I don't know her name. She lives up north of here. Close to White Oaks. She's got a couple of grown boys."

The deputy nodded. "That's Mrs. Angalee. Known her all my life. I guess she's a widow woman, least I've never heered of her having a husband. Got them two boys. Reckon there was a man around one time or t'other."

Muñoz finished stabling the horses and now stood at the edge of the porch, listening. "Who's this?" the deputy asked. "Part of this will reading business, too?"

"Yes, we work together," Chapman said. "We're going to get a room, then I guess we'll come back over here in the morning—see who shows up."

The law officer briefly studied the two Slash Q riders. "Yeah. I reckon that's a good idea—see who shows up in the morning. I'm gonna save you two old boys some money. Come on with me. Let you fellows be a guest of the citizens of Lincoln County tonight. Some folks find our jail cells to be downright comfortable. Have a lot of return customers." The deputy laughed at his own joke and added, "Repeat business, and we don't even have to advertise."

Muñoz said, "That's nice of you but if it's all the same—"

The deputy shook his head, "It ain't all the same with me. Stand beside each other. Unbuckle your gun belts and let them slide to the ground. Then back five steps toward the middle of the street and turn around."

Muñoz and Chapman dropped their belts. The deputy picked them up and looped them over his shoulder.

"Now, you boys just walk ahead of me. There's the jail over on the other side of the street. All right, git."

Lincoln County Sheriff Earnest Banks was a devotee of the Apostle Paul and took to heart the admonition about suffering fools gladly. An ideal morning, and most were, consisted of sitting in the Carrizozo Café's toilet and watching the sunrise cast moving beams of light through the cracks in the door and across the floor. When the first shaft of light fell on his boots, he took it an omen that it was time for him to start the day.

He owned two clay-fired mugs, and each morning at the café he swapped a dirty one for a clean one filled with coffee. This morning, he stood on the front porch of the café and discussed the lack of rain with a rancher. Both agreed it was so dry that piss from a tall horse would evaporate before it reached the ground. They'd had this same conversation three times within the past two months. Truths don't seem to age.

Sheriff Banks stepped out into the street, careful not to spill a drop of coffee. Mrs. Banks had decided the sheriff drank too much coffee: Made him jittery, and he had to get up twice each night. The cook at the café helped Mrs. Banks enforce the one-cup-per-morning edict. The sheriff grumbled he had been ganged up on by two women. The whole damn thing was unconstitutional.

By now, the sun was high enough the sheriff had to pull his hat brim low over his eyes, and he didn't see the deputy standing on the jailhouse porch until he almost bumped into him. " 'Bout time you was getting here, Sheriff. I been up all night guarding a couple of prisoners."

The chief lawman steadied his coffee cup. "Prisoners? Why, hell, we ain't got nobody in jail. Earl, what're you talking about?"

Deputy Earl Averill opened the jail door and, with a grand gesture, motioned the sheriff inside. "There," he said. "Caught 'em plundering around in Diuguid's office late yesterday. They musta come back to try to bust the safe again. Reckon I've pretty much solved the case. And I'm betting there'll be a reward."

Sheriff Banks stood in the doorway and looked into the jail's single cell. "What in the name of God are you talking about, Earl? You didn't lock these two up, did you?"

Things were sinking in on Earl, and he hung his head like a dog that had been caught sucking eggs. "Dadgummit," he said, "caught them dead to rights, Sheriff. The tall one was plundering around in the office, and the little one was standing lookout—'cept wasn't doing a very good job of it."

"Shit! Let 'em out. Feller on the left is Quezada's *jefe*. You saw both of them right recent. They'd come up here buying horses. I believe they're dealing with Mrs. Angalee."

Earl made a great pretense of removing the key ring from his belt—he wanted the sheriff to notice how carefully he discharged his duties as a deputy.

Muñoz and Chapman stepped from the cell into the office. The sheriff nodded toward a desk drawer, and the deputy retrieved their gun belts. "It was just a misunderstanding," the sheriff said. "Man can't be too careful these days. Still a few owlhoots wandering around, never plumb got over the Lincoln County range wars . . . holding a grudge, you might say."

Chapman watched the verbal exchange between the two lawmen and knew Earl hadn't heard the last of this. "It's OK," he said. "Reckon that's not his first or last mistake. Only man that doesn't make a mistake is the man that don't do nothing. Now if it's all right, we'll go back and sit on Diuguid's porch and wait for the woman to show up."

Earl brightened considerably. "I'll go with 'em. See that everything works out. Kinda make up for my mistake."

"I'll handle it, Earl," the sheriff said. "You probably need some sleep, seeing as how you were up last night guarding prisoners."

Muñoz, the sheriff, and Chapman sat on the rickety bench on Diuguid's front porch until noon. Diuguid nor anyone else showed up. "Not surprised," the sheriff said. "Mrs. Angalee is not one to take orders from a lawyer or anybody else. You ever met her?"

Chapman nodded. "Once. At her ranch."

The sheriff looked at his pocket watch. "Then I reckon you know where to find her. You ought to get there by mid-afternoon."

White Oaks

White Oaks had once been a booming gold mining town with stage service to Las Vegas and Socorro. But the mines had petered out, and now it was inhabited by recluses, broke-down cowboys, and folks who didn't want to be found. Mrs. Anga-lee's ranch lay at the base of the mountains and was watered by White Oak Springs, the source of the town's name.

The riders followed a dirt trail leading northward out of town. "You sure you know where we're going?" Muñoz asked.

Chapman grunted. They topped a low rise, and the ranch spread out before them: a wood frame house, three sheds, and a narrow, irrigated pasture. "Gotta learn to trust me," Chapman said to his partner, grinning. "Never led you wrong yet, have I?"

Muñoz smiled and said, "You didn't do a very good job yesterday afternoon and last night. But at least I can brag that I've been in jail. Thanks to you."

From a quarter a mile away, they could hear the rhythmic clang-clang-clang of a shop hammer against an anvil. As they approached the ranch, two dogs—a rat terrier and a shepherd-mix—stood in the road and barked at the unaccustomed visitors. The clanging stopped. A gray-haired, lithe-bodied woman and a bearded, shirtless man wearing a leather farrier's apron came out from behind a shed. The woman spoke sharply to the dogs, and they stopped barking.

The riders waited at the corral gate. The man and woman advanced, shading their eyes against the sun; the man still carried the hammer. "Can we help you?" the woman said.

"Yes, ma'am, my name is Chapman. I talked with you sometime back. I was here with Quezada."

"You've come for the horses," the woman voiced, somewhere between a statement and a question. She poked stray strands of silver up under the sweatband of her hat. An awkward and nervous movement. "My goodness. Where're my manners? Get down and water your horses." She turned to the man beside her. "Sam. Go up to the spring and get a bucket of fresh drinking water for these people."

The riders dismounted and led their horses over to the tank. A creaky windmill labored most of the day in the light breeze, and now the tank stood half full. Tadpoles and slender, striped minnows swam in the warm water, causing the surface to corrugate and reflect wrinkled, white, summertime clouds.

Chapman felt the need to reestablish himself. "I was up here with Quezada. We . . . uh . . . paid for the horses . . . and . . . uh—"

"Yes," the woman said, "you never picked them up. Joe, he's my oldest, has gone up to one of our upper pastures to bring some horses down. Couple of them need shoeing. Sam," she nodded to the son that had gone to get water, "he does all the shoeing. Not the best, but he's learning."

Muñoz stepped forward and shook hands with the woman. "I'm Muñoz—Chapman didn't see it necessary to introduce me."

"Pleased to meet you," the woman said. "I'm Angalee. I kinda run things here, when my boys will let me. Which is most of the time."

Chapman eyed Sam returning with the bucket of water. He spoke in a low voice that carried no further than to Angalee. "We've . . . uh . . . we've not come about the horses. We've come about the will. Mr. Diuguid was supposed to have sent you a letter. We were to meet at his office in Carrizozo this morning."

Angalee shook her head. "Didn't get a letter. Post office in White Oaks burned. Government hasn't got around to building another one. What's this about a will?"

"It's Quezada's. He is dead."

Angalee repeated the word as if she'd misunderstood. "Dead. Quezada is dead? Ab Quezada? Dead?"

Chapman nodded. "Yes, ma'am. The letter was to inform you about that . . . and about the will."

Angalee leaned against the corral gate, and buried her face in her hands. Muñoz moved hesitantly to comfort the shocked woman, then stepped away awkwardly.

Angalee took a deep breath. "I'm all right," she said. "It's just that he seemed like a man that might never die. I'd have thought that he would have demanded . . . or scared death into passing him by. To take somebody else." She shook her head. "I can't believe . . . just can't believe it."

Sam hurried around the side of the corral, water from the swinging bucket sloshing against his leg and darkening one leg of his pants. "Mama, what is it, what's wrong?" He'd dropped to his knees in front of his mother and stared up into her down-turned face. "What's wrong?"

"It's a friend," she said. "A friend has died."

Sam stood and stepped away from his mother, then turned to Chapman and mouthed, "Who?"

Chapman stammered, "Well, it was—"

"Our friend, Mr. Quezada," Angalee interrupted. "The man who bought our horses."

From behind the house a herd of mustangs came galloping out of the timber, pale-hued dust trailing them like low-lying smoke. A man appeared out of the dust like an apparition, his wide-looped lasso singing above his head, urging the horses onward. Angalee and Sam moved quickly, opened the gate, and then waved their arms to turn the horses into the corral.

Joe was simply the pattern from which Sam was struck. He was broad through the shoulders, heavily muscled, dark hair almost blond from the dust, beard curling just above his collar. He sat on the horse as if merely an extension of the animal. He stepped down, stripped the scarred leather *chaparejos*, hung them across the pommel of his saddle, then walked over to the group standing by the corral.

Late afternoon, the five of them—Muñoz, Chapman, Angalee, and her sons—sat on the porch and talked. Chapman was careful when discussing the will. He simply relayed what he remembered Quezada telling him about the division of the ranches. He did not mention any history about Quezada's relationship with Angalee nor his fathering the two boys.

Angalee listened, noncommittal, emotions masked. Her sons were mystified and sat looking questioningly at their mother. They had been raised in this isolated part of the country, and, until now, their mother controlled most of life's happenings.

A coyote, teats heavy with milk, squeezed under the chicken house fence and loped across the barnyard, a lifeless Rhode Island Red hanging from her mouth.

"Finally caught her," Joe said. He clawed the pistol from his holster, rested it across his forearm, and aimed at the retreating coyote.

Angalee leaned forward and pushed the pistol aside. "Joe, you're not going to shoot her." It was not a question; it was a directive. "She's braved daylight to catch that hen. She's not dumb; knows what a dangerous thing she's done. But she must eat because she is suckling pups, and she'll do anything for them. It's instinct." She smiled. "They don't learn it; they're born with it."

Suppertime came, and Angalee insisted the visitors eat. "It'll be warmed-over beans and beef, fried pies," she said, "but it's too late for you to ride back to Carrizozo, and it'll beat anything you could find there to eat, anyway."

The meal ended, but no one left the table. The conversation carried well into the night. As usual, Muñoz had little to say, but Angalee drew the Argentine out and listened closely to the accent.

The kitchen-shelf clock struck eleven. Angalee dispatched her sons to sleep in the hay shed. Muñoz got the sons' room, and

Chapman got the living room's battered chesterfield.

It was not a restful night for Chapman, as he lay awake staring into the nothingness of the dark. Yesterday morning when they'd left the Fort Stanton Ranch, he'd looked forward to getting the reading of the will and the disposition of the property behind him. He'd not felt comfortable managing Quezada's ranches. The burden was even heavier because of the involvement of the sons and the unknown qualities of their mother. Then the disappearance of Diuguid and the night in jail made things even worse. But he'd liked Mrs. Angalee and their . . . her sons. Now, he was ready to move on. Ready to take charge of the Bitter Lakes Ranch, to see if he could make it on his own.

He heard the clock strike three and then the quarter hour. The firebox door on the kitchen stove creaked open, a minute later closed. Soon, he smelled coffee. He pulled his pants and boots on before moving through the short hallway to the kitchen.

Angalee stood at the stove, pouring coffee from a blue, enameled coffeepot into a mug of the same making. She turned, raised her eyebrows, and asked, "Want some?" She wore the same denim pants as yesterday, but now the tail of her work shirt was untucked. Her hair was pulled back and held in place with a slender strip of tooled rawhide, a single-stone turquoise Navajo pendant hung at her throat. She poured a second cup, opened the warming closet door, and removed the remains of last night's fried peach pie. "Would you like to sit on the front porch while it is still cool?"

The soft light of a kerosene lamp washed across her face, creating the illusion of smooth, unwrinkled skin. Her fingers were long, their movements graceful. Mentally, Chapman subtracted twenty-some years—years of childbirth, exposure to the wicked desert sun, and the harsh life of a ranch woman—and he could see the woman who Quezada fathered children

201

with. And he wondered what devils possessed his friend to desert this woman. Even today, she was much more than a faded rose, and he was sorry he ever thought her that.

They sat on the porch in the dark, holding a fried pie in one hand and coffee cup in the other. "You couldn't sleep, either?" Chapman asked.

"No," the woman said. "I've got a lot of decisions to make. Lot of things to think about."

"The land?" Chapman asked. "The ranches are in good shape, well-stocked. May need to sell off some of the older broodmares."

She looked at Chapman and smiled. "I'm kinda partial to old broodmares."

Chapman studied his knuckles and tried to find words that would soften his assessment about the old mares.

She took his cup into the kitchen and refilled it, her bare feet silent on the wooden floor. She returned and sat in the rocker and sighed. "I wish that was it . . . all I had to worry about. I can tell by the way you look at my boys . . . my men . . . that you know that Quezada is their daddy. I'm guessing that he told you when you were last here. You may know more about him than I did. At least his recent life." She sipped her coffee and rocked for almost a minute, a soft sound of wood against wood in the early morning air. "They don't know he is their father. And I've got to tell them. I don't know what they will think of me; I don't even know what I think of me."

"They're not going to change their opinion of you. I've watched them; they would accept your word if you said the moon was made of turkey feathers."

She took a shallow sip of coffee. "You really think so? You think they'll understand? Or forgive, whichever the case."

It was getting lighter now, and Chapman could see the woman looking at him, waiting for an answer. "I really think that. I really do. If they have a hard time with it now, they'll come to an understanding. Maybe later; but they'll come around."

She asked, "Tell me how he died?"

Angalee sat, one leg folded under, one foot flat against the coolness of the porch floor. Chapman realized he was staring at the delicate veins that crossed her instep. "I . . . I . . . I hoped you wouldn't ask that question. But you are going to find out sooner or later anyway." Chapman hesitated, looking for the right words: "He was sick. In awful pain. He . . . it was by his own hand."

She was quiet for a while, then cleared her throat and said, "I figured as much. He was a *pistolero,* you know. I always thought he would get shot by someone. Never thought he would be the one to do it. Looks like I've got another thing to tell the boys." She paused. Then a little low laugh. "I've led a quiet life here for a long time. Chapman, you've complicated things greatly."

Now it was daylight. Chapman stood and gathered the coffee mugs. "Quezada said it was your own choosing. Said he looked after you, left a stack of gold coins. And you knew about the gold bars. Said you could have lived anywhere you wanted to. But you chose here."

"That's all true." Angalee's fingers worried the turquoise pendant.

Chapman was almost sorry he'd gotten into their private lives. "We'll never know," he said, "but I think if he'd had it to do over . . . maybe things might have ended different between you two."

She opened the screen door, and they went into the kitchen. "I'm afraid you didn't know Quezada as well as you think. We'll . . . the boys and I . . . get through this. I'm like that mama coyote, you know."

Chapman smiled and looked at her. "I know. And, like that

coyote, nobody will ever shoot at you."

She squatted and added wood to the cookstove firebox. "I'm probably old enough to be your mother, but you know that. I've shared my heart with you. I haven't let a man see my heart since . . . in years."

She stood and faced him, dark eyes misty. She put both hands on his shoulders, leaned forward, and kissed his cheek. "You're a good and kind man, Chapman, but you are a generation too late."

Angalee fried eggs, baked sourdough biscuits, cooked steaks, and made a pot of coffee. "Eat your fill," Chapman told Muñoz. "You'll be a long time 'fore you'll have a meal like this again." The biscuits and jelly made their last round, and the coffeepot was drained.

Joe and Sam saddled the Slash Q riders' horses and led them to the house. Chapman tightened his horse's girth again and stepped up into the saddle. Angalee and Muñoz stood on the porch talking as long-lost friends reunited. "Reckon we'd better be going," Chapman called to Muñoz. The two left the shade of the porch, and Muñoz swung up into the saddle.

"I'll get the land titles worked out," Chapman said. "It all came to Quezada through land grants and community grants. Diuguid had it all written down, but that doesn't do us much good right now. It'll take a while. But by the time you all decide on what's what, it'll be straightened out. I'll write, and you write me back. Sorry we had to get acquainted the way we did. Anyway, it'll be better next time." Both riders touched the brims of their hats, put the spurs to their horses, and rode down the dusty road leading south.

Late morning, they stopped by the sheriff's office in Carrizozo. The sheriff discovered Diuguid boasted to the local barber that he was soon meeting with investors from Chicago—gonna close a deal that would make him the wealthiest man in Lincoln County.

"Don't know where the shyster is right now, but we're on it," Sheriff Banks said. "Right now, Deputy Averill is sitting over at the café eating a chicken fried steak and planning his next move."

The sun was at its zenith, lizards were sunning in the heat, ground squirrels and gophers had taken to the coolness of their underground burrows. Sheriff Banks removed a red-checked bandana from a hip pocket and mopped his brow. "Reckon you didn't have any trouble finding Mrs. Angalee, did you?"

"Easy as pie, wasn't it, Muñoz?" Chapman chided and got a nod and a weak smile in return. "Nice little spread and right pretty, sitting there at the base of the mountains and all. We got a lot of things worked out and some more to come. Give Mr. Diuguid my regards when—if—you see him."

"Yeah. I'll do that. If you see him first, do the same for me. Tell him to stop by when he's in town," the sheriff said and laughed aloud at his own joke.

Santa Rosa

After he mailed the letters to Chapman and Angalee, Diuguid had packed his grip, bundled several papers and maps in his leather briefcase, and, just after midnight, ridden up to Ancho. He left his horse at the livery stable beside the depot and breakfasted at a café that catered mostly to gypsum miners and early-stirring employees of the brick plant. He stopped by the bank and inquired about mineral rights claims; wanted to know if any were for sale and the price. He catalogued the information in his childish scrawl, had another cup of coffee, and purchased a round-trip train ticket to Santa Rosa.

Diuguid commandeered two facing, unoccupied seats. He sat

in one and put his feet in the other. He pulled his hat over his eyes and dozed the hundred miles to his destination, ranches and small towns sweeping silently past the train windows. The train rumbled northward, leaving a thin trail of gray smoke in the prairie air and the howl of steel against steel rising from the rail bed.

Santa Rosa, perched on the western edge of the Llano Estacado, connected directly to Chicago and El Paso by rail. Diuguid had not seen such prosperity. He reserved three rooms at the Aqua Negra hotel. He stopped at the bank, introduced himself as an attorney with an Albuquerque law firm, and requested the use of a private meeting area for the afternoon. From an easily impressed junior officer of the bank, he gathered details on opening a business account—in the vicinity of fifty thousand dollars. The necessary papers would be prepared at day's end, the officer assured him. The small-town lawyer, impressed with his own guile, walked back to the depot to await the potential investors from Chicago.

Nineteen people climbed off the train: three ranchers, four children, two schoolteachers, four cavalrymen, a survey party of three, and three swarthy men wearing suits. The three men stood expectantly by the loading platform. Diuguid adjusted his tie and polished soot from his briefcase. "I believe you will be representatives of The Great Chicago Land Company?" he said, and extended his hand. "I'm attorney X. L. Diuguid of Carrizozo, New Mexico Territory."

The men introduced themselves: Vito Abbatiello, Manfredo Lumetta, and Ameilio Zunino. The youngest of the three, Manfredo, stepped forward and shook Diuguid's hand. "Just call me Manny," he said. "My associates speak limited English, and occasionally I will translate for them. Do not be uncomfortable when this happens. They are financiers from Italy." He smiled. "Long trip down. Please excuse our appearance."

Diuguid studied the three men. They wore business suits, white shirts, blue neckties, and shiny black shoes. Manny and Vito wore bowlers; Ameilio wore a peculiar cap, the crown slumping forward over the short bill. All three were smooth shaven, but their jowls glistened blue-black. While they had no resemblance to any of Diuguid's previous clientele, it was obvious they were moneyed. This was the most important thing.

He had made a recent sale of a small claim to the Great Chicago Land Company. Two thousand dollars. The company paid promptly. Most of all, they seemed to have no understanding of territorial land transactions and could not tell a worthless mining claim document from Lincoln's *Gettysburg Address*. He decided that today, along with fake deeds for Quezada's ranches, he would unload some bogus Ancho gypsum options. He was rather proud of the title work and maps he could exhibit for the ranches. He'd prepared fraudulent mineral options while waiting for the train this morning. An option is an option to the uneducated.

"I have secured lodging at the Aqua Negra. It is the finest hotel in Santa Rosa. It won't measure up to Chicago standards, but you should be comfortable." The men moved along the dirt street, Freddy and Diuguid in front followed by Vito and Ameilio. "And," the lawyer continued, "they have an excellent bar and an outstanding restaurant. I assure you it will be a pleasant stay. Perhaps we can conclude our transactions this afternoon and then you will allow me to secure a hack and give you a chance to see the countryside. Out east of here, some pretty impressive springs you might enjoy seeing." Now, Diuguid spoke in a low voice, unsure if his next suggestion would be well received, "I . . . I've . . . I've been told that ladies of the evening might be available, and I would be glad to investigate it further."

Manny spoke rapidly in Italian to his fellow travelers. They chattered a response. "They find that to be a wonderful idea—the trip out to see the countryside and perhaps later . . ." He turned his hands palms up and shrugged his shoulders.

At the hotel, the men registered and went upstairs. "We should freshen up," Manny said.

Diuguid sat in the lobby, briefcase between his feet, and waited. He closed his eyes and leaned back in a large, overstuffed chair. His mind raced. If he could manage to get . . . his brain was awhirl with numbers . . . say, thirty-five thousand total from these men along with the fifteen thousand sewed in the bottom of his briefcase, he would be set for life. San Francisco. He would go to San Francisco. He dreamed of smelling the ocean air since he was a child picking bumble-bee cotton on a hardscrabble farm in the blazing sun at Portales. Perhaps even buy a home. Maybe open a land office and sell territory land to rich Californians. Fifty thousand dollars! My God. Diuguid mopped his brow with a rumpled handkerchief and willed himself to breathe slowly.

After the noon meal, the four crossed the street to the bank, Diuguid made the introductions, and the junior officer ushered them into a private, paneled meeting room. The lawyer spread the maps on a long table, and the men traced the boundaries with their fingers. "The land by itself is worth twenty-five thousand," Diuguid explained. "I'll throw in the livestock for nothing." He displayed the claims options. "While the options are worth"—he paused to measure the anticipation in their faces—"a minimum of fifteen thousand, I'll let you have them for ten thousand."

Manny consulted briefly with his companions. "If you do not object, Mr. Diuguid," he said, "the three of us need a short time to consider your offer. If we might have a few minutes of privacy?" he said and raised his eyebrows. "I will discuss the value of American money versus the Italian lira with my associates."

"Yes," Diuguid said, "take all the time you need. I'll go down the street and rent a hack for our afternoon trip. Back in half an hour." His heart hammered in his chest. Perhaps he could have gotten more money. Then maybe not, but if this deal worked, the sky just might be the limit. He would stay briefly in Santa Rosa, complete a couple more transactions with Manny and the Italians, and then—poof—look out, San Francisco.

Briefcase clutched tightly in his hand, Diuguid hurried up the street. He'd rented a horse and buggy for considerably more than he'd expected—but he was about to be a rich man, so to hell with it; he could afford it. He passed the telegraph office just as Manny stepped onto the plank sidewalk. "Through with your meeting?" he asked.

Manny responded with a wave. "I have wonderful news," he said. "I've wired our office in Chicago, and they have responded. Telegraph is quick—a wonderful way to conduct business. Chicago has approved of our deal." He smiled and nudged Diuguid in the ribs with his elbow. "They are impressed with your work. Mightily impressed. Here is the great part: they want you to represent us in additional acquisitions. As a partner, of course."

Diuguid could not control his sharp intake of air. "A partner," he almost shouted. "They want me as a partner. With the Great Chicago Land Company? Why, I'm greatly honored and almost speechless."

Manny smiled and shook Diuguid's hand vigorously. "It will be wonderful to have you as a part of our firm. A great asset, a great asset. I had a hunch this might happen when the company vice president sent blank partnership papers with me. Just need your signature in a couple of places. And, of course, a small deposit to change the charter papers and cover other legal costs."

Diuguid almost trotted to keep up with the long-striding Manny. "A small deposit?"

"It's customary," Manny said. "But in your case, I suggested that the fee be reduced to twenty thousand. Since you are so well established and widely respected in the area."

"Twenty thousand? Dollars?" Diuguid sputtered. "That seems—just about right. I have just invested heavily in other ventures. I might have a slight problem in arriving at that amount. Right now, I mean. I can easily pay fifteen thousand now and"—Diuguid improvised—"I've got plenty more in my office safe in Carrizozo. We can take the train back to Ancho and—"

Manny made a fluttery motion with his hands. "To secure the services of a man such as yourself, I believe Chicago will be understanding. If it's acceptable, we will withhold payment for the lands we were to purchase today. Just to stabilize the accounting. Of course, you can understand, we will have to complete the transaction this afternoon because, in matters like this, time is very important. Others are vying for this same position, as I'm sure you can understand. We will simply credit your account." He winked at Diuguid. "I covet your salary check at the end of this month."

Manny and Diuguid entered the room where the Italian financiers were waiting, furiously manipulating columns of numbers on two legal pads. "Well, it's official," Manny announced. The two Italians bowed, shook Diuguid's hand, and ripped off a couple of dozen words. Manny nodded and smiled.

For the first time since leaving Carrizozo, Diuguid loosened his grip on his briefcase. He set it on the table and slit the lining. The bundles of bills tumbled out onto the table, and he shoved them toward the financiers. They carefully counted the money and, with a series of great flourishes, drew up a receipt, which Diuguid slipped back into his case.

Everyone at the table shook hands again. "Well, with that consummated," Manny said, "I think we will enjoy your hospitality and welcome a tour of the countryside. My associates will accompany you to the livery while I get a cashier's check for deposit into your account in Chicago."

A half hour later, Diuguid and the two financiers drove up to the front door of the bank where Manny waited. "Glad to deposit all that cash safely," Manny said. Diuguid slapped the reins across the horse's rump, and the happy foursome departed toward the country.

Peculiar to this dry country, east of Santa Rosa, is a series of sinkholes filled with water and connected by a network of natural tunnels. The most famous is the Blue Hole. The small lake is no more than one hundred feet wide but is almost ninety feet deep. It was late in the afternoon when the men arrived. They got out of the buggy and, with Diuguid walking in front, strolled to the water's edge.

Manny and his two companions dropped the hack off at the livery. Traveling by train and buggy, they arrived at Diuguid's dusty office before dawn. They ransacked his belongings and unsuccessfully hammered on his rusty safe. Nothing of value.

The Chicagoans left before the town awoke. They paused briefly at the bottom of an arroyo to burn the deeds, maps, and worthless options. The gray ashes of the papers scattered before the wind that accompanied the dawn. The three men arrived in Ancho in time for breakfast. Richer by fifteen thousand, they caught the train northward toward Chicago.

Two weeks later on a fine, sunny Sunday afternoon, Diuguid rose face first and rested sluggishly on the placid surface of the

Blue Hole. The Santa Rosa sheriff's office was never able to make identification of the body.

Ciudad Juárez

Shadrach was accustomed to difficulty and did not see it as an adversary, simply as an unpleasant fact. After the gunfight at Fort Bliss, he'd lived in the Franklin Mountains for weeks with little to eat or drink. The pain in his lacerated cheek was nothing compared to his broken leg, but he survived.

His earlier trip from Sierra del Tigre eastward to Ciudad Juárez and El Paso would have been an enormous undertaking for most men, but he remembered it as simply a long trip across a desert.

He withstood the beating and mutilation in Ciudad Juárez, recovered, and took revenge against his tormentors. He thought about his time in the city; it had not been tough. Occasionally he thought of *Poco Coño* and wondered where she was; he did not concern himself with her safety, only thought of lying with her again and wondered if her breasts had grown.

He'd survived the heathenish abuse at the hands of the Soto brothers and humiliation by their vermin nephew.

Although highly improbable, he just might have been the only human on earth who enjoyed hardship. There might have been others, but they were religious zealots, wore sackcloth, and heaped ashes on their head. And they disappeared centuries ago.

Today, he crossed over the peak of the mountain, and the great cities of El Paso and Ciudad Juárez lay in front of him to the south. Although the sun had not reached the midpoint, heat waves rose from the desert floor and caused the cities to shimmer with a false brightness. The brown waters of Rio Bravo del Norte sliced between the two towns on its silt-laden, 1,900-mile journey eastward to the sea. He would cross this river tonight, and tomorrow he would be in a more comfortable place.

He'd grown a beard, scraggly at best, and he'd let his hair grow long. The beard did little to mask the angry and hideous scar that creased his cheek; he shaved. Long hair did not hide that he had no ears, so he whacked the hair from his head with a knife. As strange as he looked, no one stared at him or made light of his appearance. Perhaps a glance—never lingering, eyes never pausing, a quick sweep and a hurried averting of the gaze. The haunting hollowness of his eyes, the nickel-colored nothingness, made an impression on the most strong hearted.

He stripped, a night-darkened sinewy predator, and swam the river. A small raft of woven cattails ferried his rifle and meager possessions. On the Mexican side, he raked the muddy water from his body with his spade-shaped hands, dressed, and climbed the sandy bank. Only an inquisitive dog and a wandering rag picker welcomed him to Ciudad Juárez. Both slunk away from the specter.

The city was just as he'd left it. The narrow dirt streets were filthy as he remembered; the stables little more than pens made of scrap lumber and salvaged tin. Even at this late hour, the cantinas were busy, and women stood outside beckoning, stained skirts raised almost to their crotches. A slender-ribbed, shirtless boy picked through the garbage behind a closed café. Two young men, eyes wolf-wary, emptied the pockets of a drunk in a dead-end alley. Shadrach felt at home.

He slept in an abandoned house, and yellow flies woke him at first light. He was broke and hungry.

A *prestamista*, a pawnbroker, with a medal of Saint Nicholas draped around his fat neck offered him 150 pesos for the engraved Winchester. Shadrach shook his head. The man examined the rifle and ran his fingers over the etched inscription: *Winner Slash Q Shooting.* He increased the offer to 225 pesos. Midmorning, Shadrach feasted on beans, eggs, and tortillas washed down with water.

Shadrach had no skills other than those he developed as a child: a timber cutter or a laborer in underground mines. In this wasted country, these jobs did not exist. He could neither read nor write, which put him in the same class of most residents of Ciudad Juárez. Working at his previous job at the tannery was definitely out. He could herd livestock, but that was a tiresome and lonely job, and while he did not particularly care for people, he did prefer their company to sheep and cattle.

Other than the disastrous robbery attempt at Fort Bliss, he had been a successful thief. However, most of the potential street victims in Ciudad Juárez had little money, and there was always the danger of attempting to rob someone more violent and stronger than he was.

He remembered the fat man who owned the whorehouse. The man always had *compañeros* to protect him and the loose women who worked for him. Shadrach was aware that, because of his size and fearsome appearance, someone might hire him for protection. After all, he was not the only man in Ciudad Juárez who was handy with a knife and gun.

But he would need his rifle—and the redemption cost would be two for one. He watched the pawnbroker's shop until dark, when the man waddled out carrying a long slender object wrapped in a blanket. Shadrach followed him.

When the *prestamista* opened his yard gate, he heard a movement behind him and turned. He saw the strange earless man but not soon enough to clear the derringer from beneath his coat. Shadrach's large hand wrapped around the pawnbroker's and forced the barrel of the gun into the man's mouth. The discharge of the .32 caliber was muffled by facial tissue and bone.

Three young men came along the dusty road carrying red and yellow fighting roosters in canvas sacks. They found the blanket-shrouded body under a mesquite bush. "Look at the cut across his forehead and the strange way his head is turned to the side," one of the men said, leaning forward and lifting the blanket with thumb and forefinger. "He must have been struck by a wagon." The men cautiously scanned the deserted street before removing the blanket. "*Mi Dios,*" one exclaimed, "his face must have exploded." The dead man's pockets had been ripped open. The empty money belt was under the body, and his shoulder holster was empty. The young men pulled the blanket across the dead man, made the sign of the cross, and continued to the cockfight.

Shadrach rented a hotel room that was little more than a hovel: no windows, unsheathed mattress, dirt floor, flea infested.

The next day, he became *el enforcer* at a small house of prostitution that catered to *Americanos del Norte*. North Americans, he learned, were easy to extort and frighten.

Shadrach had neither the intelligence nor ambition to run a business. The owner of a competing whorehouse asked him to help control the boisterous Saturday night crowd, who came across the river to find female companionship and blow off steam. Shadrach considered the impossibility of being in two places at the same time. "I will find someone to help you," he said, "but he will work for me, and I want half the amount of money you pay him." In two months, he was supplying enforcers to four other houses.

Now, he lived with a former prostitute who had quit the profession; truthfully, her profession quit her. But she could do math; a skill Shadrach never mastered. She did not approve of his friends coming by her house; she knew evil when she saw it because she had seen so much.

Her name was Belzora and on the very best day of her life—entering her sixteenth year, when she was of fair skin, had all her teeth—she couldn't have been described as pretty. As a young woman, she had been religious and God-fearing. Her grandmother insisted her grandchild accompany her to mass each day. She revered the padre and did not question when he asked her to disrobe. The old grandmother beat her granddaughter with a leather strap, but Belzora refused to attend church again; she did not rebel against the faith but against the faithful.

Belzora was a superstitious woman. She was terrified of Black Witch moths and believed one of the moths flying into the house of someone sick meant their death was close. She feared going near the river at night, afraid Morgana La Llorona—the one who drowns children—would catch her. After the padre abused her, she had nightmares, but she never told anyone. A nightmare retold would recur in real life, she believed. A black cat crossing her path caused her to return home and start the trip anew.

Shadrach was moody, almost impossible to live with, and, at times, violent. She learned his dispositions; she knew when to press for her way or when to stay out of his sight. Occasionally, he would drink too much tequila, and it was on those times he would talk about the evils cast upon him. The loss of his ears and much of his hearing nagged at him. He particularly despised the uncles at Las Cruces and the little devil, Alberto. But even more, he hated Quezada and the two who were with him at Fort Bliss on the night he was shot. He felt the ragged scar on his cheek and then rubbed his stiff leg.

His hate was so great, and he did such despicable things, Belzora wondered if the earless man had been a priest in an earlier life.

White Oaks

In age, they were little more than a year apart, but Joe and Sam were as close as if they had exited their mother holding hands. Angalee raised them to be independent—except of her. At times, she was ashamed she'd kept them so close. She knew it was selfish and despised this weakness, but not enough to push them away or encourage them to marry. While she was not quite domineering, it was within sight.

Since their birth, she'd lavished her undivided love on her two sons.

The sun invaded the dark valleys and caused the eastern sky to flood with a pinkish-rose hue. A small herd of pronghorn antelope, three females and a wily old buck, silently gathered to drink from a pool of White Oak Creek. Their vigilance heightened last week; a cougar had reduced their herd by one. Now they suspiciously watched every unfamiliar movement. The buck finished drinking and stood sentry on the creek bank, his eyes moving constantly and nostrils relentlessly searching for enemy scent. The females carefully picked their way down the slope, lowered their heads, and quickly drank. The morning wind stirred a weed-captured strip of cloth, and the buck stiffened, head raised high. The cloth moved again. The buck flashed his tail skyward and snorted: a low *burrrrr*. While pronghorns can clear a ten-foot obstacle, they tend to run through or crawl under barbed wire fences.

Their panicked flight devastated ten yards of Angalee's garden fence.

Joe leaned into the barbed-wire stretchers, and the wire tightened with the pressure. Sam drove staples into the cedar post, securing the wire, and Joe eased the tension on the stretchers. "Well, that ought to hold it," Sam said and dropped his hammer into a canvas bucket.

The two men stood and looked at their work.

Joe rolled a cigarette. "That feller Chapman. What you think of him?"

"Reckon he's all right," Sam said. "Seems nice enough. That Muñoz that was with him . . . sits on a horse about as good as anybody I ever saw."

"I ain't talking about that kinda stuff." Joe rolled his sleeves down and buttoned the cuffs. "I'm talking about the way he looked at Mama. Then I ain't sure, but I kinda think she took to it."

"Yeah. I know what you're talking about, I guess. 'Course she hadn't had a man around much that paid her no attention. Or not that I ever noticed."

"Well, we'd have damned sure noticed."

The brothers walked through the garden salvaging antelope-trampled tomatoes and replacing the bean stakes. They stood at the end of the rows and surveyed the damage. "Damn," Joe said, "hope next time they get scared they run in the other direction." Sam shouldered the fence stretchers, and Joe gathered the other tools. They walked up the path from the garden toward the house.

"We ain't talked about the ranches that feller Quezada supposed to have left to us," Sam said. "I'm wondering why he did such a thing."

Joe looked at his brother. "Shit, Sam, don't you ever look around or nothing? You look just like him. Whole lot more than you look like Mama. You ever thought he might be your daddy?"

"You reckon?" Sam stopped and the stretchers slid off his shoulder and to the ground. "I thought you looked a lot like him. You act contrary a lot like he did."

Joe furrowed his brow and grimaced. "I'll ask Mama 'bout it right after you do."

Sam looked at his brother, shouldered the stretchers, and continued walking. "Yeah, well, don't hold your breath till that happens."

"OK. First thing when we get to the house. I'll just walk right in the kitchen and say look here, Mama, me and Sam was talking and—"

"—no, keep my name outta this. Mama's gonna tell you to mind your own damn business. If I was you, I believe I'd keep my mouth shut."

They walked on a bit further, and the sweat dampened their shirts between their shoulder blades. "We still haven't settled that little matter of Chapman," Joe said. "I believe I'll talk to him."

"Yeah. I reckon you ought to talk to him. You do that. Tell me what the hell you're gonna say to him. Tell him that Mama is 'bout old enough to be his mother? That what you're gonna tell him?"

"Well, OK, then. You talk to him."

"Nope. I ain't gonna do that, neither." Sam might have been the younger brother, but he wasn't going to be pushed around.

"Well, what are you gonna do?" Joe said.

"Ain't gonna do nothing," Sam said. "Mama has looked after business pretty good. She'll handle it."

They were storing tools in the shed. Joe couldn't let it go. "Well, I still want to know—"

Sam interrupted. "Tell you what: you want in one hand and shit in the other and see which one fills up first."

The Fort Stanton Ranch

It took a year and one month to get the deeds and other paperwork in order. It agitated Chapman to no end that an Albuquerque law firm dipped into Quezada's bank account. "Two hundred and fifty damn dollars," he fumed. "We could have taken that money and bought five head of cattle or two good horses. What did we get in return? Some kind of mumbo-jumbo words that nobody understands." Chapman rested his forearm on a fence post and looked out across the valley. "Let this be a lesson to you," he warned Muñoz. "Stay as far away from lawyers as you can. They're either worthless as Diuguid must have been, or they are money grubbers like that bloodsucking bunch in Albuquerque."

Chapman sent Angalee receipts for sales and purchases every three months. He asked for advice about the management of the ranches. Her response: Do as you see fit. He did note that Muñoz received more letters from Angalee than he did.

He enjoyed managing the three ranches, but he wanted to get to Bitter Lakes and start running his own outfit.

And then one day, she just appeared.

Muñoz delivered three geldings to the commanding officer at Fort Stanton earlier in the day and now came out of the fort to angle southward up the river toward the Slash Q headquarters. At the intersection of the Carrizozo and Bonito roads, Muñoz heard horsemen approaching and waited, curious at travelers along this seldom used road. Angalee and Joe crossed the creek and waved. The three rode up the river to the ranch and dismounted in front of the house that once belonged to Quezada.

Chapman was working with a mustang in the corral. He beat the dust from his pants with his gloves, then washed his face and arms at the horse tank. "Been looking for you," he said. "Want to welcome you to your ranch." Then he laughed at the absurdity of the welcome.

"Looks like you are one short. Leave Sam at home?" Chapman asked.

Angalee unfastened the top button of her shirt and ran an index finger around the collar. "We thought somebody should stay with the place at White Oaks. Not that we don't trust folks up there, but you know how it is. Sam will come next time. Wouldn't want to gang up on you. Make you think we were running you off."

She loosened the stampede string and removed her hat, then untied the rawhide thong and shook her hair loose. The sunlight heightened the silver at her temples. She became aware of Chapman staring at her and nervously smoothed the front of her blouse. "We . . . uh . . . we won't be bringing any cattle down. Probably sell them to a neighbor. After we see the pasture and how many head of horses you're running, we'll decide if we need to move more." She could have kicked herself for allowing her nervousness to surface. It had been more than a year since she had given him that awkward kiss on the forehead.

"Don't know what your plans are," Chapman said, "but after you rest, we can get out and see the pasture. I mean you, Joe, and me. And we don't have to do everything in one day. We've— I've got plenty of time." Now it was Chapman who found it difficult to make a sensible sentence.

"We've got four bedrooms here in the main house and plenty of extra beds in the bunkhouse," Muñoz said. "Felipe sleeps in the back bedroom here at the main house, since he needs to be near the kitchen. Wouldn't want the cook to travel a long ways."

"I'll sleep in the bunkhouse," Chapman said. "Don't mind giving up my room."

"No. No," Joe said. "Keep your bedroom. Mama claims that I'm not plumb housebroke, so that will fit me better. I'll get the saddlebags, take Mama's clothes to her room, then I'll go spread in the bunkhouse."

Filipe cooked brisket, potatoes, squash, and chopped fresh greens. He topped the meal off with a pecan pie. After the meal, Muñoz, Angalee, Joe, and Chapman sat at the kitchen table discussing the transition. The inventory books spread before them, the four went over the head count of both ranches.

"I believe we've got a pretty good balance," Chapman said.

"It's a lot cooler up here and easier on the grass. On the other hand, we can irrigate out of the river down at La Mesilla. So I reckon that is the best pasture for the cows. But I reckon we'll sell more horses down at Fort Bliss. Fort Stanton is pretty much shut down. I don't look for the army to staff up here again."

Angalee finished looking at the figures. "Let's keep most of the horses at La Mesilla, hoping we can get a jump on the other ranchers that are selling to the army. Save us some shipping time and cost."

"That makes sense," Chapman quickly agreed. "So, what do you want me to do?"

"It's four days down to Cruces," she said. "Go ahead and take Joe down there. Show him around. That way he can take Sam on the next trip. Save your time for other things. I'll look for you two back in a couple of weeks."

Chapman went to the stove and got the coffeepot, trying to hide his disappointment. He felt dismissed; he'd wanted to spend time around Angalee; now he felt like just a ranch hand. "We'll leave first thing in the morning. Joe, you can pick fresh horses outta the *remuda*."

For the first time since Quezada's death, Chapman had trouble sleeping. He was aware of the night sounds and a stranger in the house.

El Paso

Joe and Chapman followed a freighter's road southward. "Might as well stay on this side of the mountains," Chapman told Joe. At Alamogordo, they paralleled the railroad to Fort Bliss and two days later reached the army headquarters. "We'll see if the army needs horses; we can just cut them out at La Mesilla and ship them by rail. Save a bunch of time that way. Just send a couple of Slash Q riders down with them."

Joe grunted an agreement.

There was little conversation between the two men. Even at night after they unrolled their tarps and sat before a fire heating beans and drinking boiled coffee, Chapman found it difficult to talk with Joe. It was not that Joe was uncooperative; he simply had almost nothing to say. He observed the countryside with interest and listened when Chapman explained the range and carrying capacity of the brushland.

But he sat a horse well, and that went a long way in Chapman's mind. Man didn't have to talk to be a good ranch hand.

They found the purchasing agent in the little bar just outside the fort's gate. "Well, how's my friend Quezada?" he asked.

"Died some time ago," Chapman said. He didn't see any need to go into the details. Man's gone, he's gone. The agent bought whiskey for his two visitors. Joe shook his head and pushed the glass away. Chapman didn't want the agent to think they were highfalutin, so he drank his, then Joe's.

"Good to meet up with you again," the agent said. "Been thinkin' about you. We've got this new garrison down on the border 'bout halfway 'tween El Paso and Columbus. Them Mexican bastards are comin' across the border and stealin' livestock like ants runnin' off with cornbread crumbs. Man named Guillermo Arreola, claims to be some kind of general or other, is leadin' them. The army's gonna put a part of the 13th Cavalry down there. We gonna need 'bout a hundred more head of horses." He bought two more drinks and squinted at Chapman. "How's that sit with you? You ready to start gettin' rich off the army again?"

"Hadn't ever heard of anybody getting rich when dealing with the army, especially with a purchasing agent smart as you are," Chapman said and watched the agent swell up at this flattery. The agent brought a half pint to the table, leaned back in his chair, and hooked his thumbs behind his belt.

"How much you figuring on paying a head?" Chapman asked. Always better to get another man's thinking first in a horse deal.

The agent took a leather book from his shirt pocket and looked at past transactions. He licked his lips before saying, "I reckon 'bout seventy-five a head."

Chapman folded his hands on the table. "Whoa. I thought you said you needed cavalry horses. You're pricing pack mules. Slash Q doesn't have anything like that. We've just got strong, big-boned horses. Carry a trooper and his gear most of a day."

The agent shrugged his shoulders. "Can't blame a man for tryin'. What would you say to . . . a hundred a head?"

"I'd say you are getting better. What would you say to a hundred-and-a-half a head. And you can cull out any five. What would you say to that?"

"Too high," the agent said. "But I know your horses. All of them are good. What say . . . hundred-and-quarter?"

Chapman knew the deal was done. "OK. At that price, you don't get to do any culling. But you know I won't send you anything that isn't top-notch."

The agent drained the last drops from the bottle. "All right. But you've got to deliver them a month from today."

"You okay with all this?" Chapman asked Joe.

Joe nodded. "Okay with me. Mama trusts you. Be a good way to get the White Oaks's horses on the market."

Bordering on drunk, the agent said, "What's this about White Oaks? I never contracted for anything except Slash Q horses. You ain't gonna—"

"No." Chapman raised both hands. "Still the same horses. Just a little farther north, that's all."

★ ★ ★ ★ ★

They bedded down in a nearly vacant barrack. The next morning Chapman and Joe left Fort Bliss bound for the ranch at La Mesilla.

Midday, Joe asked, "How much?"

Chapman reined his horse to a stop. "How much what?" he asked.

"The horses," Joe said. "How much we getting for the horses? Dollars. How many dollars is the army gonna pay?"

"It comes to"—Chapman tried to make it appear as if he were figuring—"comes to about twelve thousand five hundred."

"Dollars?" Joe said. "That many dollars?"

Chapman turned his horse. "That sound about right?"

Joe spurred his horse and caught up. "That much. Damn." He repositioned his hat. "Shit fire."

For the first time it was clear to Chapman how much Angalee controlled her sons' lives. None of my business, he thought. But it doesn't seem quite right. Almost like she raised them naked of the world.

It took Joe and Chapman little more than a day to go over the La Mesilla Ranch. Chapman explained the irrigation head gates and pointed out the corners and boundary lines. Joe listened and seldom commented. "Here is what we'll do about getting the horses to the army—if it is all right with Angalee," Chapman said. "I'll order a couple of cattle cars. You and Sam can load twenty head at Carrizozo. I'll meet you at Oscura with about forty head. There is a loading siding there and pretty good pens. I'll get the hands at La Mesilla to meet us outside El Paso with forty head. We'll bunch them and take them over to the garrison at East Portrillo."

"I reckon that will be all right," Joe said. "Sam and me'll just stay with them the whole trip. You know, Chapman, I ain't never been on a train. Sam hasn't either."

The Fort Stanton Ranch

Three hard days' travel, Chapman and Joe rode into the Fort Stanton Ranch as the sun was setting. Angalee and Muñoz watched them ride up the river road.

"You know you are not doing right," Angalee said to Muñoz, as the riders approached. "Sooner you tell them, get this behind you, the better off you'll be."

"That's a good plan," Angalee said, when Chapman told of the proposed sale to the army. "Twenty head is about what we've got up at White Oaks. I believe we'll sell the cattle to a rancher up in the edge of the mountains."

"Then what'll you do with the ranch?" Chapman asked. "It'll grow up without livestock grazing. Buildings will go down pretty quick. You've got this place here and the one over in the valley. Be about all you can say grace over, I'd guess."

"I'd sure be sorry to see it go," Angalee said. "It was the first and about the only thing I ever owned. It was kinda a hiding place."

"You won't have to—" Chapman didn't know how to finish the sentence. "I know a sergeant that's retiring from the cavalry. I think he'd be interested in the place. I can talk with him and see. He's gone back east but will be back in a month. Give you some more time to make up your mind."

Mexico Border Land

In near silence, the fifty raiders came out of the desert just after two on a moonless morning. They removed their spurs and muted the horses' bits with cloth. Low-lying clouds and a whipping wind from the southwest combined with a temperature in the low thirties made it ideal for the marauders.

It had been their intent to shell the garrison with the 12-pound Mountain howitzer. Guillermo Arreola's cannoniers set up in a shallow draw less than a half mile from the garrison gate and charged the weapon with a half pound of black powder. General U. S. Grant deployed the weapon in 1847 to fire at native forces defending Mexico City. It was ineffective then; today was no different. The fuse did not burn properly and failed to ignite the powder. Arreola threw his hat to the ground in disgust. He slapped the sides of his head and cursed. *Pendejo. Cabrón. Hijo de puta.*

One American trooper stood guard at the garrison gate, and one stood guard at the corral; both were huddled under horse blankets, asleep. Arreola's men breached the corral fence and rode among the trooper's horses, slashing at them with their quirts. Three of the cavalry tents were set ablaze. The night winds increased the intensity of the fire and ignited the horses' fodder. Most of the troopers had never been under a night attack, and their panic fed the chaos.

The fight was brief. Neither undisciplined raiders nor sleepy troopers were effective marksmen in the dark, especially in the midst of stampeding horses. The raiders retreated southward into Mexico, driving almost fifty of the garrison's seventy-five horses ahead of them. Three troopers and two civilians died in the attack. None of General Arreola's raiders suffered serious injuries.

The officer in charge of the garrison was inexperienced. After the raid, he wandered about bootless in a cloud of uncertainty, searching for the bugler. He failed to mount a retaliatory pursuit force.

White Oaks
Joe was excited. He left Fort Stanton well before daylight. "Get

as many miles behind me as I can while it's still in the cool of the day." His gelding was lathered when the horse and rider reached White Oaks.

"Gonna take twenty head down to Carrizozo," he told Sam. "Chapman will have a cattle car waiting for us. We'll get forty more head at a siding . . . then get the rest in El Paso."

"Damn," Sam said when Joe explained the plans. "We gonna take the train all the way to El Paso? You know, we'll have a hundred head all together. I don't reckon I've ever seen a herd that size. And you think we'll have enough time to see El Paso after we get the horses out to the garrison? Maybe Ciudad Juárez."

"Wouldn't be a bit surprised," Joe said. "I'll see what I can do. I saw them places . . . 'course it was pretty far away—just looked like a big town, that's all." He didn't see any need to tell that Chapman was running the whole show. Big brothers can be like that sometimes.

The next morning they turned the calf into the pasture with the milk cow and fed the chickens extra grain. "Might be a week or more until we get back," Joe told Sam as they loped down the trail toward Carrizozo, twenty head of horses moving smoothly ahead of them.

Just as Chapman said, a cattle car was waiting. The brothers loaded the horses and partitioned off an area for their horses and themselves. Coal smoke from the engine swept through the car as Sam, happily peering between the slats, watched the desert sweep by.

Oscura

Life-changing events can be as monumental as a meteor crashing into the earth, changing the climate and obliterating the dinosaurs. Or as simple as the brazenness of a hungry cat.

The train from Carrizozo to El Paso was made up of a steam

locomotive, one passenger car, three cattle cars, two ore cars, and a caboose. Every Tuesday and Saturday, it made a 325-mile round trip from the mines at Ancho to the El Paso main yard. The engineer, George Powell, took pride in not having missed but three days' work in five years. The fireman-brakeman, Oliver Tomshack, was almost as dependable, excluding the three weeks in the hottest part of the summer that he devoted to the consumption of tequila and rutting with a black woman over in Silver City. The two men harbored an intense dislike for the other and spoke only when necessary.

Southbound, the train was scheduled at Oscura at 9:08 in the morning.

Chapman, Tollafson, Evans, and forty head of horses spent the night five miles to the east at Rocky Springs in the edge of the Godfrey Hills. The palisades rose up behind them like hooded women, their cloaks etched with 1,000-year-old Mogollon petroglyphs and more recent Spanish conquistadors' crosses. The barren peaks stood and witnessed the unchanging desert for ten thousand years without shifting their position.

Chapman ran a rawhide *riata* between two trees, and the riders tied their horses for the night. Tired after a long day's ride, the men unrolled their tarps and bedded, the purple night sky a blanket. "Get up 'fore daylight, have the horses at the Oscura siding way before the train is due," Chapman said.

The smoke from their cook fire dwindled, and only a faint scent drifted toward the apex predator crouching a hundred yards away behind a volcanic rock.

The 250-pound jaguar stood just less than thirty inches at the shoulders. His yellowish coat with the tan rosette spots perfectly camouflaged him in the scrub brush and brown rocks. He was powerfully built, extremely aggressive, and solitary. For eight years, he controlled fifty square miles of the mountain range. He followed the men and the horses across the mountains yesterday afternoon. Although he recognized the horsemen as natural enemies, he had taken horses from a herd before; the men were more a nuisance than a danger.

A three-year-old mare grazed toward the rocky outcrop where the big cat waited. The horse stopped and sampled the air: her brain failed to correctly categorize the scent of the jaguar. Without dislodging a single stone or a particle of dirt, the cat leaped from the boulder and took the horse to the ground. There was a brief struggle. The horse squealed once before the jaguar crushed her skull.

The cowboys scrambled to their feet, levering cartridges into their rifles. Terrified by the screams of the mare, thirty-nine horses stampeded.

It took Chapman and the two other riders until sundown to round up the panicked horses.

At Oscura, the train pulled onto the siding, connected to the empty cattle car, and waited thirty minutes. Powell stood beside the engine and checked his watch each five minutes. "Well, hell," he said, "we're running a railroad here. Ain't gonna wait on some cowboy to load a bunch of nags." Finally, Tomshack opened the switch, and the train chugged out of the siding southward toward El Paso.

El Paso

Joe was lost. He stood in the El Paso rail yard and watched the train disappear northward toward Ancho. He had no idea what to do. He depended on Chapman, and when the twenty horses were unloaded at the stockyards, he stood by the pen fence trying to figure out what to do next.

Sam was in awe of everything. He'd never seen a town as large as the rail yard. Now he could see the city lights ran far beyond the cattle pens. "Believe I'll walk down yonder toward that café, see if I can get a cup of coffee." Miserable, Joe watched his brother walk down a stock alley toward a small frame building. This was Saturday night, and it would be Tuesday before the train came back. Mama and Chapman were counting on him. Here he sat like a knot on a log; he'd never felt so lost in his life. He rolled a cigarette and looked into the distance.

Thirty minutes later, Sam came back up the alley; he had the rolling, bowlegged walk of a man that spent more time horseback than afoot. "Feller down at the café said we ought to go over into Ciudad Juárez," Sam said. "See what a Saturday night looked like up real close. Said we could pen the horses here and wait till the Tuesday train. Said we could—"

"Shut up," Joe said. "We ain't got no business over there. Mama didn't send us down here to go 'cross the river whoring around. What in the hell is wrong with you? You crazy?"

Sam frowned. "I wadn't saying we ought to, I was just telling you what the man—"

Joe pointed at Sam, "Well, I'll tell you what we're gonna do. We gonna bed down with these horses. Come daylight, we gonna head west toward East Portrillo Garrison. Chapman said it wadn't more than forty miles. We'll just do this ourselves. Come back on Tuesday and help Chapman with his bunch."

This was not what Sam wanted to hear. He pushed his sweat-stained, black hat back on his forehead. "Shucks, Joe, looks like we could just go across for a—"

Joe had left his saddle hanging from the loading gate, now he propped it against a bale of hay and used it as a pillow. "Only place you're goin' tonight is bed. Now shut up."

Sam grumbled something unintelligible. He lay in the straw, arms folded across his chest. Within minutes, Joe snored. Sam stood and brushed the chaff from his shirt.

Ciudad Juárez

Shadrach leaned against the door frame of the *Buen Momento,* thumbs hooked behind his gun belt. It was almost two in the morning, and the streets were emptying of all but the drunkest of the Saturday night crowd, most of them stone broke. Three soldiers from Fort Bliss sat inside at a rickety table. An almost empty bottle of watered-down tequila had fallen to the floor, and the last drops of the evil smelling liquid were soaking into the dirt.

He watched them earlier in the evening as they combined their money so that the older trooper, a sergeant, could visit the emaciated woman lying on the filthy blanket behind the darkened doorway. They were broke; most of his customers that night were broke before midnight. This had not been a profitable night, and Belzora would accuse him of spending his money on the women down at the end of *Tercera Calle.* Her tongue was becoming sharper, and she was becoming a burden. He just might pitch her in the river.

A cowboy, black hat ringed with salt stains, came from a dimly lighted alley. A *vaquero Americano* by himself on these Ciudad Juárez streets was unusual. Usually, they traveled in small packs like dogs and were dangerous when drunk. But this one—this one seemed like a bird on the ground—except he was a cowboy.

Shadrach whistled, caught the man's attention, motioned to him. *"Hola."*

The cowboy pressed his thumb against his chest. "Me? You mean me?"

The Mexican nodded, and the cowboy crossed the street. "Buy you a drink?" Shadrach's English was barely understandable, but he made a universal sign of drinking by putting his extended thumb against his lips and tilting his head. The cowboy understood and smiled.

The two men—the earless Mexican and the adventuresome cowboy—sat at a dirty table well removed from the Fort Bliss troopers. Shadrach looked toward the bar and nodded.

The saloon smelled of beer and tobacco smoke. Kerosene lamps. Sweat. Sour. Something unidentifiable and rancid. A heavily-rouged woman with flowing, black hair brought a partially-empty bottle of tequila and two smudged glasses. The cowboy looked at the woman's low-cut blouse and heavy bosom and thought there was no way to compare the excitement of this place to White Oaks. She smiled and revealed rotten teeth.

Shadrach poured two drinks. At first, the cowboy did not understand when the Mexican lifted his glass, but when the man nodded and extended his glass further across the table, he did the same, and the glasses clinked together.

In his broken English, Shadrach talked with the cowboy. "I'm thinking you are a successful rancher and brought a large herd of cattle to the El Paso market. Probably are the *jefe* over many *vaqueros*. And you are a very wealthy man."

The fiery liquid set the cowboy's throat ablaze; he sputtered, his eyes awash. "Horses," he said and took another sip. "We've brought horses down to sell to the army."

"Fort Bliss?' the Mexican asked. "I have friends at Fort Bliss. I've sold many horses to the men at that fort."

"No. We're taking our horses over to the garrison at East Portrillo. Gonna take some tomorrow and some more on Tuesday."

The Mexican nodded and poured the cowboy another drink. "There are many of you?"

"Right now? Just two." He drained the first shot. "Just me and my brother, Joe. Chapman and some of his boys will be here next week."

The cowboy leaned across the table and extended his hand. "My name is Sam."

The Mexican leaned toward the cowboy, shook his hand, and

refilled his glass. "Chapman? You know Chapman? American *vaquero,* Chapman?"

Sam emptied the glass in one gulp. He propped his elbows against the table and rested his chin against his palms. "Yeah. Well, I don't know him much. Joe knows him real good. He's been runnin' couple of ranches me and my brother own."

Shadrach sat back in his chair and studied this new information. "Chapman and I were *amigos.* And Quezada. You know Quezada? We were friends also. Drank together at Fort Bliss."

"You did? Reckon you know he's dead. Dead and buried."

The Mexican furrowed his brow. "No! He was a very good man. We liked each other much. Dead . . . that's hard to understand."

"Been dead some more than a year. Said he got shot at Bliss. Never got over it. Some kinda robbery, they say."

Shadrach lowered his head, shook it slowly, face grimaced in sorrow. "But Chapman. He is still alive?"

The cowboy tilted the empty bottle against his lips. "Yeah. Puts in a day's work every time the sun comes up. Stays mostly at our ranch up at Fort Stanton. Foreman there. Pretty soon, he's goin' to Roswell. Got a little spread at Bitter Lakes. Me and Joe might even give 'im a few head just to get 'im started."

Eyes shadowed by his hat, Shadrach said, " 'Spect man like you travels with many pesos in his pocket? Rich *gringo,* owner of much cattle."

The American did not know the consequences of his braggadocio answer. "Some folks would think so. Carry enough to buy 'bout anything I want." He giggled and felt proud of his new position in life: a man that traveled Ciudad Juárez in the darkness, a man who had strangers buying tequila for him, a man more than capable of looking after himself.

Shadrach ran his hand along his back sheath, assuring himself the knife was still there. "We were talking about Chapman. He didn't get shot?"

"Nah. Just Quezada. In the back. Never got over it, I reckon."

"Then, if I wanted to visit Chapman, he would be at this place you name—Roswell?"

The cowboy's stomach rolled like a dog turning around and around before he lies down. "Yeah. You miss 'im at Fort Stanton, he will done be gone to Roswell, I reckon. We'll have done let him go."

"Do you know the Soto brothers at Las Cruces? They have a nephew called Alberto. They are known to steal cattle. Very bad men. We would call them *banditos*. You, I think, call them rustlers."

Sam slid to the tabletop, rested his head, one eye making a desperate attempt to focus on the earless Mexican. "No. Chapman might, maybe . . . I'll . . ."

It was nearing daylight, and the morning birds were chirping— encouraging the sun to break the horizon. An occasional window warmed with the dull glow of a kerosene lamp. Behind the cantinas, a pig farmer poured swill into a tub sitting on his ground sled and then wandered down the alley to the next slop bucket.

Shadrach was in a particularly foul mood. He sat on the edge of the bed and held one leg stiffly out in front. Belzora straddled his leg, grasped his boot, and pulled. He never owned socks, and the boot came loose with a sucking sound. She repeated her stance, and the second boot loosened.

"I do not understand," Shadrach said. "Why do *gringos* believe it necessary to lie? I have a man tonight who bragged about his wealth, said he would buy anything he wanted. You know what he had in his pockets? A rusty knife. A worn-out pocket knife and two American coins. Almost nothing." He shook his head in disgust.

Belzora left the room and returned with a pan of water. She

washed the filth from Shadrach's feet. "I've known men like that," she said. "Sometime they are stupid. Sometime they want to seem more than they are."

Shadrach nodded. "This was such a man," he said. "He died for this. Can you believe that a man died for a hat, an old black hat with sweat stains? This hat." He removed the hat from his head and gave it to Belzoria. "When you start the fire for breakfast, I want you to burn this. And let this be a lesson to you about ever lying to me."

He tumbled over onto the center of the bed, closed his eyes, and slept as a baby with a full stomach of warm milk.

Joe knew something wasn't right before he even opened his eyes. He rolled to his side to wake his brother. It was just getting light, and Sam was gone.

Oscura

"Well, there you are," Chapman said. "On account of one dumb mare and a hungry mountain lion, we've missed the train. Here we are out in the middle of nowhere." He counted the days off on his fingers. "Take us a day to get back to the ranch. That would make it Sunday evening. Then we'd have to turn right around and leave to get here on Tuesday morning. Wear the dang horses to a frazzle."

Tollafson nodded. "Yeah. And our asses, too."

Chapman had put a bullet into the big cat's skull and one behind a front leg, and now the lanky carcass hung from a pine tree, skinned.

Evans washed the hide in a pool of water, spread it across a boulder, and scoured away the bits of flesh and fat. "Knew my old trapping skills would be worthwhile someday," he said. "I'll rub the cat's brains into it pretty good. Hang it up where nothing can get to it. Pick it up on the way back. Make a rug you'll really be proud of."

"Still a pretty sorry trade for a dead mare and missing the train," Chapman grumbled.

That afternoon, Tollafson killed a pronghorn antelope yearling. "Kinda give us something to go with them beans and wore-out coffee grounds," he bragged.

They kept a closer watch over their horse herd. On Tuesday, Chapman rode up the train tracks and flagged down the southbound freight.

"Hung in an extra car this morning just in case you decided to show up today," the engineer said. "Bet them two green cowboys from White Oaks will be glad to see you. They was looking like lost pups when I left them the other day."

They loaded the forty horses, climbed into the passenger car, and—three days late—left for El Paso.

El Paso

When they unloaded, two La Mesilla riders were waiting, while the third held their forty-horse herd penned at a ranch near the river. Chapman and his men searched the rail stockyard and found the twenty White Oaks ranch's horses, a large overlapping WO burned into the right flank of each.

Chapman found the cattle pen boss, the man who was in charge—when they came and when they left—of all livestock at the yard. He hadn't seen but one of the White Oaks cowboys since early Sunday morning. "Said his name was Joe. Had brung some horses down for the garrison out west of here. Told me he was looking for his brother.

"Wait a minute," he said. "Man that cooks down at the café told me a young cowboy come in 'fore ten on Saturday night. Said the man was lookin for something to do. Cook asked him if he'd ever been in Mexico. Kid said no. Cook told him if he ever got grown, he ought to try it."

The Fort Stanton Ranch

Angalee and Muñoz had searched for a cow and calf but had no luck. Felipe told them his bones felt like a rain was coming, and they wanted the newborn calf in the barn. The mama cow had a different idea and had hidden in a salt-cedar thicket along the river, chewing her cud and slowly blinking her large eyes as the riders searched a nearby arroyo.

"You think they'll be back this afternoon? Or tomorrow?" Angalee asked as she scooped feed into a wooden trough for the two horses.

"Way too early," Muñoz said. "If everybody got there Saturday, they'd have got the horses over to the garrison on Sunday. Probably took a day to settle up. Day back to El Paso. That's just if everything went right, and most of the time it doesn't. I'd bet on Saturday. If then."

Mexico

Under a moonless sky, Guillermo Arreola's cannoniers disassembled the 12-pounder and hauled it back to the guerrilla's camp. The next day, they removed the charge, cleaned the piece, reloaded, and fired the weapon. There was a tremendous eruption of fire from the muzzle. Eight hundred yards away, a mesquite tree blew up in a cloud of leaves, splinters, and a brown thrasher's nest. The cannoniers were overjoyed; the thrasher flew in erratic circles above her demolished nest.

El Paso

"Okay, boys," Chapman said. "This is the way it is: we've got two cowboys missing, and neither one of them knows his ass from a hole in the ground when it comes to a town size of El Paso or Ciudad Juárez. I'm guessing here's what took place. One of them, probably Sam, might have left out of here sometime Saturday night, and the other one Sunday morning.

Sounds like Sam went across the river, and Joe went to hunt for him. If they did, and they're not back by now, they're probably not coming back in one piece. You can bet on that."

"You think they ain't got no more sense than that?" Evans asked.

Chapman shook his head. "I'd have thought Joe would have known better. Don't know much about Sam."

"I was with a bunch that got into it once down here. Followed some stolen horses back south of the border," Tollafson said. "We had a hell'va time. Like not to have got out of there alive. Sheriff and 'bout ten deputies come across and got us outta jail. But them was different times. Hear they don't do that now. Things have changed. Ain't none of that back and forth stuff now." He shook his head. "Man gets in trouble over there now, he's just fell in the shit far as the county sheriff is concerned."

"Well, that's where we'll start, anyway," Chapman said. "Maybe he knows something."

"Yeah," Evans said, "he'll know a whole lot more than we do. Bet your boots on that."

The El Paso County sheriff's office was an unimpressive, two-story, brick building with the jail on the top floor and offices and holding cells on the ground floor. Sheriff Memphis Stottlemeyer was a large man, had broad shoulders, and wore a three-piece suit with a cutaway coat. His foul disposition was legendary. He wore two pistols and was deadly with either.

"Dammit, you're the second man that's come in here asking the same question," the sheriff said. "What in the hell is the matter with you cowboys? You come in here from up the river acting like you are in a church town full of Baptists. Don't you know a stranger can't just go wandering around here by hisself? There's folks here in this town right here that'll cut a man's throat just for his hat."

Chapman had gone into the sheriff's office by himself. Tollafson, Evans, and the La Mesilla riders waited outside in the shade of the building. "Hate to be of trouble to you. But these two fellers I'm looking for are about my age, maybe a little younger, and . . . well, they're pretty green. Raised up north here round White Oaks. Hadn't been around much."

Stottlemeyer sat on the edge of his desk, rifling through arrest warrants. "Yeah, I know the kind," he said. "Greener than goose shit. First thing they do is get drunk. Then they go across the river to have a little fun. But what they find ain't fun. Next time anybody sees them—if they're seen at all—dogs are feeding on them in an alley."

"Naw, these men wouldn't do that, they're—"

The sheriff stood and pulled a watch from his vest pocket, made a great show of winding the timepiece. "I'm running outta time with you. Got to go eat dinner over at the hotel. Meeting a rancher that's got a big problem with somebody cutting his fence." He slipped the watch back into his pocket and adjusted the gold chain and heavy fob. "These men, are they brothers?"

"Yes, sir. They are. You seen them?"

"Might. Where you from, son?"

"Little place up north of here. Fort Stanton."

Stottlemeyer sat back on the edge of the desk. "Fort Stanton, huh? You happen to know a man up there that owns a large ranch? Big rascal 'bout my size. Man's probably around sixty . . . maybe as much as seventy. Named Quezada."

"Yes, sir. Used to work for him. He died a while back."

The sheriff stared at Chapman. "Died. The hell you say. You ain't yarning me, are you?"

"No. I helped bury him on a hill back from the Slash Q headquarters. I'm telling you the truth."

Sheriff Stottlemeyer went behind his desk and sat in a wooden swivel chair. He opened a desk drawer, rummaged around, and pulled out a faded photograph. He looked at it briefly before blowing the dust away from the faded image. Chapman could see four young men. A bearded man sat in a chair; the three others, smooth shaven and hatless, stood behind him. They wore dark coats and white shirts and string ties. Printing at the bottom of the photograph read: *Best Photographer Wichita Kansas.*

"Damn salty looking bunch, ain't they? That's Quezada with the beard. Me on the left. Virgil and Morgan is the two other men. Earps. I hear that Virgil got shot up, and I know for a fact that Morgan is dead. Hell, I don't know how I'm still alive. Now you tell me Quezada is dead. I figured he'd way outlive us all. He was a damn stem-winder, I'll tell you that." He shoved the picture back in the drawer. "Just shows you never can tell."

Chapman waited. It was clear things moved at the sheriff's pace.

Sheriff Stottlemeyer took a ring of heavy keys from a wooden cabinet. "We got a law about carrying saddle guns down the street here in El Paso. 'Bout every man carries some kind of pistol in his pocket or hung from his belt. But, hell, most of them can't hit their own shadow. And you just can't walk down the street carrying a loaded rifle. For every man here in Texas that's been killed by a pistol, bet there's been a dozen killed with a saddle gun. Or a shotgun. Damn shotguns scare me. Everybody ought to be scared of a man that'll carry a scatter-gun.

"Believe I've got your cowboy. Ain't got no holes in him or nothing."

"You got Joe and Sam locked up? Here? They're okay?"

"Never said that. Don't know about the other one. But Joe is locked up in the back. Deputy found him the other night walking down the street, going in and out of saloons, carrying a saddle gun. Hunting his brother. Cost you five dollars to get him out."

The men sat in a German saloon, glasses of beer and a plate of boiled eggs and crackers on the table. "Just woke up and he was gone," Joe said, then snapped his fingers. "Gone just like that. He'd left his gun, his horse . . . didn't have nothing except the clothes on his back. Plumb silly. Don't know what in the heck he was thinking."

"And you looked pretty much everywhere here in town?" Chapman asked.

Joe nodded. "Did till that danged deputy come up on me. First thing I knew my rifle was on the sidewalk and my arm was twisted up behind my back. You pretty much know the rest of it. I believe I'd have found him by now if I hadn't been in that stinking cell." His lower lip quivered like a little boy that's stubbed his toe. He wiped his nose on his shirt cuff. "Chapman, I . . . I ain't got no idea where he's at."

"I . . . I hung out down here when I was young and didn't have any damn sense," Evans said. "Dad had a little spread over just south of Fabens. Me and my brothers would come over here when we could get away from Dad. First thing we'd do was go cross the river to Ciudad Juárez. There was four of us. Thought we was tough. Growed up rasslin' steers and ridin' buckin' horses. We done all right as long as we stayed together. But if anybody strayed off by theirselves, wadn't no end to the trouble he could get in. And I mean bad trouble."

"You think that's where he went?" Chapman asked.

Evans shrugged. "It's what I'd have done. 'Course, I don't even know the feller. But I was full of piss and vinegar, and I'd have done it in a heartbeat."

"We'll go back to the stockyard and get our horses. Go up the river a little bit outta town and cross." Chapman drew a crude map in the dirt. "Damn sure carry our saddle guns. Reckon long as we stay outta town, the sheriff won't give a hoot. We get on the other side, we'll sure stay together."

The riders saddled their horses and rode up the river in the darkness, found a sandbar, and crossed. They rode along the road, the horses' hooves kicking up little ghosts of dust that disappeared in the night. "Look like a bunch of cowboys lookin' for trouble," Tollafson joked, then added, "and hoping they don't find it."

Chapman turned to Joe. "You stay with me. I'm not going back to Fort Stanton and have to tell Angalee that I've lost both her boys."

Ciudad Juárez
It had been a long night for Shadrach. There had been two fights in the whorehouse—the worst kind: women. He'd separated the first two women and kicked the ugliest out the back door into the alley but not before she tore the buttons from his shirt and scratched his face. If she showed up again, he'd break her arms and stuff her head first into a rain barrel. The second fight was over a four-peso, skinny drunk. More hair pulling. More scratching. This time he kept his distance until the women tired. Because he wanted them to come to work tomorrow night, he gave both two pesos and sent them home.

He and one of the bouncers from a competitor's house of ill repute stood at the edge of the street, smoking. Shadrach did not find it amusing when the man laughed and called him a *coño;* asked if he needed help in controlling his house.

At the sound of horses, both men turned and looked along the street. People mostly walked in the street this time of night, and there were no freight wagons or buggies. Now eight riders came toward them, filling the narrow roadway. Both Mexicans stepped back into the shadows and ground their cigarettes into the dust.

The riders dismounted, tied their horses, and talked briefly. They pulled their saddle guns from the leather scabbards and divided into two groups. They worked both sides of the street. Two stood guard while two went inside the saloons and whorehouses. No one claimed to have seen Sam or anyone that resembled him.

Shadrach noted the similarities of Sam and one of the riders. That would be Joe, Sam's brother, he thought. The Mexican retreated down the alley and faded into the maze of twisting streets.

In less than an hour, the riders completed the search. They gathered and discussed the futility of their hunt. Joe kept his head lowered and didn't contribute to the discussion. He was way outside wherever he was supposed to be and wished neither he nor Sam had ever left White Oaks.

Eventually, Chapman and the others mounted and retraced their route back to the sandbar crossing. The front-yard cooking fires along the way were dying for the night, leaving only thin plumes of almost translucent smoke. Occasionally a dog came to the edge of the street and barked, voice uncertain, barely threatening. A small boy came from a ramshackle house and relieved himself in the dust while watching the horsemen. He gave a tentative wave with the unoccupied hand. It was unacknowledged in the darkness.

El Paso

Sheriff Stottlemeyer sat in the lobby of the Pierson Hotel and looked down Kansas Street. His shoulders drooped, and he grimaced at the sight of Chapman waiting for the streetcar to pass so he and his men could cross the street. "Look there, Deputy," he said. "We'll be lucky if we can get these boys outta town 'fore there's a shootin'. They ain't got no more sense than to think they are goin' to find that man's brother."

Joe and the Slash Q riders sat on the broad front porch while Chapman came inside.

"Sit down here with us," Stottlemeyer said. "I'll get Francine to bring you a cup of coffee. Maybe some eggs."

Chapman smiled and shook his head. "Ain't got time, but I appreciate that. Just wanted you to know we're gonna look for Sam on this side of the river today. We don't find him, we'll go back to Ciudad Juárez tonight. Hate to have to do that; just wanted you to know."

Stottlemeyer looked up at the rangy cowboy standing in front of him. Unshaven. Bloodshot eyes. Tired. Edgy. "Son, let me tell you something. I wouldn't even bother with you if you weren't a friend of Quezada," the lawman said. "You see that mule pullin' that streetcar? He ain't got no choice. But you're different, and you're wasting your time. And mine. Had my boys look around last night. Nothing. If they didn't find anything, you ain't gonna find anything. I ain't telling you how to run your business, but if I was you, I'd deliver them damn horses and git on back up the river where you belong. This ain't no place for you. 'Specially over across the river at night—don't care how tough you are; they're tougher over there on that side."

The sheriff drained his cup and raised it above his head. Francine brought a cup of fresh coffee and carried the empty away. "I know you want to find that other feller. That you somehow feel responsible and stuff like that. But look at it this way. You stand to lose more than just one man. I'll feel a lot better when you get your boys outta town. You hear what I'm sayin?"

Chapman leaned across the table and shook the lawman's hand. "I thank you, Mr. Stottlemeyer. Thank you for your advice. But . . . I . . . I ain't really got no choice. So, we'll see you later. No, take that back, hope we don't."

Stottlemeyer pulled a thin black cigar from his coat pocket and did a ceremonial routine of cutting the end off, moistening the outside, then lighting it with a wooden match. He took a deep pull. Smoke drifted lazily from his nose. "I'm gonna tell you something else. I'm telling you 'cause you would go back over there whether I told you or not. Deputy talked to a cavalry-man from Bliss this morning. Man said he saw a *gringo* at a joint over in Ciudad Juárez the other night. Young man in a black hat. Bad thing about it is he was so drunk he ain't got no idea which joint it was."

Chapman tipped his hat. "I appreciate you, Sheriff."

While it was daylight, Chapman used the same routine to search the bawdy houses and saloons in El Paso as he used in Ciudad Juárez, except without carrying saddle guns. Nothing. No bartenders, no women, nobody had seen a man matching Sam's description.

Ciudad Juárez

Dark came, and they entered the Mexican town at the same point as the night before. Eight riders armed with pistols and each carrying a saddle gun across the pommel of their saddles presented a show of force.

The streets were breathing, coming alive with the night denizens.

Although his hearing was impaired, Shadrach was not an easy man to surprise. He knew what kind of humans haunted the streets after the sun slid below the crest of the barren mountains to the west. He knew because he made a living off those people, the same way the white-winged vampire bats drained the blood from the unwary cow.

He watched from the end of the street. The riders split into two groups just as they'd previously done. But tonight, two cowboys walked the alleys behind the buildings, a third went inside, and the fourth stood at the front door with his rifle resting in the crook of his arm. The Slash Q riders worked their way down the street toward him, methodically checking each building.

A grove of cottonwood trees lined the bank along the river. When the riders were a block away, Shadrach went around the building and hid in the underbrush, the river raggedly gurgling behind him. If they got too close, he would slip into the sluggish river and cross into El Paso. If not, and after they called the search to an end, he would emerge from the darkness like a black cat hunting a place to hide.

Shadrach identified Chapman; he was tall, and the riders apparently took their orders from him. He would remember the *vaquero*, the way he walked, the way he carried himself. In the future and when the cowboy was alone, he would deal with him. Tonight, he would hide and wait for another day. He savored waiting for another day. It was a satisfying thought. It gave him more time to plan. It was like waiting for a drink of water after crossing the desert and then feeling the flowing coolness and the satisfaction.

An hour after midnight, the riders surrendered their battle. "He's not here, Joe," Chapman said. "This is twice we've pretty much turned this town upside down. We're not gonna find Sam. I'm awful sorry."

Joe slumped in the saddle, chin against his chest. "What am I gonna tell our mother? He's my younger brother. Shit, I was supposed to look after him. What kind of man does that make me?"

Chapman patted Joe's shoulder. "We'll figure something out. We'll just do the best we can for right now. We'll look some more later, after we've delivered the horses."

Mexico Border Land

A hundred head of horses crossing the desert raises a considerable cloud of dust. The Slash Q men left El Paso going westward toward the garrison. Water, Clark's Cradle, lay twenty miles ahead. A spring rose out of the rocks and settled into a tepid, alkaline pool. If it had been any worse, the horses couldn't have drunk it; if it had been any better, the desert burros and stray cattle would have drained it. Or a rancher would have set up a headquarters near it. 'Course the Mexican bandits would have loved that—always good for a hungry man to know where his next meal was coming from. Or know where another man is pasturing his stock.

Chapman was happy with small blessings. And any watering place in the desert is a blessing.

Star Valley, Wyoming

It wasn't that she didn't want to marry—it was just she didn't want to marry Rulon.

Star Valley lay between the Salt River Range in western Wyoming and the Webster Range of eastern Idaho. The Salt, the Greys, and the Snake Rivers coursed the valley. Shoshone Indians hunted there until the nineteenth century. Then the bearded men with round brim hats and many wives ran them out.

Initially, the Church of Jesus Christ of Latter-Day Saints proclaimed the area as the Star of All Valleys. Later the name was shortened after the bitter winters of the late 1880s, when as much as four feet of snow fell within a two-day period; some called it Starve Valley.

Rulon was fifty-five; Zella had just crossed the cusp of womanhood. The man had five wives, weepy-eyed and prone to staring vacantly, and he wanted Zella to be the sixth. Her father thought Rulon would make a fine husband—after all, he owned a grist mill and was a carpenter of sorts—and the father believed his daughter would learn from the sister wives.

Zella wanted nothing to do with the old man. "Smells worse than a sick goat," she told her mother. She'd seen how he abused his livestock. His wives seldom smiled and were pregnant most of the time. She thought his children the ugliest in the valley: blond-haired and freckled, snotty noses, weak-eyed. She didn't want him as a husband, didn't want to bear his children, didn't want to look at him.

She was a strong-willed woman: defiant enough to take three of her father's horses, two for riding and one for selling. It took all summer to reach Cheyenne. She taught school in a one-room schoolhouse, and when the spring thaws came she continued southward toward Denver. She was eighteen.

It was easy to get a job teaching in the small-town schools. In the next two years, she worked in Colorado Springs and Pueblo. In the fourth year of her freedom, she clerked at a dry goods store in Walsenburg.

She met a rancher, a widower, who took a fancy to her. But the treelessness and barrenness of the eastern Colorado Plains reminded her of the Star Valley. The scattered towns gave this part of the country an isolated feel, a feel of hunger, a feel of desperation. She wanted more.

Had she been a man, she would have been called a saddle tramp. She thought of herself as having an itching foot. She simply wanted to see what was over the next ridge or around the next curve.

Years after escaping Rulon and his snotty-nosed children, Zella, still single and virginity intact, arrived in the part of New Mexico where the Southern Plains meets the high Chihuahuan Desert. In this Valley of the Pecos her foot stopped itching.

She dusted off her worn copy of *The Blue Back Speller* and a tattered copy of *McGuffey's Eclectic Primer*, fudged some about her educational background, and convinced the Chaves County school board she was times-over qualified to teach.

East Portrillo Garrison

Still two miles east of the garrison, the horse herd smelled the water, tossed their heads, and broke into a trot.

A sentry glassed the scrub-covered plains and alerted the garrison commanding officer. "They're coming. Must be a thousand of them."

Chapman and Joe rode in front of the herd. The other riders rode flank or drag, their knotted kerchiefs pulled over their mouths and noses. The rising dust caked in the corners of their eyes. Every man coughed frequently, hawked and spit dust-ingrained phlegm. Twice in the last ten miles, Tollafson halted his horse, dismounted, and wiped sand from the animal's nostrils.

The sun was setting, color and size magnified by the swirling dust. Five troopers rode out from the garrison, their silhouettes coronated by the fierceness and passion of the dying sun.

The camp was a mishmash of wooden corrals, wire fences, poorly constructed barracks, and ragged tents. The officer in charge met them at the edge of the parade ground, his troopers standing behind in a ragged formation. "I'm Captain Augustus Herrman Zimmerlee. In the absence of the contracting officer, I will represent the U. S. government."

Eyes raw from the clouds of sand and dust, Chapman surveyed the disarrayed camp. "Don't reckon you all aim to be here very long?"

"Just long enough to get the damned Mexicans under control," the officer replied.

Chapman looked at the charred tents and disrepair of the horse lots. "At the rate you're going, looks like that might be a long time."

"You may see that as humorous," the officer said, lips tightened into a thin line.

"No, just the truth," Chapman replied.

Captain Zimmerlee stared at Chapman. He'd always thought his stare was one of the best parts of his leadership ability—first thing I learned at West Point, he'd told his wife. But it didn't work today, and he was sorry that he'd tried it with this Slash Q rider. There was something about Chapman he found unsettling. Stress. He decided it was stress—mixed with irritation.

"You going to do the counting and sign our receipt or we gotta wait till somebody else gets here?" Chapman asked. All his men were tired, dusty, dry, and irritable. The officer failed to take this into consideration and did not have the common courtesy to offer water to the men or their horses—a supreme breach of etiquette in this desert country. It infuriated Chapman.

"I have that authority," Captain Zimmerlee said. "Did you bring the proper papers with you?"

"Yeah, I did. While I'm getting them outta my saddlebags, the boys here are gonna water their horses. And if you got any drinking water for them—" he let the last part of the sentence hang.

"I'll have my troopers water them. We are kinda particular 'bout civilians within our compound. The cook will bring water for your men."

Chapman took the papers from his saddlebags. They were wrinkled, sand-covered, and smelled of a sweaty horse.

Zimmerlee looked at them and blew the grit away. He made a great show of reading all the words, pausing frequently to stroke his scraggly chin whiskers. "You got a pencil?" he asked Chapman.

"No. I'm too damn ignorant to carry any such item. I figured you had about a hundred, being's how you are so damn smart and the army has trusted you to such a high position—heading up an outfit out in this important bit of our country and all."

Zimmerlee didn't want to get in a pissing contest. He struggled to maintain honor after the Mexican raiders stole the horses during their first raid. Now, this rangy cowboy was making him look ridiculous. He was losing respect—maybe he had already lost.

"I accept the horses, and the count is accurate," the captain said. "Here's your receipt with my official signature."

"Appreciate that," Chapman said. "But what we'd druther have is our money. Your signature won't buy beans and blankets. You are prepared to pay, aren't you?"

"I . . . uh . . . I don't have those funds available. Currently, I mean. A courier will make payment to you. He will be from Fort Bliss, and when they—headquarters at Fort Bliss—receive my approval, it will be taken care of as soon as possible. In fact, I will dispatch a messenger tonight."

"You don't have the funds? You knew we were coming, and now you tell me you can't pay for the horses." Chapman leaned into the captain. "I gotta good mind to take the horses back with me in the morning. No, that isn't right. Just turn around and leave now. Your approval don't mean diddly-squat to me. Can't buy a damn thing with 'your approval.' You know what I'm saying?"

The officer took a half step backward. "There's no reason for you to raise your voice. There are enlisted men present. Disrespect is not acceptable."

Chapman stepped forward and put two fingers against the officer's chest. "You will send a messenger to Fort Bliss tonight. No, right now. If by noon tomorrow our money is not waiting for us at the cattlemen's office at the El Paso train yards, we'll be back for the horses. And you don't want us to have to do that. I don't have any fear of this raggedy-ass bunch of soldiers. If I have to do that, you can explain to whoever you explain things to why you are riding stick horses."

"Yes. I believe that will be the appropriate method to handle this." The captain turned to an enlisted man and said, "You will take a message to Fort Bliss. Prepare your mount, and the message will be waiting. This is the highest priority."

"We'll spread our bedrolls over yonder, on top of that rise," Chapman told his men. "Damn sure wouldn't want to infringe on the goodness of the U. S. cavalry by getting too close to their property. I'll talk to their wrangler later. See if we can put our horses where they can get fodder and maybe some grain. Tell you fellers something. Knowing folks like Captain Zimmerlee is enough to make a man pull for the Indians or the Mexicans— whoever he's fighting.

"We got bacon, beans, bread. Got coffee. Probably more than those troopers have. Not much else man would want. Less it might be a soft bed."

"Or thirty minutes of womanly companionship. Believe I'd skip the bacon and beans for that," Evans said. All but two of the men laughed: Joe was dealing with his conscience and the loss of his brother; Chapman was pissed at Zimmerlee and the reception his men had received.

Three weeks after the first attack, Guillermo Arreola's cannoniers disassembled the 725-pound mountain howitzer. One mule carried the barrel; two carried the carriage and wheels. A fourth mule carried the ammunition. They moved two hours before midnight, crossed a dry creek bed, and followed a sandy wash until they were within a quarter mile of the garrison. They assembled the howitzer, loaded it with a half pound of powder and a spherical shell. The shell would destroy any wooden building by setting it on fire. The second shell, a double canister, would be fired at the troopers who pursued the raiders—if they pursued. At close range with the double canister, the gun was devastating.

Arreola planned to fire on the garrison and then have his horsemen attack from the east, driving the cavalry horses out onto the open prairie. A dozen men would come out of the shallow ravine and fire their rifles into the fort. Any troopers that counterattacked would be killed by the howitzer's second shot.

Tollafson built a fire and cooked. The riders ate and sat watching the fire fade into dully glowing embers. It had been a long day. The distance back to El Paso tomorrow would be the same distance as they covered today, but they would not be eating the dust from a hundred head of horses.

Chapman stood and beat the dust from his pants and shirt with his leather gloves. "I'll go talk with their wrangler about feeding our horses." He had removed his boots and now was having trouble finding the second one in the dark.

Joe scrambled to his feet. "Let me talk with him," he said. "I feel like I ain't done nothing but just hinder folks on this whole trip. Least I can do is hunt him up. Bet I can talk him into some fodder."

"OK," Chapman said. "But if you get into any trouble with the wrangler, come back and let me know. I ain't too popular with them anyway, so I won't have nothing to lose."

Heat lightning quivered in the sky to the west, and the hollow rumble of thunder cohabitated with the night sky.

Joe walked across the prairie toward the dim lights of the garrison. A three-hundred-yard walk; three-hundred-seventy-five steps; just over the crest of a low hill. The die was cast, and the roller was at the mercy of fate.

The Fort Stanton Ranch

"I'm having a hard time waiting. Sitting around doing nothing," Angalee told Muñoz. "Let's ride over to Oscura and meet Chapman and my boys. I've just got a feeling they'll show up tomorrow. They'll be on the northbound from El Paso. There's always an empty cattle car."

"We'll be taking a chance," Muñoz said. "What if they're late? Couple of days late, maybe."

Angalee laughed. "Then we will have taken a long day's ride for nothing. But if I'm right"—she shrugged and smiled—"it'll be worth it."

East Portrillo Garrison

The corral erupted in a ball of fire and intense heat. Sand sprayed skyward; bits of horsehide and bones rose upward, hung at their apogee, then dropped to earth in the midst of the roiling, crippled cavalry mounts. Crazed horses fled the explosion and the licking flames. Near the horse tank, they trampled the lifeless bodies of two men pierced by shards of shrapnel.

At the sound of the cannon, Chapman and the Slash Q riders scrambled to their feet and faced the garrison fire and the mass of panicked horses.

As the fireball rose, the earthshaking pounding of the marauders' horses came toward the cowboys from the east. The raiders were racing toward the fort, a scimitar of horsemen intent on overrunning the confused troopers. Twenty marauders dug their sharply roweled spurs into the sides of their horses and lay low over the necks of their mounts, clutching the reins between their teeth, pistols firing wildly toward the garrison.

★ ★ ★ ★ ★

As the guerrillas came closer, the raging fires lit their faces, and redness danced off their horses.

Evans dropped to one knee and levered a shell into the chamber of his rifle. "They're comin' from behind us," he shouted. "Whatever the hell they are, they're comin.'"

The horsemen veered when they recognized the backlit silhouettes in their path as men. But it was too late. The Slash Q riders fired their rifles, chambered rounds, and fired again. Six of the horsemen died with the first salvo; three more in the second.

What had been a concerted charge evolved into a melee. Riderless horses plunged into the darkness. One continued its charge toward the garrison, a wounded marauder, foot trapped by a heavy wooden stirrup, being dragged beneath the hooves of the panicked animal. A second horse, its rider dead from the first salvo, bolted through the line of cowboys. Tollafson was trampled, and, when he regained his feet, his left arm flopped uselessly at his side. Other horses lay on the ground, thrashing in pain, their high-pitched squeals of agony erupting eerily from the night.

The barrage of bullets was too great, and the guerrillas turned south in panic. The Mexican riflemen guarding the cannon fired into the darkness and killed three of their own horsemen. The canonniers lit the fuse, and the second round, the double canister, roared from the mouth of the howitzer. The Mexicans who survived the hail of bullets from the Slash Q riders and the undisciplined rifle fire from their companions were shredded.

Guillermo Arreola was horrified. He'd buttoned his coat, polished his belt buckle, shined his buttons and medals. He was prepared to accept a gentlemanly surrender from the garrison. Now he had lost most of his cavalry, and what troops that remained were terrified of a counterattack.

Arreola climbed on one of the mules and raced away. The canonniers and the riflemen who guarded the battery fled southward, afoot in the darkness of the desert.

Had an hourglass been upended at the sound of the first explosion and the sand continued to flow through the narrow neck until the sound of the cannoniers' mules disappeared in the distance, there would have been little perceptible difference in the upper chamber.

Dawn. Smoke drifted across the garrison. The acrid stench of burned horsehair was so strong it stung the nostrils of the survivors.

Captain Zimmerlee sent a reconnaissance squad in search of the howitzer; they returned dragging the antiquated weapon through the sand. The garrison's armorer dropped a charge down the barrel, spiked it with wooden staves, and then fired. The barrel split; the gun would never be used in battle again.

The final inventory of deaths in the brief battle: twenty-eight horses, twenty guerrillas, three troopers, and Angalee's oldest son, Joe.

The burial detail dug two mass graves, stripped the guerrillas of weapons, mounded sand over their remains, and then did the same for the horses. The troopers, two killed by undetermined rifle fire and the one killed when the howitzer shell exploded against a grain crib, were buried in separate graves. The company bugler played *Butterfield's Lullaby*, the last notes flattened out across the desert, disappearing into the vast nothingness.

"Although it is not our obligation or custom," Captain Zimmerlee said to Chapman, "we will bury the civilian."

"He had a name. It was Joe. He was one of us. He wouldn't have been killed if you hadn't been such a mule's ass. He would

257

have been with us and not out blundering around in the dark trying to get hay and water for our horses. We look after our own. I'd take him back with us to Fort Stanton, but his body . . . he couldn't take the heat. And I don't want his mother to see him like this.

"I don't know what kinda report you'll file on this whole mess," Chapman continued. "But if you got any damn sense, you won't try to take any credit. My men saved your sorry ass. If it hadn't been for them, your whole bunch would be on foot or, worse yet, marching in front of them Mexicans across the sands south of the border. Come to think of it, I believe you're probably better suited to sell women's drawers than to lead men."

The Slash Q riders gathered all the pieces of Joe that they could find and bound them in a sheet of canvas. They tied the sheet across his horse and took him back toward El Paso. Mid-afternoon, they reached Clark's Cradle and dug a grave above the springs. They buried his battered remains, piled boulders atop the grave, and left no marker.

El Paso

A government purchasing agent waited at the El Paso yard. "Heard you did some straightening out on Captain Zimmerlee. Then we had a courier come into the fort not an hour ago. Sounds like one hell of a fight you boys put up. You men decide you'd like to be cavalrymen, I'd be glad to put in a good word for you."

"Yeah, we'll do that," Chapman said. "But I don't reckon that's gonna happen."

The two men crossed the street and went into the coolness of the Bank of El Paso. "Need to open an account," Chapman said.

The teller considered the man standing in front of him. Tall.

Burnt deep brown by the sun. A week's growth of beard. Flecks of gray showing in the stubble. A smoky odor. Tired eyes.

"Glad to help," the teller said. "We . . . the bank has a policy. Ten dollars is the minimum deposit for a new account."

The purchasing agent stepped to the cage and pushed a government draft through the shallow opening. "I reckon this will meet the bank's requirements," he said.

The teller had been at the bank for three months. He'd never seen a check for five hundred dollars, much less one for twelve thousand five hundred.

Chapman and Tollafson hunted Sheriff Stottlemeyer and found him getting a shave and haircut. The barber removed the towel from Stottlemeyer's neck, dusted stray hair with a fine-haired brush, took a bottle of green liquid from a shelf, poured a generous amount in his hands, and noisily slapped it across the sheriff's neck and jowls. "Haircut's for you; smell good is for the women."

The lawman stood, stepped away from the chair, turned, and looked at himself in the mirror—"Hell of an improvement if I do say so myself."

The barber helped him slip into his black cutaway.

The sheriff shot his cuffs from the coat. "Okay, boys," he said. "I'm officially open for business. What can I do for you?"

"We'll be going back up the valley this evening," Chapman said. "Need to check with you, just to see if you'd come across Joe's brother or heard anything. We were just hoping that you might—"

The sheriff interrupted. "No. Like I told you before, man goes to Ciudad Juárez and don't come back the same night, he most likely ain't comin back. Sorry, that's just the way it is."

Chapman slumped and turned away. "Just thought I'd ask. Appreciate what help you gave us."

"Hold on just a minute. I've seen some bedraggled cowboys in my time, but you two just might take the cake. What in hell you boys been into? Look like something the dogs drug up. And your buddy there. Got his arm tied against his belly. I do believe it looks like it's broke."

"He got run over by a horse out at the garrison the other night. This whole trip has pretty much been a damn wreck."

"All riiiight, now I understand. It was you fellers that took on the Mexes the other night. Heard there wasn't more than a handful what got away. That Zimmerlee feller has been out there nigh onto a year. You boys took out more in one night than his men even shot at the whole time?"

Chapman nodded. "Yeah, guess that's true. But we lost a man I wouldn't have traded for every horse in Texas. Or every army officer."

Chapman paid off the La Mesilla hands. Evans, Tollafson, and Chapman stopped for a beer at a bar near the railroad yard. Nobody had much to say. They'd come down here with a hundred head of horses and nine men. They'd be going home with nothing but their road horses and a receipt for twelve thousand five hundred dollars in an El Paso bank. Joe was buried out in the desert at Clark's Cradle; Sam was somewhere over in Ciudad Juárez, probably dead.

They loaded their horses in a cattle car on the northbound at the El Paso stock pens. The train pulled out of the yards, the rugged Franklins to the east and the flat nothingness of the Chihuahua Desert stretching westward far past the horizon.

The Slash Q men watched the countryside slip by; it was a sad and long ride.

Oscura

Three days earlier, Angalee and Muñoz waited at the siding at

Oscura until the train steamed past on the northward run toward Carrizozo. Angalee's shoulders slumped in dejection as she sat and watched the train until it diminished to a dark thread trailed by a drifting ribbon of smoke. She turned away from Muñoz, and, when she spoke, her voice was timid. "I don't have a good feeling about this. They should have been on this train."

"It's all right. They probably had trouble keeping the horses together. Or there was a delay in getting paid. A thousand things could happen. There is a simple reason, and you'll feel silly for worrying soon as you see them." Muñoz's voice was reassuring, but inside there was a hollow feeling of something dark.

The train swung into the siding and, with a great screeching of iron against iron, stopped, the cattle car door slid back, and three cowboys led the horses down the cattle chute into the afternoon sun. Before them lay the mountains, pale green and comforting. Beyond them, Fort Stanton, the ranch, and Angalee.

They followed the same trail to Fort Stanton over which they'd driven the horses a week ago. The men rode single file: Evans in front, Tollafson in the middle, Chapman behind.

Slumped in the saddle, Chapman revisited the happenings. He and his men had gotten to Oscura in time to meet the train, but the jaguar stampeded the horses, and it took almost a day to round them up. Then Sam had gotten a wild hair in his ass and crossed the river into Mexico. Chapman had gotten Joe outta jail, and the bunch made two trips into Ciudad Juárez. Nothing. Then that mess out at the garrison. Joe was just trying to help. It could have been any of the Slash Q riders who went to talk with the wrangler. Luck of the draw. Boom. Never knew what hit him. Just gone.

Now he had to tell Angalee.

The night was crisp; the moon was nearing full; the scent of pine and spruce washed across the horsemen. The ride through the mountains was uneventful other than an encounter with a black bear and her two cubs. She faked a couple of charges, woofing toward the horses, then growling and snapping her teeth menacingly.

Evans jacked a shell into his saddle gun and aimed at the advancing bear. The animal stopped, reared to her full height, slinging her head, saliva stringing from her jaws in the moonlight.

"She's bluffing," Chapman told Evans. "Just back off a bit. She's just holding ground while the cubs get away."

It was easy to back off a bit. Although the horses were accustomed to a charging steer or an overprotective cow, the rank smell of the bear was a warning of something more dangerous. The squeal of the horse mauled by the jaguar was still in their ears, and now the smell of something wild and treacherous added to their uneasiness. Had the cowboys not kept a tight rein, the horses would have fled like aspen leaves before a storm.

Like teenagers who had not yet mastered their growing feet, the cubs galloped downhill through the woods in an ungainly scramble. Mama surrendered the roadway when the cubs were out of sight.

It was after midnight when Chapman and the Slash Q riders reached the ranch headquarters at Fort Stanton. A yellowish-orange glowed through the front windows of the ranch house, and, as the riders approached, they could make out two ghost-like figures standing on the porch.

Tollafson and Evans pulled alongside Chapman. One said, "We've decided we'll swing down along the river. Gonna take a dip. Try to get some of this desert grit off us. Get the Ciudad Juárez and that damned garrison taste outta our mouths. We'll be along directly."

Chapman continued toward the house. He removed his hat

and dragged his shirtsleeve across his salty forehead.

Muñoz and Angalee stepped off the porch and stood in the moon-washed front yard, waiting.

Roswell

The students called Zella, Mrs. Z. She was the first person at the school each morning, the last to leave in the afternoon. Her auburn hair did not dull under the desert sun, but she freckled.

After school, she tended her garden with the same passion as she tended the schoolchildren. For three years, she rented a small adobe house on the outskirts of town. It was comfortable, but she was a woman of the plains and the wide-open spaces.

She was frugal, and with her meager savings she bought a quarter section of land on the northeastern side of Roswell. The house needed work, but she had time and patience.

She taught herself to weave wool into intricately patterned blankets and colorful scarves. She wore a concho belt, a flat brimmed hat, and a brightly colored blouse when she sat on the hotel veranda and sold her watercolors. "Worth a second look," cowboys said.

Zella leaned against the horse trough and watched the heat lightning play across the mountains to the west. She often wondered how her life would have been if she had married the Walsenburg rancher. There would have been children, but there would have been isolation. And she would have wondered forever about the country to the south.

What if her foot continued to itch? What if, on some dark night, she had taken three horses and fled to God only knows where? There would have been guilt, unhappiness, and motherless children. She convinced herself that she'd done right. And so, she willed herself to be happy here in the Valley of the Pecos.

The Fort Stanton Ranch

"There's only one man," Angalee said. "There were others; I know I heard more than one horse." Her eyes strained against the darkness along the moonlit road. "Now I can see the others. Bet that's Joe and Sam. They are crossing the pasture going to the river. They don't want to show up here with all that trail grime on them."

Chapman took his horse inside the corral, stripped the blanket and saddle, and removed the bridle. There was stiffness in his walk as he moved up the path toward the house. Two barn cats danced around his feet, and he paid them no mind. He would have given ten years off his life if this wasn't in front of him. Angalee and Muñoz met him halfway.

"Well, you were gone long enough," Angalee said. "I believe I could have walked a round trip to El Paso, and you and the boys were traveling by train. Hope you didn't have any trouble. Everything is all right, isn't it?"

"We . . . uh . . . we had trouble," Chapman said, voice little more than a whisper. He rubbed the corners of his mouth and shook his head. "It . . . it was . . . was pretty bad."

"My boys. It wasn't one of my boys, was it? They're not hurt?"

Chapman looked away from Angalee toward Muñoz and spread his hands in a pleading motion. "There wasn't anything I could do. Sam must have decided to go . . . uh, go across the river . . . we . . . the boys and me, we hunted . . . two days and we . . . uh . . . we never found—"

"You left him down there? Don't tell me you left him. I know Joe wouldn't leave without him."

Chapman shook his head. "We was gonna go back. And look again. Joe was plumb set on that. Then we were attacked at the garrison. It was a cannon of some kind. We never knew anything . . . right after we delivered the horses . . . and there was this big explosion . . . and—"

Angalee stepped forward and grasped Chapman's shirt. "What're you saying? Are you telling me Joe is hurt?"

"It wasn't nothing anybody could do . . . it was just one shell. Joe and one of the troopers . . . they . . . they never knew what happened."

Angalee screamed something unintelligible and pounded her fists against Chapman's chest. Muñoz tried to hold the distraught woman, but she pulled away and slapped Chapman. "God damn you, you're lying. Why are you lying to me like this? Why are you doing this to me?

"My boys are at the river washing. They wanted to be clean . . . they are down there now . . . they're shaving. One of them is climbing the bank . . . it's Joe . . . no, it's Sam . . . it's blurred but I can tell. It's one of my boys." She slapped Chapman again, turned toward the river, and started running.

Chapman caught Angalee by the wrist, and, with Muñoz's help, they overpowered the woman. Her body went limp. She slumped to the ground, clutched at her hair, and screamed and screamed into the darkness.

Chapman carried the unconscious Angalee to her bedroom and stood awkwardly while Muñoz turned the cover back.

"This will take a while," Muñoz said. "A long while. I've had such grief. When Mama and Papa and my . . . everybody died in Galveston . . . got blown away. I wandered the streets for days. Sometimes when I think back, I don't understand . . . can't remember . . . anything much. I could have been anywhere . . . been anybody."

Chapman laid Angalee in the bed. He stood uncomfortably shifting his weight from one boot to the other. "I just didn't know how to tell her . . . didn't know how to make it easier."

Muñoz smoothed Angalee's hair. "There wasn't a good way. This was one of those times when . . . when there was nothing anyone could say."

"What can I do? To help, I mean?"

Muñoz leaned forward and removed Angalee's shoes. "I can handle this. You just need to leave for right now."

Chapman nodded. Somehow, he needed to reassure himself. "You are a good hand with the sick. Took care of Quezada there at the end. Did a good job, too."

Muñoz took Chapman's arm and led him to the door. "Thank you for saying that. We women have a gentle touch that you men will never have. It's a natural thing with us."

Chapman stood in the hallway, leaned toward the wall, braced with one hand and played Muñoz's words over and over. *We women have a gentle touch that you men will never have—we women—we women.*

It had been almost twenty-four hours since Chapman had eaten, and now he thought he might be on the verge of starvation. He rummaged around the warming closet of the kitchen stove and found bread and a strip of beef. A half pot of tepid coffee sat on the stove; its bitter smell rose up in great strength as he filled a cup. He went to the springhouse and returned with a pint of cold sweet milk, the jar beading with sweat as he set it on the table. He poured two fingers of milk into the cup and the coffee lightened barely one shade.

Chapman ate the meat and bread and drank more sweet milk than coffee. He went to his bedroom, dragged the boot jack from the corner and removed his boots, then went back into the kitchen and refilled the coffee cup. Chapman was not a man given to tobacco, but tonight he went to Quezada's desk and found a stale cigar. Barefoot, he padded to the front porch and lit up, the sulfur odor of the match blending with the harshness of the coffee.

The front door squeaked, and Muñoz moved noiselessly

across the porch to sit in a willow chair. "She's all right. She'll sleep a while. It just hit her so hard; it was her sons, all of her family. I . . . I lost my whole family in an instant during the hurricane. I remember the shock."

The cigar glowed dully in the dark and then faded. The smoke lifted and moved as a narrow sheet across the porch and into the freedom of the night.

Chapman said, "I came home and pretty much ruined Angalee's life in just one lick. It is haunting the hell outta me. I couldn't do anything about Sam. He was more than likely dead when we got to El Paso. Only way I could have helped things would've been to have Sam and Joe meet the other hands in La Mesilla. They would've stopped Sam from crossing the river—or at least gone with him. They all speak Spanish, know where to go and where not to."

The cigar glowed, and this time Chapman coughed at the harshness of the tobacco. "Don't know about Joe. Seems like the whole damn affair at the garrison was loused up. That damn army feller. If he'd gone after those Mexicans the first time and taken care of them, they wouldn't have come back for a second helping. But he didn't. It was like he was scared to get out of the fort. Mexicans figured he was easy pickings; probably thought they would get all his horses this time."

"Fate. It was fate," Muñoz said. "No one could have predicted any of this."

The cigar bloomed once more and then made a series of tight ovals as it arched out into the darkness. "It could have been any of us easy as it was Joe. He wanted to go and dicker with the trooper about water and feed. He figured he'd caused enough trouble. Letting his brother slip away and all. Wasn't his fault, but he thought it was, and that's why he wanted to go. I figured I was starting to fill Quezada's boots. Managing stuff like he would have. Shit, I can't even hold a candle to him."

"You're being too hard on yourself. Everything about Joe's death was like flipping a coin or turning a card. No one could have known. You need to put this behind you the best you can."

Chapman grunted a muted *yeah,* then said, "While ago you said 'we women.' "

Muñoz stood and paced the porch. "Yes, I said that, didn't I? So now we need to talk about me. I've got to figure out about my life. What I'm gonna do."

"What do you mean—'your life'?"

"I can't stay here. Can't stay on the ranch and work as a hand. The men wouldn't put up with it."

"Well, they haven't fussed in the past."

"And they haven't known I was a woman, either."

Chapman blew air from between his lips with a puffing sound. "Pfft! Who is going to tell them? I'm not. Bet Angalee's not. It's nobody's damn business. You can ride and rope good as you ever could. You're a good hand. Better than most."

The front door creaked again. Felipe was on his way to the woodpile. He always started breakfast at four. *"Buenos dias,"* he said.

"Morning to you," Muñoz replied.

They waited until Felipe gathered his wood to return to their conversation.

"Who knows you are a woman?" Chapman asked.

"Besides Angalee? Quezada. He knew. Talked to me about it toward the end of his life."

"Yeah. What did he say?"

"Pretty much same as what you said. Said it was nobody's business. Said I could be a bird if I wanted to—long as I could rope and herd cattle."

Chapman laughed. "At least I can see some things like he did. Makes me feel a little better."

Muñoz stopped pacing and sat. The chair rustled as she

shifted her weight. "I've thought about how all this started. Me trying to act like a man, I mean. I loved my daddy, and I guess I was his favorite. But in his old ways, he believed that man was superior to woman. But it did him good to see me outride, outshoot, or just best a man in any way.

"He told me once that if I'd been born a boy instead of a girl, I would have been a top officer in the army. Instead, I would just have babies." She paused and swallowed. "Just have babies." She swallowed again. "But until then, it was all right for me to embarrass men. To best them in any way I could. So when Galveston blew away, and I was on my own, I believed I could survive as a man but not as a woman. So, here I am. A woman pretending to be a man."

They sat for several minutes, neither talking. Up the river, a rooster crowed. Downriver, the old Indian woman's rooster answered the challenge. As if waiting for those signals, the sun rimmed the top of the mountains to the east. A light breeze drifted down the valley, the vane of the windmill aligned, and the blades rotated lazily. A trickle of water splashed into the horse tank; Chapman's horse came to investigate and drink the blessedness of home.

Chapman, Evans, and Chance worked the shallow valleys of the mountains rounding up stray cattle. Chapman was glad to have something to do; something to take his mind off the past few days.

At midmorning, they brought nine head of cows, four calves, and two young bulls into the corral. Chance built a fire and, when the coals were just right, heated two branding irons. Evans roped the calves, tied their feet, and dragged them to the fire. Dust rose from the pen, and the bawling of the calves mixed with the stench of scorched hair and burning hide.

Muñoz rode into the corral and helped Chapman with the

"headin' and heelin' " on a couple of young bulls that had previously escaped the castrating knife and branding iron. An hour after branding started, the freshly marked livestock were grazing in the pasture beside the river.

Felipe rang the dinner bell, and the ranch hands washed up at the horse tank.

Angalee did not share the noon meal.

The recording of purchases and sales and monthly payment to the Slash Q riders had been Quezada's duty. He had a fine hand, and Chapman marveled at the ranch register's neat columns of figures. Now that it was his duty, he wished he'd spent more time practicing writing and less time reading western novels. But, like so many things he'd learned lately, there was no going back.

He finished the monthly tally, closed the thick ledger, and slid the tambour of the rolltop desk closed. He swiveled his chair and faced the center of the room; Angalee stood in the doorway watching him.

"Afternoon," he said.

She didn't answer, just stared at him for a long moment, nodded curtly, slipped from the doorway, and disappeared.

As was customary, supper was just the noon meal warmed over. Chapman paid the hands their monthly wages, and they saddled up for the short ride down to Fort Stanton. He stood on the porch and watched them leave. "Don't send somebody for me if you get thrown in jail. Once you are outta my sight, you are outta my mind."

He and Muñoz sat on the front porch. Neither had much to say because most everything was said the previous night. Muñoz rocked, the chair moving quietly. Chapman took his boots off and sat, clenching and unclenching his toes against the smooth floor.

"I've been studying about things here," Chapman said. "I reckon these two ranches are in about as good shape as I can get them in. Quezada left me this little place outside of Roswell. Out near Bitter Lakes. Been some time since I've been there, and I'm kinda worried about things. Hadn't heard from the man running it lately—not a good sign, not a good sign at all. It's not much and, at best, gonna need a lot of work, stocking it and everything. 'Course it won't handle more than a double handful of cattle. I think it would be best if I went on over there and got started on things. I'm thinking about Angalee, too. Every time she looks at me, she's gonna think about her boys— gonna think that if I'd have done better, looked after them better, they'd still be here."

"No, she's not gonna think that."

"I think she will. It'll ease her feelings."

"I think you should stay. You give any credence to what I think?"

Chapman weighed his answer. "I do. But if I stay here, I'm gonna always be walking in Quezada's shadow. Folks will measure me by him, even if they don't mean to. It's gonna be easier on everybody this way."

"So, it'll just be us?"

"I believe Tollafson and Chance will stay on here. Evans will probably go with me—'course it'll be their choice. Ranch hands are dime a dozen. Cowboys will show up here looking for work like bees after honey."

"And me?" Muñoz asked. "What about me?"

"You're just teasing me. You know where you'll be. Right here. You and Angalee will make a good pair. You'll do good together."

"But you're not giving me a choice. You're like Daddy. I'm a woman, not qualified to make my own decisions. That's what you are thinking, isn't it?"

"Yeah, you're kinda right and kinda wrong at the same time. You're qualified to decide anything you want to. But we both know where the best place is for you. Angalee will need you, and, when it comes right down to it, you'll need her."

"I think I could change, Chapman. You will need a woman, and I could . . ."

The moon had not risen, and the porch was dark; Muñoz could not see Chapman shake his head. "Yeah. You could change some. But you wouldn't be happy. It's best this way."

Muñoz was quiet. Finally, "I think you're probably right."

After Quezada's death, Chapman became a light sleeper. The bawling of a steer, the whinny of a horse, unusual movement in the house—anything would wake him.

There was movement in the hall, and he opened his eyes. Something white in his bedroom doorway. He could hear breathing. "Who is it?" he asked.

There was no answer. His gun belt hung from a chair beside his bed. He pulled the revolver from the holster. *"Quién es?"* he said and cocked the pistol.

"It's me."

The door squeaked shut; the lock clicked. Slowly, the figure shed the white covering and came toward his bed.

CHAPTER THREE:
1900s

The Pecos River Valley

"Damn. This is pretty rough," Evans said.

Chapman dismounted and now stood in the doorway of the Bitter Springs ranch house, looking inside at the vacantness and rag-strewn floor. "Well, at least the sumbitch didn't leave us a bunch of broke-down furniture to haul off. But I do wish he hadn't stole what few cows I had. Reckon that's why I hadn't heard from him lately; he's been busy selling my cattle."

The two men rode a quarter mile eastward along the sagging fence that made up the southern boundary of the pasture. Before them stood the growth that marked the edge of the Pecos River. They stopped, and Evans turned in the saddle and hooked one leg around the horn. "Leastways, you got water," he said.

Chapman nodded. "If that's what you want to call it. Don't look so good to me. Bet it's salty as all get-out. But we got that little artesian well for drinking water, such as it is."

"I ain't griping. You ought not to, either. You knew we weren't coming to no Garden of Eden when we left Fort Stanton. You'll not see that much green again for a while. Quezada kinda gave this place to you backhanded anyways."

The two men rode back to the dilapidated, four-room adobe house. The pole barn was in good enough shape to shade their horses. "Maybe we ought to live in the barn and stable our horses in the house," Evans observed, and Chapman gave him a dirty look.

Evans grinned. "Flip you to see who cooks next week."

The first year on the ranch, the two men learned to make adobe bricks and repaired the house to a livable condition. Their part-time job was keeping garter snakes, lizards, and hand-sized tarantulas out of the house. They ran twenty mama cows that year and had thirteen calves. "Pretty damn grim, if you ask me," Evans said after coyotes got two newborn calves.

"I didn't ask you," Chapman said. "And I ain't tying you here. And I don't want to hear them words anymore. 'Nother thing, I won't tolerate griping. Any griping needs to be done, I'll do it."

Evans might have complained about things after that, but he was careful Chapman didn't hear it.

Chapman leased another section and a half the next year, and now, with 2,200 acres in pasture, they had enough to run thirty-five head. "We can squeeze by if we save all the calves," Chapman said one night after supper.

Just before sunrise the next morning, the coyotes got two young calves, and a third fell into a sinkhole and died from a broken neck.

The year after Chapman leased the section and a half was the driest anyone had ever seen. Early January brought a couple inches of snow, and the temperature dropped to twenty below for four consecutive nights. The artesian well choked to no more than a trickle.

Migratory birds that usually wintered on the shallow lakes gave up. They could not penetrate the ice; anything swimming or growing beneath the frozen surface was far from their reach. They flew in confusion before trailing the wiser and more seasoned leaders south to the Texas coast.

"Reckon we ought to follow them?" Evans said, but the words came with a grin.

Old men, hands mittened, congregated around the stove at the feed store, coat collars turned up, earflaps pushed up against their cap crown. They chose to share their wisdom with Chapman and Evans. "Watch your bull," one of them said. "Freeze his thang off. Look like a milk cow when spring comes."

Evans and Chapman checked on the cattle twice a day. But it wasn't enough. Nine cows and eight calves, driven by a north wind, drifted south, piled up in a hedgerow, and froze on their feet. February wasn't much better, except it didn't snow. The cattle were weak, and five more died. It didn't rain in March, April, or May.

"We'll get rain in June," an old rancher told Chapman. "Most always do."

They did—an inch. But the temperature climbed to 105 degrees, and what little grass survived the winter turned brittle underfoot and the color of an old boot. July was just as hot; three inches of rain fell, but it was too late.

After that, it didn't matter. Nothing mattered. The cows stood in the burnt pasture and looked toward the barn, mournfully bawling their misery.

"Count ever' damn rib they got," Evans said.

In August, Chapman sold all of his cattle he could gather to a rancher down the Pecos. The man insisted on delivery, and five cows died during the trip. The market had never been this low. Almost every rancher in the valley was in the same shape— starving cattle and no grass.

Hawks patrolled the barren prairie and on most days found no prey. The bitter winter destroyed almost all of the burrowing animals: kangaroo rats, prairie dogs, and mice; the birds of prey were reduced to eating grasshoppers and beetles. Even the great owl, a bird of the night accustomed to feeding on sly rodents, grew accustomed to unsuccessful forays. He sulked in the barn, became a day hunter living off grasshoppers.

"Well, there's one good thing," Evans said. "Them damn buzzards are fatter this year than they've ever been."

"Yeah," Chapman said. "But I ain't eating buzzards. You might, but I ain't."

Zella, her head bonneted against the summer sun, straightened from her tomato vines and watched as Chapman and Evans drove their emaciated herd southward down the Pecos. She hadn't enjoyed the winter, but she'd seen worse up in Star Valley.

Last week, she'd lost a frying-size chicken to an owl that took it in broad daylight, right before her eyes. She'd seen the owl flying toward Chapman's barn, but she figured the man had enough trouble without a neighbor bitching about the loss of a chicken. It would work itself out.

With the loss of his herd, Chapman was reduced to owning nothing but two sections of rangeland that would not revegetate for five years. He might be able to run a half dozen cows, but this would not provide enough income to support him and Evans.

He explained this to Evans one afternoon when they were fishing in the scarcely moving, reddish flow of the Pecos. "It's just not there," he said. "We won't make enough cash money to feed two horses, much less two men and their horses. I feel I've let you down. Let both of us down, far as that's concerned."

Evans baited his hook and dropped it into a sluggish eddy. "Hell, don't feel bad. I knowed it was comin'. Just a matter of time. I been through hard times before. My folks was starved off a little farm in the edge of the Ozarks. We run a whole year on just peas, hickory nuts, and cabbage. Finally had to sell the milk cow. Reckon that was the last straw for Papa. He . . . he hung hisself in a holler down below the barn. I was sixteen."

"Well, this isn't that bad," Chapman said. "We'll get by, just won't be pretty for a few years."

Evans watched his floater drift toward the bank and then back toward the middle of the river. "I'm not worried about getting by. I've got by on my own for thirty years. You don't need to worry about me. Might say, I was lookin for a job when I found this one. I got a cousin that owns a little farm over at Clovis. Might ride over there and see if he needs a hired hand."

Chapman sat and watched a willow bend in the river's current. "You're not a farmer," he said. "You're a cowboy, and a damn good one at that. You ain't the kind of man that ought to be walking cotton rows. Bet you can get on at one of the big spreads."

"Might. We'll see."

It was Chapman's turn to cook breakfast. He pulled on his pants, checked his boots for scorpions, started a fire in the cookstove, and walked out into the backyard to pee. Evans's horse was gone. Back inside, his bed hadn't been slept in, and both Evans's shirts were gone from the nail where they hung.

Chapman didn't fix breakfast. He went out to the barn and fed his horse a handful of grain. He leaned against the side of the building and looked up into the dull blue sky. "Well, that's that."

In the years following the horrible winter, Chapman scrambled to make ends meet.

He drove a six-mule grader and scraper on irrigation projects south of Roswell. This was man-and-mule-killing work. Summer temperature hovered around 100 degrees. The air was so dry, men drank water by the quart, and their shirts were never wet with sweat. Mules simply quit pulling before they fell from heat exhaustion; horses did not have the same self-preservation mindset—they fell dead in their traces.

Many days, Zella watched the weary man return home well after sundown and wondered at his stubbornness.

CHAPTER FOUR:
1910s

Ciudad Juárez

Shadrach was alone; Belzora finally had had enough. He came home one night, supper was not ready, and she was sitting on the back porch asleep, soaking her feet in a pan of water. He kicked the chair from under her.

"You lazy *perra!*" he shouted. "Worthless dog."

She scrambled to her feet, grabbed the battling stick from the wash pot, and came after him. "*Agujero de culo.* Asshole," she screamed. Her fury did not match his; she was left whimpering in the kitchen, both eyes blackened, split lip, and two broken teeth.

He took to the street in a rage, looking for a fight with anyone who crossed him.

When she was sure he was gone, she went to the bedroom and dragged the wooden box from under their bed. It contained 250 pesos and 101 U.S. dollars. She stashed the money in a cotton bag and tied it around her midriff. She stopped in the kitchen and looked at her swollen eyes and split lip in a mirror. A bowl of butter sat beside the saltcellar, and she smeared the grease on her face.

She hurried back to the bedroom, laid the moneybox on the bed, dropped a single peso into its emptiness. "*Bastardo,*" she sneered.

Belzora walked eastward from Ciudad Juárez. By noon the next day, the battered woman was at her cousin's house in

Senecú. She'd never told Shadrach anything about her family or where she lived as a girl. If he lived to be a hundred, he would never strike her again.

Shadrach was successful in his search for trouble. He found two Fort Bliss troopers in a cantina. For less than two minutes, they gave as well as they took, and then the savageness of the earless Mexican became too much for them; one crumpled to the floor, one fled.

He prowled the streets until daylight. The word spread quickly about his rage, and even the most pugnacious street brawlers fled into the dark alleys at his approach.

It was almost midmorning when Shadrach returned to the house he'd shared with Belzora.

"You *puta*," he yelled into the empty house. "*Perra*, where are you?"

He found the box on the bed and the single peso. He rampaged through the house, destroying rickety furniture, battering doors off their hinges, smashing Belzora's dishes. He would have given the sight from one eye to have her neck between his hands.

His hangover was growing as his pulse hammered from the exertion of destroying the house, and he lay under a mesquite tree in the backyard, sleeping until dark. The sound of a braying burro woke him, and he cursed. Neither water nor tequila could quench his thirst.

The woman had stolen his money. The brothers and their vermin nephew, Alberto, wounded his dignity, and he worried the account of their treatment of him would come across the river. People would lose their respect for him. The drunken *gringo*, Sam, the one who bragged, told him Quezada was dead, so only Chapman remained to tell of his defeat at Fort Bliss. Muñoz was probably still alive but was nothing more than a blowfly on a carcass. A passing of the hand and the fly would disappear.

He could clearly see it: first, the Soto brothers at Las Cruces; second, Chapman in this place called Roswell.

He took his rifle—the one with the etching *Winner Slash Q Shooting*—across the street and leaned it against a bush. The gun was a constant reminder of the wicked Soto brothers in Las Cruces, and, if not for its great value, he would have thrown it in the river. He gathered his pistols and knife, wrapped them in a ragged jacket, and placed them by the rifle. Back in the house, he found a tintype, and, with a coarse thumbnail, scratched away the likeness of Belzora, leaving only his scowling image staring from the photograph. He gathered Belzora's few clothes, piled them in the center of the bedroom floor, and poured kerosene on their miserableness.

The Rio Grande Valley

He took his weapons and, with the house behind him consumed in writhing flames, crossed the Rio Grande and started his trip, the scorching desert to the west and the purple mountains to the east, bitterness in his mouth.

He traveled northward, vigilant for farms and small ranches; he needed horses and food.

He thought about Alberto and the two remaining uncles. The boy did not deserve to grow into manhood; he would be like his uncles. He was evil, scheming and would be a despicable man. Thoughts of the uncles, the Soto brothers, sickened him; arrogance was something Shadrach could not tolerate. The brothers were common cattle thieves, dependent upon their aged mother. They had no honor.

At San Miguel, he swaggered into the isolated post office, panicked the postmistress, and walked out into the sunlight with just over seventeen dollars of U.S. postal funds and a small bag of mail. The postmistress could identify him only as an ugly, earless man with depthless eyes the color of slate.

He found the Soto brothers' ranch, the hovel of a house, the dilapidated barn, the unkempt corrals. For two days, he watched. On the third day, the brothers rode into the stock lot in a buckboard. Alberto, now a gawky young man not yet twenty, sat on the tailgate, bare feet dangling just above the packed sand.

"You will attend to the horses," the uncles told the nephew. "It is a disease of the young. They are always given the opportunity to assist their elders." The men left Alberto at the barn and disappeared into the darkness of the filthy and windowless house.

Shadrach stepped from behind a wooden crib and clasped his hand over Alberto's mouth. "Remember me?"

The young man's eyes rolled in terror as he recognized the raspy voice.

Shadrach bound Alberto to a post, stuffed corn shucks into his mouth, and whispered into his ear. "I want you to be very still and quiet. If you move or make a sound, I will come back, slit your throat, pull your tongue through the cut, and leave you here for the barn rats to harvest. Do you understand me?"

Alberto understood, and tears welled in his eyes. He wished he'd not lorded over the earless man those years ago. Maybe his other two uncles would be alive today; maybe he would not be tied to this post; maybe the empty-eyed man would not be here today. If he lived, he would attend Mass each day; even more, he would become a priest, minister to the poor and sick and the lowest of the low, protect the widows and orphans; he would be humble but revered by all in the valley. This was the deal he proposed to God. But He must have been busy herding a dust storm or watching over the ocean on that day; Alberto's supplications got no higher than the top of the post to which he was bound.

El Paso

The U.S. marshal's office in El Paso was a converted tack room at Fort Bliss. It would be temporary, he'd been assured. That was five years ago. Ellison McCavran liked it that way; he didn't have to put up with jangling streetcars, overflowing beer joints, and hollering whores hanging out of windows. It was not that he disliked bar rooms and whores, but if someone was having a beer, he wanted it to be him.

The U.S. postal rider who made the daily run from Las Cruces to El Paso knocked on McCavran's office door, pushed it open, and reluctantly shuffled inside. The rider was a nervous man, too thick in the middle, almost too hairy to be seen in public. "Got some trouble up the valley," he said. He hung his thumbs under his suspenders and slipped them to the side. Two parallel lines of salt coursed his shirtfront and, after a break atop his shoulders, crisscrossed his back. "Some nasty sumbitch robbed the office at San Miguel. Liked to have upset Old Lady Parker plumb outta her drawers."

This was not the kind of news McCavran liked. Whole lotta paperwork. No action. Boring as watching minnows swimming in a ditch. The marshal had been what was referred to in his prime as *a stem-winder.*

"Kicked asses and didn't take no names," said Sterling Hill, chief U.S. marshal in charge of West Texas and some parts of the country west of that. The *kicking asses* part was what got Marshal McCavran in trouble most of the time. "Run wild and loose," Marshal Hill remarked on more than one occasion. He continued, "Good at shootin', bad at judgin' who to shoot at."

"A post station, you say." McCavran didn't take his feet down from the desk. "Scared a woman! What do you think I oughta do about some little pissant thing like that?"

"Well, Mrs. Parker is the sister of Texas Senator Ajax Chilton." The postal rider emphasized the words "sister" and "senator."

McCavran's boots came off the desk and thumped against the floor. "Well, why didn't you say so in the first place? Turkey! That dirty shithead won't get away with abusing a fine woman, 'specially a U.S. senator's sister."

So, Marshal Ellison McCavran strapped on his pistols, got his saddle gun, shotgun, and two horses and rode around the tip of the Franklins upriver to San Miguel.

Mrs. Parker lived by herself just down the road from the post station. She was a bit on the skinny side and a lot on the ugly side. Turns out Mr. Parker went to milk the goat one night and never came back. "I think a bear got him 'cause we never found hide or hair," she told the preacher—every Sunday.

McCavran sat on the shady end of the post station porch and listened to her whine. His mind was back at Fort Bliss having a beer.

"He was a brute of a man," she said, describing the thief. "Had no more regard for an unprotected female than nothing. I was scared I was gonna be raped, me being here by myself and all."

The marshal wanted to tell her that her looks protected her from being raped better than a .44, but he was trying to be more civil these days. "Can you describe this monster?" he asked. He'd taken out his little notebook and was looking interested but was drawing uppercase *ABC*s as she talked.

"He was the biggest man I ever saw. Ugly. Mexican, I think. Eyes the color of slate. Smelled awful. He took all the money. It belonged to the United States government, you know. And all the mail. Every piece."

"Anything else?"

"Oh, yes—he didn't have any ears."

It had taken McCavran an hour to find the trail of bent grass and broken bushes alongside the river. It was almost a quarter of a mile before he came upon the first piece of discarded mail—a wadded envelope. Two miles farther, he found the second piece. The robber crossed the river twice, and the marshal rode bent over the saddle horn, eyes watching for tracks and broken weeds.

Almost dark and Marshal McCavran discovered grass broken and bent at the foot of a tree where the man slept, sitting up, back protected, vigilant. Envelopes were used as kindling for his frugal campfire—no bigger than the crown of a man's hat—the fire of a man accustomed to hiding in the darkness, a man accustomed to being secretive. McCavran found the shell of one egg and a sliver of potato skin—nothing else.

The marshal slept in the same place, covered by his duster, pistols resting in his lap. He was up and moving before the morning birds stirred.

It was noon on the following day when he found the last camp. There was a broader area of matted grass but no fire. The robber stayed two nights, eating raw potatoes and kernels of dried corn, watching, waiting. He moved from this hiding place twice, once to visit the river and once to answer a call to nature.

The lawman felt in his bones that he was close and spent most of the afternoon creeping through the cane along the river, looking for trail. The wind shifted to the north. The scent of fresh ashes came with the first breeze. Cautiously, he moved forward and then saw the burned house, the wind lifting ribbons of gray ashes and flinging them across the barnyard. A movement beyond that. McCavran could see a young man tied to a locust post, head slumped forward, swollen tongue exposed between blood-encased lips, a corn shuck stuffed into his mouth.

The marshal walked back a half mile to where he'd tied his horse, got his scattergun, dropped a double-ought shell into each chamber, and moved back to where he'd seen the man tied to the post. He waited fifteen minutes; still nothing but the one man. The lawman backed fifty yards away and walked a semi-circle to where he could see the smoking remains and beyond that, the bound man. Sure there was no one else at the small yard, he stepped forward and held his hand over the ashes—no more heat than a fresh boiled egg.

He took a charred fence slat and raked the ashes. Scattered bones. A mostly burned head. A Bowie knife. A pistol. A belt buckle. He studied the remains and decided two people were in the building when it burned. He looked at the bones again. Two adults.

Behind him, a groan. The lawman spun, dropped to one knee, and cocked both barrels of his scattergun. The bound man raised his head slightly and moaned again.

McCavran cut the cotton rope and gently lowered the young man to a sitting position. He studied the bloodied corn shuck. There was no easy way; he pulled it from the man's mouth. There was a feeble groan, then nothing. The marshal squatted in the horse-lot dust, watching; there was no movement except for the shallow breathing. He went to the river, filled his hat with water and, using his bandana, washed the man's face. The ropes had cut cruelly into his flesh; water would neither help nor cure.

Marshal McCavran bent over the injured man and was startled when his eyes fluttered twice, then opened, dullness behind swollen and narrow slits. "Damn," the lawman said, sucked in his breath, and straightened.

Then he moved closer. "What's your name, son?"

The young man gingerly touched his eyes, then ran his fingers across his lips; the dried blood flaked away, small deep-crimson flecks. "Alberto," he whispered.

"You live here," the marshal said, more than asked.

Alberto managed a shallow nod. He moved his swollen tongue across the parched lips and left no dampness. "Is he gone?"

The marshal dripped water on Alberto's lips. "Who? Is who gone?"

Alberto moved his lips twice before whispering, "Shadrach."

Roswell

"Say there. Your name Chapman?" The U.S. marshal stood at the edge of a barrow ditch, duster open just enough so the badge glinted, thumbs hooked behind the leather gun belt.

Chapman lowered the grader blade and pulled back on the reins. "Whoa. Whoa." The mules dropped their heads, and the trace chains went slack. "Yeah, I reckon I'm guilty. What can I do for you?"

The marshal stepped out into the freshly turned dirt and extended his hand. "McCavran. Ellison McCavran. U.S. marshal. El Paso."

"Mighty long way from the house, aren't you?" Chapman said and shook the marshal's hand. "You'll not sleep in your own bed tonight, I'd say."

McCavran smiled, teeth shockingly white against his saddle-colored face. He removed his flat-brimmed hat and waved at a swarm of sand flies. "Son, I ain't slept in my own bed for so long, I ain't sure my wife would know me from Adam's off ox."

"Damn, Marshal, you'd best be getting home rather than blundering around here in these irrigation canals."

"Yeah, you're probably right. But I didn't stop here to discuss my love life with a stranger."

Chapman wiped his face with a salt-streaked bandana. "Well,

I'm not selling any cows, 'cause I don't have any. And till it rains, I'm not buying any. The Eddy Company owns these mules, so I'm not selling them. Looks like if you want to deal livestock, you are gonna have to find a man that's better off than I am."

"I don't deal in cows," the marshal said. "I deal in justice. Protecting the poor, orphans, widow women, rich bankers, shit like that."

"Don't reckon I know any of them. Know a bunch of poor ranchers needing money. That count?"

"Depends," the marshal said. "I might be able to help at least one."

"Well, if it is me, get on with it. I've got a lot of dirt to move before dark."

"OK, here goes. Me and Sheriff Memphis Stottlemeyer down in El Paso are pretty good buddies. Well, was, 'till he got took by a drifter with a scatter gun. He told me 'bout you losing a man 'cross the river. Man named Sam something-or-other. He kinda kept it in the back of his mind. Always sorry that he couldn't help you. Never had anything real tight to go on, but some troopers from Bliss saw a fellow fittin' your man's descrip-tion at a bar in Ciudad Juárez. Bar run by an earless Mex. Anyway, he always figured it was your man—the one that you lost, I mean. So, that's kinda my first knowin' of you."

"We dang sure hated losing Sam. Looked the best we could. You know how things are over there."

"Damned straight I do. Well, be that as it may, you fellers played hell with a bunch of Mexicans 'bout that time out at East Portrillo Garrison, didn't you? Purty near wiped them out, Memphis said. Said you stood your ground with them comin' at you a-horseback. And in the dark to boot."

"Yeah, reckon so. We was pushed into it, didn't have any choice, and we was just looking after our own best interest. I'd like to think I'm smarter than that now. Not get caught up in anything like that again. Don't look it, but I am."

"Probably right. We'd all like to think that, anyway." The marshal went back to his horse, fished around in his saddlebags, pulled out a packet of papers, and sorted through them. He found what he was searching for and took it to Chapman. "You know this feller?"

Chapman squinted at the tintype photograph, half of it scratched away. He tilted it so the light shown on the image differently and then nodded. "Believe I do. It was several years ago. Twice on the same night. A saloon in Fort Bliss and then again outside."

"His name is Shadrach."

"I don't know his name. Never introduced to the gentleman. But I did note the sumbitch never grew any ears back."

"What else you remember about him?"

"He was trying to rob a friend of mine. Somehow, he put a bullet in Ab Quezada. It put him in such bad shape he . . . he . . . uh . . . he died."

The marshal took the photograph, brushed dust from it with his coat sleeve, and slipped it back in the packet of papers. "Such bad shape, he killed hisself. That's what you started to say, wadn't it? Killed hisself?"

Chapman looked at his palms and ran his thumbs across the thick calluses. "Yeah. Killed himself. I . . . I don't like to think of it . . . that way."

"Then how do you think of it?"

"I . . . uh . . . I like to think he got tired of hurting and decided to do something else."

"Do something else? Well, by God, I never heard it called that."

"Now you have. I reckon I'd better get back at this ditch. Boss man don't pay for me to stand around and educate strang-

ers about something I'd rather not talk about." Chapman laced
the reins through his fingers. "Anyway, the mules are tired of
hearing your mouth."

The marshal adjusted his hat to keep the sun out of his eyes.
"How you like driving mules? Being a dumbass farmer? Wearing overalls. Stepping over mule turds and the such."

Chapman looked down at his threadbare overalls and worn,
high-top leather shoes, uppers pulling away from the soles. "You
didn't hunt me down to make fun of me. Least I hope that's
true. Your badge is big, but it isn't that damn big. What do you
want?"

"Me and Memphis, we figured we know who killed your
buddy. Same man that shot up your other friend, Quezada. I
wonder if you would like a little revenge?"

"Well, I believe I might be owed a little," Chapman said.
"Why you telling me all this?"

"Because I want you to help me kill Shadrach."

Just after daylight on the last day Chapman was to drive the
mules at the irrigation canal project, he pulled a galvanized
washtub under the stream of the artesian well. By twilight, the
twenty-eight gallon tub was brimming with water warmed from
the relentless sun.

He took a wash pan of warm water into his house and shaved
by lamplight. When dark came, he went back to the tub,
stripped, sat in the still-warm water, and washed a week's worth
of grime from his body.

Three miles to the west across the prairie, a dim light
twinkled. He'd noticed a woman around that place but hadn't
seen a man. He figured she was married. Wasn't many single
women in this part of the country.

He put on his least dirty pants and shirt, saddled his horse,
and rode to the neighbor's house. He stood at the edge of the

porch, rapped with his knuckles, and called out, "Anybody home?"

A woman came to the door. "Can I help you?"

"Yes, ma'am. Like to talk with your husband, if I could."

The woman looked at him as if he'd said a cuss word. "No man has been fortunate enough to marry me yet. Is there something I can help you with?"

The yellow glow from the living room lamp backlit her, made her hair a dusty red, and Chapman wished he'd introduced himself earlier. He shifted from one foot to the other and looked at the ground; anything not to stare at the curves of the woman's silhouetted body.

"Yes, ma'am. My name is Chapman. I live over yonder." He motioned back to the east with his head. "We been neighbors some time now. I've . . . I've been meaning to stop by and meet you, and I guess I've been pretty slow about it. I know it's late, and I won't take up much of your time. I got a favor to ask."

"Good evening, Mr. Chapman," the woman said. "I've intended to stop by and introduce myself to you, too. Seems like you've been at it pretty hard. Always late when you come by. Anyway, we've finally met. What kinda favor you asking?"

"It's kinda big. I've got this milk cow, and she's just come fresh. The calf will take most of her milk. But if you could kinda watch her, I'd appreciate it. I'm betting there's enough milk for the calf and you, too. She's mostly Jersey, and her milk is rich. Make good butter."

"I think I can handle that. I was raised on a farm, and I speak cow pretty good," she said, and then smiled at her own joke.

The cowboy shuffled his feet again, an awkward miniature dance, and busied himself adjusting his hatband.

She watched him, amused at his awkwardness. "I'd have you in," she said, "but I was getting ready to go to bed; besides, the house is a mess. Anything else I can do for you?"

"Eggs," he said. "Would you mind . . . uh . . . ?"

"Gathering your eggs. You've got some hens, and you'd like for me to gather the eggs."

Chapman cleared his throat. He couldn't get his mind off her red hair . . . the outline of her body, and it seemed the inside of his mouth had turned to cotton. "Yes, ma'am, if you don't mind."

"No, I can use the eggs. How long you need me to do your chores?"

"I never thought of it that way. Does sound like I'm asking you to do my chores, don't . . . doesn't it?"

"How long?" she repeated. He reminded her of a starving cat: stringy, eyes catching the lamp light and shining in his burned face. Then she thought of *nervous as a long-tailed cat in a room full of rocking chairs.* Her Grandma used those words. She didn't laugh, but she wanted to.

"Oh. Yeah . . . how long. Maybe a month, little more or less."

"Just let me know when you get back," she said. "Oh, by the way, Mr. Chapman, my name is Zella."

Chapman touched a forefinger to his hat brim and stepped up into the saddle. "Good to meet you, Miz Zella." He touched his hat brim again and rode off into the darkness toward his ranch.

At home, he turned his horse loose in the barn lot and went inside the house. The lonesomeness came to him, and he still missed Evans, his smart mouth, his cheerfulness.

Chapman dragged a quilt from under the bed, unrolled it, took his revolver and rifle from the folds, and laid the guns on the kitchen table. He disassembled the revolver and cleaned it, then cleaned the rifle and counted his cartridges. Sixty-three— ought to be enough. Way more than enough. If he needed more than that, he was probably a goner.

He brought his saddlebags into the kitchen, wiped the sand and cobwebs from each pocket, put a little coffeepot, a metal cup, and a flat pan in one side, wrapped the cartridges with pants and shirt and stored them in the other side.

Now he lay in the darkness, staring at the ceiling, fingers laced behind his head. He thought about Marshal McCavran, Quezada, Muñoz, Joe, Sam, Angalee, and Shadrach. The last thing he thought about before going to sleep was the red-haired woman—Zella.

His sleep was restless. To the west, thunder whispered hoarsely; a finger of hot light trembled along the peaks of distant mountains.

After drinking his fill, Chapman's horse stood beside the barn, nostrils flared, taking in an unfamiliar man scent. The horse pricked his ears forward and moved uneasily as the stranger shifted his position in the hay.

Toward the end of the 1800s, Roswell was little more than a dusty town where you were as likely to encounter a coyote walking down the street as a human. The village boasted a general store and part-time mortuary, a post office, a courthouse, a three-cell jail, a twelve-room hotel, a saloon, and scattered residences in various stages of completion or dereliction. Then old man Jaffa tried to set out a pecan tree, punched a hole in his backyard, and, to his astonishment, a small artesian well boiled up out of the sand. Next year, the railroad came, and Roswell almost became a real town.

The weather was hellishly hot in the summer and colder than a witch's tit in the winter. In late summer, the monsoons came though, bringing high winds, hail, and an occasional tornado. Fall was nice unless there was an October snow.

Marshal McCavran stood in the shadow of the courthouse

belfry, beads of sweat growing on his neck, and dog gnats swarming around his head. He had little patience and most of it evaporated with the day's heat.

Chapman rode down the dusty street, his wide hat and long-sleeved shirt giving some protection from the baking sun.

The marshal removed his hat, dried the sweatband with a soiled handkerchief, then used the same handkerchief to mop his brow. " 'Bout time you showed up. How in hell am I gonna administer the oath to make you a special deputy United States marshal if you can't show up on time?"

"You said three o'clock." Chapman pulled a watch from his pocket and checked it. "It's fifteen till. I'm early."

"No, you ain't—you're late. When I say three, I mean a half hour before. I got men inside gonna witness the swearin' in. You're holding up everything. I got things to do 'fore dark. Now let's get this show on the road." The marshal opened the courthouse door, put his head inside, and shouted, "All right, we're ready."

Two men, a bearded and bedraggled sheepherder and the local undertaker, came out into the brightness of the street, shaded their eyes, and looked at the marshal. The sheepherder spoke no English. The undertaker, who hated his smelly job with a passion, said, "Remember, Marshal McCavran, you're paying us two bits for this witnessing, and we'd like to have it in advance."

The lawman grumbled something about the responsibility of a good citizen and gave the men their money. He turned to Chapman. "We gonna start now. Guess I'd better get your whole name. Help make the swearing in more official."

Chapman replied, "Francis Elmore Chapman."

McCavran looked up from the yellowed and creased paper he held in his left hand. "The hell you say. What kinda name is that? I believe you made that up."

"That's what Mama named me."

"Well. If it's just the same with you, I believe I'll just use Chapman. Make this proceeding shorter." He consulted the paper again and cleared his throat. "Raise your right hand and repeat after me:

"I, state your name, do solemnly swear that I will faithfully execute all lawful precepts directed to the marshal of the western district of Texas, under the authority of the United States and true returns, and in all things well and truly, and without malice or partiality perform the duties of the office of special deputy United States marshal of New Mexico."

Chapman repeated the words best as he could.

The lawman stopped, mopped his brow, and waved at the gnats. "It says a lot more about lawful fees and defending the Constitution and faithfully discharging duties. Stuff like that, which I ain't gonna read, 'cause it don't make any sense to anybody 'cept the man what wrote it."

McCavran folded the paper. "You gonna do all that stuff, ain't you?"

Chapman would like to have heard the rest of what he was swearing to, but it was plain Marshal McCavran had lost patience. Instead, he said, "Yes, sir," and the lawman pinned a badge on his shirt.

The sheepherder sat cross-legged in the sand sharpening his knife on the sole of his boot, and the undertaker's eyes had partially glazed over. "You witnesses are free to go. Be careful where you spend all that money."

McCavran and Chapman sat under the shade of a cottonwood tree that grew by the store, drinking Dr Pepper and watching their horses grazing along a barrow ditch.

"How did I get tangled up in this mess? I haven't seen this Shadrach fellow in years, and then just that one night. I'm not sure I'd know him if he came walking down the road over yonder."

Marshal McCavran nodded. "Well, he damn sure remembers you. Guess you could say he wants to see you bad. Real bad."

"Do tell? You been talking to him?"

"Yeah," the marshal nodded. "Well, I'll take that back and say sorta."

The marshal rambled along with his story of the pursuit of Shadrach, finding the bodies of the Soto brothers, and the horribly mutilated body of their nephew.

Occasionally Chapman ran his fingers under his vest to feel the hardness of the star. "That's a real good story and all, Marshal, and I really appreciate you telling me. But where do I fit in all this? You want me to go over into the Valley and hunt this post station robber or whoever the hell was burning these folks? Maybe so you can go back to Bliss and sit in that fine office? Act like a big shot?"

The lawman rubbed his moustache. "No. Do you remember me telling you about Mrs. Parker's story about how the bear got Mr. Parker when he went to milk the goat? Look at it this way. You're Mr. Parker; Shadrach is the bear."

"So, what does that make you? How do you fit in?"

The marshal drained his soda. "I'm gonna kill the damn bear, and here's how I'm gonna get the sumbitch to come into the goat pen."

"What in heck are you talking about?"

"Don't be asking questions before I finish with my story."

McCavran left the shade and came back with two more Dr Peppers. "I just about knew it was that sumbitch. He'd tried to hide his trail, but I'm pretty good at that sort of thing. If that rascal had been a day later, I'd have caught him. Things work out that way sometimes."

Chapman took a drink and asked, "So this Alberto feller, did he live?"

"Yeah. I guess he will. There wasn't anything I could do for him; couldn't tell if he needed a doctor or priest the worst. I put some hay on the ground and laid him down in it. Kinda made a tent outta my duster so the flies couldn't get to him so bad. Rode over to Cruces and found the doctor in his office. And the priest had just finished Mass. Doctor took his buggy. Priest sitting there on the seat reared back like a big old owl on a salt box. Wasn't gone more than two hours. Got back, Alberto had rolled outta the hay and was layin in the dirt."

"Why, heck, Marshal, you been longer than that telling me the story. Which one did Alberto need the most: doctor or priest?"

Marshal McCavran grinned. "Patience, son, you gotta learn patience. This was serious business. Doc got him cleaned up. Rope burns were awful, but the worst thing: Shadrach had split the boy's tongue. I couldn't understand nothing he was saying, just a bunch of sputtering far as I was concerned. Sounded like *sith—sith—sith*. 'Course my Spanish ain't too hot anyway. That's where the priest come in pretty good."

Chapman took the horses down to a tank, watered them, and moved them over to the shade of a cottonwood tree. The animals stood there on three legs, one hip cocked and resting a hind leg, head down, swishing their tails. Man that ran the store came outside and looked up at the sky like he was expecting rain. There wasn't a cloud anywhere to be seen, hadn't been in a couple of weeks; he was just hoping.

The marshal continued. "Alberto couldn't talk worth a shit. But I done told you that. He tried to draw pictures in the dirt. But I couldn't follow 'em.

" 'Tween him drawing pictures in the dirt and the priest tryin' to translate all the *sith-sith*s, we finally figured out that

Shadrach slipped up on him and tied him to the post. Alberto pointed to his eyes and showed he watched as Shadrach set the house on fire—wiggled his hands in the air like a fire blazing. One uncle came through the door, Shadrach shot him in the head; other uncle tried to come out and got the same thing."

"Dang. I never heard of such."

"Well, you have now, and that ain't all. He cut their ears off, right there in front of the boy. Put 'em on a necklace with some other things that looked like dried apricots. Told the boy he was coming over to Roswell to see you. Gonna settle something. Seems like you kinda made a fool of him down at Fort Bliss. Said since Quezada was dead, that you'd have to do in his place.

"Oh, something else. That tintype picture of Shadrach? He'd propped it up against a post. Said he wanted the boy to remember what he looked like."

Chapman chewed on his bottom lip and thought about the night Quezada was shot. "He don't know me. That was a long time ago, better than ten years."

"Not what he told the boy. Said he saw you in Ciudad Juárez. Saw you twice. Said a man named Sam told him where you'd be living. Told Alberto that after he killed you, he'd come back and see how he was feeling. I've run across some bad ones, but this one takes the cake. Like he is proud to be a sumbitch."

"Sam! He said that name? You knew all that? Knew he was coming after me? Didn't tell me? Why, hell, he could have slipped up on me last night while I was asleep. Killed me dead as a hammer."

The marshal grinned. "Yeah, he could have. But wasn't very likely. While you was visiting that redheaded neighbor last night, I climbed up in your hay shed. I'd have put a bullet in him iffen he'd got in fifty yards of your house."

"In the dark?"

"Yeah. Well, I'd have done the best I could. You know how it is?"

"Well, that makes me feel a lot better. You gonna shoot at some man in the dark. Fifty yards away. If I'd known all that, I'd have slept much better last night. Now I find out you're using me like honey trying to draw a man in so you can shoot him. You ever think about doing this on your own and leaving me outta your fight?"

The marshal pared his thumbnail with a knife, then looked at the results. "I've thought about that. For 'bout a week. If I could've found the sumbitch 'fore I found you, I'd have done shot him."

Shadrach

After leaving the Soto brothers, Shadrach's trip through the Organ Mountains had been almost easy. He moved over on the east side and worked generally northward, always checking his back trail for any pursuers—had to trust his eyes more because his hearing was getting worse. Food had been no problem. He raided chicken houses, gardens, and vegetable cellars.

While not as strenuous as the mountains for the horses, the rugged *colinas* still took their toll. Shadrach found it necessary to procure a horse. He chose a rancher who had several horses; his thinking: a small number would not be missed from a large herd.

He left the ranch with a fresh mount, leaving his worn-out horse and twistedly seeing the whole thing as a form of barter. Primitive, but effective.

Turning eastward, he looked across the expanse of white sand that lay before him, desolate and shimmering brightly in the morning sun. At an isolated ranch, he discarded his spent horse and took three fresh ones and a mule. The rancher, a man deep into his seventies and crippled with arthritis, protested briefly.

The necklace of ears grew by two.

Shadrach skirted the southern edge of the great gypsum dunes, but it was still an unpleasant trip. The blowing sand and sparse growth added to his irritation. His disposition soured more as the sand burs punished his horses and the blinding whiteness attacked his eyes. He'd tied a bandana around his head, unsuccessfully trying to keep the sand out of the gaping holes where his ears once were.

He traveled simply. At night, he roasted two potatoes and an egg in the campfire. He boiled day-old grounds in a tin can, drank the bitter coffee, always careful to leave enough for morning to wash down the roasted egg. He took comfort—almost pride—in his miserableness.

Working his way northeastward through the Sacramento range and just south of Alto, he met a man with a three-team hitch hauling timber.

The teamster dismounted and made pretense as if to tighten the trace chains. What he really wanted was to get a better look at the snake-headed man. "Scariest looking sumbitch I ever seed," he would tell people later, after it was all over. "Had a rag tied around his head like a granny-woman. I'm telling you, he looked as dangerous as a scorpion."

Shadrach had no need to talk to anyone; he knew his destination. He put the spurs to his horse and loped northward.

Roswell

"So rather than us runnin' all over the country looking for him, we're gonna let him know where you are," the marshal said. "Gonna let him come to you."

"I might have been born at night, but not last night. You gonna use me like I was Mr. Parker. A damn goat. Feed me to

Shadrach, the bear."

The marshal grimaced. "You're tryin' to put me in a bad light, son. Not gonna be like that. I'll shoot the bear 'fore he gets to you."

"And if you miss? What you want me to do?"

The marshal thought a bit. "Well, I reckon you ought to start runnin' or shootin'. Whichever one suits you best."

Chapman watched the marshal's face, hoping to see a smile; there wasn't one.

"Not gonna be that bad, Chapman, I'm not gonna have it on my record that I let a deputy marshal get shot by some border-crossing killer. Here's the way we are gonna do it. 'Bout ten miles west of town, there's a canyon that's pretty much boxed. Half mile or so long.

"Gonna let you work some of those little dry spreads out there—buying steers. Spread your name round pretty good. Let folks know where you're gathering the cattle. You can set up a little camp kinda out in the open half way up the canyon. Want folks to be able to find it easy. 'Specially Shadrach."

"You want me to camp out in the open? Easy found?"

"Yep. I'm gonna look out for you. I've got a Sharp's .50. Buffalo hunters used them. Got a tripod. Five hundred yards, I can shoot a gnat in the ass."

Chapman laughed, but not much. "I'm not worried about a gnat's ass. I'm worried 'bout my ass."

Unless one developed a love for the desert and its barrenness, there was little to enjoy west of Roswell. The ranches were scattered, and most of the people wondered why in the hell they'd settled in this wasteland. Of course, there were reasons: hiding from something or someone; solitude seekers; orneriness; or just too plain stubborn to give up.

Chapman stopped by a half-dozen ranches and introduced

himself, always saying, "Name's Chapman. Used to live down near Fort Stanton and worked with a rancher named Quezada. I'll be holding my cattle out in Tom Elder Canyon. Down there close to that little creek. Water will run out in a few days, so my stay won't be very long." He told the ranchers, "Spread the word among your neighbors. Any of your friends got anything to sell, tell them where I am, and that I pay honest prices. Probably need a couple dozen more head before I'll take off north."

He camped out in the nearly treeless, yellowish-gray rangeland under a mesquite that must have been growing here when conquistador Francisco Vázquez de Coronado was searching for the Seven Cities of Cibola. In three days, four ranchers came by, and Chapman bought an ill-tempered bull, a dozen cows, and a calf with the scours. An Indian stopped by and tried to sell him two goats.

Inwardly, Chapman cringed at the sight of the goats, and the story of Mr. Parker and the bear came clanging through his mind. Quezada had given him a telescope—Civil War vintage—and a battered leather case. He glassed the hillsides without success trying to find where the marshal was hiding—hoping he was a whole lot less than 500 yards away.

"You'll not see me," McCavran promised, then, "Shadrach won't either. Little cave up there. I've stocked it with water. I am a very patient man. Think of me as a rattler waiting to strike."

Late afternoon and the desert lost its crisp smell; there was nothing now but heat and the faint scent of creosote brush and sage. Chapman built a sparse fire and boiled coffee. He had ground staked his horse, and now the animal raised his head to face down toward the mouth of the canyon. The horse's ears moved forward, listening to something Chapman could not hear.

★ ★ ★ ★ ★

The marshal's .50 caliber boomed from the rim of the canyon. A mesquite branch fell to the ground—five feet behind Shadrach. Boom—this time the shot was too low, and it smothered in the sand.

Chapman could hear a horse pounding toward him. *Oomp-oomp-oomp.* Steel horseshoes striking rocks. Bushes slapping against leather.

Zella

Zella checked on Chapman's milk cow each day and gathered the eggs. For a week, she rode by his house and out to the barn. Her curiosity increased, and one afternoon she got off her horse and peered in the window. He was surprisingly neat; he'd made the bed and hung his clothes. She pushed the door open and went inside. His dishes were upside down on the kitchen table, protecting them from blowing sand and insects. No pictures. Nothing personal. A straightforward and uncluttered man, she thought. Probably past trainable.

Not that it was of any interest to her.

Tom Elder Canyon

Yesterday, Chapman paced the distance between the boulders—the place he intended to take his stand—and the entrance into the box canyon. Just a little less than a hundred and fifty yards. His Winchester had a flat trajectory up to one hundred and twenty-five yards. If he took a fine sight on the head, the bullet would strike the target at no less than eye level.

Deeper up the canyon, the cattle were restless and bawling for water. The herd bull, an ill-tempered roan and white animal with a seven-foot horn span, was leading the thirsty cows out of the canyon and toward Chapman. If the oncoming rider got in with the herd, it would be much more difficult shooting.

Chapman crawled upon the boulders. With the sun now at his back, he lay across a room-sized rock and rested the rifle on his folded jacket.

The rider raced from the canyon entrance, standing in the stirrups, searching the rim rock for the source of the rifle fire. His hat had blown off and was held against his back by the stampede string. His red head rag made a fine target.

Chapman's first shot took Shadrach high on the top of his shoulder, the bullet reaching him before the sound of the rifle. He crumpled forward just as Chapman took aim and fired again. Dust poofed from the Mexican's shirt.

He slipped to the side, his boot caught between the stirrup and the tapadero, and the frightened horse went crow-hopping through the brush, the broken rider bouncing without rhythm against the rock-strewn sand. Chapman levered a third cartridge into the chamber, cursed, and fired at the horse, but the bullet, deflected by a mesquite bush, went whining away.

Spooked by the gunfire and the panicked horse, the bawling cattle retreated and milled in a circle, cloven hooves churning the sand into a fine dust that rose skyward above the rim of the canyon.

Chapman mopped the sweat from his brow and reloaded. He climbed higher up on the boulder, rested his rifle, shaded his eyes from the brightness, and glassed the brush with his telescope. Shadrach's horse stood a hundred yards away, head hung low, sides heaving as it tried to regain its breath after the long run through the sand and brush. The saddle was gone from the horse's back.

Chapman looked back along the route the horse had taken and saw a glint of silver and then a motionless man, leg twisted, foot still trapped in the stirrup. From the rim of the canyon, Marshal McCavran shouted, "Good shootin', man; you got him."

Chapman stepped into the saddle and rode toward the broken body, his horse skittish from the gunfire and the metallic scent of blood. An early evening breeze whispered down the canyon, the mesquite leaves quivered, and Shadrach's shirt rippled slightly. Chapman rode closer and sat looking at the twisted body before he dismounted. He pulled his handgun and thumbed the hammer back.

Shadrach moved ever so slightly and blankly stared out into the distance past Chapman. Blood gathered at the corner of his mouth and trickled into the sand, leaving a rust-colored blotch against the whiteness. He cupped his lips and exhaled. An intake of breath, then, *"Agua, por favor."*

Chapman untied the canteen from his saddle, took it in one hand, cocked pistol in the other, and advanced slowly. Keeping his distance, he leaned over ever so slightly and splashed water across the dying man's lips.

Shadrach lay on his side, left hand under his shirt; his right hand shifted to shade the sun away from his nickel-colored eyes. *"Más, por favor,"* he whispered.

Chapman holstered his pistol, dropped to his knees, and poured more water into Shadrach's mouth.

"Más," he whispered once more.

Chapman tilted the canteen again.

Without taking his hand from beneath his shirt, Shadrach fired a shot from the derringer he'd taken from the pawnbroker in Ciudad Juárez. The bullet entered Chapman's body just above his right pap and exited just below his right shoulder blade.

Chapman grunted in surprise. He remembered Quezada's maxim: "Always shoot 'em one more time." He snatched his revolver from his holster and fired once. The bullet passed between Shadrach's eyes, and sand geysered behind his head.

Chapman's pain was not immediate; it was more a feeling of

being shoved. He sat back on his heels, the canteen falling to the sand, water gurgling and convulsing out its narrow mouth. The explosion from the derringer seemed to last for seconds, booming in his head and reverberating. He took a shallow breath; the pain pulsated and then stayed. He toppled over and lay on his side, his cheek indenting the sand. A desert flea scurried past his eye, and he couldn't focus—couldn't remember how.

Death

On rare occasions, people have journeyed through a dark tunnel to arrive at the border between this world and the other world. From this darkness and confusion, they have peered into the other side. Without exception, they report seeing a bright light and feeling a sense of calm. Then the light dims, and they encounter softness, warmth, tranquility. They feel translucent, and there is a sense of peace and being lifted.

His father, Lathel, dressed in khaki, straightened from a transit and waved. His mother, sitting in a rocker with a shawl across her shoulders, looked up from her poetry book and gave a weak smile. Quezada sat on his horse, a soft fog floated stirrup high, and the rider touched his thumb and forefinger to the tip of his gray hat. Behind them were people he'd never seen: women in gingham dresses and bonnets, bearded men in buckskin shirts, a sea captain, a lamplighter, a sheepherder, a fisherman, a gladiator, a shoe cobbler, a stonemason—most smiling; all beckoning.

He reached from the darkness and tasted the light with his fingertips. It would be easy, he thought. Leave the darkness and the pain. Turn loose.

The Women

The two women walked across the pasture toward a barn, a

cow, and a newly born, wobbly-legged calf moving up the path before them.

"Have you ever done something, and you are ashamed of yourself?" Angalee asked Muñoz. "Something you can't take back. Something selfish. Something where you were only thinking of yourself."

"Or afraid to face something?" Muñoz said. "Afraid to do something you knew was right. That's selfish. I've done that. Did it for years."

"Kinda makes you wish you were Catholic, doesn't it?" Angalee said. "Have a priest to confess to, get it off your shoulders. Get rid of the guilt."

Muñoz laughed. "It's not that easy. I come from a Catholic family. Too simple. If it worked that easy, everybody would be Catholic."

Belzora sat cross-legged on the ground, working burrs from a ram's fleece. At her feet, a little girl played in the dirt. Her sister's child. She would never have a child of her own. There were many things she'd never had or would have.

But she'd never be beaten by a man again. Shadrach or any other man.

If she ever had any dignity, he'd taken it away. But she'd taken his money—his precious money—and with that, she'd put a hole in the man he thought he was.

She picked her niece up and sat her on the fleece.

Zella walked the path from her barn, quarter full milk pail swinging from her arm. A black and white cat she'd named "Brother" trailed, his tail rigid in anticipation of a saucer of milk. Except for a dull reflection in the kitchen window from the setting sun, her house was little more than a silhouette.

Loneliness never bothered her. She'd lived by herself for so many years; quietness had almost become an acceptable companion. Now she wondered if sharing a supper table with a man . . . having a mister to talk with . . . maybe a man in her bed . . . how would that be?

She moved these thoughts away to the place where she stored dreams and forgot about them. Almost.

Tom Elder Canyon

"There's no other way to do this," the marshal said. "It's gonna hurt like hell or maybe worse. In a way, you're lucky. The bullet went plumb through—bigger hole where it come out than where it went in. Took part of your shirt in with it. I pulled it out, and I've stuffed a rag in the top side. Left the low one open—stop blood from puddlin up in your innards."

He helped Chapman to his feet, then up into the saddle. "You lean over now, son. Hold your hand here. Keep as much pressure as we can on where the bullet went in. We're gonna walk the horses. Not gonna shake you more than we have to."

Roswell

It took almost six hours to get to Roswell. Two lit windows and three curs greeted them. Chapman's clothing was sweat and blood soaked. His horse continued to look back, spooked by the lethargic rider.

"You know any kind of doctor in this town?" the marshal asked.

"Woman helps deliver babies," Chapman said. "Folks go see her. Call her PV. Not her real name. Folks call her that anyway. Claims she can stop blood. She is married to a seventh son of a seventh son. His name is Wayne. Claims he can take off warts."

"Well, we ain't worried about none of that 'cept stopping blood. You're tougher than an old razor strop and are gonna be fine." The marshal said all that, just meaning half of it—the part about being tough.

It took three minutes of the lawman's pounding on the front door and shouting "U.S. Marshal, Ellison McCavran" for the midwife to answer. Her husband, the man who could cure warts, stood behind her, a scattergun across the crook of his arm. "What you want?" she said, holding a lantern at eye level.

"Got a man here who's hurt. Got shot. Understand you deal with such matters."

The woman looked to the edge of the porch where Chapman's horse stood, its rider slumped over the saddle horn, shirt and pants dark with blood. "Where did he get shot at?" she asked.

The marshal turned and reached up for Chapman before stopping to answer the question. "It was out in the country in Tom Elder canyon, 'bout half—"

"You silly shit," the old woman snorted. "I don't care what part of the country. Where'd the bullet take him? In the head? In the back? Side of the ass? Where?"

"Oh, I misunderstood; looks like the bullet went in 'bout here," he placed his hand over his chest, "and come out his back."

The old woman stepped to the side and motioned for her husband to help the marshal. "He been sittin' up all this time?" she asked.

"Yeah. He's been a-horseback pretty much since he was shot," the marshal said, and the old man helped Chapman off the horse and onto the porch. The woman looked at Chapman's shirt. "Set him over there in that chair. Don't tilt him none." She turned to the marshal. "Cut his shirt off. I gotta get some stuff. Be right back."

By the time the marshal completed his task, the old woman had come back to the porch carrying a yellow-flamed kerosene lamp. She set it on the floor next to Chapman. Her high cheekbones shadowed the light from her eyes and deepened her wrinkles. She wore an apron, its whiteness marred with brown, vertical streaks.

"She's good at this kind of stuff," her husband said.

The old woman went back into the house and returned carrying a sugar bowl, a clean pillowcase, and a quart of whiskey. "I want you to hold him up straight in the chair. And hold him tight, 'cause he may try to buck some in a minute."

She took short scissors from her apron pocket, cut the pillowcase into broad strips, and laid them across her arm. "Now, I'm gonna take me a little nip of whiskey and a dip of snuff to steady my hand," she said. "Then I want you to get a good holt."

She took a slug of whiskey, shuddered, then took a metal snuffbox from her pocket, tilted her head back, and deposited a thumb-size amount of snuff behind her lower lip. She cupped her hand and made a funnel, then poured whiskey down into the gullet of the ragged bullet wound near the top of Chapman's shoulder. He lunged forward, cursing, yelling in pain. "Just keep holding him," she said. "I ain't done yet."

She took another slug of the whiskey, then poured a tablespoon of sugar into the open wound and bound the shoulder with two strips of cloth. "Now, I'm just gonna pour a little whiskey where the bullet came out. It won't hurt too much but you'd best hold on tight 'case he decides to run off. Or act a damn fool."

She poured; he cringed a bit but didn't shout or cuss or anything.

"Not gonna wrap this up like I did the top," she said. "Not gonna pour any sugar 'cause I don't want it to clot over. If it needs to drain, we'll just let it drain on this rag. And that, Marshal, is all I can do for him. You stay out with him tonight and be sure he sets up straight. We goin' back to bed. I'll bring you some hot coffee and couple of sugar-biscuits in the morning. Your man make it through the night and he ain't spitting or coughing blood tomorrow, he gonna be all right. Sore for a while. Can't ride no buckin' horses. Best not cough too big or try to strain out a fart."

The marshal sat on the floor beside Chapman for what was left of the night. Right after daylight, the old woman came out with the coffee and biscuits just as she promised.

"He's gonna get sorer for a couple of days. I believe it best you get him where he's gonna stay this mornin'. 'Sides, I don't want no marshal and his shot-up buddy sittin' on my porch drawin' flies and buzzards. Ain't good for my bidness." She squatted beside Chapman and pulled the bandage away from his shoulder; he gritted his teeth and sucked air. "Got a good seal growin' up there where I poured the sugar and don't see much drainin' down his ribs. Me and the old man are goin' fishin' directly. Oh, last thing. You owe me a dollar and six bits."

The Pecos Valley

The marshal brought Chapman's horse and helped the wounded man up into the saddle. Chapman was not too happy about it, but he was tired of sitting on the old woman's porch. Anyway, she didn't want them out there, so it made leaving easier.

But there was a problem. Chapman's shirt had been sliced into three pieces before it could be removed from his body on the previous night. And it was stiff with dried blood.

"Never be fit to wear again," PV said as she carried it on the end of a stick and threw the garment under the porch. "I'd loan you one of my husband's, but he ain't got but one and he is wearing it."

"Don't look at me," the marshal said. "I haven't got another one, either. You done a good job Chapman, but I'm not giving you the shirt off my back."

"Loan you couple of my aprons," the old woman volunteered. "Tie one on frontwards and one on backwards. It'll do till you git home. I'll not charge you nothing. Jest bring 'em back in first passing."

They walked their horses through town, Chapman sitting slumped over in the saddle, wearing two aprons, gritting his teeth, sweating. "Gonna let you rest here in the shade for a minute," the marshal said. "Talk with those two cowboys over there at the blacksmith's tent. Now, don't you run off 'fore I get back." The marshal laughed; Chapman didn't even smile.

Five minutes later, the marshal returned. "Cut a sweet deal with those two fellers," he said. "They gonna go out to Tom Elder canyon, bury that mean-assed Mexican, and bring whatever is left outta those cows back to your place. I got his pistols and that fancy engraved rifle he was carrying. Told them they could have the ornery bull for their trouble. They figured they was driving a hard trade, said they wanted a calf, too. I give them the one with the scours."

"Where are we going?" Chapman asked.

"Hell fire, man, I'm carrying you home. I ain't no nurse. Might stay around couple of days, 'case you come down with some kinda ague. Then I gotta get back down to El Paso. 'Spect there will be a bad man needs catching."

Chapman shifted gingerly in the saddle and adjusted the front apron. "Like you caught Shadrach?"

The marshal looked at the upcoming road and ignored Chapman's comment.

The two crossed the Pecos. The sun was just three hours high, and slender heat waves were causing the horizon to dance. They rode along in the low hills, horses glad for the slow pace in this heat.

"How come you are bringing the cows to my place?"

Chapman asked. "I don't feel like seeing after any of your livestock."

"They ain't mine; they're yours," the marshal said. "You bought them. You ain't got a bill of sale. I can't take them, can't sell them. They was bought with government money, but the government don't know that. So I'm giving them to you. And if you tell anybody where you got them, I'll swear you are a damned liar."

The two got to Chapman's house before dark. The marshal helped the wounded man off the horse and into the coolness of the house. "I'll go get us some groceries. Be back in a couple of hours," he told Chapman. "You sit right still until I get back. Might even look for a nursemaid for you." He lit a lamp. "Don't want you stumbling around in the dark. And try to not be wearing an apron when I get back."

He came back and found Chapman sprawled on the bed, asleep. The lawman made cathead biscuits, fried two steaks and six eggs, boiled a pot of coffee, and woke Chapman. Both men ate like they were starving.

The next day about noon, the two cowboys came down the lane with fourteen head of cattle, a shapeless cloud of reddish dust following like a ragged apparition. They turned the cows into the lot and shook hands with the marshal. "How's that Chapman feller?" they asked, secretly wanting to talk with him.

There's always been something fascinating about a man that'll hunt another man, legally. Chapman was one of those men. Anybody can buy a gun and go out and shoot a rabbit or an antelope. But when a man is hunting something that can shoot back, it puts a little different light on things—sets the man apart. The two cowboys figured even if they could not talk to the man hunter, maybe they would at least see him. Give 'em braggin' rights down at the saloon.

While the cowboys didn't know much about Shadrach, the dead Mexican was impressive even in death—his earless head, empty eyes open in death, and face scarred from street fights. That it took three bullets to kill him told a lot about his constitution.

"He'd have scared a bad dream," one of the men said.

"I'd druther not think about him," the other said.

The cowboys watered their horses and saw Chapman sitting in the porch shade, two blood stained bandages across his body. They raised their hands in greeting; Chapman nodded.

"Don't look all that tough to me," one of the riders whispered. "Eyeballs sunk way back in his head like that. He's skinnier than a range bull."

The other cowboy squatted, his back toward Chapman, and inspected his horse's hoof. "Why don't you go up there and aggravate him a little—see if you can make him come outta the shade."

"Yeah. Yeah, I'll do it next time Christmas comes in July."

Both men stepped up into their saddles and turned down the dusty road toward Roswell. "You reckon he's as bad as folks say?" one asked.

The other replied, "I'd say he was badder and worser."

This was Saturday: a day free of school teaching duties; a day Zella caught up on housework and chores around the place. She saw the riders pass with the cattle, and then later when the two came back.

She saddled her horse and rode down the lane to Chapman's house. It was time to see after his milk cow and calf. And to see what all the commotion was about. She thought of it being neighborly and not nosey—not that what anyone else thought made a difference.

She stopped in front of the house and, when no one came out, circled her mouth with her hands and shouted "Hello."

Then, "I've come to see about the cow."

The marshal stepped out of the house, into the yard, and introduced himself. "U.S. Marshal Ellison McCavran El Paso," he said, like it was one long word. "You that redheaded woman that lives on the next ranch, ain't you?"

"No. I'm *the* woman, not *that* woman."

"Yes, ma'am. The woman. I got Chapman inside. He's been up some, but now he's took to the bed for a while. Got shot up some."

"What do you mean *shot up some*? Is he hurt bad?"

"Well, I don't think it's very serious," the marshal said. "But then it's him that was shot, and I believe he might see it some different. He ain't taking on much, but he ain't laughing much, either."

The woman pulled herself back up in the saddle. "Maybe I could see him in the morning after I look after the milk cow."

Considering his wound and the nursing care of Marshal McCavran, Chapman slept reasonably well. The lawman fried bread in butter and boiled coffee before going to the lot to check on the cattle. He came back to the house and saw Zella's horse tied to the garden fence. Inside, Chapman sat propped up in bed, a platter of *huevos rancheros* balanced across his lap. The woman sat in a wooden straight chair watching him eat.

"Put you a plate on the kitchen table," Zella said. "Kinda light on the chili sauce and refried beans. Wouldn't want to ruin Chapman's day."

McCavran ate and came back into the room, where Chapman was picking at his food. "Don't look like the man's got much of an appetite," he said.

"Maybe he's got better manners than you," Zella said, and everybody except Chapman laughed.

"Don't be too hard on me," McCavran said. "Let me show

315

you something that I risked life and limb for." He pulled a rifle scabbard from under the bed, laid it on a table, and slipped the Winchester '73 out. "There you are," he said. "One in One Hundred. Got a helluva history behind it. I know for a fact Ab Quezada paid a hundred-twenty dollars for it. Look at the engraving: *Winner Slash Q Shooting.*"

Zella studied the rifle and handed it back to McCavran. "Who's Quezada, and what is 'Slash Q Shooting'?"

The marshal slid the rifle in the scabbard and then everything back under the bed. "On another day, Chapman can tell you about Quezada. But I probably know more about the rifle than Chapman. I've heard he won it fair and square. But one of the Soto brothers stole it before he even got to touch it. I know that from what Alberto sputtered while he was in a confessing mood. Then I reckon Shadrach took it when he killed one of the brothers."

"And I'm supposed to know who Shadrach and Alberto are? And the Soto brothers." Zella asked. "Or is that something I'll find about later, too?"

"If you can get Chapman to talk."

"So, this Shadrach man, he had it all this time?"

"Lot of the time, I guess. He had it with him when Chapman shot him off his horse the other day. I got it and brought it here. Figured it was about time the rightful owner possessed it."

"Took a while, didn't it?" Chapman said and tried to laugh. The laugh never got past a sick grin, and he clutched his side.

Zella felt his forehead; it was warm.

The marshal stood at the window watching summer ducks circling out over the shallow lakes. He turned and neatened the corners of his moustache with the side of his index finger. "I've been thinking about you looking after Chapman's hens and milk cow. If you are making a trip up here every day anyway, probably wouldn't be too much trouble if you looked in on him. See if he needed anything to eat and stuff like that. Wouldn't be putting you out too much, would it?"

"You putting him in the same class with a cow and a flock of hens?"

"No. Well. Not exactly. But you see what I mean, don't you?"

Zella took Chapman's plate to the kitchen and came back. "Yes, I know what you mean. You mean you're fixing to ride out of here and leave me with a sick man. That's what you're saying, isn't it?"

"Miss Zella, you're making it sound a lot worse that it is. He's not that sick."

The woman tidied up the bed covers some before answering. "If I can see after a cow, surely, I can look after a man."

"Then it's, yes, you'll see after him some."

"Some."

The marshal gathered his duster, gun belt, rifle, and scatter-gun. He touched his hat brim. "Mighty kind of you, ma'am," he said and was out the front door before Zella could qualify her answer.

He was an easy patient. Zella brought him breakfast before leaving for her teaching job in Roswell. In the afternoon, at a time when she was accustomed to seeing after his cow and chickens, she brought him supper. During the times she was not there, he sat on the porch, moving ahead of the sun, staying in the shade. He found himself looking forward to their twice-daily visits; secretly, she did, too.

Three weeks after the shooting, Chapman could cough without holding his right side and tears coming into his eyes. "I believe tomorrow I can start looking after myself and the livestock. You've been a good nurse, and you're a good cook. Don't see how I can ever repay you."

Zella had started letting her hair flow around her shoulders, the severe schoolteacher bun a thing of yesterday. "Oh, you'll find a way. Neighbors have a way of seeing after neighbors."

The next morning he pulled the tub back under the artesian pipe. By late afternoon, it was full of sun-heated water. He reserved a full pail, looked out across the flatness, saw no one, stripped naked, and climbed into the warmness. He washed his hair and the stench from his body. Chapman pulled his drawers on and sat on the edge of the horse trough; the sun dried his body.

He took the bucket to the back porch, poured the warm water into a tin washbasin sitting on a wooden shelf next to his shaving mug and straight razor. He went back inside and returned with a piece of broken mirror and his razor strop. He hung the metallic ring of the strop on a nail and commenced to pull his straight razor across the leather.

He lathered his face and stood looking at his gauntness in the mirror, his eyes recessed, and his cheekbones sharp. He guided the razor through the lather; it built up on the back of the blade, and he washed it clean in the basin. He tilted his head and pulled his mouth to the side, tightening the jawline skin. He straightened his sideburns and poured fresh water into the basin. Finally, he washed the remaining lather from his face.

She stood at the edge of the porch and watched. His dark hands and face contrasted sharply with his skin as if misplaced on the wrong body. The ribs rose against his skin, the exit wound still angry on his back. He needs feeding, she thought.

Before she could speak, he turned and saw her. "Good evening," she said. "Bet you forgot it was Saturday, and I'd be by early."

He nodded, embarrassed she'd seen him like this. "Go on in," he said. "Soon as I find my pants and shirt, we . . . we'll . . . uh—"

"Continue our conversation," she said.

He echoed, "Continue our conversation."

Things changed after that. She'd get home from school, and he'd be hoeing her garden or cutting stovewood. Sometimes, he would have boiled a chicken and made dumplings—slicks, he called them. They sat on the porch in the coolness of the late afternoon, and she patched his shirts.

He learned of her early life: escape from Star Valley and the Mormons, school teaching in Colorado, and working in a dry-goods store. He talked of his Tennessee upbringing and told her about Quezada. He talked of Angalee and her boys and their early deaths. He told her about Evans, Tollafson, Chance and the other Fort Stanton cowboys, and Fort Bliss and the Argentinean, Muñoz. He didn't say much about Shadrach, except to say he was a bad man who finally got what was coming to him.

They never talked about the future.

On these early fall nights, when the coyotes cried and sang in the distance and the night birds swung through the dark sky, they sat at the kitchen table, played dominos, and drank coffee. At ten, he would saddle up and ride back to his house. It had never seemed really lonely. Until now.

One night he didn't go home. The next morning he woke, and they were sharing a pillow, Zella's head resting in the hollow of his shoulder. Her red hair lay in folds across his chest; her lines contouring beneath the sheets. He looked at the patternless freckles dusting her shoulders. Then he lay staring at the ceiling for what seemed hours, almost afraid to breathe.

She stirred, the straw of the mattress rattled softly, and she could see his face. His eyes were open, but he had not disturbed her sleep. Something about this contented Zella. She shifted her head until her breath slipped across his neck, and a smile crinkled at the corners of his eyes.

The next week they married.

If they had known of the lean years that lay before them, it would not have affected their decision to marry.

Zella continued to teach; Chapman fought the arid land. They bought five sections of pasture in ten years, mostly from ranchers who admitted defeat and moved on to something they hoped would not torture their souls with visions of semi-starved cows and ungodly dryness.

"We'd have been run out years ago if I'd not been smart enough to marry a school teacher," Chapman told anyone who would listen. "Being married to a teacher runs in my family," he said but never elaborated on his mother.

He broke horses for neighbors. "Two dollars four bits, I'll make them so tame your mother-in-law could ride them to church," he boasted. But it came at a cost of both collar bones broken, sprained knees, and dislocated hips.

"I'm a better nurse than teacher," Zella told a neighbor. The next week a steer ran a horn between Chapman's thigh bone and muscle, and Zella was back in the patch-up-the-cowboy business.

Together, they could overcome everything except the barrenness.

"If I were a cow and never had a calf, you'd sell me," Zella told Chapman.

He rubbed that special place in the small of her back and laughed. "If you were running a ranch and had a bull like me around for all these years with no calves, why, you'd make a steer outta me 'fore I could turn around twice."

CHAPTER FIVE:
1920s

The Pecos River Valley

They'd almost quit thinking of ever having children when Zella became pregnant. Then life seemed to mock them again; the baby boy was stillborn. Zella was strong, Chapman crushed. Maybe it was because she mothered children at school that she coped better. Sometimes she would wake at night and he would not be in their bed. She would find him sitting on the porch, face buried in his hands, shoulders heaving, sobbing quietly.

"I'll be better," he said. But he wasn't.

He was still a commissioned deputy U.S. marshal. Now the lawmen rode in cars, but occasionally, when they could not find their fugitive because he had taken to the brushy canyons, desert, or the mountains, they would come by and ask Chapman for help. "He can track a last week's dream," they told Zella. It made her proud of the man who had become taciturn and moody.

He'd return in a week, sometimes two, cooked almost black by the desert sun. Haggard. Silent. Exhausted. Horses spent.

She never questioned him about his search; he never talked about it. But she learned things from the man at the post station. "Marshals say he's the best. Called him coldhearted. Wouldn't want him trailing me."

Zella met a parent of one of her students on the street. "My husband tells me Chapman is the toughest man he's ever seen. Sheriff told him he would give up a Yankee nickel from Mary

Pickford 'fore he'd let Chapman come hunting him."

Zella didn't want to hear this kind of talk about her husband. She'd never seen this side of him.

She watched him make his bedroll, clean his rifle and pistol, gather bullets in a leather sack, and swing up into the saddle. At times like this, she wondered if she really knew this man Chapman, this man she'd married, this man with a heart broken over the loss of a child who never breathed.

Once he was gone ten days. Zella was on her way to the well when she found him asleep on the porch, arm crooked across his eyes, a horse blanket covering his thin body. She went back inside, came out with a cup of coffee, and sat by him, smoothing his matted hair with her hand.

He sat up, bleary eyed, a month's growth of beard, lips chapped. "I can't do this anymore," he said. "It's killing me. It's killing you. You never signed on for a life like this."

She gave him the coffee, and he took a long drink. He hooked the top of his spurs on the edge of the porch steps, pulled until the boots slipped off with a sucking sound and lay in the sand, the shafts gapped open and oval-shaped like the mouth of a prairie dog's den. He took another drink, and she saw his nails were uncut and dirty.

They sat side by side in the woven willow swing. She leaned forward, removed his socks, and tossed them into a pool of sunlight. While she was still stooped, he laid his hand softly across her back and then with both arms encircled her, the side of his face resting against the nape of her neck.

She felt his body tremble once and then a second time. Then he sniffed like a little boy will do when he's trying to stop his nose from running or has stubbed a toe and needs to cry.

Finally, he loosened his grip, and she straightened to lean in against him. "You need to talk about it?" she asked.

He drained his coffee cup, and she went inside and returned

with a fresh cup. Her collie came onto the porch, sniffed Chapman's feet, and settled with his head touching Zella's shoe.

Chapman looked across the plains and began.

"I met a marshal, the Lincoln County sheriff, and one of his deputies over in Hondo. They had lost the track of a man who'd stolen a truck and a couple of old man Hale's fancy horses. Didn't get ten miles outta town 'till the rustler got the truck hung up. Unloaded the horses and took to the mountains. The lawmen were a little scared of him; he'd shot one deputy. Didn't kill him but spooked the rest of them. They are not used to being shot at, much less being hit."

Chapman stood and walked to the edge of the porch and looked down the dusty road like he was expecting somebody. He came back, sat, then crawled his fingers along the dog's side. He straightened and laid his hand, palm up, on Zella's lap.

"I finally picked his trail up and the next day found where he'd laid up for the night, campfire ashes still barely warm. He turned northwest and went just south of Carrizozo. I knew we had him; wasn't anything in front of him but El Malpais. I figured surely to God he'd turn up the valley and not try to cross that rough country. Guess he panicked and just quit thinking. He wasn't three hundred yards out into the lava beds before both his horses gave out. He was sitting out there in the edge of one of those lava-tube caves. And, damn him, he opened up on us, bullets gouging the sand and whining off the rocks.

"Sheriff and his deputy went north of him; marshal went south. We figured he'd try to get out the same way he'd gone in there, and I'd be waiting on him. Sure enough, that's what he did. I let him get about fifty yards from me, and I stood up and hollered, 'United States marshal, put your gun down.' He fired on me with his Winchester. I took a shot at him.

"He shot at me three more times without taking time to

aim—*bam, bam, bam*—like a man will do when he's scared. I waited until he moved to the edge of the lava. I shot again and saw his hat go sailing off. He dropped his rifle. Put his hand to his forehead and staggered. Took a couple more steps toward me, his head lolled to the side. He fell. Never got up.

"Sheriff and his deputy eased up on him and had a look. Deputy waved his hand and hollered that I'd got him. Said he was dead. I leaned against a rock and shook for a bit. There is something about killing another man that will get to you sooner or later; don't think anybody ever gets used to it. Marshal went on up, and they dragged the man outta the rocks back to where I was sitting."

Chapman left the porch and went to the side of the house and out of her sight. Zella could hear him retching.

He came back, hobbling barefoot across the yard, and went to the horse trough. He washed his face and hands. Retched again and washed up a second time.

Zella didn't go to him, didn't want to embarrass him, but stood in the edge of the yard, not looking at him but, instead, out across the prairie.

He came back to the edge of the porch, drying his beard on his shirtsleeves. "The horse thief, the man who'd shot the deputy and then pulled down on me . . . man I'd shot—" Chapman wiped his faced again and rubbed his hands on the side of his pants. "Tollafson . . . dumb sumbitch was Tollafson."

This time when he buried his face in his hands, Zella went to him.

He slept through the day, Zella frequently checking through a partially opened door. It was not a restful sleep—most men can't sleep for a while after killing another man—as he tossed and moaned, grimaced, hands rolling and unrolling the top of the sheet. His lips moved, but the words were unintelligible.

The sun no more than two hours high in the western sky, Zella opened the door and went into their bedroom. Chapman sat on the edge of the bed, hands splayed across his knees. "What time of day is it?" he asked.

"Almost supper time," she said. "I've warmed your water out at the well. If you are interested."

He stood. " 'Spect I ought to be interested. I smell so bad I couldn't hardly stay in the bed with myself." He smelled his armpit. "Have mercy!"

A nice thing about living in the desolate part of the country is privacy. The next neighbor lived four miles to the west, and, if Zella wasn't teaching, it might be a week before they saw another human. Sometimes, women found the solitude overpowering, and if they had no children and a rambling husband, they would carry on in-depth, one-sided conversations with the chickens or a horse.

Chapman crossed the yard, barefoot, his drawers hanging loosely from his thin shanks. He climbed in the galvanized tub and slid down until only his head was visible. Zella brought his razor, soap, and two bath cloths and knelt beside the tub. She soaked his beard and then shaved his face as expertly as a barber. She wiped the shaving lather against one of the bath cloths, then washed his hair.

They did not talk.

When she finished rinsing his hair, he sat upright and motioned her to step over into the tub with him. She pulled the hem of her dress up, tucked it in under her belt, and stood between his raised knees, facing him. He washed her calves, her knees, and then her thighs. He stood and removed her dress, and they sat in the warm water, her back to him. He washed her neck and breasts, and the soapy water slid down her arms, then dripped from her elbows.

They ate a cold and late supper that night.

He slept until noon the next day.

She left early morning for her school teaching and apologized to the children for her absence the previous week. *My husband was sick; I was needed at home,* she said, and the children questioned. "Was he shot?" a fourth-grade boy asked. *No, he'd been gone for a while and was tired and sick.* "Did he shoot anybody this time?" a girl asked. *That's not something people talk about.* A seventh grade boy stated, "My Daddy says Chapman is coldblooded, a man hunter." *He helps the marshals sometimes when they need him. He is a good man with a kind heart.* Another boy, bolder, "I saw him at the feed store other day; he's kinda scary." *Must have been somebody else; my husband isn't like that.*

Shadows were lengthening when she came into the yard; Chapman unhitched her buggy and took the horse to the barn. "We'll be having leftovers tonight," she said, "if that is OK?" He grinned and rubbed the special place in the small of her back.

"Will you sit here?" he said and motioned to the swing. He stood behind her and brushed her hair.

They finished supper, washed, dried the dishes. "Want you to take a little ride with me," he said. "Won't be gone long, just down to the lakes." He saddled his horse and came back with her spotted mare. The air lost its heat; a coolness was setting in. They stopped at the edge of a sinkhole to watch a flight of dragonflies skim the surface of the placid water, their flight uniform as if choreographed.

They rode down to the bottomland, the crusty grayness of the flatness broken by the scattered, stagnant pools. Chapman dismounted and rummaged in his saddlebag until he found the marshal's badge. He threw it sidearm; it twinkled in fading sunlight, danced across the water, for a second seemed to float, then disappeared beneath the surface.

"There," he said.

Zella waited for more—something . . . some explanation. Then she knew he didn't need to say anything else. He'd said it all.

He pulled himself back into the saddle, and they turned the horses toward home.

Fall came. The demons haunting Chapman slipped away; Zella hoped they had become mired somewhere in the quicksand along the Pecos River and drowned.

He went back to digging post holes and breaking horses.

Zella fed Chapman biscuits and steak slathered in white gravy. His belt no longer tightened to the last hole. "I'm about to reach frying size," he joked and walked about the kitchen, thumbs buried in his armpits, arms flapping, chicken-like.

"Could I interest you in a vacation away from the cookstove?" he asked one morning as they finished their second cup of coffee. "I'd love to carry you west, over the mountains. Where I got my first cowboy lessons. Need to look at Fort Stanton and Quezada's old ranch. It's been a long time since I was there. Some folks I want to see. How they've got along. What's happened to them. That was an earlier part of my life, and I want you to be a part of that."

A week later, they loaded the buggy, stowed a tent and cooking supplies in the back, took an extra horse, and set out westward across the grayish desert. Once they reached the Capitan Mountains, their pace slowed. They fished for trout in the mountain streams and swam naked in pools still tinged with last winter's snowmelt. They pitched their tent in the mouths of narrow valleys and sometimes didn't talk, just sat and watched as the shadows worked their miracles.

"Over there," he said. "That's the old parade grounds. Aw,

look at the buildings; that kinda hurts. It was on the way down when I first saw it, but at least it wasn't falling down. See that tree? Saw my first Indian right there. Bought a turquoise pendant from her. One dollar. Wonder where it ever got off to.

"Post station sat right there. No. No, it was a little farther down. There. There it is. I'll be damned—it's still standing." He got out of the buggy and walked around the building, looking at it as if it were a Christmas present from his childhood. "A wrinkled old woman was the postmistress. Probably about my age now. I thought she was ancient."

He climbed back in the buggy. "I asked her where Quezada's ranch was. She told me to follow the river, said there was a couple of windmills out in the pasture. Headquarters was across the river."

He pulled the horse to a stop. "There," he said. "See it. Looks as good as it ever did. Dang, you don't know how seeing it makes me feel. I wasn't much more than a pup when I first came here."

Zella slid across the buggy seat and gripped his arm. "Now you're an old dog, gray around the muzzle."

They moved forward, and another building showed between the trees. "There's the bunkhouse. Slept there the first night I was here. Thought I was a real cowboy. Found out later I had a bunch of learning ahead of me. A whole bunch."

"You made it," Zella said. "You made it a long time ago."

"The hands were eating dinner. Potatoes and beef. Eating like they were starving."

"Remember who they were?"

"Yeah. Chance and Evans . . . and . . . uh . . . Tollafson. He showed me how to saddle a horse. Told me he had a brother and a first cousin hanged for stealing livestock and changing brands with a running iron."

"A brother?"

"Yeah. Reckon in a way, it kinda ran in the family." Chapman waited, cleared his throat, and then continued. "I wish it hadn't . . . I . . . I really wish it hadn't."

They pulled into the front yard and tied the horse to a long hitching rail. A three-legged dog came from beneath the house, gave a couple of perfunctory barks, then sat and stared at them, seemingly satisfied he'd done his duty. A horseman came from the barn and rode up to the buggy.

Chance leaned forward, resting his hands against the pommel of his saddle. "Well, by God, if it ain't Chapman. A sight for sore eyes if I ever saw one. And I'm betting this is your wife. You shore done good for yourself, old son. Real good."

Chapman reached across the buggy wheel and shook Chance's hand. "This is Zella. And yeah, I did good. After I married her, folks around Roswell started calling me Lucky. You married yet?"

"Married? Me? Married? You gotta be joshing. Ain't a woman in four states would have me. I reckon I'll die a bachelor. 'Sides, I'm way too old to try to break in a wife."

"Well, hell. What's wrong with me? Get down and come in the house. Seeing the way your rig's covered with dust, I'm betting you're way past tired."

"Anybody else around the place I'd know?" Chapman asked.

"Well, I guess. Angalee and Muñoz probably down at the garden by the river. I'll go and get them. Ab will be back pretty soon. Mare had a colt last night in the back pasture. He's gone to get 'em."

Chapman crawled down from the buggy and held his hand up to steady Zella as she stepped to the ground. "Ab? Don't remember anybody named Ab," Chapman said.

Chance grinned and turned his horse. "You'll like him. He's a hell of a fine hand. Sits a horse 'bout good as anybody I ever saw. Muñoz is responsible for that; ain't a better teacher around.

Go on in the house. I'll be back pretty quick."

Zella and Chapman walked across the yard to the side lot. "Yep, branded my first calf right over there," Chapman said, hooking his thumbs in his belt and walking with exaggerated bowed legs to the fence. "Good job, if I do say so myself. 'Course the smell of scorched hair liked to have made me throw up."

Zella laughed and gave him a little shove.

"There's the well. It's the one we used while I lived here. I'd come out here to get fresh water the night Quezada died. I heard his gun go off, and I dropped the bucket right there and ran back into his bedroom. He never took another breath. Worst hour of my life. I remember it like . . . like it happened five minutes ago."

A rider came from the tree line leading a mare, a spindly-legged colt closely following. "Hey," he shouted, "be right there soon as I stable this mare."

Behind them, a wagon rumbled up the caliche road from the river, two women sitting in the spring seat, Chance on horseback to the side. They stopped in the edge of the yard, and Chance helped one of the women to the ground, then crossed behind the wagon and helped the other.

The younger of the two women hurried across the yard and awkwardly hugged Chapman, head against his shoulder, patting his back.

"This is Zella, my wife," he said, then, "This is Carla Mu-ñoz." The two women shook hands.

Angalee came from behind the wagon, smoothing her silver hair along the sides of her temples. She shyly extended her hand to Chapman. "After all these years," she said. "You haven't changed that much, kinda weathered." She turned to Zella. "And this is your wife; Chance told me," she said and smiled. "I hoped you had a wife. And a family? You have children?"

Chapman put an arm around Zella and pulled her against him. "Not yet," he said. "Just haven't gotten around to it yet. Zella teaches. We been putting some land together. Busy. You know how ranching is, got no idea one day to the next what's going to happen."

Angalee nodded, embarrassed at her thoughtless question and sorry she'd put him in a position he had to answer. "I do. Been on a ranch almost my whole life," she said and turned again to smile at Zella. "It's not the easiest way to make a living. But I'm sure you've found that out by now."

The young man finished tending to the mare, and now he came from the barn to where the others stood beside the house. He stopped beside Angalee, removed his hat, and dragged a shirtsleeve across his forehead. "Still hot," he said.

She dusted hay from his shoulders and combed his brown, curly hair with her fingers. "This is an old friend, Chapman, and his wife, Zella," she said. Then, "Chapman, I don't believe you've ever met my son, Ab."

Chance took the wagon to the barn, and Chapman followed with the buggy. Ab had ridden along the river, checking the fences and looking for a cow that strayed during the night. Muñoz took the last of the fall tomatoes into the kitchen, while Angalee and Zella sat on the front porch.

The two men took the gear off the horses and fed them grain. "Reckon you heard about Tollafson," Chance said.

"Hadn't been over this way for a while," Chapman said, evading the question.

"Not too long ago, the marshals cornered him up in the *Malpais*. He'd stolen a couple of horses. And a truck. A damn truck. Didn't know no more about driving a truck than I do 'bout having a baby. Dumbest thing I ever heard of."

"They arrested him?" Chapman asked, closely watching

Chance's expression.

"No. They killed him. I heard one marshal was from El Paso and the other one from Albuquerque. Heard the sheriff's deputy said it was the one from Albuquerque that done it. Just come in and done their job and left. You know how they are. Arrogant bastards."

"Yeah. I do," Chapman said, glad that Chance was fastening the barn door and not looking at him. "I'm glad you told me. But I'm awful sorry to hear it. He was good to me, you know."

"Well, he had this streak in him. Angalee let him go years ago. Got to where she couldn't trust him. Drinking too much and shit like that."

They walked toward the house together, a trip they'd made hundreds of times. "I didn't know about Ab. Seems like a nice young man," Chapman said.

"Yeah, he's a good 'un. Got a little wild streak in him. Guess not too much for a feller his age, 'bout right I reckon. Angalee's raised him different than she did her other boys. He's not been under her thumb. She cut the apron strings early. He's a good man and gonna make a hell of a rancher when he gets a little more experience."

"Angalee remarry?" Chapman asked.

Chance stopped walking and turned to Chapman. "You know better than that. Don't believe she married with the first two boys. Wadn't no need to start now. And I bet you gotta 'nother dumb question. And I ain't gonna answer it either."

They resumed their walk. Chapman, hands in his pockets, was looking at the ground. Thinking. Counting the years. His eyes welled. "Not gonna ask you any more questions," he said.

They ate supper on the porch that night, the lamplight drawing bugs that charged relentlessly against the screen wire.

Soon after they finished eating, Chance and Ab left for the

bunkhouse—got a game of dominoes hanging from last night was the excuse.

Muñoz and Zella cleared the table, then stayed in the kitchen to wash the dishes. Chapman and Angalee sat at the table, cups of coffee growing cold. The weak lamplight softened Angalee's wrinkles and filtered the years. Openly, each studied the other's face.

"We've done this before," she said, "sit like this," and Chapman nodded. "I told you then you were a generation too late, and you didn't believe me. Now you understand what I was telling you. Time does not wait for anybody nor gain on anybody. It moves at its own pace. I want you to know right now, I never regretted having Ab. Not for a minute. But I would have regretted having you here." She watched his face, waiting for a response. "Am I making sense—you know what I'm saying?"

"I would have made a good daddy," he said.

"You might. Might not. We'll never know. But I raised two boys, and I'd learned some things. Young men have to have wings before they try to fly."

"But it's not fair—"

"It's not a fair world. It's not fair Joe and Sam died down there in that border country. It's not fair Quezada and I couldn't get along. It wouldn't have been any different with you. I've always been set in my ways, from the very beginning. I'm an old woman now. You've got years ahead of you. You and Zella. Your time will come. Mine did."

"Then, I don't understand. If you knew all this, why did you come and . . . ?" His voice trailed away.

". . . come to your bed; that's what you are asking, isn't it? Why did I come to your bed? Everything I had was gone. Quezada. Joe. Sam. You were the only thing left that had any love for me. I needed you that night. I needed help. For one night, I needed someone to prop me up. I didn't care what was wrong or right. I didn't worry about the next day or the day after. On that one night, I needed you. I'm a quick healer. Always have been and always will be. Can you understand what I'm telling you? Maybe you can't now, but you will someday."

"Did you ever think anything about me?"

"I did. I thought about you. You would have hung around here, following me like a puppy. I didn't need that. You didn't need that."

"But, it was so sudden. The next morning, you told me to pack up and get. It was like . . . like you . . . like you didn't care."

"But I did care. Cared enough to send you on your way before you made a fool of both of us."

She turned in her chair, and her face was shadowed. "But you were just a young stud. I knew how you felt about me. But it could have been any other woman. I know how the sap rises in most men, necks swell like a buck deer in rut. I've watched them all my life. Learned from my mama, and that wasn't good.

"I saw a man up at White Oaks get taken by Mama. That was a rip-roaring town then. Man came into town, suit, tie, shined shoes. Mama rubbed up against him just once in a saloon, and that was it. He never had any sense again. Asked Mama to marry him. Said he'd look after me like he was my own father. We went over to Carrizozo, and they married. We stayed in the hotel there, had two rooms."

"But that's not like us," Chapman protested.

"Shows what you know. Women are women. Mama came to my room the second night, said for me to get up and be quiet about it. We left the hotel, got the man's buggy, and went back to White Oaks. Man showed up two days later and said that Mama had taken thirty-five hundred dollars from his suitcase. Had her arrested. She sent for me to bring the man to the jail.

Sheriff let him into Mama's cell, and they sat on the bunk together. She whispered in his ear for a couple of minutes. He frowned and hollered for the jailer to let him out. Next morning he told the sheriff to turn Mama loose, said he didn't want to press any charges."

"What did she say to him?"

"Don't know to this day. But whatever it was scared him so bad he left the country. Couple of weeks later, Mama bought the ranch where I was living the first time you saw me. Paid thirty-five hundred. Cash."

"And I'm supposed to get something from that story?" Chapman asked.

"A normal man would, man that understood women. If that doesn't, maybe this will help. Quezada told me about showing you the gold. Nobody ever bothered it; not Quezada, not me, not my boys. But when you all left after buying the horses, I moved the gold. Got suspicious. Didn't even tell my boys."

"You mistrusted me? Quezada's friend?"

"Yes. Women don't trust anybody. Even another woman. But, anyway, I put the gold in a lava tube that opened up between two sotols and a yucca 'bout a mile from where you saw it. Looked around and figured I'd remember the place forever. Years ago during that hard winter, all three of those bushes froze and died the next year. Then the wind blew the tops off, so my hiding spot looks exactly like the rest of the *malpais*."

"Lost out there in all those badlands?"

"Yes. Lost just like almost everything else in my life. But as you can see, I'm a strong woman. And strong women move ahead."

With his index finger, Chapman rounded up stray grains of sugar into a black square of the checked tablecloth. "Don't you think a boy ought to know his daddy? I mean, after all—"

Angalee shook her head. A quick, decisive movement. "There

is no after all." She stood from the table, raised the lamp globe, blew the flame out, and took their dishes into the kitchen.

Before breakfast the next morning, Muñoz and Chapman walked to the top of the hill where Quezada was buried. A marker sat at the head of the grave with nothing but the single word, *Quezada*, chiseled into the face of the native stone.

"He influenced a lot of people's lives," Chapman said. "Couldn't say that he was all good, but you always knew where he stood—nothing watered down. A hundred years from now, I doubt that anyone will remember that he passed this way. I think his bloodline ended with him in this part of the country."

"You can never tell," Muñoz said. "Bloodlines are funny. Sometimes they seem to go on by themselves. Something just pops up occasionally."

"Sometimes. But not this time, I think."

They started down the steep trail toward the headquarters, the mountains rising purple behind them.

"Do you ever think of that night down at Fort Bliss?" Muñoz asked Chapman. "Every once in a while, I dream of it. That scary man, it . . . it marked me—might have made me who I am. Not something I've been able to put behind me. I'd . . . I'd never been handled like that. I thought I might die."

Chapman nodded. "My first time to shoot at anybody. I couldn't have hit my boot with a pistol. I'd have done better throwing rocks at him."

They came to a gate and stopped. "What do you think ever happened to that man?" Muñoz asked.

"His name was Shadrach. He's dead. Died out west of Roswell sometime back. You can put him out of your nightmares for good."

"Dead? You sure?"

"Sure as I'm standing here."

"That's good. Mayhaps not too good for him," she said, then laughed. "Mayhaps. Sounds like Quezada, doesn't it? Perchance I'll sleep better now."

They passed through the gate, shut it, and continued on.

"I know you won't ask," Muñoz said looking away from Chapman and across the valley, "but I've been happy here. Angalee is not as strong as she puts on. I've been needed here. Maybe that's what I was cut out for—just be needed. I've taught Ab some things about horses. He kinda thinks of me as an uncle—or an aunt. We don't talk about it. Never had a need to."

"I'm . . . uh . . . I'm glad for you. Zella and all. Things have a way of working for the best, don't they?"

Chapman nodded. "I believe it's really time. Just give things time, and mostly it'll turn out OK."

Angalee and Zella sat on the screened porch, drinking coffee as Chapman and Muñoz came down the trail from the cemetery.

"I'm glad you came with him," Angalee said. "You've . . . you . . . you've married a good man. He's solid. Started to say you were lucky, but fortunate might be more fitting."

"Thank you. We've had a good life. Few bumps. Probably less than most married folks."

Angalee smiled and reached across the table and patted the back of Zella's hand. "Well, you got him early. Wasn't too old and set in his ways. Gave you plenty of time to break him in right."

Ab came across the yard with a pail of water. "Drawed a fresh bucket for you, Mama. You and Mrs. Chapman. I'll put it in the kitchen."

Zella watched him. Brown, curly hair. Rail thin. Sun-kissed dark as any Indian.

"Handsome, isn't he?" Angalee said.

"Takes after his daddy," Zella said.

Angalee nodded. "I . . . I . . . uh . . . never knew his daddy when he was that age."

Zella looked at Angalee and smiled. "I've been around horses about all my life. Show me a yearling, take me down to the pasture, and I can pick out his daddy."

"You think that holds true in humans?"

"Pretty much," Zella said and then nodded, agreeing with herself.

Angalee drank and looked across the top of the cup at Zella and caught her direct gaze. Open. Non-accusatory. Calm. Frank.

"It doesn't bother you . . . I mean . . . knowing that Ab's father . . . knowing that I . . . that we—"

Zella leaned forward, her elbows on the tabletop, chin resting on her clasped hands, and smiled at Angalee. "I've bought and sold horses most of my life. The best horse I ever bought was owned by a widow woman who lived over at Caprock. I've still got that spotted horse. Never bothered me at all knowing that another woman once owned him. Guess you could say that I know a good one when I find it."

Angalee digested the other woman's words. "You're a fine horse trader, Zella. A fine horse trader. Hope I never have to bargain against you."

Zella chuckled and said, "Don't worry. You never have and never will."

After breakfast, Ab brought the rig into the front yard. The women hugged; Chapman and the men shook hands.

"Been a pleasure meeting you, sir," Ab said to Chapman. "I've heard a lot about you. From Chance, mostly. He says you are a crack shot. Me, I'm usually low and to the left. Perchance you can help me sometime."

Chapman didn't look at Ab. "Mayhaps."

Angalee stared at Chapman, a smile, and a slight shake of the head. "Perchance. Mayhaps. You sound just like a man I used to know."

There was a heavy sense of finality—a feeling this would not happen again, these people would never be in the same place after this moment.

Chapman and Zella rode along the river road; crumbling Fort Sheldon came into view. They stopped and looked at the parade ground now covered in brush and weeds. The feeling of emptiness was overwhelming.

Zella took Chapman's hand. "I think Ab is a handsome young man. I liked him. When we have children, and if we have a son, he'll look like Ab."

She continued. "I would have liked to have known Angalee. When she was younger, I mean. She told me that she had two other sons, but they both died years ago. I knew most of that story. I let it go and didn't question her any more.

"And Muñoz would make a great neighbor. There is softness beneath all that hard exterior."

They rode northward, the buggy wheels cutting into the dust, the fort disappearing behind them. Chapman was lost in the road unwinding across the rolling prairie before them.

"In a way," he said, "it seems as if everything happened yesterday. Quezada, the cowboying, gunfights along the border, selling those horses to the army, the shooting at Fort Bliss." He looked across the range. "Everybody was young—least a lot younger than they are now. Then again, it seems like it happened a lifetime ago. Maybe even to somebody else.

"I've learned a lot. Lot of folks helped me learn. You've taught me about the good and loving things in this life. Durn near completed my education. I believe my daddy would approve."

She smiled and leaned into him. He put his arm around her.

They turned eastward toward home. They rode along in silence, and, finally, Zella said, "Do you feel better now?"

"Yes. I needed to do that. And I needed you with me."

Late morning, they stopped, and Chapman built a small fire and boiled a pot of coffee. "You remember me telling you about Felipe, the *vaquero* that was always around? Chance tells me that when the old Mexican died, they buried him just down the hill from Quezada. Marked his grave with a wooden cross. It musta rotted away 'cause I never saw it. Anyway, he wound up close to Quezada. Guess that was good. He's probably still looking out for his old *jefe*, playing songs on the old beat-up guitar and fetching tequila for him."

"That's the way it's supposed to be," Zella said. "We keep the ones we love with us forever."

"Even after we're dead?"

"Yes, even after we're dead."

Chapman raked ashes over the fire, then poured the last of the coffee into the shallow fire pit. "I kinda like the sound of that. Me and you being together forever."

Chapter Six:
1930s

The Pecos River Valley

In 1930, a mild year with green pastures and greater than normal rainfall, Zella gave birth to a son. Chapman was fifty-five, and she was forty-five. It was the twentieth year of their marriage.

They named the boy Martin. Neither of his parents had a Martin in their family, nor had they ever known anyone with that name. They just liked the way Martin Chapman sounded. He read before he started to school; teachers' children are like that. He rode a horse at five months, sitting in the saddle in front of Chapman and holding on to the horn. "Cowboys need to start learning pretty quick," his father said. "There's lots to learn about being a man—don't want him to wait as long as I did."

"I would like for him to be a doctor," Zella said. "I've always wanted to have a son who chose medicine as a career. A man who could help people."

"Would you settle for him to be an average rancher and a good man?" Chapman asked.

He can make up his own mind, they agreed.

But Martin never left Chapman's shadow, and Zella knew the boy's destination long before he did.

"I've traded a calf for a red pony," Chapman said one night after supper. "Zella, you think we can find a little boy who'll want to ride it? 'Course, it'll take a lot of looking after. Feeding and watering and stuff like that. Be a big job, lots of responsibility."

Martin was gathering the supper dishes and stacking them in the dish pan. "Me," he shouted. "Me. I can do it. Why, if I've got my own horse I can help round up strays. First thing you know, I'll be breaking wild horses. Be a regular hand."

"I don't know, son. You're pretty young for something like that."

"Daddy, I'm almost seven. And I'm eating everything that Mama puts on my plate. And I can tie my own shoes.

"Tell him, Mama. Tell him how I feed the chickens and gather the eggs. And I help you gather the tomatoes. Pick peas. Look after the dog. Tell him, Mama."

"He does all that, Chapman. Pretty handy fellow to have around. He just might be ready to start working on being a cowboy."

Martin could barely breathe. Daddy put pretty high stock in whatever Mama said. He'd lot rather have her on his side than 'bout anybody he knew—'cept Daddy, of course.

"I don't know, Zella. We can give it a try. See what happens. But I'm telling you, son, it's a big job."

Over the coming twelve years, Martin would progress from the red pony to the rankest of horses in the Pecos Valley.

Life on the ranch wasn't easy. It hadn't been in the past; it wouldn't be, ever.

"Cowboys are cursed," Chapman would say. "We always need rain, and if we get enough for the grass to grow, cattle prices are down. Looks like it's one damned thing after the other."

"Why don't you quit? Do something else," Zella said, knowing the answer in advance because they'd had this dance before.

"Quit. Woman, did you say quit? Why, I don't even know

what that word means. Say, if I did quit, what'd I do? Work at a grocery store? Maybe sell shoes? You want a man that'd do stuff like that?"

Zella grinned. "No. I didn't say anything like that."

Chapman continued as if she hadn't said a word. "This is all I know, and here you are, trying to make a sissy man outta me. Next thing I know, you'll be trying to put a tie around my neck."

Zella poked her finger in her husband's ribs. "You'd look good with a necktie. White shirt. Get rid of those calluses in the palms of your hands. Why, I can see you now."

"No, you can't. You wouldn't let me put my feet under your supper table if I was like that. And another thing. What kinda example would that set for Martin? I'll not have my boy saying that his dad got starved outta ranching and took to clerking in a store. No, sir. I'll not have it."

Zella poked him again. "Well, if you say so. If you got your mind made up, I'll not try to change it."

Chapman tilted his head back and jutted his jaw. "Well, I hope not. The very idea."

Chapman was a good teacher, patient almost to a fault. "No, son. Make your loop like this. Let it grow a little, a little more. Two swings. Now, easy. Good. Good. Now let the loop go." The rope dropped over the stubby post. "Now take the slack out with your right hand. Keep your left hand in front of you. Let it slide through your front hand. That's good. Now, we gonna do it again."

It was getting dark; the sun had set, pulling the redness of the evening sky with it. Zella stood in the edge of the barn lot. "I've called you the last time," she said. "Supper is getting cold. No, that's not right; it is cold. Nothing worse than cold, chicken-fried steak. You don't come on, I'm going to feed it to the cats."

Chapman raised his hand, palm toward Zella. "One more

time, Mama. Just one more time. He's about got the hang of it." He turned back toward his son. "Little bigger loop, Martin; let it grow a little more."

Zella went back into the kitchen and put the food in the stove's warming closet. She knew "One more time, Mama" really meant we'll be in when it gets so dark we can't see the post.

Secretly, she didn't care. She and Chapman could eat warm food after Martin was grown.

Chapman taught Martin lessons that went far beyond roping and riding wild horses. "You'll never be a man until you know the right way to treat a woman," he lectured Martin. "You got one woman in your life right now, and that's your mama. And that makes her special. You're not gonna ever have another mama. She carried you in her belly, son. She gave you life.

"But someday, you're gonna have a new woman in your life. That'll be your wife. And that makes her special."

They sat horseback on the bluff overlooking the Pecos River as it coursed southward, a reddish-brown snake languid in movement. The summer sun had yet to bake the vegetation, and a breeze swept across the grass causing it to undulate—now green, now gold, now green again.

"And then," Chapman paused. "Then someday you'll have a child with this new woman. That'll make her even more special 'cause this'll be something you've made together."

The dinner bell rang at the ranch house. Both horses turned their heads and pricked their ears toward the sound.

"That'll be for us, Dad. Don't want our dinner to start getting cold. Don't want Mama feeding it to the cats."

Chapman grinned at his son, and they turned their horses toward home.

★ ★ ★ ★ ★

"Being a good parent is like being a good horse trainer. It's important to teach the horse but not break the spirit," Chapman told Zella. They sat on the porch swing, and, in the dusk, they could see Martin leaning against the corral gate, talking to his pony.

"You're right," Zella said. "Just to show you how right you are, I believe I said the same thing last week."

Chapman slid closer to Zella and laid his arm across her shoulder. "I was just checking your memory," he said. "Still pretty good."

Zella looked at her son on his thirteenth birthday. His voice had started to change—that now-high, now-low sound boys find so embarrassing. The fuzz on his upper lip had thickened and darkened. She was careful not to point out the obvious.

"I'd like to put a rock on top of your head," she joked. "A heavy rock. One with enough weight to stop you from shooting up like one of those weeds growing along the riverbank."

In the back of his mind, the talk his father had given him earlier about Zella being a special woman grew stronger. "I've been thinking, Dad. What you said 'bout Mama. What if I just stayed here on the ranch and looked after her? I mean, I know you do a good job, but when she gets older, she'll need a little help—drawing water, looking after the new calves, things like that. I'm not real sure that I'll ever want to marry."

Chapman grinned. "You think that now, but when you get older, you'll find a woman of your own. You'll change your mind about getting married. 'Sides, I don't want to share Zella with you all my life."

CHAPTER SEVEN:
1940s

The Pecos River Valley

When Martin was fourteen, Zella died sitting in her rocker in front of the fireplace. A skein of green woolen yarn coiled in her lap and spilled onto the floor. No one would ever know, but she inherited her family's weak heart, and that was what killed her. Chapman found her, knitting needles still clutched in her arthritic fingers, a peaceful smile pulled at the corners of her mouth.

"Dad never grieved openly after Mama's death," Martin told Matilda after they married. "I'd come in from looking after the stock, and he'd be sitting on the back porch, looking out across the pasture. I wouldn't say nothing, and he wouldn't, either. Both of us would just kinda nod. He was just like that, but sometimes I'd hear him at night, talking to Mama. Telling her what had gone on that day. Talking to her about the pastures and the rain. The price of cattle. Sometimes, he'd ride down to the river bluff in the evenings, look out over the sinks and all that dryness. Watch the dragonflies till it got plumb dark.

"He'd come back to the house. Tend to his horse. Go straight to bed."

Matilda looked away from Martin because she did not want to see the tears in his eyes.

"I can tell you, he wasn't always the man you see now. He was a different man when Mama was around. She made him shine. Don't think I can tell you how much he loved her. Maybe I didn't even know myself."

The person who benefitted the most from Chapman's outlook on women was Matilda. She'd been pampered—"Papá's Pet," her siblings called her—but she'd never truly experienced love until her marriage to Martin. "He is such a kind and gentle man," she told her sister. "Did you know that he brings *café* to my bed on cold mornings?"

The sister felt envy; her own marriage ended shortly after it started. Her husband preferred crap games and the tawdry women with tight dresses who sat at the corner tables in bars. The women who wore too much makeup and saw every married man as a challenge.

"He is never angry, at least not with me," Matilda continued. "Never has he raised a hand to me. He cares about my happiness. He loves me as much as he loves our son—just different. I didn't know such loving men existed."

"But he's a young man," her sister argued. "Young men are always hungry for other women and—"

Matilda shook her head. "Not Martin."

"Then he is very strange," the sister said.

Matilda patted her sister's hand. "No, that's not it. He learned the ways of a man from his father."

Martin Chapman caught the train in Roswell for Fort Sill, Oklahoma, on an overcast September day. The wind blew sand across the depot waiting room floor, and it eddied in the building corners unable to escape, trapped with bits of paper, grass seed, and cigarette butts.

He and Matilda sat on a wooden bench in the station's waiting room, and he wiped the tears from her face. "Two years, three at the most, I'll be back. We'll build a ranch, run a bunch of cows; I'll be somebody you'll be proud of. We'll still be young, have more kids," he said. "Pete'll need brothers and sisters."

The little boy climbed up on his father's lap and ran his fingers across his face.

"Pete, you be good now, you hear?" Martin told his son. "You mind your mama. See Grandpa Chapman behaves himself. Don't let him try to ride any wild horses. Help him around the ranch."

Chapman came into the waiting room. He was seventy-four, stooped, had a bad hip, and walked like a man with one boot heel missing. Martin stood, and the two men hugged. Neither patted the other's back. Not a word passed between them.

"I'll take Pete with me," the older man finally said to Matilda. "Give you two a chance to do a proper good-bye."

The train's whistle moaned, a low wavering call the wind whipped eastward toward the river, and the conductor came through the room calling, "Board. All aboard."

Four other men, faces smooth with youthfulness, climbed the three steps into the passenger car and chose seats isolated from the other occupants. A cattle buyer from Socorro guessed the young men's final destination, closed his eyes, and, looking downward, shook his head. In 1942, he, himself, commenced the northward trip along with two other young men. He returned to New Mexico in 1945; the others never came back— one died at Normandy and one blown to bits on a sandy beach on Iwo Jima.

Martin lowered the window and waved at his wife. "See you soon, honey," he shouted.

She blew him a kiss and called, "I'll love you forever." But her final words were lost in the clamor and churning of the locomotive's drive wheels.

The train moved northeastward. Martin saw his father on horseback at a road crossing on the north edge of town, Pete sitting in the saddle in front of him holding onto the old man's hand. The horse stood with his rump to the gust, tail blowing between his back legs and mane tilting forward into whatever the future had in store. Chapman's collar tilted with the wind and leaned against his graying hair.

Pete waved, little chubby fingers clenching and unclenching in the fading light; Chapman nodded and touched his index finger to his hat brim.

CHAPTER EIGHT:
1970s

Washington, D.C.

Jill Bateman, the nurse, married on the ninth day of April when the cherry blossoms burdened the branches and caused them to bow and nod gracefully in the wind. She, the groom, Amon Barlar, and the navy chaplain stood in the grass under the pink glory, and the Washington Monument rose up behind them, a silent and eternal sentinel—the only witness to the ceremony.

The marine major was dashing, she thought, in his evening dress uniform, and he thought she, wearing a long white skirt and barefooted, was the most beautiful woman he would ever see. The chaplain was almost envious of the aura that washed across the ceremony, for he too had once been young and in love.

After the vows, the newlyweds held hands and strolled along the lake. He bought coffee at a refreshment stand. A cherry blossom petal blew into her cup, and an old memory rose up from her past. She'd seen this before. A petal had blown into the soldier's cup. And for a moment, even in her happiness, an image of the crippled man surfaced.

"Santa Fe, New Mexico? You want to go to Santa Fe for our honeymoon?" he said, then laughed. The major would have taken her to Timbuktu or any other place in the world.

The Rio Grande Valley

Their plane dropped over the Sandias and settled onto the runway at Albuquerque Sunport. Inside the terminal, the wooden beams, tile floors, and Indian art were a stark contrast to the sterility of this morning's Dulles International.

They bought coffee and *churros* and sat on a balcony overlooking the concourse. Below, children played hide-and-seek games amid the throng of deplaning travelers. Trailing the stream of passengers, a young woman pushed a wheelchair, its occupant a prematurely gray, thin man who leaned forward staring listlessly at the floor, his legs covered with a gray blanket.

The nurse took her husband's hand and said, "Our reservations are not until tomorrow night in Santa Fe. You've never been in the West. I'd like to take a short side trip . . . maybe let you see the mountains and deserts south of here . . . might even show you off to an old friend."

They rented a car and drove southward along the Rio Grande through the Chihuahua desert to Socorro, then eastward across the rugged desolation of the Valley of Fire, and finally through Carrizozo to Capitan.

"You've brought me from the hustle and bustle of Washington to spend the night in the Smokey Bear Motel, right here in the middle of downtown nowhere?" he said.

His wife laughed and kidded him about riding a desk and now he might have an opportunity to ride a horse. They had *chimichangas* and a bottle of wine that night, then walked to the park and sat holding hands in the moonlight.

He'd heard part of the story before. But tonight she gave all the details and, for the first time, made him realize her emotional attachment to the happenings surrounding the soldier. He suggested they see if he was in the phone book at the motel. Give him a call.

"I can't," she said. "If he is not at his dad's old place, then I don't know where to look. We've got to go out there—I've got to see. I'll know the turn-off to the ranch when I see it. Assuming it's still there. If we don't find him in the morning, we'll go up to Santa Fe and create memories we can relish as long as either of us breathe.

"Then go home. I'll put all this to rest—it won't be easy, but I can do it." She looked down and picked at an invisible thread on her blouse. A minute passed before she said, "But down deep I'll know somehow my best effort was not enough. And I'm not accustomed to failing, you know."

The next morning they breakfasted on *huevos rancheros*. She seemed reluctant to start the search: brushing her teeth, a touch of lipstick, adjusting her neckerchief, tucking a strand of hair under her cap. He threatened to go without her. "Not in your wildest dreams; the mountain lions and the coyotes would eat your socks off," she said.

Driving eastward, their automobile reeled in the dark ribbon that was Highway 380.

"It's just over this little rise and around the next bend in the road," she said twice, and disappointment showed in her face when no side road appeared. "It's up here where the creek bed runs parallel with the road; I can feel it." She leaned forward, and her entire body supplicated.

And the gravel road was there.

The entrance to the ranch was framed by two pinyon posts and a cross timber. A weathered plank with the crude image of a dragonfly cut into it swung by two rusty chains from the cross timber. "Chapman's mark," she exclaimed. "It's his father's mark." She covered her face and cried.

They turned through the gate and drove across the pasture road, made a sharp turn beside the husk of a burned car, and there was the house perched on a narrow bench of rock overlooking the creek. They passed two stock barns and a herd of cows that suspiciously eyed their unfamiliar vehicle. Beyond the house, two men were in the midst of a furious cloud of dust while working steers through a gate and into a holding pen. As the car approached, both men dismounted and shaded their eyes against the glare of the late morning sun. The larger man tied the horses to the corral fence; the other man stripped his tan work gloves and walked toward the car, an Australian blue heeler shadowing at his side.

"That your man?" her husband asked and at the same time knew it wasn't.

Jill slowly shook her head. How foolish, she thought, driving out into this isolation and expecting a miracle, expecting to find someone who demons surely repossessed years ago.

She studied the man as he approached the car. He had the bowed legs and the pitched-forward gait of a man born into cowboy boots. Obviously, he was someone more comfortable riding a horse than walking. Faded denim shirt and jeans draped his whippet-lean frame. Curly hair dropped over his ears when he removed his broad-brimmed, sweat-stained hat. He hooked his index finger and scooped sweat from his forehead. A week's growth stubbled his face. His batwing leather chaps—she remembered the soldier had told her the correct pronunciation was *shaps*—were scratched and the edges tattered. He would never appear in a fashion magazine but it wasn't because he was unattractive. He fit the land.

The cowboy walked to the driver's side and asked, "Can I help you folks?" He leaned down and rested his forearms against the car door. He looked at the driver, then across to the passenger. Before they could answer, he smiled and said, " 'Scuse me, I don't know where my manners went. I'm Pete. Pete Chapman."

★ ★ ★ ★ ★

The three sat on the veranda, and, after the older cowboy tended to the horses, he walked across the yard to the house, the rowels of his spurs making a jingling, musical sound. He'd taken his hat off and now looked at her for a second, forehead wrinkled with concentration, and then exclaimed, "Well, hellfire, you're the nurse. I'd knowed you anywhere. Bet you don't remember me. I'm Rudy, Rudy Vega."

The nurse stood and shook his hand. "Sure, I remember you," she said. "You were a pen rider down at Seven Rivers. You were his buddy."

"That's me," he said and turned to Pete. "What you think about me dragging a cooler of beer out here—kinda help wash this dust outta our guzzle?"

There was strangeness. Pete had been a boy when she last saw him, and now he was a man. Rudy had been a sidekick and still was—except to a different man and in a different time.

The nurse almost intimidated Pete—here was this woman that saved his dad's life. He didn't remember her much . . . mostly what his mother told him.

Amon was impressed with everything: the real cowboys, the ranch, the cold beer, and the reverence the men were showing his wife.

They each had a beer and watched the heat of the midday sun cause thin dancing devils to rise from the corral dust and swirl aimlessly away toward the distant mountains.

Pete rolled a cigarette, lit it with a wooden match. He stripped his brush-scarred chaps, dropping them on the edge of the porch. "I reckon I know why you're here. You've come to see Dad. Well, he ain't here. Ain't been in a long time."

She felt a choking in her throat, and her chest filled; took a drink of beer, and it soured in her mouth. We should leave now, she thought—right now—just get in the car and drive back to

Albuquerque, and I can pretend none of this ever happened.

Pete had seen the tightness gather around the nurse's mouth, the tremble of her chin, and the tears welling in her eyes. "I'm sorry," he said, "maybe I kinda got my words tangled up. Let me explain it to you, and Rudy can jump in when he needs to. Fill in the blanks with the stuff I don't know."

He punctured the top of another beer can, sucked the foam, and laid the opener in front of her. "Probably best if Rudy starts. I wasn't around here for the beginning."

Rudy was a large man, thick through the shoulders, with big, work-worn hands. The timbre of his voice corresponded with his size. His horseshoe moustache was thick and mostly gray. He smoothed it down toward his chin before he spoke. "We come out here, and things was in a mess. 'Course, I don't have to tell you this; you saw it yourself. I wanted to bust the house up and start from scratch. But he argued that Chapman had built it, and he wanted to save as much of his daddy's work as he could. It was hard work. Naturally, he couldn't help much.

"Sometimes, I wished I was still at the feed lot. But he was doing all he could do, them nubby fingers and all—hobbling around carrying planks and using a handsaw. But he got stronger. Laid the rocks for the fireplace and split pine shingles. And he started doing the cooking. Started gaining weight. I told him one night it was my biscuits that had been holdin' him back."

The four had a good laugh about the cooking. Both the nurse and her husband looked at Rudy's big, calloused hands and could not imagine them in biscuit dough.

"He planted more peach and apple trees at Chapman's orchard, and, in the afternoons after work ended, he brought five-gallon buckets of water, two at a time up from the creek to water the saplings," Rudy said. "He didn't want no help. Said Chapman had done it by hisself, and he would, too. I figured them trees would do him in, but they didn't.

"We patched up the house so we could live in it. Got the fences stretched back where they'd hold livestock. Cobbled up the dam down on the creek; built a couple of barns. After a while, he was like a brother. We'd go over to Lincoln or Carrizozo and have a couple of beers, but I'd have to watch him. He'd get pissed off at something and want to fight. Busted up as he was, he'd still fight a buzz saw, but he didn't fare none too good, and I'd have to take up for him."

The blue heeler was sniffing the beer cooler, and Pete called him away. "Tell them about coming over to Artesia," Pete said.

"We'd go over there once a month. It was a hundred miles one way," Rudy said. "It was a lot longer going than coming back. We'd get a couple of six-packs to shorten the trip back to Capitan.

"I'd go by the lumber shed, and he'd meet with Pete at Jamaica Park on the south side of Artesia. He was paying twenty-five dollars a month child support—and for that, got to spend two hours a month with Pete; his own boy—two hours a damn month. Osweldo had to have the money in hand before the visit even started. He insisted that Pete and Martin sit at a certain picnic table so he could park in the shade and watch them—*protecting my stepson,* he said." Rudy spit off the edge of the porch and rearranged the snuff behind his lower lip. "He was one ignorant sumbitch."

Pete smiled and gave Rudy a thumbs-up. "Go ahead, old son, tell 'em what you really think."

Rudy drained his beer and crushed the can. "I don't know everything that was happening in everybody's life at that time. And if I ever knew it, I probably forgot most of it. But I can tell you one damn thing, Osweldo was a revolving asshole. Anyway you looked at him, he was an asshole."

1958

Osweldo had kinda hit a bad patch. He thought his nickname, *El Calculadora*, had been cool. Now he decided *El Tigre* was cooler. Most of the boys at the poolroom had given themselves fancy nicknames, too, each striving for one more sinister than the other. Then the word got around the nurse called him a *culo cobardes*, a cowardly ass, at Romero Luna's house, embarrassed him, called him out, and told him she could see through him— told him he was no more than smoke. Gotta get my reputation back, he thought, and started plotting.

Pete was a happy kid now that he had a real father and was living most of the time with his Grandfather Luna. He brought a ball and two gloves to the park, and he and his dad played catch. His dad brought peanut butter and grape jelly sandwiches and Cokes so cold that ice gathered in the necks of the bottles when they were opened. Osweldo always drove him to the park. It made Pete uncomfortable that his stepfather sat in his car and stared at them.

Matilda wrote faithfully to the nurse each month and got an immediate response. But when she started working full time at the motel and her life busied with the two girls, she wrote less frequently and finally stopped. Osweldo drove by the motel a couple of times each day—"Just keeping a close watch on you," he told her.

Matilda's father, Romero, decided he would not plant peppers this year. But still, Freddy came each day, and the two would sit under the shade of the big pecan tree. "If you are going to enjoy *la sombra* of my tree," Romero said, "it is only *justo* that you help me give it a drink." The two old men would trudge down to the Pecos and together bring back a five-gallon bucket of reddish-brown water to quench the tree's thirst. Late in the day when the desert coolness approached from the east and fanned out over the valley like a blessing hand, the old men would half-fill two glasses with cold buttermilk and top them off with crumbled, yesterday's cornbread. They ate the mixture with long-handled spoons, and, when Freddy finished, he always commented, "Ahh, that must have been God's dessert when He was a little boy."

Although Rudy and the soldier were almost the same age, Rudy felt like a big brother looking out for a younger one. He'd played football for the Carlsbad Cavemen. He'd been an offensive lineman and, at six-feet-four, two-hundred-forty pounds, had been, as a local sports writer called him, a man among boys. He wore the same size jeans as when in high school but had gotten thicker through chest and shoulders. He was now a big man among men. He was not comfortable leaving the soldier at the park while Osweldo was sitting there in his polished Hudson trying to act like some kind of badass—upturned shirt collar, greasy hair looking like a question mark hanging over his forehead, and hiding behind aviator sunglasses.

Osweldo couldn't stop thinking about how the nurse threatened him—called him a coward and smoke. Perhaps he'd start charging the soldier fifty a month instead of twenty-five, or maybe even a hundred. If the soldier balked, it might happen he'd just take it out of his hide. Right there in the park in front of Pete. Show the boy what kinda man his father was—the word would get around. Once people knew the full fury of *El Tigre,* the guys at the poolroom would show respect to him again.

Rudy dropped the soldier off at the park and drove over to the feed store to buy alfalfa pellets for the horses. Osweldo and Pete were late. It was one of those rare days in the desert when the wind was lazy and not blowing sand and dust across the parched prairie, and the air was so clean you could almost taste its freshness. The soldier rolled his jacket into a pillow and stretched out on a picnic table, the warmth of the sun tingling him. It reminded him of how nice it was to be alive. The sound of car doors slamming did not interrupt his peace.

"Daddy." It was Pete whispering in his ear. "Osweldo wants to talk to you. He's over there by his car, waiting."

Osweldo measured the soldier as he limped across the grass and thought, no problem. The soldier wondered why Osweldo was waiting with such a peculiar stance, feet spread apart, hands on hips.

"I am responsible for this boy's welfare." Osweldo nodded toward Pete. "It is expensive to feed and clothe him. I am a hardworking businessman, and it is a great inconvenience to me to leave my important job and bring him over here. And then to stay here and protect him."

The soldier thought: what in the hell is wrong with this man? He knew Osweldo was worthless and had not held a regular job—maybe ever. "I'm sorry that this meeting is such an inconvenience to you. I'd be glad to meet Pete at Mr. Romero's house, if that would help."

Osweldo started talking out of the corner of his mouth with a half snarl like some bad man in a John Wayne movie and gave the soldier his best impersonation of a tough man. "I don't want to do that," he said. "I've never trusted that old bastard. Nor his buddy, Freddy. We can keep our meeting as it is now, but I'll need more money. I will need . . . at least one hundred dollars each time we meet."

Martin looked at Osweldo as if he had just asked for the moon.

"Fellow, I don't have that kind of money. I'm just getting started. Trying to buy a few cows along, finishing up the house, and just barely scraping by." He shrugged his shoulders and grimaced. "I can't do that. It's too much."

Osweldo stepped forward, put both hands in the soldier's chest, and pushed. "Well, can you do this?" he said, as the soldier stumbled backward across the curb and fell into the street, the sharp gravel cutting his hands. Osweldo took another step forward and kicked the fallen man twice in the side. He could almost feel his reputation rising; hear his amigos saying, "Man, did you hear? *El Tigre* kicked the crap out of that *gringo*— right there in front of his son. Man, that *El Tigre*, he's one bad dude."

That's what he heard in his mind. What he didn't hear was the sound of Rudy's Dodge pickup as it slid sideways to a stop in the middle of the street behind him and the crunch of gravel as Rudy ran toward them.

Sometimes, Romero Luna sat on a straight-backed chair in his front yard, a frayed towel spread across his shoulders, while Matilda gave him his monthly haircut. Freddy would sit patiently and wait his turn. She did this on most Saturdays that Osweldo took Pete to the park to visit his father. It lowered her anxiety level if she could keep her mind occupied with other things. Today, the two men had missed their cuts because they decided to go to the park and shake a few bones.

For months, the visits had gone smoothly, but she could sense Osweldo was itching to cause trouble. He referred to Pete's father as "that damned cripple *culo.*" She learned to hold her tongue and not disagree with Osweldo when he was in one of his "moods."

Today, the men were gone no more than an hour before they clattered up the drive in Freddy's beat-up car. They stood under the pecan tree and talked—moving their hands up and down as if they were stuffing something into a basket—before they came into the house, grinning as if they were sharing a secret.

She did not recognize the pickup that stopped at the edge of the road. Pete scrambled out and raced excitedly across the yard. On first look, she did not identify Martin: his limp was not as pronounced as it had been earlier, and he was not as thin. He removed his hat, and his gray hair slipped down and curled about his ears.

"Afternoon, Mr. Luna, Freddy, Matilda. There was a dust-up at the park today," he said. "I'm sorry it happened in front of Pete. Reckon Osweldo was trying to make some kind of point or something. Rudy got in it and . . . well, I'm sorry it happened. To keep peace, and so I can still see Pete . . . I'll try to pay the hundred dollars Osweldo wants. Sometimes I may come up a little short. Mm-hmm—but I'll make it up next time."

For a moment, Matilda placed her hand over her mouth. "A hundred dollars! That's ridiculous." She stepped forward and touched his face. "You were not hurt?" she asked.

He was embarrassed. "Well, Rudy got kinda rough, but I reckon Osweldo's feelings might be hurt some. But he'll get over it."

There was a silence, one of that uncomfortable kind where everyone nods and waits for someone else to talk. Rudy rescued everyone by tapping the Dodge's horn, and Martin turned and limped across the yard to the truck.

In a small town like Artesia, the words about a fight kind of take legs, and it was not long until everyone knew. Pete told his grandfather and Matilda what he'd seen, while Freddy listened. Freddy told his biased version at the poolroom that night. One of Osweldo's friends was crossing the park and saw everything: he had his own version. Two oilfield roughnecks were drinking beer across the park, and they had their own recollections.

With all the exaggerations discarded, the consensus was: Rudy picked Osweldo up by the neck and butt and stuffed him headfirst into a fifty-five gallon metal trash can. Every time Osweldo tried to get out, Rudy poked him back in the can again and kicked the sides a couple of times, for good measure. This went on for five minutes until Osweldo stopped squirming and cussing and remained quietly, upside down in the trash can in the midst of beer cans and apple cores.

With the *El Tigre* name deteriorating quickly, Osweldo became known as "Trashcan" at the pool hall. He needed backup, he told a couple of friends, and then tried to convince them Rudy and the crippled soldier jumped him; that he was kicking Rudy's ass before the cripple sucker punched him.

When Martin next met his son at the park, Osweldo's two friends sat in the back of his Hudson, and, when he approached the car with money, they made a gesture of drawing a knife across their throats.

Romero, Freddy, and two friends were playing Texas 42 at the park pavilion. "Did you see that?" Freddy asked. "See those two trying to scare Pete's daddy?"

Romero nodded. He shook the dominos, and each man drew seven tiles. "I am saddened for my family," he said. "I have not asked for much *en mi vida*. I prayed at the birth of each child—both for the child and my *esposa*. The year my wife and Freddy's wife died, I prayed their end would be peaceful and *llena de misericordia*. I think because I ask for so little, most of my prayers have been answered."

The man to his left bid thirty. Freddy and the next man passed.

Romero studied his dominoes. "It sickens me that Matilda married such a *vida baja*," he muttered. "I wish he would just go away."

"¿Quién ofrece?" Freddy said kindly because he could feel his friend's unhappiness. He loved Romero as he would have loved a brother—maybe even more. It made his stomach hurt to see Romero like this. If only he were younger and stronger, then he would ask Osweldo to be a better man. And if he refused and continued to disrespect Romero and Matilda, well then . . . some other measures would have to be taken. "Will you bid?" Freddy asked his partner again.

Romero studied his dominos. "I believe we'll play . . . sevens," he said. Freddy groaned, turned his dominos face down, and leaned forward to watch his partner play the hand. Romero placed his four-and-three-spot domino face up on the table and announced, *"Siete."*

"Did he talk about his time as a prisoner?" the nurse asked Rudy.

"We was real close—talked about most everything. But he never talked about the war. Prison camp and stuff like that. There's times in the winter where he'd just sit and look into the fireplace at night . . . wouldn't talk. I asked him once what he was studying about so hard, and he said the prison and some Oklahoma boys he'd known . . . and then he'd start sayin' other names. Then he just tuned up and cried. I never asked him again.

"He was always cold; started wearin' this little thin denim jacket all summer. Always cold."

The nurse looked at her husband.

Amon leaned forward and rested his forearms on the table. Sweat dampened the underarms of his shirt.

The nurse went to their car and got a packet of Kleenex before coming back to the table. She dug around in the cooler, pulled out a beer, and pressed its coolness against her forehead. "Please go on," she said.

Rudy smoothed his mustache again. "We got to where we didn't go to Artesia more than once every six weeks. We took to meeting Pete at his Granddaddy Luna's house. Most of the time, Matilda would be there. She'd got to where she'd look at Pete's dad outta the sides of her eyes. And he'd always bathed down at the creek and be smooth shaved when we got there."

We need to move this along, the nurse thought. She needed to get to the end. She needed to know where he was. What happened to him.

Rudy continued. "I kinda had a feeling where this was going to wind up, but it wasn't none of my business. I'd sit out on the porch and talk to Mr. Luna . . . and Freddy, if he was there. Osweldo would drive past the house real slow, music playing so loud I know he couldn't hear a damn thing 'cept that *boom . . . boom . . . boom*. Always had a couple of his poolroom buddies with him. Slimy looking little shits. I'd stand up and move to the edge of the porch when they came by. I had one of them big old .45 Peacemakers stuck down behind my belt, and the handle was showing. They didn't want none of me. They'd scoot way down in the seat where you could just barely see their heads. I reckon they thought it made them look mean or somethin'."

"Let me add something right here," Pete said. "I was just getting to be a teenager, and I thought I knew dang near everything. Mama kept a dress at Grandpa Luna's—it was red with little blue and yellow flowers around the top . . . came down low on her shoulders. She never wore it except when Dad came to visit. She had these pearl combs that were her mother's. She'd do her hair up in the back and pin it with the combs. See it right now. Most of her hair would be under the combs, but there would be a little on the low part of either side of her neck sticking out like angel wings.

"Lookin' back now, I can tell you Mama was still a good lookin' woman. I picked up on stuff pretty quick. Sometimes they'd be in the kitchen at the same time, getting a glass of water or something, and I'd see their arms brush together. But they'd not look right at each other."

Rudy laughed and then said, "So, you can see why I stayed on the porch with the two old men. Kinda keepin' them occupied. I figured whatever was between him and Matilda was . . . well . . . none of my business."

"Osweldo wasn't exactly a fool," Pete said. "He could tell the difference in Mama when she came home after Dad's visit. 'Come back here glowin' and smellin' with that perfume,' he'd holler. My sisters said that he'd slap and knock her around. But it seemed like he always did it worse on the night before Dad's visit. Mama would show up with a split lip or a black eye—she'd tried to cover it up with makeup, but it didn't do much good. It'd piss Dad off pretty bad. I could tell."

Rudy was taking up the story again. "Somebody took to sticking notes in our mail box, saying stuff like: 'I'll take care of you' and 'I'm gonna get you, you pissant' and 'Too bad your house is gonna burn down'. Osweldo had a first cousin that lived in Capitan. We figured it was him."

"How did you know that it wasn't Osweldo?" the nurse asked.

" 'Cause I caught the little fart one day stuffing something in our box," Rudy said. "Scared hell out of him. He had one of them loud, dirt motorcycles, and he run out across the pasture and through a briar thicket like the devil and his dogs was after him."

Pete popped his hands together and laughed. "We run across him the other day at the service station. He's still scared of Rudy."

Rudy boomed a laugh, and his belly shook. "When I scare them, by gosh, they stay scared."

"Things just got worse. Osweldo would tell Mama that he needed more and more money from Dad. And he took to knocking her around more. Sometimes she'd bring my sisters and come to Grandpa Luna's house—stay for three or four days. When summer came, Mama brought me out here to help Dad. 'Course, I knew she was just trying to get me outta town. Osweldo followed us out here and then followed Mama back home.

"Reckon I might have to take back what I said about Osweldo not being a fool," Pete said. "He just didn't know when to quit, and it got him killed."

The major reached for Pete's tobacco sack and made a clumsy effort to build a cigarette. His eyes were as wide as a kid reading his first Louis L'Amour western.

Rudy continued the story. "I got a letter one day saying a cousin of mine down at Carlsbad had died, and his funeral would be on the next Monday. Wanted me to come and be a pallbearer. Heck, this cousin, Willie, and I hated each other, and I'd have been the last person in the world he'd have wanted at his funeral. I told Pete's dad that there was something fishy going on. He sat there for a minute rubbing them nubby fingers across his chin and then told me to go on; said he'd be all right. Said him and Pete would be fine until I got back."

"That was the second summer Mama had brought me up here," Pete said. "I thought that Dad was getting worse. Kept his jacket buttoned all the way up to his neck . . . didn't talk as much. He was a whole lot tougher on the livestock. I'd catch him just sitting at the barn lookin' out at the hay field, kinda mumbling like he was talking to hisself. Sometimes, I could understand him. He told a man named Billy that he needed a hand grenade. He begged the lieutenant and a chaplain to get up and walk, told them they weren't dead. He wanted somebody to look for morphine. Strange stuff like that. He'd found Grandpa Chapman's old rifle—the one that was engraved—wrapped in a tarp under a plank in the hay barn. He spent a lot of time cleaning that rifle and ran a lot of shells through it.

"I pretty much got used to Dad doing strange things. Hiding food. Wearing three pair of socks. Stuff like that. One night, I woke up hearing the *whack, whack, whack* of a pick bouncing off hard dirt. Come outside and Dad was digging a hole at the edge of the barn. Took him two days working pretty steady. I asked him what he was doing, and he mumbled something about digging a fox hole."

"A fox hole? Whatever for?" The major was puzzled.

"I didn't know, exactly. He'd get in it and practice shooting. We'd set up paper plate targets down there at the sharp bend in the road 'bout where that burned-out car is. I wasn't much good at it, but Dad would hunker down in that fox hole and put five of five shots pretty close to the middle of a paper plate 'bout every time. He was a helluva shot."

"The military gave him an expert marksmanship and distinguished shot badge," the nurse said. "I've seen the records."

The beer supply was running low. Rudy went into the house and came back with two more six-packs. He iced them down in the cooler.

Pete sat and looked at the cooler like he was deciding if he wanted . . . needed another one. He convinced himself that one more would be fine.

"I'd had a case of the chicken pox that summer," Pete said. "Most days, I laid on a pallet in the shade of that pine tree right out yonder reading comic books. Dad was out at the barn, and Rudy had been gone to the funeral for about an hour when Osweldo's Hudson come roarin' up the road toward the house. He was driving awful fast, and his radio was turned about as loud as it would go. I never even had time to sit up 'fore Dad started shooting."

The nurse was breathing through her mouth, and her hands came up as if to cover her face, then fell and grasped the table's edge. Perspiration gathered on her forehead, and she wiped a drop from her cheek. "He just started firing?" she asked.

Pete nodded. "Just *blam, blam, blam.* Shots was 'bout quick as you could snap your fingers three times."

The nurse flinched and turned away.

"First shot took out the windshield on the driver's side. Next two shots was probably right 'bout in the same place. I don't believe Osweldo heard none of them. Reckon the windshield just blew up in his face, and the next two bullets was in his head 'fore he could blink his eyes."

The nurse put her hands over her ears, leaned back in the chair, and closed her eyes. *Oh, my God. Oh, my God.*

Amon was taking quick, shallow breaths and couldn't look away from Pete.

Pete sat quietly, rubbed his hands together, and then took a deep breath. "The passenger door and both back doors flew open. Three men jumped out of the car and ran across the pasture toward the road. And I mean these men were flat-out running; you could have played a game of marbles on their shirttails. Dad fired one more time—not at the men, 'cause if he'd been shooting at one of them, that man would have died. He's shooting at the back end of the car. There was a helluva explosion, and a rolling fireball that I'll bet was a hundred feet high just rose up. Man that did the investigation said there was four five-gallon cans of gas in the trunk.

"The three men got back to the highway—got lucky—and flagged down a trooper. Wasn't more than a half hour until three cars came up the road traveling real slow like the drivers was expecting something bad. Had them red lights flashing. They stopped before they got to the burning car. The sheriff talked over a bullhorn. Told who he was and said they'd just come to help. Wanted Dad to show himself. Asked him to drop his weapon. I didn't know anything about stuff like this, no more than I'd read in comic books. I put one of my white socks on a stick and waved it. Sheriff had a pair of binoculars, and I could see that he was looking at me. I walked out to the barn. Dad was cleaning his rifle, acted like I wadn't nowhere around."

Pete took a deep breath as if he were reliving everything. "Dad went back into the barn to get—I don't know, a rag or something. I snatched that gun up and took off down the hill to where the sheriff was hunkered down behind his car. I was running, carrying the rifle, hollering 'don't shoot,' and waving that white sock all at the same time. They questioned me a lot, 'bout who did the shooting, and if he had any more weapons.

"I was scared to death—seeing all them men with guns and their radios all talking at the same time. Sheriff told me to get in his car, and we just eased along up to the barn. Dad was sitting on the edge of his foxhole, smoking a cigarette and smiling. He didn't know where he was any more than a goose. Sheriff kept the car between them, leaning across the hood, and talked to him. Dad was chattering some kind of foreign language. Sheriff had been in the war, and he said it sounded like Korean."

The sun was starting to seek refuge behind the mountains. A chaparral bird chased a desert rattler across the driveway and then fought a second roadrunner over the kill. The wind was settling for the day, and the smell of sage and creosote bush rose up to drift across the veranda, invisible spirits rising from the dust.

Just above a whisper, the nurse asked, "And your dad?"

Pete opened another beer and took a couple of swallows. "Handcuffed him. Put him in the back of the sheriff's car. All that stuff. 'Course, they took him to jail. Tried to question him. Dad just kept talking Korean—wouldn't answer in English. He was tried and found guilty. Nobody ever knew a word he was saying."

Now the nurse broke down in deep, shuddering sobs, and the major held her against his chest. While she gained control of her emotions, the cowboys looked away.

Pete motioned to Rudy and said, "You go."

Rudy took a deep breath and shrugged his shoulders. "He was out on bail. Somebody over in Artesia—we never knew exactly who it was 'cause a oil company's lawyer handled it—went his bond. Took the jury three days to reach a decision.

Hell, the law had his rifle and the ballistics test. Pretty open and shut case, I figured. Understand there was two fistfights and some hair pullin' while the jury was deliberating. He was found guilty one day about dinnertime, and the sentencing was to be the next morning. They let him come back out here for the night."

"They let him come home on the day before the sentencing?" the major asked.

Pete flashed a tobacco-stained smile. "Well, yeah. More than half the folks around hated Osweldo. Most of them figured he got what he deserved. Dad had kinda become a local hero—taking out a badass and all. Judge Reyes figured Dad would just show in the morning for sentencing. 'Course the judge didn't know Rudy very well, did he, Rudy? He didn't know you worth a crap."

"One of the deputies brought him out here—said he'd be back in the morning to pick him up." Rudy had trouble with his voice and kept clearing his throat. "Him . . . him being found guilty and all stuck in my craw mighty damn bad. I . . . uh . . . I . . . I put him in my truck. Sometime 'round midnight, we got into El Paso and cleared the bridge over the Rio Grande into Ciudad Juarez. We had breakfast in Chihuahua."

"Where is he now?" the nurse asked.

Pete answered. "Samalayuca. Little town sets out on the north edge of them big sand dunes down in Mexico. 'Bout an hour south of Ciudad Juarez."

Amon wrinkled his brow. "But aren't there extradition rights between the United States and—?"

Pete interrupted. "New Mexico won't fool with this. Hell, considering everything, they probably wouldn't even take him back if Mexico offered."

"Is he in some kind of facility?" the nurse questioned.

"No," Pete said. "Him and Mama run this little bar. Well,

really Mama does. Not but two bars in town. They do all right."

"*Matilda* is there with him?!"

"Yep," Rudy answered. "I stopped in Artesia that night and got her. Her and the two girls. If I hadn't had a crew cab truck, we'd have smothered to death all piled up in one seat."

"Is he . . . happy? Is he all right?"

Pete shook his head. "Not really. He's about crazy as a peach-orchard boar. But Mama does good with him. He follows her around kinda like a child. He'll touch her shoulder and ask when the bandages will come off—when he can be released. Needs to go home, he says. Still wears that denim jacket fastened up to the top button. He don't speak nothing but Korean. She's learned enough of it that they can get by. Mama is a good 'un.

"She says sometimes he almost comes back for a few hours. He'll talk about the house at Seven Rivers and how happy they are. Talk to her about the next day's rodeo. Wants to know where she will be sitting in the stands. And if she will wear his favorite blouse. Then he'll just quit talking and go back to the hell of wherever he lives. 'Course he'd never really come back to this world in the first place."

The blue heeler seemed to sense the sadness in Pete's voice, padded across the coolness of the veranda floor and laid his head on the man's knee.

The nurse took the Kleenex wrapper from her pocket. It was empty. She had wadded the damp ones and pressed them into a ball. She searched and found the driest, then blew her nose. "I'm so sorry," she said. "There is no reason it had to come to this. Not after all he'd been through. One of the things I've learned to hate about this world is the unfairness."

The nighthawks launched into their flamboyant, nocturnal, aerial acrobatics. Amon, returning from the car with a fresh supply of Kleenex, stood and watched their flights and listened to their victorious cries as they snatched insects from the dusk.

"Do you see him often?" the nurse asked.

"Naw, not really. Couple times a year, me and Rudy will drive down there. Take them a side of beef. A little money. Toothpaste. Cosmetics for Mama and my half-sisters. Stuff like that. Dad'll shake hands with Rudy. Offer him a cigarette. But it upsets him to see me. He'll wave a white napkin or anything white. Get back in the corner of a room and chatter in Korean.

"Some while back, Dad started dusting. He'll get this old feather duster and dust the window sills out in front of the bar. Then he'll just keep on dusting window sills right on down the street. Everybody in town kinda watches out for him. He gets too far from the bar, they shoo him back up the sidewalk. 'Course, the sand blows all the time down there, them big dunes sitting outside of town and shifting all the time. Dad can't make no more progress against whatever is going on in his head than he can against the blowing desert sand.

"But I spend some time with Mama. She don't change much. We'll go for a drive and talk while Rudy rides herd on Dad."

Amon asked, "Does he do other things—with his time, I mean?"

Pete smiled. "He plays with the little kids some. He'll flip the eye patch up on his forehead. Kids will pretend to be afraid of him. Call him *mal de ojo*. Evil eye. But they love him. Lots of the time, they are the ones that rescues him from just dusting plumb out of sight.

"Mostly though, he sits out in front of the bar in the sunshine. He's got an old red, wooden, straight-backed chair. He sits in it and leans back against the wall. Watches the people go by. Doesn't matter what the weather is, he's right there, jacket buttoned up to his chin."

"Trying to get warm," the nurse said.

Pete nodded. "Trying to get warm."

"Demons be with him forever?"

"Yeah, I reckon."

They drove back to the motel. Jill smoked and watched the rugged countryside slide by; Amon watched her from the corner of his eye.

They poured the leftover wine into paper cups and sat on the motel porch. The sun dropped beneath the horizon, and the air chilled.

"Shall we?" Amon asked and swept his hand toward their motel door.

They showered and then made love. Later, he lay on his back and extended his arm. She snuggled in against him, her face nestled in the hollow of his shoulder. Minutes later, his breathing became regular and deep. She moved closer to him and pulled her leg across his body.

The next morning, while Amon paid the bill, Jill flipped through the postcards on the motel counter.

A battered pickup towing a gooseneck trailer filled with bawling steers swung into the graveled parking lot. Pete stepped out of the truck cab, a coffee mug in one hand and a manila envelope under his arm.

Jill crossed the parking lot and met him. "What a surprise," she said. "I wasn't sure we would see you again."

Pete gave her the envelope. "Thought you might like to have this," he said. "Some time ago, Dad started drawing dragonflies. If you remember, that was Grandpa Chapman's mark? He'd cut one in the board across his gate post. Think it came from the time he and Grandma Chapman lived at Bitter Lakes. Those things swarmed around the lakes like mosquitos.

"Anyway, Dad draws them on cardboard and gives them to kids. Or really, just anybody passing by Mom's little bar down in Mexico. Thought you might like to have a couple of them. Something to remember Dad by 'case you never get down to Samalayuca."

ABOUT THE AUTHOR

John Neely Davis was raised in the sandy hills of West Tennessee, an area east of the edge of the Mississippi Delta. Most of his working years were spent in government land acquisition stretching from the Appalachians to the river valleys of New Mexico.

Previously published novels include *Stephen Dennison, The Sixth William,* and *Bear Shadow.* The latter novel won the Janice Keck Literary Award.

He has also contributed to numerous anthologies: *Filtered Through Time, By Blood or by Marriage, Comanchero Trail, Western Trail Blazer* Series, and the recently released *Showdown.*

He lives with his wife, Jayne, in historic Franklin, Tennessee.

The employees of Five Star Publishing hope you have enjoyed this book.

Our Five Star novels explore little-known chapters from America's history, stories told from unique perspectives that will entertain a broad range of readers.

Other Five Star books are available at your local library, bookstore, all major book distributors, and directly from Five Star/Gale.

Connect with Five Star Publishing

Visit us on Facebook:
   https://www.facebook.com/FiveStarCengage

Email:
   FiveStar@cengage.com

For information about titles and placing orders:
   (800) 223-1244
   gale.orders@cengage.com

To share your comments, write to us:
   Five Star Publishing
   Attn: Publisher
   10 Water St., Suite 310
   Waterville, ME 04901